D1090758

Burrows

Books by Reavis Z. Wortham

The Rock Hole
Burrows

Burrows

A Red River Mystery

Reavis Z. Wortham

3 1489 00634 3030

Poisoned Pen Press

Copyright © 2012 by Reavis Z. Wortham

First Edition 2012

10 9 8 7 6 5 4 3 2 1

Library of Congress Catalog Card Number: 2011942735

ISBN: 9781464200052   Hardcover
       9781464200076   Trade Paperback

All rights reserved. No part of this publication may be reproduced, stored in, or introduced into a retrieval system, or
transmitted in any form, or by any means (electronic, mechanical, photocopying, recording, or otherwise) without the prior
written permission of both the copyright owner and the pub-
lisher of this book.

Poisoned Pen Press
6962 E. First Ave., Ste. 103
Scottsdale, AZ 85251
www.poisonedpenpress.com
info@poisonedpenpress.com

Printed in the United States of America

This one is for two educators who impacted my life and set me on this writing course. Miss Russell, the redheaded elementary librarian who is no longer with us, and Miss Adams, my most influential high school English teacher who is still exactly the same as she was in 1970.

Chapter One

Drip.

Though slight, the wet splat was clearly audible on the warm front porch of the small Lamar County farmhouse. Josh Brooks rocked ever so slowly as the late evening breeze waved the long grass along the nearby fence row and ruffled his curly brown hair. He stared at his lap, breathing as if trying to save energy or control his emotions.

Drip.

A Hereford on the other side of the barbed wire scratched her chin on a bodark fence post and swished her tail at a pestering cloud of late season flies. Josh's boyhood friend Kendal stepped outside through the wooden screen door and allowed it to slam shut.

For a moment Kendal stopped, expecting a scolding for banging the door. When they were children, it was almost impossible to remember to close it softly, and every kid that raced through Mrs. Brook's living room allowed the door to slap shut about every third time.

"Sorry Miss Onie!" Kendal called through the screen to Josh's mother.

The neat, elderly house in the small farming community of Forest Chapel belonged to Josh, who had never lived anywhere else. His dad, Oscar, had farmed the one hundred eighty acres until a heart attack felled him one soft spring morning as he fed the cows. Josh turned twenty-one a year after the funeral and married the prettiest girl in Forest Chapel, Beth Dearborn. Miss Onie Mae let them have the master bedroom, moved to the other side of the house, and they never looked back.

Drip.

Sporting a burr haircut, Kendal sipped on a glass of sweet tea. Everyone said Miss Onie Mae Brooks made the best tea in the county. "You need to get that drip fixed, Josh."

The young farmer didn't respond as Kendal strolled across the wooden boards of the pier and beam farmhouse and settled into a mismatched rocker beside Josh. The setting sun cast long autumn shadows across the yard, bathing it and the pasture in a warm glow.

A tinny radio in the background played a Chuck Berry song.

"You know, Josh, it's been good to see you again after all these years. Remember how it was here in the evenings when we were kids? I really enjoyed those summer nights; catching lightning bugs in jars and playing chase."

Drip.

Kendal sighed, enjoying the tinkle of ice against the glass that once held store-bought jelly. "Most of the time anyway. When Randal Wicker and Merle Clark played with us it kinda irritated me. Seems like with the four of us, I was always low man on the totem pole. You think it was because I was different? I suppose it's the nature of kids to gang up on one for some reason. Anyway, it don't matter none anymore, does it?

"I thought about those days when I was in the hospital. There was nothing else to do all those years except lay there and think, or listen to the radio. Most of the time I wished I was back here with you, being a kid again."

Kendal rocked and grinned at a sudden memory. "You know, Randal really wasn't as good a friend as you were. I guess he and Merle were more like a team, like you and me should have been. That came to mind the other day, too. The radio was on when I was coming down here from Nebraska and I found a station playing that new song 'And I Love Her' by the Beatles. That's when a memory clicked and it was the four of us playing ball out here in the grass, but we weren't listening to them long hairs back then, were we?

"But anyway, it was that song, this time of the year, and the weather that made me think to myself 'You need to stop by and see them boys because it's been a long, long time since y'all last visited.' So here I am.

"You remember that day Merle got an extension cord and brought the Philco outside and put it right there by Miss Onie Mae's peonies and turned it up loud while we played baseball?"

The pleasant demeanor crumbled for a moment, and Kendal chuckled. "I've always thought Randal was kinda jealous of me, especially because I got a new glove for Christmas that year."

Hey sissy, are you stupid or what? Is somethin' wrong with you? C'mon and catch the ball ya moron! Don't be afraid of it!

"You remember that? I *loved* the smell of a new ball glove fresh out of the box. I don't even think girls ever smelled so good, except for Beth that is.

"Man, wasn't she something? I especially remember how she'd run her fingers through that Esther Williams hair of hers and pull it back behind one ear, real sexy-like. Oh, yeah, I guess you do, since you wound up marrying her. She was crazy about you from the get-go, even when we were little. I wish things had been different for me, but I can't quit thinking that if things were normal she might have liked me best."

Josh let the comment go without answering. His finger twitched on the rocker's armrest, then he settled back again.

Drip.

Kendal laughed and called through the door. "Ain't that right, Beth? We had some times all right. But y'all were always playing those jokes on me, calling me sissy or sister-girl. I never did learn to tell when you were kidding or pulling a prank."

They rocked while Josh allowed the conversation to be monopolized.

"The best one was when y'all sprinkled those leaves over the limbs and trash washed across that little draw down by the creek bottoms and convinced me it was solid enough to walk across. Whooee! I thought I wouldn't stop falling until I landed in China. That draw must have been fifteen feet deep. Busted my lip and I nearly bit through my tongue. You boys were practical jokers all right."

A sudden gust blew across the road, threatening to snatch Josh's cap.

Drip.

"That danged drip is really getting annoying. We'll need to fix it pretty soon. Anyway, Merle was kinda mean sometimes. Like when y'all told me you didn't want to play. Oh hell, I knew y'all were sneaking off together without me, and don't think I didn't see what you did when no one was watching. That's what hurt the worst, me wanting to be with you and y'all stringin' off alone and leaving me."

They sat for a moment longer, watching the sun settle toward the tree tops. Kendal drained the glass and set it carefully on the painted two-by-four serving as the porch rail. "Well, we had our secrets, didn't we? But the things you did...the things you said...well, that's why I'm here.

"My therapist told me it was best to lay the ghosts, and that's what I'm trying to do. Matter of fact, he's right and I feel pretty good right now. Going by Randal's yesterday and this stopover did wonders for me; seeing you, Beth, and your mama. Well, I need to keep moving and there's a lot of people to visit before I have to move on."

The driver in the two-tone 1958 Buick Roadmaster convertible honked impatiently and then returned to slapping spilled flour from his sleeve. Behind the wheel, Kevin's tolerance was wearing thin because they had places to go. And besides, he was hungry. He wanted to run up to the Center Springs store. He had his mouth set for rat cheese and crackers, something he hadn't tasted in months.

"All *right*, Kevin, you dumb bastard." Kendal stood and stared down at Josh. "I made a mistake getting that aggravating son of a bitch out of Tulsa. He's worrisome and I'm about tired of traveling with him. You know Kevin, though, he's from over in Boggy Bend. His daddy is Don Jennings."

Kendal adjusted the .22 revolver stuck in the waistband of half-damp, slightly oversized jeans stolen from Beth's clothes line. A razor sharp Old Hickory butcher knife from the kitchen rode snug behind a plain leather belt. With a forefinger, Kendal reached out, caught a small drip hanging on the end of Josh's nose, and carefully wiped the red liquid on his already soaked pants.

"All right. I'm gonna drop by and see Merle here in a little bit. You know, y'all shouldn't a-done me the way you did, but I reckon that's about settled, and then I'm going to Mexico for a while.

"Anyway, you don't look so good, boy. Guess a .22 bullet rattling around in there behind your eyes will do that. But you still need to get that drip fixed." Kendal laughed, chewed an almost non-existent fingernail for a moment and started down the steps. "Oh, one more thing I need to do before I go. Won't take a minute. Hold your horses, Kevin and don't you get up either, Beth! You and Ma lay there by the fire where it's comfortable. Good to see y'all again."

Drip.

Crackle.

Splash.

Chapter Two

I was in the pasture, sneaking up on a field lark in the tall tickle grass, when I heard Grandpa's tractor turn onto the oil road leading out of the bottoms. I got the idea from television the night before when I saw a soldier on *Combat* use his rifle to push down the grass as he crawled up on a German machine gun nest.

I was making a pretty fair belly sneak for an eleven year old, but Hootie made things harder as he raced around sniffing for quail in the November sunshine.

Truthfully, I was out there because Miss Becky had gotten a call and when I heard who was on the other end of the line, I figured it would be best to make myself scarce. It was surprising that Mr. Elmer Hughes would take the time to pick up the phone and complain about me throwing dirt clods at the pickups passing on the highway.

Great-grandpa Will Parker built our house on a little hill overlooking the bottoms. The main highway coming over the creek bridge from the east was arrow straight for a mile before curving around our house like a stream around a boulder. The high position gave me a perfect setup to chunk clods at passing cars and trucks. I was pretending to bomb them, like in *Combat*.

The hard sand clods hadn't actually *hit* anyone, but they made dusty little puffs on the highway as the cars went by. I had the range down when Mr. Earl passed, and a pretty good sized clod hit directly in front of his truck. I didn't figure it would hurt the paint on that old wreck none if I did hit him, and I didn't, but he tapped his brakes and I skinned out of there before he could see who was hiding up near the corner post of Grandpa's overgrown barbed wire fence.

Anyway, just as I got close enough to get a shot at the bird, I heard Grandpa's old two-cylinder Popping Johnny tractor turn out of the bottoms. Because the breeze was out of the northeast, I also heard our radio through the open window over a hundred yards away. Miss Becky had it turned to a loud sermon about The Beatles and how that new rock and roll group was going to take everyone straight to hell before 1964 was done.

As I slid forward, I caught a glimpse of the tractor as it came down the oil road on the other side of the pasture.

Then a big ol' snake stuck his head out of the dry grass not two inches from my arm. I didn't recognize what kind it was. It might have been anything from a copperhead to a blue racer, but it didn't make me any difference.

It was a snake and I was always scared of snakes as I was of a bear.

We froze, almost nose to nose. It was strange, because everything suddenly snapped into crystal clarity. I took in the sharpness of its scales, the pattern they made, and the way its body expanded and contracted as it breathed.

I'd heard enough stories about them who've been bit. Doctors tie tourniquets above the bite and make deep cuts with a sharp knife into each fang mark. The arm or leg swells up and turns black. Then the flesh dies and sloughs off to reveal bone and tendons. Old Mr. Harry Nichols was missing the little and ring fingers of his left hand from where a water moccasin bit him when he was a boy and he got gangrene.

The tractor came closer and turned onto the two-lane highway. From there it was only a couple of hundred yards to the gravel drive leading up to the farmhouse. Clear as a bell I heard a scissortail singing while he jumped up and down on top of a telephone pole by the highway.

The sound was wonderfully natural while I laid there and stared at what I finally figured to be a water moccasin. The pool wasn't a hundred yards away and the snake was hunting, like me. I was fascinated by those glassy black eyes.

Its tongue flicked out.

It was too much. My face flushed with heat and I prickled all over with fear. Before it could coil, absolute terror jolted me into action. I jumped to my feet with a shriek and raced back toward the drive. Hootie saw my sudden leap and shot across the pasture, weaving in and out of the bull nettles and over the milkweeds.

Grandpa Ned waved as we ran parallel to the road. From his perch high on the tractor's hard metal seat, he had no idea I was running in panic. I was so scared I forgot to watch out for the bull-nettles and brushed one of the plants. The tiny hairs poked through my jeans.

I barely paid any attention to the burning in my leg as I ran to the barbed wire fence and realized I'd cheated death one more time. Hootie slid under the lowest strand of wire and I followed closely behind.

I was safe! No snake bite. I suddenly felt as if I could float in the air like a balloon. My fear went away in an instant and I whooped and charged the tractor, filled with relief.

Grandpa turned into the drive and stopped his John Deere as we cleared the wire. He pushed the clutch lever and grinned down at me. "Top! Did you finally get up? Hand me that rifle and climb on up here!"

Jittery from excitement and relief, I realized I still had my BB gun. I handed it up, the muzzle pointed away. Grandpa laid the air rifle at his feet, extended a sun-browned hand, and pulled me upward to stand on the wide axle beside the iron seat. His blue work shirt and overalls suited him; soft and faded from scrubbings in the team of square metal washtubs on the back porch. I grabbed hold of his gallus for balance.

"Hang on!" He pushed the tall throttle bar. Hootie ran in a wide circle around us. The virtually worn out tractor jolted forward, tires popping on the gravel.

Grandpa used to be a farmer and the constable in Center Springs until he had enough of toting the law in Precinct 3. He retired and left his badge on top of the television months before, but he hadn't escaped the plow. It was a good thing, because we all knew that he had to keep busy. If he sat down and did nothing, he'd die.

From beside Grandpa I could see directly ahead into the hay barn on top of the hill. We followed the drive's incline to the five-hundred-gallon gas tank. He shut off the engine.

"Did you kill any birds this morning with that air gun?"

"Couldn't get a shot. Them field larks know just enough to stay out of range, but I did get two big old bullfrogs down at the pool right after I got up this morning. Miss Becky showed me how to clean them. She said she'd fry the legs for our dinner."

"Hope I get a bite. Here we go." He grabbed my much smaller hand and lowered me back to the ground, letting me dangle for a moment like a monkey before he let go. He passed me the BB gun and despite his age, he climbed down like a young man and stretched the kinks out of his back. After wiping the sweat out of his hat with a faded handkerchief, he removed the nozzle from the gas pump and inserted it into the tractor's tank. Grasping the handle, he cranked it to prime the pump, and then reversed the direction to fill the tank.

I left him to his business, ran to the house, and yanked open the screen door. It slapped closed and the comfortable smells of fried meat and vegetables drew me to the table sitting square in the middle of the kitchen, surrounded by rough-hewn cabinets, a deep freeze, the ice box, and a homemade china cabinet.

"Go wash your hands," Miss Becky ordered without turning from the hot stove where she was frying my frog legs. The bun on the back of her head hung limp in the kitchen's humidity, despite the time of the year. Two box fans moved the warm air around.

"I ran into a bull nettle. My leg's stinging like fire."

"Well, we'll put some damp baking soda on it in a minute."

She kept the black plastic General Electric radio in the adjoining living room tuned to a station out of Chisum. The preaching was over, and the news and crop reports were on. Mostly background noise to me, Grandpa liked to listen to the local crime report, even though he was retired.

By the time I washed my hands, the table was set. Grandpa stomped on the porch to knock the dirt and sandburs off his brogans. He came inside, went straight to the water bucket on the counter, filled the dipper, and swallowed hard several times. He always counted on Miss Becky to draw a bucket of cold water fresh from the well and have it ready. In the heat of the summer, she kept a big chunk of store-bought ice floating on top.

He pitched his straw hat on top of the deep freeze and went to the bathroom to wash his face and hands, splashing water on the sink and wall like a duck.

"Y'all sit down and eat now." Miss Becky placed a pan of hot biscuits on the table within easy reach of Grandpa as he came in drying his face with a hand towel. He took his place and broke one open to cool.

"Mama, y'all get ready after dinner and I'll carry you to town. I need to go by the courthouse and you can get what you need at the store while I'm there."

There was always something to do in the tiny community of Center Springs where I lived with my grandparents after Mama and Daddy died in an automobile accident, but I was tickled at the idea of going to Chisum.

Every now and then during dinner, Grandpa used his spoon to dip from the bowl of black-eyed peas in the middle of the table. He was never one to mind getting a bite from a bowl once he'd finished his meal. Some didn't like that kind of behavior, but it was Grandpa's table and he figured he'd eat what he wanted.

Just to aggravate us, he'd even reach over and scoop from my cousin Pepper's plate or mine. I knew he liked getting her goat, because his blue eyes twinkled while he watched her get mad and sull up like an old possum.

"You know, Top, me and you need to go down to the creek pretty soon and catch us a stringer of white perch while it's still warm. I've been thinking that a mess of fish might taste pretty good."

"Can we go…"

He shushed me with a hand when he caught the last part of the newscaster's description of a chase through Oklahoma. "Listen a minute."

All along he'd been half listening to the news and I only paid attention to the radio once we quit talking.

"…multi-state crime spree by these three fugitives. Tulsa police and the state highway patrol think the two, Kendal Bowden and Albert Gantry, have killed four people in three states and aided in the escape of Kevin Jennings, who was also serving time in the Tulsa mental hospital. It is believed the trio might be heading toward the Kiamichi Mountains in southeast Oklahoma. At this time the highway patrol and local law enforcement agencies are assisted by a multi-state agency composed of more than one hundred officers. We'll keep you updated on this murder spree as more information comes in. Hogs are up, fall is here and the stock report is next …"

The sound of roaring engines and shrieking tires burning rubber on the highway drifted through the open doors and windows, causing Grandpa's face to get red. I knew the reason. Right after he retired and Uncle Cody got elected as constable, local kids realized that the one-mile stretch of highway from the creek bridge to the turn at our house was open game for drag racing.

For years, they knew better than to race right beside Grandpa's, except when they caught him gone to Chisum or to pick up a prisoner in one of the other little nearby burgs. Now they easily fit in a couple of quick races before he could call the laws, who always showed up long after it was over.

Miss Becky frowned, but before anyone said a word, the telephone in the living room jangled with one ring. Two rings would have let us know the call was for Miss Whitney, who shared our party line.

Miss Becky rose from the table to answer. "Hello? Oh Hidy, Bill. Y'all doing all right? Oh, all right. Wait a second." She laid the phone on the telephone table. "Ned, Bill Caldwell wants to talk to you."

"He knew I'd be eating dinner." Grandpa frowned. "Bill's old enough to know he oughta let a man finish his dinner before he calls." He drained half of his sweet tea before he left the table.

Miss Becky turned the radio down and whispered as he passed. "I heard Miss Whitney pick up the receiver." She didn't like it that Miss Whitney listened in, but there was nothing anyone could do about it.

Grandpa didn't tell us much when he was constable. The only way Miss Becky had of learning anything was to hear his one-sided conversations and figure things out for herself. She got to be pretty good at it, but unfortunately for her this time, Grandpa did most of the listening. "What time did you say you found him? Are you talking about east of where Sanders Creek comes into the river, but before the river bridge?"

I chewed on a frog leg and watched his face through the open door.

"Well, that sounds bad, but you know, I ain't constable no more. Whyn't you call Cody and get him out there." He laughed after a minute. "Well, all right. He'll probably get there before I do anyway, but I'll be out in a little bit."

He hung up the phone and came back into the kitchen. "We'll go to town when I get back. Bill caught a feller on his trotline, so I need to get on down there."

"My lands." Miss Becky raised her hands. "Does he know who it is?"

"He didn't say."

"Well, that's awful."

The phone jangled again, irritating Grandpa. "Does that thang ring all the time when I'm in the field?"

"It's usually for me." Miss Becky hurried back into the living room to answer. This time it was her turn to be silent for a long while. Grandpa didn't like it that she was in there on the phone during dinner time, but he couldn't do much more than fidget.

She asked a few more questions like "When did he do that?" and "I suspect he might."

She finally finished the call, but didn't put down the receiver. "Opal May Whitney, I know you're on the other end of this line. Now you don't say a word to nobody or I'll know who spilled the beans."

She came back to start clearing the table. Grandpa and I exchanged glances. I knew better than to ask questions, but he didn't. "Who was it, Mama?"

Miss Becky smiled and picked up my empty plate. "It was for me. I'll tell you directly."

I didn't like their adult talk one little bit, but there wasn't anything I could do about it. Grandpa might buck and snort, but she wouldn't tell anything until she was ready, so I changed the subject. "Can I go with you to see Mr. Bill?"

"Naw, I remember the last time you were with me when somebody was found dead."

I recalled the blood-splattered living room in Powderly about two months before he retired. The radio call said he was needed pretty quick. We were feeding cows, and instead of taking me home first, we went straight to Arthur City, about three miles from the pasture. We pulled up in front of a little clapboard house to find half a dozen deputy sheriffs' cars parked on the dirt road.

A shook-up highway patrol officer was standing in the yard. "Ned, you need to see this."

Grandpa must have forgot I was with him, because he went up through the door with me following. He stopped at the threshold in shock. When he realized I was coming in behind him, he pushed me back, but not before I saw a slaughterhouse in the living room. I spent the next two hours killing time in a dead man's front yard while every lawman in the county dropped by to sort out the carnage.

"Besides," Grandpa started toward the front bedroom, "bodies that come out of the river ain't for young'uns to see. Come in here a minute, Mama." Miss Becky followed him out of my earshot. Hootie came up to the table and I fed him a couple of bites of fried potatoes.

I was disappointed, because I wanted to do something else besides hunt and fish, which was the main thing for kids to do in Center Springs. Around 1870, our little community was actually a pretty good-sized town. But now less than eight hundred people still lived just off the bottoms, barely enough to keep our cotton gin going, along with two general stores on the north side of the two-lane highway with the Domino Hall in between.

Miss Becky told me that when she was a kid Center Springs even had a cobbler, a barbershop, a blacksmith, and an honest-to-god brass band. But after a long spell of rain and thunderstorms, the Red River drowned the entire valley under thirty-three feet of silt and water. Most everyone was washed away and only a handful of people returned.

When the Depression hit, folks who didn't have money worked the fields, chopping or picking cotton, or harvesting crops for pennies to buy food. Most of them lived close to the ground and raised their own vegetable gardens, barely scratching out a living in dirt floor shacks.

Families still depended on one another for help and no one lived far off from the others. On my dad's side, twenty families worked hard-scrabble farms within two square miles of one another. Each family had at least ten kids, and they all helped one another when times got hard.

I was rubbing Hootie's ears when Grandpa and Miss Becky came back into the kitchen. "You know, Top, I'd like for you to go to the courthouse with me after I get back." He picked up his hat. "I haven't seen O.C. in a coon's age and it'd tickle him to see you, too."

"That'd be great…"

Grandpa shushed me with a hand. Sometimes it was hard to get a whole sentence out around him. "Listen a minute." We heard a car crunching up the gravel drive. I looked out the door and it was Uncle James and my cousin Pepper. She and I are the same age and people sometimes think we're twins.

I went outside and watched her get out of their Bel Air. She waved when I met them in the yard. Over the past few months I'd learned to read how she was feeling. Some days, when the weight of what happened to us in the river bottoms was heavy on her shoulders, she was a sad, quiet gal.

Other times, like today, she bounced out of the car with a grin. Uncle James ruffled my hair as he walked past on his way into the kitchen and I rubbed his big belly. She motioned for me to follow her out behind the smokehouse where Miss Becky hung her clothes on the line. This time it was loaded heavy with drying sheets. I knew they'd smell good later that night. Once out of sight, Pepper reached into her jeans and dug out a couple of bent cigarettes.

She stuck one in the corner of her mouth. "Want one?"

I instinctively took the other and then panicked. Holding a toonie with my grandparents so close scared me half to death. I knew for a fact that Grandpa was going to come around the corner and catch us with them. It wasn't that we hadn't tried smoking before. She and I had been down at Uncle James' pool with a couple of other cousins a few weeks earlier, trying our best not to cough our lungs out from a pack of Camels.

"No! Golly-bum, they'll smell the smoke when they come outside. Grandpa's getting ready to leave in a minute and the wind is out of the northeast."

She rolled her eyes. "Titty baby."

"Why don't you eat a booger?"

"It don't make any difference no-how. I don't have any matches. We'd have to snitch one from the kitchen."

Miss Becky kept wooden matches in the dispenser on the kitchen wall, but I was already rattled and was sure as shootin' that she'd know we were up to no good if we went inside for one. "Where'd you get them?"

"Neal's store. He had a bunch of singles for sale on the counter and I grabbed a couple when he was slicing pickle loaf for Miss Nelson."

"You *stole* them?" The thought of a theft was almost enough to make me swimmy-headed. Grandpa hated a thief worse than anything and thinking about her stealing from Uncle Neal made me feel bad. "You ought not have done that."

"Shit, titty baby. They aren't but a penny or two apiece. It's not like I robbed a bank or nothing. We'll save 'em for later."

I heard Grandpa and we quickly stuck the cigarettes in our pockets and went back around to the front.

"Pepper!" Miss Becky called through the screen door. "Come help me clear the table. Top, you need to burn the trash."

"Well shit." Pepper stomped her foot. "I ain't been here five minutes and she's got me working."

When I went inside, Uncle James was sitting at the table, eating pinto beans. I picked a couple of matches from the dispenser and carried the trash to the burn barrel, thankful that I didn't have to do dishes with the women.

Chapter Three

Ned sat at the telephone table and made a couple of quick calls while the kids were outside. White haired Judge O.C. Rains received the first. Judge Rains was a cantankerous Lamar County judge and had been Ned Parker's good friend all his life.

Thelma Lee Fletcher, O.C.'s secretary of forty years who wore her hair like Jackie Kennedy, answered on the first ring. "Judge Rain's office."

"Howdy, Thelma Lee."

Knowing that a Saturday call from Ned meant trouble she was immediately curious. "What's wrong, Ned?"

"It ain't none of your business, but it's always good to hear your voice. Put me through to O.C."

He knew she was grinning into the receiver. "I'll find out anyway."

"I know it, but that'll have to come from O.C., so let me talk to him."

"All right, hon. Tell Becky howdy for me."

O.C. wasn't as prompt in answering his phone. He liked to make people wait. It rang half a dozen times, and that irritated Ned, because he knew the phone was right next to O.C.'s hand. The only thing closer was the fly swatter he kept by the papers he was working on.

O.C. despised a fly.

He finally picked up the receiver. "What?"

"Y'ought to say hello first, before you barge in with a bad-mannered question."

O.C. sighed and turned in his wooden chair to contemplate the screenless courthouse window. "If you wanted to visit, I'd expect to see you standing in my door, so something's wrong. You want to tell me, or do I have to wade through five minutes of pleasantries before you get to the point?"

"How'd you know it was me?"

"I heard Thelma Lee."

"Then why didn't you answer the damned phone when it rang?"

O.C. chuckled. "Because I like to aggravate you. What's the matter?"

"I'm on my way down to the river. Bill Caldwell's done pulled up a body while he was running his trotlines this morning. Said he didn't know who it was, so he left it tied off to a snag and floated down to Cody's honky-tonk and called from there."

The Sportsman's Lounge was one of half a dozen mean beer joints clustered on the Oklahoma side of the river. Sometimes referred to as Juarez, a nod toward the Rio Grande far to the south, the joints offered sawdust floors, three-two beer, a juke box, a dirt parking lot, and a good helping of trouble.

"That's Oklahoma's problem, Ned. Besides, Cody needs to run out there, not you. You remember you've retired."

"'Course I remember. My mind ain't gone yet." Ned watched through the screen door as one of the racers cruised slowly past on the highway and peered up the hill to see if anyone was home.

"I know the river belongs to Oklahoma, O.C. Bill had his lines set on the Texas side so he figured he'd let me know first." Texas had no jurisdiction beyond the south bank's drop-off to the water's edge. "I'll radio the sheriff there in Hugo and meet him on their side. We'll need to ride back out in Bill's boat. I don't intend to slide down that riverbank on my ass to see a dead man. I've seen one before."

O.C. chuckled again. The image of Ned sliding the twenty feet or so down the steep bank cheered him up. "All right, then.

Why'd he call you? Don't *he* know you've retired? You ain't the constable n'more."

"'Course he knows. But everybody out here's called me for so long that it's second nature. Cody'll be there shortly. We kinda have to wean them off of me, and some folks don't take to weanin' very quick."

"All right."

"You gonna be in your office later this afternoon?"

"Yeah, why?"

Ned doodled with a pencil on a Harvey Holmes Insurance notepad. "I'm gonna bring Top by to see you. Becky talked to his teacher a little while ago and she said that even though he's one of her best students, he's showing out this year." His voice softened. "I imagine it all has to do with the trouble we had last spring, but I'god, he's been a handful lately."

O.C. sighed. "What'd he do?"

He already had an idea his charge was getting dangerously close to what he called a butt-whoopin'. A reliable source reported that Top was seen down at the pool not far from the store, smoking with other kids. One of the smokers was Pepper. The virtual eleven-year-old twin was rough as a cob and cussed as well as any farmer in the county. Her daddy, James, was trying his best to raise her right.

"Well, it isn't any one thing in particular. He seems to be out of sorts. His grades are slipping, and he's always fooling around when he should be working. I swanny, that boy seems to think he's hard as a brick-bat all of a sudden. He's starting to puff up against a few of the older boys, and they'll likely give him a licking real quick if it keeps up. But they all feel sorry for him after what happened. One of these days though, he's going to make somebody mad and come home with another black eye, or worse.

"I intended to jerk a knot in that boy's noggin this weekend, so he'll straighten up and fly right when he gets back to his lessons Monday morning. But I got to thinkin' that if we came to see you…" He finished telling the old judge his idea.

O.C. laughed out loud and slapped his bony knee. "You betcha. I'll see you when you get here."

Ned hung up and called the Hugo courthouse. This time the phone rang straight through.

"Sheriff's office."

"Clayton Matthews, this is Ned Parker. What are you doing?"

The young sheriff sighed. "I was getting ready to go home and eat dinner, but I bet you're not hollerin' at me for a visit."

"You're right, hoss. I got a call about a body in the river. I'm heading down there in a few minutes. You want to meet me and Cody by the Sportsman?"

"You're supposed to be retired."

Ned sighed. "Don't I know it, but folks are still in the habit of turning to me first when there's trouble. Cody'll meet us there."

"All right. See y'all at the river."

The Red River bridge was ten minutes from Ned's house. He crossed to the Oklahoma side and turned right toward the cluster of dreary buildings perched on the riverbank, bumping over hard ruts until he got to a soft, deep beach-like sand bar. He shut off the engine when he saw Bill Caldwell standing beside his battered johnboat.

Bill gave a half-hearted wave and started forward. "Hidy, Ned."

Ned held up a hand. There was no reason for Bill to walk to the car. They'd just have to go back to the boat. He slammed the door and joined him at the water's edge. "You ready to go?"

"'Bout as ready as I can be. Ned, let me tell you, it liked to have scared me to death when that feller come to the top."

Bill Caldwell was a legendary cat fisherman along the river. Any time he set his lines, it was a sure bet he'd return with a boat load of fish, sometimes giant blue or flatheads, or at the very least a wash tub full of eating size channel cats. He'd fished the Red River his entire life and knew where the big ones lay in the deep holes and under washed out banks. All three of the bait houses on the Texas side sold Bill's fish, kept alive in large, aerated concrete troughs. Customers simply pointed to the ones they wanted and in minutes they were filleted and wrapped in newspaper.

"I expected a big old snappin' turtle, 'cause that's how they feel, just heavy an' still. I never imagined it'd be a body."

He stopped and glanced over Ned's shoulder. Radio antenna whipping, a low slung Oklahoma sheriff's car with worn out shocks cruised slowly past the beer joints and bounced to a stop beside Ned's Chevrolet. Sheriff Clayton Matthews emerged from the car and adjusted his Stetson. "Hidy, Ned."

"You all right, Clayton?"

Sheriff Matthews noticed the badge pinned to Ned's shirt. "Yep. Can't get away from it, can you?"

Ned sighed for the third time that day. "Naw, I cain't, even though Cody is the constable now. He'll be here directly."

"They let you wear that badge after retirement over there in Texas?"

"I didn't ask. I figured I'd put it on to make this about half-official until Cody showed up."

Sheriff Matthews wasn't sure he liked that line of thinking, but decided to hold his opinions. He squinted past Ned at the fisherman standing beside him. Ned nodded toward the old man. "Clayton, this is Bill Caldwell."

"We've not met." Bill extended his rough hand.

Matthews returned a firm grip. "Right. I've seen you on the river before, though."

"Don't doubt it. I have my license…" he reached into his back pocket.

"I don't need it." Matthews waved it away. "You can show it to the game warden when he gets here."

Bill was worried. "You called Homer Williams?"

"Well, since you caught somebody on a trotline in the river, I figured the game warden needed to be here, too."

Bill slumped sadly, as if a great burden had fallen on his shoulders. "I just want to get that feller off my line so I can go back to fishing."

Matthews nodded, understanding Bill was caught in a situation beyond his control. "How do you know he's still there? He might have come off in the current."

"Naw, them big one-ought hooks are buried deep in two or three places, and I tied with a piggin' string around his foot too, so he wouldn't come loose."

They were interrupted by the game warden's truck as it jostled across the rough parking lot. A flat-bottom johnboat stuck out over the lowered tailgate and rattled loud enough to make conversation difficult. He wasn't as concerned about the soft sand, and plowed through to stop beside the water's edge. The Sheriff met him, resting his hand on the open window. "Hello, Homer."

"He still in the water?" Homer wasn't much for pleasantries.

"That's what Bill says."

Homer nodded as Ned joined them beside the truck. "What are you doing on this side of the river? I thought you was retired."

"Bill called me first because he didn't know any better. Said he'd found that feller caught in his trotline."

Homer bit his chapped lip. "Trotline, my ass. Bill's been netting this river for the past two months and I haven't been able to catch him at it, yet."

All three men glanced toward Bill, who stood miserably beside his beached boat.

"Lordy," Ned said. "I hope he didn't accidentally drown somebody in a net."

"Only one way to find out." Still in the truck, Homer shifted into reverse and checked his mirror to make sure one of the new arrivals hadn't parked too close behind him. Word was getting out. An increasing number of cars and trucks turned off the highway to drive past the beer joints and stop close to the cluster of men beside the river. "Let me get this boat unloaded and we'll see."

Two men who'd drifted down to watch the activity helped lift the johnboat out of the truck, along with the motor and a gas tank. They carried it to the river and partially slipped it into the river. Minutes later, Homer stepped over the bench seats and hooked everything up. He wound the starter rope around the Johnson's flywheel and gave it a yank. The engine started with a roar, throwing out a cloud of blue smoke.

Cody Parker arrived and threaded his way through a crowd of loafers waiting on the sandbar. Back home from his tour of duty in Vietnam and recently elected as Constable of Precinct 3, Cody was something of a black sheep in his family.

Miss Becky spent considerable time at the Assembly of God church across the pasture from the barn, praying for Cody's salvation. She hadn't seen much progress, but her faith was as strong as Cody's free spirit.

Despite her distress, Cody took up with a married woman and purchased the nearby Sportsman Lounge, drawing sharp criticism from the residents in Lamar County. Norma Faye soon divorced her abusive husband, married Cody and they moved to Center Springs. More eyebrows rose after the election when Judge O.C. Rains swore Cody in as constable, citing the young man's experience in the military.

"Hell, he was a soldier over there in that Vietnam. I reckon being in the army is training enough to do what we need done here. Besides, I've sworn in elected constables that haven't done anything except milk cows before they pinned on a badge."

Proud of the young man with the tiny star on his chest, Ned motioned for Cody. "Climb in, Lawman. You and me'll ride with Bill."

Homer Williams and Sheriff Matthews exchanged glances, but they didn't see the need to puff up to the old constable who had been around for decades.

Ned stepped gingerly into Bill's boat that smelled strongly of fish and gasoline. He settled onto the front bench seat. Cody made his way to the middle and they soon led the way upriver, followed by the sheriff and Homer in the game warden's boat. Other boats followed the officials at a respectful distance on the wide river.

Ned watched the riverbanks pass as they slowly motored upstream, water glugging and slapping underneath the boat's flat bottom. Fall colors on the hardwoods lining the banks reminded Ned that he could be hunting squirrels instead of dealing with drowned people. This was what he wanted to get away from, but at the same time, he felt a little spark that he hadn't experienced since retirement.

Bill piloted the boat around a tree floating downriver. The Red often undercut the banks, toppling full grown trees and sweeping them along until they hung up against drifts on a bank, or against a bridge pylon.

After a while, Bill let off the gas with the hand throttle and pointed out where one of his trotlines disappeared into the depths. He angled across the river against the strong push of water.

"It's tied off on that big ol' root right there."

A large tree from the flood several months earlier lay half in and out of the water. Nearby, Ned saw a twenty-yard expanse of dark soft sandstone ledge pitted with half a dozen circular washtub-size holes full of water that he and Miss Becky used as play-pools when Top and Pepper weren't much more than toddlers.

Each hole contained a large, smooth rock that ground around and around when water submerged the ledge. Through the years, the strong current washed the rounded rock in circles, continually enlarging the tiny pools and keeping them open. It was community tradition to take the rocks out while the children played safely in the natural tubs, then replace them to continue the cycle.

It never crossed my mind that I'd be here today, pulling a dead man from the water so close to where those babies played.

Bill piloted the boat past a submerged tangle of roots and drifted back over the thick nylon cord disappearing into the river's deep channel. He leaned over the gunwale and grabbed the cord with a calloused hand. "Give me a minute and I'll have him up." He grunted at the heavy mass on the line. Cody shifted to the same side, reached deep into the water, and held onto the cord to help fight the current.

In the other boat, Williams held steady near the trotline disappearing in the red, muddy water. The game warden dropped a three-prong grappling hook straight down and hung the cord with the ease of a man who had inspected hundreds of trotlines through the years. He grasped the cord and raised it completely out of the water to see empty hooks dangling free. "Glad it isn't a net, Bill."

Bill didn't take his eyes from his end of the trotline. "I told you how he was caught. You ain't gonna catch me lying, I ain't that kind."

The body rose slowly, becoming clearer as it neared the surface. Cody and the game warden recoiled at the sight of a headless corpse. Cody shot Bill an angry glare. "You didn't say he didn't have no head!"

"Well, I didn't know if I should or not. I figured you and Ned would see that soon enough."

Ned snorted. "You oughta give a man some warning, Bill. *Goddamn*, I'd liked to have been ready for *that*!"

Turtles and fish had been at the bloated corpse. Stiffened in death, his arms stuck out from the torso. Swollen fingers splayed like evil, white sausages.

With its emergence into the air, a horrific stench enveloped Bill's boat, causing everyone to recoil.

"Can you tell who it is?" Bill pinched his nose closed.

Ned had the unusual ability to use the velum, the teardrop-shaped flap in the back the throat, to close off the passages to his nose. He was one of the few people in the county with the ability to block smells with this conscious mechanical process, while breathing through his mouth and keeping his hands free.

He leaned over the side and watched the water wash over the bloated figure. After a cursory examination, he leaned back. "Naw. Since he ain't got no head and all swole up, I can't tell if he's anybody I know, but you can bet Bill's off the hook for drowning him. Well, Sheriff, I believe you've got a murder on your hands."

"Wasn't asking for one." Matthews hadn't even peeked at the body. He had a weak stomach and didn't want to puke in front of the men.

"There's something wrong here besides what I can see and all." Ned studied the body for a long moment. "Looky here, Homer."

The game warden shifted to better see the lines. "What, besides them hooks buried in this feller?"

"Yep. Check the bait."

"There ain't none."

"That's right, Bill, there's not a single piece of bait on any of these hooks."

"Well, I hadn't gotten to this line since yesterday, so they got all my bait."

"Don't feel any fish on here, either." Any time a fisherman ran his trotlines, he knew if there was anything at the far end, because the line thrummed with the fighting fish. "Had you already run this line?"

"Naw. Dammit, Ned. I didn't have any luck in this hole at all. You think I had something to do with killing this feller?"

"I didn't say that, I was wondering is all."

"All right," Sheriff Matthews said. "Let's get off this river. Get us over there, Homer, and let's get this thing done."

Raising nearly two hundred pounds of rotting meat into a boat was completely out of the question. Homer tugged a short piece of cotton rope from a 'toe sack lying on the bottom of his boat and used it to tighten the body fast against the side.

Bill opened his pocketknife and used his sharpest blade to cut the piggin' string and the smaller drop cords tied to the large hooks buried in the man's side. The trotline snapped back to the depths and they drifted free.

"What are things coming to?" Ned asked aloud. He question was lost as Bill yanked his boat motor to life. A belch of exhaust spread across the slick river.

Homer grunted, started his own outboard, and followed slowly in their wake. Matthews turned from the body only inches away and watched the Texas side of the river go past. The stench washed over him and he shifted to the other side, gagging.

Minutes later they passed under the Highway 271 Bridge, motored through the shallow water, and onto the sandbar. Once they beached, Cody stepped out and grabbed the bow of Bill's boat. He waded out, pulling them securely onto the sand. One by one, the men climbed out.

Without a word, Sheriff Matthews pitched his life jacket onto the metal seat and trudged across the sand through a crowd of onlookers. He opened his car door and sat behind the wheel to shuffle through a dry stack of sun-curled papers in the dusty dashboard. Finding the one he wanted, he squinted at the sheet.

He returned to the waiting men. "Well, I know who he is now. I have a paper here with the description of a convict who broke out from the mental institution up in Tulsa a few days back. He had a tattoo of a hula girl on his left arm with the name of Cora under it… like that one. That there is Kevin Jennings. I guess we ain't looking for *this* escapee no more."

"Good god," a wrinkled old farmer said. "It's the Jennings boy from up on Boggy Bend. They had to send him to the nervous house years ago when he had some kind of breakdown."

"I remember that," Jimmy Foxx Wilson said. He and his brother Ty Cobb had been loafing up at the store when they heard about the body and dropped by to see if they knew who it might be. "He went haywire one day when his family was at church and killed every cow, chicken, horse, and pig on the place. He was a-waitin' on his folks to get home so he could kill them too, but a neighbor seen what happened and flagged the family down and warned 'em."

The men on the sandbar shook their heads in wonder. None of them understood how anyone allowed themselves to go insane.

"Wonder what he's doing here in the river?" Cody wondered aloud.

"He probably came back to hide out where he knows the country," Ned said.

"That don't explain why he's in that shape." Sheriff Matthews rolled up the report. "He was broke out by them two fugitives who'd been killing folks in Nebraska and Kansas before they went back to get him. I heard one of them had been in the same nuthouse and got to know Jennings there."

"So they picked him up, and came down here." Cody fished in his shirt pocket for a toothpick.

Ned sighed. "Well, with this one gone there's still two of those outlaws left and they're close by."

The sheriff turned from watching the newly arrived ambulance drivers put the decomposed body into a bag for transportation back to Hugo. "Naw. I got a report in the mail this morning that that they found another body in the same shape not far from the Little River, outside of Cloudy, near two days ago. That was Albert Gantry, the guy Kendal Bowden started this murder trip with. With this one gone, that leaves Kendal." He waved a hand toward the northeast. "I didn't think much about it until this one showed up, but it appears to me the meanest of the bunch is cleaning house."

"Makes sense."

Cody cocked his head and worked his toothpick around. "What makes you say that, Ned?"

"Because that's what I'd a done. Now he's on his own with nobody to rat him out."

"He's a mean one, killing people during robberies and cuttin' the heads off'n his own friends," the sheriff said. "The laws have been chasing him a far piece."

"Well, this goes to show that some folks just need killin'." Ned turned upriver. "He ain't the kind to have friends, and that's why this man is in the water. Bowden is finished with him and I bet you a dollar to a donut that he was headed here from the start. I imagine right now he's somewheres close by with kinfolk. They're the only ones that'll have him."

Chapter Four

Me and Pepper were watching Miss Carol's Playhouse on the black and white television when Grandpa got back from getting that feller out of the river. Without a word, he passed through the kitchen and living room and went into the bathroom. He stayed in there a good long time, washing his hands over and over, before he came out. Miss Becky went in right behind him and spent a good five minutes drying the sink, wall, and mirror that he splashed.

Instead of leaving right away, Grandpa went back outside to stand in the yard and watch the empty highway.

We followed him and fooled around in the yard while he talked to himself. Miss Becky puttered around in the kitchen, waiting, because she knew he needed to work through whatever was on his mind until he was ready to go. We've always called our grandmother Miss Becky, because that's how Grandpa always talked about her. As usual, she hadn't asked him one single question about what he'd been doing.

He finally came back to the porch. "What are y'all waiting on?" He called to Miss Becky through the kitchen's screen door. "C'mon, Mama. It's getting late."

She picked up her purse and came outside without a word, like she'd been the one holding us up. I'd already put Hootie in the corn crib so he wouldn't try and follow us to town. Pepper and I climbed into the back seat and Grandpa had the car backing up before the motor smoothed out.

Pepper leaned over the seat. "Grandpa, can we listen to the radio? They might be playing a new Beatles or Rolling Stones song."

"Naw, we ain't listening to any of that noise from them long-haired pukes." He dialed the radio for a moment and bluegrass came out of the one speaker on the dash. "That there's Bill Monroe with that new kid Del McCoury playing with him. Now that's music."

Miss Becky put an end to any further arguments when she put her hand on Grandpa's shoulder and turned around to face us. She almost caught Pepper sticking her tongue out at Grandpa's back. "Why don't you read one of them comic books like Top until we get there?"

Pepper swelled up and grabbed one of my Rawhide Kid comics from between us. When Miss Becky turned back around, she held it in front of her face. "Shit." She peeked over the top to see if Miss Becky heard her whisper.

I stifled a giggle. After the song, we heard a Pepsodent commercial that stuck in my mind until we parked beside the courthouse, half an hour later.

You'll wonder where the yellow went when you brush your teeth with Pepsodent.

We slammed doors and gathered beside the statue of a Confederate soldier.

Miss Becky checked her purse for a list. "I need to go to Woolworth's to get some thread while y'all are in there with O.C. I'm going by Duke and Ayers, too."

Grandpa seemed to barely pay attention to her because he had something on his mind. "You take Pepper with you. Top and I have business inside."

The frown Miss Becky gave Grandpa told me she didn't know what he was talking about, but she never argued with him in front of us kids. "That'll be all right." She reached back in her purse and handed me the new puffer I always carried for my asthma. "I heard you wheezing. Take a dose of this before y'all go in."

I was always wheezing because my asthma was so bad, so I squeezed the bulb, and inhaled the atomized medicine. My lungs immediately itched deep down inside for a moment and I breathed easier. I hung it out of my back pocket.

"Let's go." Grandpa turned and led the way without another word. I threw Pepper a grin as they followed the sidewalk toward the town square. She stuck her tongue out at me. Miss Becky saw it and was giving her a good talking to about acting like a lady as Grandpa and I climbed the granite courthouse steps. For a kid, the tall arches over the front doors almost reached to the sky.

Our footsteps echoed in the tiled foyer on the way to the elevator. The place always smelled like bleach and mothballs. I followed Grandpa, even though I'd been there many times before. He never turned around to see if I was behind him, but he knew I wouldn't get too far. I saw the wall-mounted water fountain and like any kid, it made me want a drink, even though I wasn't thirsty.

I trotted across the tiny black and white tiles. I'd turned the handle to sip from the stream of water when a hand grabbed the back of my collar and jerked me nearly off my feet.

Surprised, I gave a yelp.

"Shhh," Grandpa said almost in a whisper, letting go of my shirt. He pointed toward another fountain five feet away. "You don't use *this* one. We use that'un there."

They were exactly alike, and I couldn't figure out what he meant. Then I saw the "Colored Only" sign over the fountain.

"What's the difference?" Water was water.

He ignored the question. "Get you a drink over there if you're thirsty and let's go."

"I don't understand."

"I know you don't, but that's how it is right now."

The idea sounded ridiculous to me. We all drank from the same dipper out of the water bucket back home. Separate water fountains for colored and white people didn't make sense, but grownups had funny ideas about things.

"Where do the Indians get a drink?" I asked.

For a second Grandpa had a strange expression on his face, like he'd never thought of that question. It was a surprise, because Miss Becky was Choctaw. "I reckon they can…. hurry up and come on." I changed fountains and followed him to the elevator where the old Negro man opened the safety gate and gave us a big smile.

"Mornin', Mister Ned."

"Morning, Jules. How you feeling today?"

"Tolerble well. Bless you for askin'. Who's that you got with you?"

He knew me, but most adults tended to kid young'uns. I stepped into the elevator with them. "Howdy, Jules."

Grandpa's big knuckle sharply cracked the back of my noggin. "That's *Mr.* Jules to you."

With tears of embarrassment and shame in my eyes, I stared down at my Red Ball sneakers. Two reprimands in only a few minutes had me feeling sorry for myself. "I'm sorry, Mr. Jules." I swallowed a huge lump in my throat and stared at the ground.

"Thass all right, Master Top." He closed the metal gates. "Y'all going to see Mr. O.C. this afternoon?" He put his gnarled thumb on the fourth floor button.

I focused on the long, yellowed nail on that thumb to keep from crying. Grandpa put his hand on my shoulder and gave it a squeeze. "Yessir, we are, but we'd like to go to the top first, please."

Mister Jules was genuinely surprised, but when Grandpa nodded, he pushed the embossed button. The elevator groaned, jerked and squealed as we rose slowly, cables clanking overhead.

Grandpa kept his hand on my shoulder and gave it a little squeeze. "How's Lily today, Jules?"

He smiled and settled into their familiar conversation. "Fair to middlin' I reckon today. 'Leventh wife Lily was cannin' beans when I left this morning."

Grandpa chuckled. "You don't call her eleventh wife Lily at home, do you?"

I was sure Mr. Jules was around a hundred and four because he had outlived ten other wives. In my opinion, the frail old man should have been home sitting in front of the fire. Instead, he showed up every day for work as the Elevator Man at the Lamar County Courthouse.

"Aw, nawsir, I don't. She'd have a rigor if I did that. I call her 'leventh wife so's y'all know who it is I'm talkin' about." Jules stopped the elevator, adjusted it level, opened the safety gate, and then the door to reveal a floor full of jail cells. "See y'all in a little bit."

"Sure enough." Grandpa and I stepped off.

"What are we doing?" I asked. "Is Mr. O.C. up here today?"

One of the sheriff's deputies rose from behind a wooden desk a few feet away. His hair was slicked back with the Vitalis that filled the air. The man was nearly as big as Mr. John Washington, the county's only colored deputy, and his shoulders were wide as a Buick. I one time heard somebody say Mr. John was near big as a grizzly bear.

"Howdy, Ned. This the one?"

Grandpa put his hand back on my shoulder with a firm grip. "Sure is. Top, let's follow this man. I want to show you something."

The serious deputy picked up a set of keys and led us past the desk, around a corner, and into a wide aisle running the length of the concrete floor between two long lines of open jail cells. A few sorry-looking men loafed in the cells, sitting and laying on the bunks. One was standing with his back to us, his hands around the bars set in one of the many outside windows that were the only ventilation for the prisoners.

The deputy clacked his nightstick against the bars as we passed. "Don't you be yelling out the winder there, Eugene. I'll cuff you to your bed if you do."

"You can kiss my ass, Harvey." The prisoner turned around. "Well, I'll be damned, you arresting kids for playing hooky these days, Ned?"

Before he could answer, Judge O.C. Rains came up behind us. "Howdy, boys." He was breathing hard, so I figured he'd climbed up the stairs from his office on the fourth floor.

I was in awe of the old judge who was always larger than life, like a movie star. His thick white hair and matching eyebrows reminded me of those judges in movies they showed late at night on Channel 12. He always wore dark suits and thin little ties, and of course, his Stetson.

Knowing what Grandpa expected, I stuck out my hand and said hello. Judge O.C. gave me a solemn shake and turned his attention back to Grandpa. I didn't listen to their conversation, because I was watching the prisoners who all suddenly became very interested in me.

One was dressed in nothing more than rags. In the cell next to him was a black man with a huge mouse over one eye where someone caught him a solid lick.

I didn't have time to notice the other convicts, because a metallic clank echoed as Deputy Harvey unlocked an empty cell. When I turned my eyes back from the open door, Grandpa and Mr. O.C. waited there, staring down at me. Deputy Harvey stepped back with a stern face.

Mr. O.C. frowned, his white eyebrows almost touching over the bridge of his nose. "Son, your Grandpa told me you've been acting up back home."

Stunned at the turn of events, I glanced from one old man to the other. "Uh, well…"

Grandpa broke in. "I also heard you played hooky for a couple of hours with another young outlaw, and someone saw y'all smoking down at your Uncle James' pool."

Even more shocked, my ears rang and my lungs refused to cooperate. "We…"

"That right?" Mr. O.C. had me off balance. "Well, I'm sorry to see you've fallen in with a bad bunch, son. What do you have to say for yourself?"

Mr. O.C. leaned forward with his hands on his knees to get closer to my eye level. He was an expert in the courtroom and I was no match for the glaring old prosecutor's questioning. "What else have you done and thought you got away with? Have you done anything else that could be wrong in the eyes of the law? That's either a yes or no answer."

Questions came hard and fast and suddenly I couldn't think quick enough. "Uh." I peeked up at Grandpa for some relief, but he stared at me with those ice blue eyes, waiting on an answer. "Yessir."

Grandpa's shoulders slumped. "That's it, then."

Judge O.C. nodded and straightened to his full height. "Yes, it is. Texas Orrin Parker, a.k.a. Top, for your misdeeds at school, for smoking, cussin', drinking, and being a general all around scalawag, I hereby sentence you to..." he checked the pocket watch from his vest, "...one hour in jail, commencing right now, to think about all the things you've done wrong. May God have mercy on your soul."

My mouth fell open as those words echoed through the cells like the voice of doom, sounding like the hanging judge I'd watched in a western the night before. Grandpa turned his back to me and my eyes felt hot with tears.

"Wait a minute. Grandpa...?"

The big deputy stepped up, squeezed my shoulder and firmly turned me toward the cell. He put my hands on the bars. "Stand right there and don't move, prisoner. I have to frisk you."

I tried to turn and see Grandpa over my shoulder, but Deputy Harvey gripped the back of my neck with a much stronger hand and held me still. "I said don't *move!*"

Shocked, I hardly breathed. He patted under my arms, down my sides, and on down around my legs. Next, he tapped my back pockets and felt the puffer. He raised his eyebrows at Grandpa, and I guess he must have shook his head, because Deputy Harvey left it here.

With two fingers he reached in my other back pocket and removed a couple of washers, the unopened prize from a box of Cracker Jack, a small compass from an entirely different box of Cracker Jack, a roll of fishing line wrapped around a piece of wood, and half a piece of Juicy Fruit chewing gum.

He switched to my front pockets. The left one produced a couple of screws, an interesting rock, a piece of furry hard candy, and a dozen BBs. It was my other pocket that really got me in trouble. Besides my pocket knife that Uncle Cody had given me, he found Pepper's now broken cigarette and a wooden match I'd absently stuck in there only a couple of hours before.

My eyes widened and I felt as if the floor moved under my feet. "That's not mine."

The deputy handed the contraband to Judge O.C. "That's what they all say, prisoner." He pushed me into an empty cell. "Sit right down on that bunk right there and don't you move until you're released. I don't want to hear a peep out of you, neither."

Numbly, I stumbled across the cell as if going to the gallows. When I turned to sit on the edge of the hard bunk, the deputy slammed the door with a clang and turned the lock. I saw Judge O.C. hand the cigarette to Grandpa. He had an expression that about broke my heart, and the three of them left without another word.

I was alone in jail.

For the first time I noticed the scruffy men at the bars had moved closer, watching me from the adjoining cells. I'd always heard about your blood running cold, and now I knew what that meant.

"Hidy, boy." One of the prisoners scratched the stubble on his cheek. He had a crooked grin and teeth to match. I wanted to run to the door and scream for help, but I knew Grandpa and Mr. O.C. were men of their word. I'd be there for the entire hour. "I wish they'd-a put you in my cell. I'd like the company."

The wristwatch they'd left on my arm said I'd been there for only one minute.

The prisoner on the other side hung his hands through bars and rested his elbows on the cross brace. He had a wicked scar under his left eye. I was sure it came from a knife fight in one of the honky-tonks across the river in Oklahoma and his blood had run free and soaked the sawdust floor Grandpa once told me about. "You're pretty young to be an outlaw, but that's all right. I got *my* start when I was about your age. They didn't catch me till quite a bit later, though. It was my drinkin' that tripped me up. They caught me drunk down in the cane breaks and liked to have beat me to death in a ditch before they put me under arrest."

His mention of drinking brought Mr. O.C.'s words back to me. I wondered if the judge found out that me and Pepper had been sneaking into the evidence jars stored in the smokehouse to take little bitty sips of the clear white lightning on the top shelf. Grandpa always kept a small quart jar full of confiscated whiskey as a memento for each still he broke up down in the bottoms.

Crooked Teeth reached way into the cell, as far as his arm could reach. "I like the material on that shirt, boy. Scooch over here so I can feel it for a minute, would you?"

Horrified, I stared straight ahead at the cell door and didn't stir.

"Naw, don't listen to him, son." Scar hawked up a thick wad of green snot and spat. "You slide over thisaway and let me rub that fresh boys-regular haircut." He stuck his arm through the bars and wiggled his fingers at me. "I love the way that short hair feels under my hand."

I tried not to cry, I'd been through worse last year and I was hoping Grandpa would hurry up and come back soon to get me out. I sat dead in the middle of the bunk, barely beyond the two inmates' reach.

"I heard what you're in fer," Crooked Teeth said. "I wish I'd'a stayed in school and studied harder. I wouldn't be locked up here today if I had."

Scar shook the solid bars, but they didn't budge. He jumped up, put his feet on the lowest crosspiece and hung there like a monkey. "I played hooky all the time and that led to smoking, drinking, and card playing, and the next thing I knew I was in the pen. I got out, but didn't have no education so I couldn't get a job, and wound up back here again."

Crooked Teeth shuffled his feet. "I only have three more weeks on my sentence, and when I get out I have a job picking cotton. You can come when you get out and pull bolls with me if you want."

Scar wasn't interested, and I knew why. Picking cotton was one of the hottest, hardest jobs I knew of. A lifetime of working in the fields was a depressing thought. "Naw, I'll see what happens when I get out after Christmas. Hey boy, I saw that toonie they got out of your pocket. You wouldn't happen to have another smoke stuck away would you? I'd dearly love one right now. You can use them for money in here, too."

I didn't answer, because I started wheezing, feeling miserable, and scared. It was a good thing Miss Becky had given me the puffer before we came in, or I'd have been in serious trouble. I tugged it loose from my back pocket, squeezed another dose into my lungs, and continued to stare straight ahead.

The prisoners gave up reaching for me. Concentrating on my breathing, I managed to tune out their conversation and counted the seconds, then minutes. Someone came down the aisle and stopped in front of my cell. I glanced up to see Deputy John Washington standing there under his hat.

Folks called him Big John, because he was near seven feet tall and built like a mountain. He was the first official Negro deputy in the county and most of all, he was Grandpa's good friend. Tears welled and I wanted to sob when he shook his great head. "I swanny. What's this world coming to? I never thought I'd see *you* in here."

I'd lost my last friend. He was our rescuer, the self-appointed protector of all Parkers, and I felt I'd let him down. "Mr. John?"

He held his hand up to stop me, his eyes sad. "Don't say nothin'. You don't owe *me* any explanation. But you owe one to your granddaddy, and Miss Becky. This is gonna break her sweet old heart. I swan, I never would have believed it if I hadn't seen this with my own two eyes."

Looking forever lost, he turned to leave and was nearly to the corner when the colored man in the cell across the aisle stood up and put his hands on the bar.

"Tell your granddaddy it's in the bottoms."

Big John turned around. "What did you say to that boy, Norbert?"

"Nothin. I didn't say nothin' to nobody. Just singin' is all."
He sang low, almost tunelessly.

I learned a long time ago,
From someone that oughta know,
That no one knows the truth about a woman.
You know they's kinda strange,
Yeah lawd they's kinda strange,
But they say we're stranger.

He turned and lay down on the bunk facing the brick wall.

"Well, don't be saying nothin' else to that boy right there
or I'll match that mouse under your other eye." Mr. John left
without another word.

"Kinda strange," Norbert told the wall. "Kinda strange,
kinda strange."

Tears still leaked from my eyes nearly an hour later when
Grandpa and Mr. O.C. came back to get me. Deputy Harvey
fiddled with his keys and finally unlocked the iron door. Grandpa
studied me with his hands in his pockets. "Well, what did you
think about being in jail?"

I wanted to run across the cell and into his arms, but he stood
there like he was watching his cows. "I didn't like it."

Mr. O.C. scratched the back of his neck. "You want to hear
the sound of that door shutting behind you again?"

I fought down a sob and drew a deep breath. "Nossir."

"Well then," Grandpa said. "You remember what it was like
to be with these outlaws the next time you want to get into any
foolishness. Now, you straighten up and fly right so you won't
see the inside of this place no more."

"I will."

We left, me walking between the two old lawmen, followed by
the deputy. Mr. O.C. wouldn't leave it alone. "You know, Ned.
This is like when we walk a man to the gallows, him between
you and me, with a deputy behind us to shoot the prisoner in
case he tries to run."

"That's right, but Top's learned his lesson, haven't you?"

Not trusting my voice, I nodded and fought more tears until we got on the elevator Mr. Jules held for us. He gave me a sympathetic wink and took us down to Mr. O.C.'s floor. In his office, all my stuff, except for the match and cigarette, was in the only chair that wasn't full of papers. I put everything back in my pockets while they ignored me and talked law business.

"Ned, Merle Clark didn't come home three days ago and Shirley is getting worried."

"Why are you telling me, O.C.? I ain't constable no more."

"Well, dammit you cranky old fart, you know about everybody in the county, and I thought you might keep your ears open and help Cody. I done told him this morning and now I'm-a tellin' you."

"Merle's probably laid up drunk somewhere. Did Shirley think he went across the river?"

"She didn't say. He left for the field the usual time and didn't come home."

"Anybody find his truck?"

Mr. O.C. sighed and twiddled his flyswatter. "Nope. The tractor was sitting in the shade where he left it after he plowed all day. He just got in his truck and disappeared."

"I've thought about doing that myself from time to time."

"Yep, but you never did it. Keep an ear open and help Cody, if he needs it."

"He's doing fine. He'd do a lot better if people'd quit calling on me whenever they need the law. They need to get in the habit of calling Cody."

"They will."

Grandpa finally picked up his hat. "Well, I reckon we'll go. Top, you ready?"

I was more than ready. We said goodbye to Mr. O.C. He winked at me as we left. In the elevator Mr. Jules' crooked old hand gave me a little pat on the shoulder to let me know things were all right.

When we came out of the courthouse doors, Miss Becky and Pepper were waiting in the cool shade of the crepe myrtles on the north side. Pepper frowned. "Why are your eyes red? You don't look good."

"I don't feel too good, neither."

"Come here and let me see if you have fever." Miss Becky put the back of her fingers on my forehead and cheek. Embarrassed, I pulled away and glared at Pepper.

"You're fine." Miss Becky turned to Grandpa with a concerned look on her face. "Everything work out all right?"

He gave her small grin. "Ummm humm."

My breathing was finally getting back to normal when I saw the two prisoners, Scar and Crooked Teeth, from upstairs. They came down the courthouse steps, dressed like deputies. I gasped and pointed at them, thinking they were making a jailbreak and had killed men for their uniforms.

When they noticed us standing in the shade, Crooked Teeth waved at Grandpa. He smiled, nodded, and waved back. "Much obliged, boys. I'll see y'all later."

Stunned, I watched him turn toward the square without changing expression. He started to rest his right hand on the gun at his belt, then realized it was no longer there. He stuck it in his pocket, instead. "Now you know."

"What?" Miss Becky didn't understand our conversation.

"Nothin' much. Talk among menfolk. How *you* been acting in school, Pepper?"

"Fine, Grandpa."

He gave her a long eyeball before answering. "Uh huh. Let's go and get done here so we can get on home."

Chapter Five

Still feeling good about his little joke on Top, Ned was sure he'd gotten the youngster's attention. He dropped everyone at the house when they got back from town and drove up to Neal Box's general store. Ned recognized Rank Pickles and Curly Baxter, two hard working young cowboys on C.J. Emerson's ranch out west of Forest Chapel. Several other loafers gathered around the bed of Rank's battered 1940 Chevy pickup.

Ned slowed to a stop, tires crunching on the bottle-cap parking lot. He joined them beside the truck. "Boys."

They nodded a greeting in unison. "Mr. Ned."

"Whatcha got in there? Somebody shoot a lion, Harlan?"

Harlan Westlake ran a little cotton farm up near Forest Chapel. "Naw, Mr. Ned. We're admirin' Rank's new tires."

"Those are nice caissons. Rank, you boys been up on the river north of y'all's ranch in the last few days?"

Rank shrugged. "We get up there ever now and then. It all depends on where the cows are. Why?"

"Well, me and Cody helped haul a feller out of the river this morning and I doubt he drowned. His head was already gone when he went in. I was wondering if you've seen anybody on C.J.'s place lately. I believe he went in between y'all and where the river shallows up some out on Sandstone Ledge."

"I thought you was retired," Curly said.

"I am, but I figured I'd give Cody a hand with this one."

Rank leaned on the dented front fender and cleaned his nails with a pocketknife. "I haven't seen anything, Mr. Ned. Shoot, I barely get off the place these days and that's usually to come up here to the store. We only went to Chisum a little while ago because we needed tires."

"That's right." Curly fished a plug of Days Work chewing tobacco out of his shirt pocket. "What makes you think he went in there? It's a long old river."

Ned rubbed the back of his neck. "That's a good question, but if he'd gone in anywhere between Garrett's Bluff and y'all's place I figure he'd a-hung up long before he got to Center Springs."

Curly bit off a chew and tucked the remainder back in his pocket. "We'd remember if we saw anybody, because that would be an event. We just work cows and don't see too many folks."

"All right boys. Let me know if you hear anything."

"Sure will." Rank shaved off a chunk of thumbnail and eyed the new arrival with disgust. "Shoot. There's Duane."

Duane Crowly was the community's skinny little problem child who still needed to learn a few manners. It wasn't that the young man wanted to *cause* trouble. Trouble always arrived right behind the nineteen year old who didn't have a clear understanding of where the lines were drawn.

Duane annoyed them by settling one cheek on Rank's open tailgate, tilting his Stetson back, and barging right into the conversation. "What are y'all talking about? There's nothing back here but empty feed sacks and post-hole diggers."

Curly leaned over and spat a thick stream of brown tobacco juice. "We were talking about Rank's new tires, Duane."

Duane examined the tires. "Shoot. This rubber is the best part of this old heap now. Rank, why don't you sell this wreck and buy a truck that will go with them new wheels?"

Harlan Westlake backed away from the anticipated killing. Another more faint-of-heart farmer quietly left. Ned watched with interest, wondering how Rank would handle the irritating pest.

He never twitched. "Well, Duane, my daddy gave me this old truck. It's worth a lot more than you think."

To a man, besides Duane, everyone at the store knew there are things in this world shouldn't be insulted; trucks, dogs, and wives included. Duane didn't have enough sense to let it go. "Man, if it was me I'd use this beat up old wreck to give the weeds something to grow around."

Curly practiced his shallow breathing, hoping that when Rank went into a blind rage he wouldn't notice him standing nearby and shoot him for simply *knowing* Duane.

Rank causally reached out, grabbed Duane's oversize ear with a callused thumb and forefinger, and pulled his wide eyes around to the front bumper. The assemblage in the parking lot brightened at the sight.

"School just took up, son. Now you listen with that other ear. See that crease in the bumper, next to the right headlight? I put it there when I was ten years old. Daddy was teaching me how to drive a standard shift and I hit a cultivator when I was trying to remember where the brake pedal was.

"See here. These scratches along the fender and door are a matched set with the other side. I got them the night Curly, Blackie, and I graduated from high school and went flying down a dirt road in Forest Chapel like we had good sense. The road turned, but we didn't. We plowed through a five-strand bob-wire fence and stopped nearly a hundred yards deep in a pasture full of rodeo stock with bad attitudes."

Duane's eyes crossed from the pain. Rank led him toward the cab. The farmers standing nearest the truck backed away, chuckling.

"That dent in the door there perfectly fits the side of my head. On my twenty-first birthday the girth broke on my saddle while I was chasing a calf past the catch pen. Right there's where I stopped.

"About all that's left of the driver's seat is a scrap of material and a couple of springs. Dad, who's long gone now, wore out the material. I'm wearing out the springs."

Duane's eyes bugged out like a mouse in a trap when Rank squeezed harder and gave his now very red ear a little shake for emphasis.

"Dad and I put in the gun rack when I was about eight. He carried his old Winchester in the top rack, and my BB gun always rode in the bottom."

Rank pulled Duane's ear around to the passenger door. Eyes watering, Duane followed. The gathering crowd of spectators scrambled out of the way. Rank pointed. "Daddy put *that* crease in the door when his eyes got so bad he couldn't hardly see to drive. The gate by the barn wasn't quite as wide as he remembered. The post didn't give, but the sheet metal did. See this?" He pointed at one particular dent surrounded by several others.

"I think," Duane gasped. "Do you want me to?"

"Those scratches came from the night Nelda and I backed into a ditch and got stuck when we should have been home where we belonged. I jacked it up, she gunned the engine, and when I shoved it off, and the handle flipped up and hit the tailgate. I'm lucky it didn't knock my fool head off."

Rank completed his tour by returning Duane to their starting point. "With Daddy driving, I shoved hay over this tailgate to feed the stock from the time I was big enough to walk. Then when I was grown, my boys did the same while they were still in diapers. Nelda was convinced they'd fall off and get killed, but I told her no one ever died from falling into cow paddies.

"I've cleaned birds on the tailgate, hauled deer home in the bed, and carried Clay Tate to the hospital when he fell off the roof of his hay barn and broke six ribs. This truck is my office and all those tools are what I use to make a living. I like this old truck. It has a lot of memories. And if you don't annoy me any more, you can live to have a few more memories, and *dents*, too."

He let go.

Duane rubbed his newly liberated ear and settled his hat. "Nice truck."

"Thanks."

The farmers laughed and slowly scattered, breaking into smaller groups to talk about crops or the weather. Ned was about to leave when Cody Parker turned his El Camino off the highway and coasted to a stop beside the domino hall. Ned grinned at the new constable who showed up a minute late and a dollar short.

"Ned, we've been calling the house and trying to get you to answer. O.C. tried your old Motorola, too. I went by and Miss Becky told me you were here."

"What's wrong?" Ned was annoyed to see some of the loafers drifting back to better hear their conversation.

"Issac Reader went over to have supper with Miss Onie Mae Brooks and found the whole family dead."

Ned felt his face go numb and his heart beat wildly. He'd grown up with Onie Mae. He might have married her at one time when they were teenagers, if things had worked out differently. "I'god. How long ago did he find her? What happened?"

"Nearbout's an hour ago I reckon. He didn't say how they died. The funeral home has an ambulance on the way out there right now and Mr. O.C. wants me and you to meet them. Sheriff Griffin will be there directly."

"I thought you was retired, Ned," Duane said, still rubbing his ear.

The old man turned and pointed his finger. "I am, and men my age call me Ned. Boys your age generally call me Mr. Ned, or Mr. Parker. How 'bout you try one of them two."

"Yessir, Mr. Ned."

"That sounds better. C'mon Cody. You're the constable, and I ain't. Thissun's yours."

While Cody frowned at the order, Ned hurried across the parking lot to his car. Dusty inside and out, the sedan had once been his own office on wheels. He made a frustrated sound in his throat when he turned the key and the Motorola remained silent. He'd paid for the unit himself, and when he retired, Ned left it in the car so he could listen in on the chatter at night. It was a comfortable security blanket that took the edge off retirement.

However, for the past month the radio worked fitfully one day and not at all the next. Since the county no longer paid for repairs, Ned used the local shade tree mechanic, Rod Post, to keep the radio alive. Rod assured Ned he'd figure out what was wrong, but so far, his attempts at chasing down the electronic gremlins were disappointing.

Frustrated, Ned slapped the side of the unit a couple of times and the power light came on. He snatched the microphone off the mount and keyed the thumb switch. "Martha, this is Ned."

The radio crackled and the dispatcher came on. Depending on the situation, the sheriff's office communicated over the radio through a mix of plain talk, code numbers, and small town familiarity. "Ned, for god's sake, O.C.'s about to bust a gut because he hasn't been able to talk to you. We got a call that said somebody killed Onie Mae Brooks and her whole family. He wants you to get over there right now."

Forgetting that Cody should have led the way, he keyed the mike again as his tires squalled on the pavement. "I know. Cody told me. We'll be there directly."

"Holler and tell us what you find." Ned recognized O.C.'s voice through the tinny speaker.

"I'll have Cody call in when we know more. He's the constable now, not me."

O.C. didn't answer and Ned replaced the microphone on its metal bracket. Seeing Cody behind, he stomped the accelerator and the big engine roared.

Chapter Six

Onie Mae lived with her son Josh and his wife in the family home in Forest Chapel, overlooking the fertile bottomland he farmed after his dad passed.

She had been part of Ned's life ever since they were kids attending the one-room schoolhouse in Center Springs. The thought of her murder sat like a lump of clay in Ned's stomach as his sedan flew down the highway at more than eighty miles per hour.

The winding country roads weren't made for speed, and after each turn Ned breathed a sigh of relief when there wasn't a cow, or a slow-moving farm truck, or a tractor puttering along in his lane. He pushed the accelerator even harder each time he saw the highway was clear, feeling the front end loose and shaky through the steering wheel.

The two-lane concrete split to a farm to market blacktop that narrowed into a skinny tree-lined county road. Ned steered onto the gravel, forcing himself to slow down on the curves, knowing he'd quickly slide into the steep cut banks, especially if he hit a thick blanket of fallen leaves. A cloud of dust filled his rearview mirror as gravel rattled against the undercarriage.

He braked to make a fishhook left-hand turn up the hill, barely avoided the ditch, shot up the Brooks' steep tree-lined drive, and slid to a stop in the open yard. Issac Reader's battered farm truck sat beside Josh's newer Ford. A normally jerky little man, Reader was even more animated as he jumped out of the cab at the sight of Ned's car.

"Listen, Ned! They was dead when I got here!"

As usual, Isaac started talking before he was close enough to be understood, which always annoyed Ned to no end. He opened the door and killed the engine. Isaac closed the distance, still talking.

"Slow down, Ike. I didn't hear a word you said. What was it?"

The nervous little farmer grabbed Ned's door frame and stood in the way. "I said they was all dead when I got here."

"Well, get out of the way so's I can get out and stand up."

Isaac backed up as Cody slid to a stop behind Ned's car. Leaving the El Camino door open, he joined them. "You know, Ned, you really should have let me lead. I have lights on this thing."

Ned shot a glance at the single red light on the driver's side of Cody's El Camino. "We didn't pass a single car on the way over here and besides, nobody'll get out of the way of that thing. They know my car."

"Y'ain't the *law* no more, Ned."

That slowed the old man down as he realized the truth. "That's what I keep telling folks."

Ignoring their exchange, Reader backed away and waved his hand toward the house. "Listen, I wasn't paying any attention when I got here. When I glanced up I thought Josh was asleep up there, but when I got out of the car and saw him like that and the flies…and…everthang."

Cody considered Josh's remains across the roof of his car. Reader was right. The man almost looked normal in his rocker, except that his head was gone.

The three paused in the yard. Cody cleared his throat. "I suspect he's for sure dead."

Reader nodded. "He's cold as clay."

"Did you touch anything, Isaac?"

"Listen, Cody, you know better than that. Listen, I scatted off the porch right after I saw them in there and come out here to the car."

"Then how'd you call the sheriff's office?" Ned knew his old friend better than most folks. "Did you go call from somewhere else and drive back here?"

Isaac dropped his gaze to stare at his dress shoes. He wore his best clothes for the visit. "Well, I *might* have stepped inside to use the phone there by the door."

Ned sighed. Talking to Isaac always made him tired, even though he'd known the man since they were kids. In fact, Isaac too had been in Onie Mae's class in school, but she always had eyes for Edward.

"Did you touch anything you haven't told us about, or see anything else?" Cody led the two men across the yard.

Isaac followed closely behind. Ned trailed in the rear. "Yeah, I saw Beth and Onie Mae laying in there in front of the fireplace like they was taking a nap. Listen, there's blood everywhere in the kitchen."

"You went in the kitchen, too?" Ned felt the heat rising in his face.

"Listen, listen, it smelled like there was something burning on the stove since I was here for dinner, so I wanted to turn it off in case the house caught afire, but the pans was cold, so somebody turned them off after dinner had done burnt up, but I don't think she was cooking today, so I bet it happened yesterday."

"You may be right, but you need to slow down now and let us handle this. Stay out here while me and Cody check things out. If anybody comes up, you keep them in the yard. Better yet, stop them back there at the top of the drive."

"Listen, I won't let no-one else up here lessen you say so."

Ned started up the well-worn steps behind Cody and stopped. "Do they have their heads, inside?"

Isaac nodded quickly. "They're whole."

"Thank the lord." Relieved that he wouldn't have to endure still another horror, Ned joined Cody and knelt beside the rocker and Josh's remains.

Isaac was right. The man had been dead for hours and flies droned in a cloud around the body. At the moment Ned didn't know how or why, but he was sure the murders were tied to the escapees from Tulsa.

Leaving Josh, Ned opened the screen door and Cody followed him inside the immaculate living room, closing the screen quickly to keep as many flies as possible outside.

Apparently Isaac hadn't taken such care, for they crawled on the bodies carefully laid out on a gray and blue rag rug in front of the fireplace. The women hadn't died easily, and Ned figured they probably heard the murderer kill Josh, giving them time to fight back.

Ned felt light-headed. "I'god, look at this."

"Lordy. I've never seen so much blood."

"Folks have a lot in 'em."

A lake of congealed blood in the living room of the country home told the story of Onie Mae's arthritic struggle with the assailant who cut her throat. Ned noted the marks where the killer dragged her to where she now rested. He edged around the enormous pool and stepped into the kitchen.

Beth died in there, but she went down fighting. The knife drawer was open and a pump twelve-gauge with a broken stock lay covered in flour. Neither man entered, preferring to let the sheriff's department and the Texas Rangers make that investigation later.

Despite his military experience, Cody had never seen such a slaughter in his community and wasn't even close to being prepared for the sheer violence in the farmhouse. He breathed deeply to clear his head.

They returned to the living room. Pulling a yellowed handkerchief from his back pocket, Ned knelt and gently wiped a small spot of blood from Onie Mae's forehead. Then he carefully draped the handkerchief over her face, hiding his old friend's half-open eyes.

"Should you be doing that?"

Ned rose on cracking knees and wished he had another one for Beth. "I shouldn't be doing a lot of things here."

The sound of crunching gravel signaled the arrival of another vehicle. Ned carefully picked his way back around the blood and bodies when he heard Isaac's voice. Through the screen he saw Isaac Reader standing with his hand out in front of a deputy sheriff's car. Unfortunately, the little farmer was taking Ned at his word.

"Nossir, you cain't drive no futher. Listen, I got my orders from both Constable Parkers and they said no one drives in this yard."

The highly agitated deputy had opened his door and was obviously about to put Isaac in handcuffs. Cody stepped outside. "It's all right, Isaac. Good job, but let the deputy on up here, and the ambulance too when it gets here."

"Listen, you can drive on in now. Cody said it's all right. No hard feelings. Listen, listen, I was just following orders."

Instead of venting his anger on Isaac, the deputy punched the gas. He shot into the yard and parked beside Ned's car. He stepped out. "We got a call that a family was dead here."

"That's right." Ned came down the steps, more to get away from the flies than to make conversation easier. "That's what's left of Josh Brooks dead there in the chair, and his wife and mama are laid out inside."

"How'd they die?"

"Hard."

The deputy thumbed his hat back. "Are they…like that?"

"They're just dead."

Cody joined Ned at the car, breathing deeply to rid himself of the smell, and his mind of the sight they'd witnessed. "I'm liable to have bad dreams tonight."

"I have 'em ever night."

The younger constable studied Ned's lined face for a long moment. It hadn't occurred to him that the old man carried the burden of many years' worth of incidents and horrors on his shoulders. "I might need to talk to you about that later."

"Any time." Ned passed the deputy's vehicle and opened the door to his own car. He unhooked the microphone and pressed the key. This time it worked. "Martha. This is Ned. Tell O.C.

they're all dead here for sure and have been for a day or two. We'll need Arthur Myers to pronounce them."

The deputy left his car and stopped. "Hey, what are you doing with a radio? I thought you was retired."

Ned blew like a horse. "I'god, I thought I was too."

The fitful Motorola's speaker crackled. "All right, Ned. The ambulance will be there in a little bit and Arthur won't be far behind. You need anything else other than them and the Justice of the Peace? Is Cody there with you?"

"Yep, him and Deputy...?" he raised his eyebrows.

"Collier. Peter Collier."

"Deputy Pete Collier. I'm gonna let him and Cody take this over and get out of the way. You tell O.C. I suspect this is the work of whoever killed that feller we found in the river this morning."

Martha's voice sounded sad through the tinny speaker. "This is a busy day for you, ain't it? I thought retirement was supposed to be relaxing."

"Well, it ain't."

Chapter Seven

Even before the horrific Brooks murders, Cody Parker was often awakened by screams in the night; shrill screams borne of terror and ghostly pain. No matter how long he lay there in the darkness, heart beating fast enough to explode in his chest, the shrieks never repeated. He was surprised that Norma Faye didn't feel his heart pounding on her side of the bed.

It wasn't always mental screams that jolted him awake in the early morning hours. At first he marked it down to too much work, but each time he awoke with a strong emotional residue from those subconscious experiences.

If that wasn't bad enough, he constantly dreamed of houses. He recognized them in his sleep, structures as familiar as if he'd lived in them all his life. Once, Cody attempted to draw on the collected memories of those nightmares and the rough set of floor plans quickly sprawled beyond the paper's edges.

Maybe he built them with his own hands in other dreams.

Hidden rooms filled his dreams, rooms that he knew and recognized, but had never entered. Sometimes he moved confidently though spacious, well-lit attics, bright with golden yellow light, and planned to add bedrooms designed to fit the roof's slope. He walked confidently through the bright spaces, striking the rafters with the sure feet of a mountain goat. The rafters often led to enormous floored areas smooth as those in a ballroom.

A number of forgotten items waited there, things he remembered from *other* dreams. Lost backpacks, toys, tools, household items, and boxes never opened, yet he knew the contents.

Desiccated rats. Disgusting bundles of bones and hair.

The night after finding the bodies at Onie Mae's farmhouse, he dreamed of a long, coffin-like box in an attic, positioned near a crumbling brick chimney. The lid lifted slowly, silently, and a long, four-fingered hand emerged to reach over a pile of rubble to pluck a wriggling rat from its nest in the insulation. The door slammed closed and he heard obscene slurping sounds.

He opened the lid.

A horrible caricature of a clown emerged and attempted to paralyze him with its eyes. Cody backed around the chimney, closed his own eyes so he couldn't see the monster hiding behind a false face, and emptied his .45 at the creature.

Unopened boxes and lost items.

Those kinds of dreams weren't unusual for the Parkers. The foreboding "gift" they handed down allowed them to sense only fuzzy details of a coming calamity without the luxury of knowing when, where, or *if* the incident would occur. The sheer uncertainty was frustrating, because like Top's dreams of drowning in the Rock Hole, it gave him nothing more than a sense of dread.

The finely detailed dreams themselves were relentless.

From childhood his subconscious entered dark warrens burrowing *under* houses as he slept. He'd been in them, also. The tunnels began at the dream building's foundation and led downward toward even darker, unexplored recesses. Sometimes he wormed through a mine, and other times he wriggled like a mole through confining spaces barely wide enough for his shoulders.

One familiar passageway led to a large, cave-like area with a constant dribble of pure, drinkable water and boxes of ammunition stored off the damp floor. There, a large tree grew high on a ridge overlooking an unpainted, rundown house. Behind it, a wide pasture bordered by leafless trees ended at a fence row, and beyond that, a cultivated field led to a river.

He suspected his newest tunnel dreams came from his experiences in Vietnam. After being shot down in a helicopter, Cody liked being on the ground best. He volunteered and spent months exploring tunnels originally dug during the war against the French. But upon the arrival of the Americans in that tropical jungle, the tunnels quickly expanded into a network of mazes hiding those who fought against the U.S. military.

In Center Springs, as he lay awake in the darkness for hours beside the red-headed wife he loved so much, Cody wondered why he specifically dreamed of burrows.

His family had always dreamed.

At times their dreams and nightmares came true.

Chapter Eight

Pepper and I had been playing in the hay barn most of the morning one soft rainy Saturday. I made sure to stay on the alfalfa side. The Johnson grass baled and stacked on the right was full of dust that made my asthma act up. When we spent all day on the sweet smelling alfalfa bales, I never once wheezed.

The weather was cool enough that we played on the bales near the rafters without worrying about the heat coming through the sheet metal. It was safe there, because by fall, the yellow jackets and wasps mysteriously vanished in anticipation of the coming winter.

We built a fort, but after that, there was nothing to do but sit inside the walls and shoot my BB gun at the deserted wasp nests. Great-grandpa built the barn, and after years of baking in the sun, the rough sawn oak rafters were like iron. If I happened to hit one with a BB, it whanged off the hard wood like I shot an anvil.

I was listening to the rain shower on the tin roof when a splash in the nearby pool caught my attention. Peering through the open side, a swirl right beside the bank told me a fish was feeding. "Did you see that?"

Pepper turned around and shrugged. "The rain on the water?"

"No, a big fish just broke the water down there. We oughta go try and catch him."

"Have you forgot it's raining?"

"It ain't much more than a shower now. I don't intend to spend a long time down there getting wet, but our crawdad poles are right there by the feed barrels. Let's go down and see if we can catch that fish."

Our crawdad poles weren't anything more than two long sticks with heavy twine wrapped around one end. When the weather was nice, we snitched a couple of strips of bacon from Miss Becky's icebox and tied them onto the twine. Crawdads love bacon, so we spent hours sitting on the pool bank waiting for the line to twitch. When it did, that meant a crawdad was on the bait and we'd lift it carefully out of the water and onto the bank, hopefully before they let go with their big claws.

"Listen dumbass, twine on a crawdad pole won't hold a *fish*, and besides, we'll need a hook."

I thought of the smokehouse, where we kept the fishing gear. "Let's run down and get the poles then."

"Miss Becky'll make us stay in if she sees us out in the rain."

"We'll loop around behind the smokehouse. She won't be able to see us if we go that way."

Pepper gave in and we slipped out of the barn. I was surprised to see two extra cars in the drive. I thought I recognized one of them. It belonged to Miss Ethel Fay, who was older than dirt. She still drove, but most folks tended to get over on the shoulder whenever they saw her coming. I didn't recognize the other car.

"Shit," Pepper said. "The place is full of them old quilting women again."

It was one of those gray days that made women want to yap, so they rounded one another up to drive over and gather around the quilt rack hanging from Miss Becky's living room ceiling. That old living room saw a lot of uses, both happy and sad. It was full of laughter when they were quilting, or during Christmas and reunions, but it also was where they laid out great Uncle Vestal when an Hereford bull went crazy and stomped him to death one hot summer day during the war. They always said that even though they fixed Uncle Vestal's head, it was lopsided during the viewing. For once Grandpa didn't have to listen to folks say, "Don't he look natural?"

"Good." I realized the quilting party was working in our favor. "They'll all be in the living room and not paying attention to what's going on outside the window."

We cut through the wet grass behind the chicken house and from there it was nothing to slide carefully through the barbed wire instead of getting muddy by slipping under the gate.

Pepper waited while I peeked around to be sure the coast was clear. It was, and I darted through the partially open door, grabbed the rods, and ran back outside in seconds. Handing Pepper one of the rods, we slipped back through the fence and repeated our route back behind the barn. From there it was only a hundred yards to the pool.

We were soaking wet from the rain by the time we got there. I slowed down. "Shhh, there's crawdads peeking out of the water. That's what the fish are eating. All this rain is drawing them out of their holes."

"You run over there and grab us a couple. The last big crawdad I picked up pinched the piss out of me and I don't intend to get pinched again today."

"All right, titty-baby." It felt good to be able to call her that for once. I crouched down and walked carefully up to the bank and stood real still for a minute. It didn't take long for a big old crawdad to work its way through the shallow water. I snatched him up and in less than a minute later, I had two.

I handed one to Pepper and she carefully held it between two fingers, so it couldn't pinch her. After I threaded the hook through my bait, I did the same with hers, and we cast toward the middle of the rain's dimples.

It didn't take more than two or three minutes before Pepper's crawdad attracted the attention of a bass. It slammed her bait with a hard thump and the rod bent toward the water. Pepper reared back and the line snapped with a crack.

"Shit! I done lost my whole rig!" She slammed the butt of her rod into the mud, stomped her foot, and marched over to the shelter of a big red oak to finish working out her mad.

Trying not to let her see my grin, I twitched my rod tip and felt the hard pull of a big fish. I set the hook and the rod bent almost double. But unlike Pepper's, the drag on my reel was set properly. The line sang through the guides for a moment, and I was in a fight. It didn't take long for the fish to tire, and I soon brought to hand the biggest bass I'd ever seen in that pool.

"Woo hoo! What a fish!"

Pepper was still mad about losing hers, but she quickly joined me in the rain to admire the bass. I grabbed it by the lower jaw, the way Uncle Cody taught me, and held it up. "I bet this thing weighs ten pounds."

"More like five. But that fish is neato."

"Don't matter. Let's go show it to Miss Becky! And don't say neato. You ain't one of them Beatniks."

She stuck her tongue out at me. "She'll wear us out for getting wet."

"No, she won't. She'll want another one for a fish fry tonight."

I took off, leading the way. Already muddy, we wriggled under the gate and jogged up the drive. Once there, I peeked through the screen door. The dinner dishes were already washed and put away, so I knew that gaggle of women had the whole afternoon to gossip and sew on a quilt.

Miss Sara Hemphill's scratchy voice came through the open screen. "Well, I swanny."

Pepper made a face and moved real jittery like Miss Sara when she talks. "Well I swanny," she hissed quietly.

Hearing that old lady's voice drained all the excitement out of me. Aggravated, I put the rods away back where we got them. After I thought about it for a minute, I decided that dealing with a bunch of old women over the fish would be too much.

"Wait here."

"Where you going?"

"I'm letting this old bass go."

Her eyes widened. "Don't you want to show it off?"

"Naw. We'll just tell Uncle Cody about it later." Lucky for the fish, the cool, wet weather kept it alive until I got back to the pool. I lowered it into the muddy water and pushed and pulled it for a minute to get water through its gills, like I'd seen Uncle Cody do. The bass soon regained its senses and twisted out of my hand to disappear back into the pool.

When I returned, we sat on the porch and watched the leaves fall as the rain got heavier. The cackling old ladies set our nerves on edge as their voices came to us through the screens.

"Elizabeth Dawson is pregnant again."

"Don't she know what causes that?"

A wave of old lady giggling washed through the screen.

I blushed when Pepper leaned over and whispered in my ear. "They all know what causes babies." I didn't like to think about such things, so instead I watched water drip off the eaves.

"I heard Phyllis Steele and them got back from Port Arthur a day or so ago. They was down there nearly three weeks and when she come in, she was brown as a Mexican."

"I couldn't stand the humidity that long."

"I couldn't stand *Phyllis* that long."

More gales of laughter. That one made me smile.

"Did you hear that Martin Davis' cousin came to visit from California? She don't have much to do with anybody except Martin, who she dotes on, but he's in bad shape and they don't think he'll see Christmas. Sammy told me she's a little cleaning cyclone. They say you don't hardly see her without a rag tied around her head. Cleans all day, every day. She's living with Donny Wayne Foster and them. Him and his wife moved here from Kiomatia a while back."

"Lord child, I wish she'd come over here and help me clean." That was Miss Becky's voice.

"After she does mine." Miss Sara's scratchy voice made Pepper stick her finger down her throat, pretending to gag.

Grandpa turned off the highway and onto the gravel drive, his old truck running smoothly in the moist air. He always said damp air helped a carburetor breathe. He saw us on the porch, stopped at the gate leading up to the hay barn, and honked for us to come unlatch it. We raced through the rain, opened the gate, and rode the running boards up to the barn to help him get a load of hay.

He didn't say anything about us being wet, and that was fine by us.

It turned chilly late that night, more from the dampness than the weather. I woke after midnight, about to pop. Pepper and I had stayed up to watch Gorgon the Gruesome host a Nightmare episode on Channel 11 out of Dallas. We usually didn't get that channel, but the weather helped the signal, so we watched Abbott and Costello in a movie about Dr. Jekyll and Mr. Hyde. It wasn't scary, but it was fun.

We drank two RC's apiece and that's why I had to go to the bathroom so bad. When my feet hit the linoleum, I was glad they didn't have an outhouse anymore like they did when I was little. I always hated going out to the back after dark. Grandpa wasn't much for changing things, so it was a long time before he put in a bathroom.

In fact, Miss Becky still washed clothes in an old wash tub with a ringer that Grandpa set up for her each Tuesday morning. She filled it from a hose and added boiling water from the stove. I only heard her one time say she wished she had a new washer, but she'd never say it around Grandpa.

I was still half asleep when I went into the bathroom, but I didn't turn on the light. There was a glow from the kitchen, so after I finished, I walked through the chilly living room and found Grandpa sitting at the table all by himself, wearing only his dukins.

"What are you doing running around this time of night in your drawers, hoss?"

"I had to pee. You get hungry?"

He nudged an empty saucer away with a finger. "Not really. I was thinking and ate a piece of Miss Becky's cake because it was there."

He looked awful sad to me, so I sat down at the table even though I had on nothing but my underwear. "What's the matter, Grandpa?"

"Nothing, son. I's sitting here, looking outside."

The upper half of the wooden door was glass, but all I saw was the dark. I didn't know what to do, so I licked my finger and picked up crumbs from his plate. Forgetting I was there, he stared out into the darkness and talked quietly to himself like he always did.

His words usually weren't clear, but I caught a piece of what he was saying. "Never should have quit."

"Quit what, Grandpa?"

He frowned, surprised. "Nothin'. Just thinkin'."

I sat with him for a while longer until he stood up as quick as if he'd been stung. "Let's get to bed. Daylight comes early."

Chapter Nine

Two days later Ned, Cody, and Judge O.C. Rains sat in the rearmost booth of Frenchie's café, half a block down from the courthouse, laughing about Top's jail sentence. It was the first Cody had heard of the incident, and though O.C.'s recollection was hilarious, he couldn't help but feel sorry for his young nephew.

Ned noticed the brief frown on Cody's forehead and understood that he was remembering the night at the Rock Hole. Cody had already put two and two together to figure out that Top's behavior were a direct result of that traumatic night. "O.C., have you found out any more about that crazy killer that came through Tulsa?"

O.C. cautiously sipped the steaming coffee. "The one they're after is for sure Kendal Bowden. He was in the nervous house there for a lot of reasons, mostly because he's plumb crazy."

Cody watched Frenchie wiping the counter. The men's Stetsons lined up, crowns down, in front of one empty stool that kept anyone from sitting right beside their booth. Frenchie moved each hat, wiped the surface, and carefully replaced the hats exactly as she found them.

"Lots of crazy people are still on the streets."

"That's true, Cody, but this one's completely out of his mind, even though they said he was all right when they let him out of the sanitarium. I reckon their treatments didn't take and they turned him loose before he was done. He headed off north for a while and got into some meanness up in Nebraska when he teamed up with a hitchhiker, then he turned around and headed back south, making a bee-line for the river." O.C. planted his elbow on the table and wagged a forefinger.

"Them two went plain nuts up there in Nebraska as if Bowden wasn't crazy enough already. The first murder they hung on him was when they killed a Fuller Brush man for his car, and hadn't drove it but for an hour when a tire blew out. When *another* feller stopped to help him change it, they killed him, too, and stole *his* car. The next thing they know, Kendal and that other feller…"

"Don't he have a name?" Ned asked.

O.C. shrugged. "Gantry, I believe. They hid out on a farm in Kansas for a day or two, before they killed the folks who lived there. The sheriff still hasn't found out if they knew them people or not. Before breaking Jennings out, they stopped at a Tulsa store for ice and robbed the man that owned it. They don't know if he tried to fight, argue, or pick his nose, but they shot and killed him, too."

"Did they cut their heads off, like they did Jennings and Josh Brooks?" Cody asked.

"Naw, just left 'em laying there."

"Then how are they sure these are the same ones?"

"They are. And to top it all off, he's from here in Chisum. Kendal Bowden is George Hart's stepson."

"That the same George Hart that used to own Hart and Hart Funeral Home with his brother Alvin?" A sizzle of fear ran up Cody's spine. He hated undertakers, those solemn men who stood around in dark suits and handled dead people who weren't kinfolk. "Wasn't he kin to Sheriff Poole?"

"The same. They was first cousins. And you know all those boys are crazy as Bessie bugs. Somehow they're kin to the Fosters, who's kin to the Martins and Davises."

"They're all somehow kin us, too, I imagine, if we dig deep enough." Ned stirred his coffee slowly, remembering Cody's fistfight involving Donny Wayne a few months earlier. Small-town connections were sometimes as tangled as overgrown briars on a fencerow.

"Anyway, they broke that Jennings boy out, after cutting a guard's throat. The Oklahoma highway patrol found Gantry in a ditch up near Cloudy. The other two got away, that is, they thought so until y'all found Jennings in the river." O.C. held his cup aloft. Frenchie came around the counter with a fresh pot.

"I remember hearing Kendal was a strange little kid," Ned recalled. "Stayed out of sight most of the time after his mama died and I heard something was wrong with him when he was a kid. Miss Sweet knew, because she was the midwife when he come squalling into this world, but she never said a word about what was wrong. Right there toward the end, something went on inside the funeral home that no one would talk about, but whatever it was, they sent him off and didn't want him back."

John Washington's auntie, Miss Sweet, served as a midwife and acted as a healer in the county. Mostly called to duty by the colored population, poor whites often trusted her skills instead of trained doctors. Sometimes even those with money turned to her for discretion, or embarrassing ills or pregnancies. The old woman didn't care about color or family problems. She trusted in her Lord and served those who came for help.

Because the fresh coffee was too hot to drink, O.C. poured a splash from the cup and into the saucer. He delicately picked it up with his fingertips, blew across the surface and sipped the cooler liquid. Cody grinned at the old man and the saucer. He'd seen Ned do it a hundred times in Miss Becky's kitchen, but he'd never watched anyone cool coffee like that in a café.

"It was a nasty affair." O.C. sniffed the coffee and Cody grinned again. "Come to find out, Alvin Hart had been messin' with that kid for years." When he saw the questioning frown on Cody's forehead, he checked to be sure Frenchie wasn't within earshot and lowered his voice. "You know, he was diddlin' Kendal. I heard George had a part in it, too, but they never pinned anything on *him*."

Immediately uncomfortable, Cody unconsciously leaned back, as if to distance himself from the disgusting topic.

"Something snapped inside Kendal, and before long they had to send him to the Crazy House, but it was all hush hush. I tried to find out what else was going on, but those state boys kept close-mouthed about the whole thing. It wasn't my case and I didn't have no business nosing around, but I knew something was up when that son-of-a-bitchin' Val Jackson got involved and changed the venue to Potter County.

"They sent Alvin to the pen for a couple of years over Kendal. Then, while all the state investigators were digging around, they found out that instead of burying or cremating the bodies of folks who didn't have any money, or who died alone, the Harts hauled them out to a sand pit on an old farm not far from Blossom and dumped the bodies there." O.C. picked up the cup again, taking a quick sip to see if the liquid had cooled. It hadn't. He set the cup down sharply and licked his burned lips.

Shocked, Cody looked to Ned for confirmation. "It sure 'nough happened. I saw it. It was pitiful the way they done those poor people. Pitched them in that hole and covered the bodies with a little lime. They deserved time in the pen for that one, too, but they never convicted George. I still can't figure out why not."

"Because they had the trial outside of Lamar County, that's why." O.C.'s face reddened at the memory. "That was Val Jackson's doings, too."

Cody gave Ned a questioning look. "Val was a judge here with O.C. for a while, until he got voted out. They didn't gee haw too well together."

"Because he was a no'count son-of-a-bitch," O.C. repeated. "The Harts still had money, then, until they spent it all on the trial. Why, George Hart was a world-wide hunter back when he was younger. He went to Alaska, Canada, and all over Africa, bringing home heads and hanging them on walls. He had one whole room full of animal heads that he bragged about, saying everyone should hang trophies to show what kind of men they are. Never saw the likes of it, and him leaving his son home with Alvin and his doings. The trials and fines cost them everything they had and they lost the funeral home, but through their daddy, they owned the Cotton Exchange down on the tracks, and that's where they've lived from then on.

"You'll see George out every now and then, but I heard Alvin is so bad off now from old timer's disease that he stays inside. George walks around late at night, picking up odds and ends that people throw out. Kids have taken to calling him the Ghost Man, but those brothers haven't socialized with anyone in so long that people have mostly forgot 'em."

"I heard about the Ghost Man when I was in high school," Cody recalled. "But kids are always talking about ghosts at the hanging tree in Center Springs, or the well that's haunted by the ghost of a slave." He shivered.

Ned and O.C. chuckled. "Possum run over your grave?" They'd told similar stories when they were kids.

"Nobody sees the Ghost Man in the light," Cody said in a spooky voice. He switched back to his normal tone as the memories returned. "He only shows up at night, slipping around town, still wearing a ratty old black undertaker's suit and carrying a sack, or pulling an old homemade wagon full of junk down the street. Us kids tried to scare each other by thinking he was still fooling with dead bodies after the funeral home closed down, or stealing them from the graveyard, and maybe he is."

O.C. was finally able to sip his coffee. "You ain't the only one he makes nervous. From time to time people call and want something done about him, but when I ask what laws he's broke, they don't know. They just want him arrested and off the streets, but if we start hauling everybody in that we don't like, we'll have to build another jail.

"Most of the complaints fell off when Hart took to spending his time on the colored side of the tracks. Our folks don't care what goes on over *there*, as long as it don't come across to the north side. John's people ain't much for complaining about the Ghost Man. They let him alone, and George tends to his business…whatever *that* is."

O.C. sipped his coffee, letting his eyes wander around the café. Frenchie raised her eyebrows when she caught his gaze. He shook his head. He didn't need any more coffee right then. He'd gotten the temperature just right.

"Well, anyway, back to what we were talking about. Kendal is still out there and I've got a pretty good idea him and that partner of his killed Josh and them, and that Jennings boy. Now we can't find hide nor hair of Kendal, and all those investigators think he's still around here. He has enough kinfolk in this county that he can stay hid the rest of his life.

"The investigators have set up shop down in the basement at the courthouse, but they're thinking he's gone back north. They'll be out moving tomorrow and searching up in the Kiamichi, because they got a tip he was hiding back up around Cloudy."

"I'm not sure of that." Cody worried his coffee cup. "I'll nose around and see what I turn up, but I doubt we'll see him though, unless he gets drunk and runs into somebody."

"That's what might happen," Ned told him. "It's the screwy things that get people caught. I've seen it."

"You saw a lot when you were constable." Cody tried to change the subject. "Which of those old stories have stuck with you the most?"

Ned's eyes twinkled. "The ones I ain't telling you."

They laughed again.

Ned motioned for O.C. to lean in. They spoke quietly for a moment, knowing that everyone in the café listened to their conversations. "I'm hearing that folks are starting to worry that The Skinner might have come back to town and killed that feller and dumped his body in the river."

O.C.'s eyebrows rose.

"What have you said?"

"Told the ones that asted me that it wasn't nothin' like what The Skinner had done, and that I thought he'd gone to Mexico."

"They say anything else?"

Ned glanced around at the customers. "Naw, they usually shrug and say he'll eventually come back."

They leaned back to study on the conversation. O.C. examined his coffee cup for a long moment. "Well, you think The Skinner might have killed that feller in the river, and Onie Mae's family!?"

Startled for a moment at the O.C.'s volume, Ned quickly realized what he'd done. He answered in a loud and clear voice. "Naw, O.C. He's most likely in Mexico right now, or dead down on the border somewhere. He went down there to get away from us and the Mexicans probably got him trying to cross the river."

They knew the other customers were doing their best to listen. "That's what I expect, because I ain't heard a word from the FBI or any other laws since the Skinner got away that night."

They studied their coffee again.

"Well, things are bad," O.C. said in a normal tone of voice.

"Not everthang. Here's one, then, I gotta go." Ned wrapped his rough brown hands around his cup. "Cody got called out about suppertime one night not too long ago when Delilah Harrison thought she had a burglar. He wasn't sure how to get out to where they live in the dark, so he come got me and I went with him." He leaned back and nodded toward Cody. "Tell him the rest of it."

"Well, come to find out when we got there, her old man Ezra Lee is still having hard dreams about the war over Germany and came home drunk again. She wouldn't put up with it, so she sent him upstairs to sleep it off while she did the dishes.

"Ezra Lee passed out on the bed and dreamed that he was back in one of them bombers. He woke up, still drunk, a-hollerin' 'we're hit, we're hit, we're going down!' He grabbed a bedsheet thinking it was a parachute and jumped out the second floor window and landed in Delilah's rose bushes and broke his leg."

They chuckled for a moment.

"Well that ain't all. The fall sobered him up enough to limp around and beat on the kitchen door to get in. You know how everybody in Center Springs is on edge about these killings.

Well, Delilah heard the commotion and thought someone was kicking their way in. She grabbed an iron skillet and hid behind the door. When Ezra Lee finally saw it was unlocked, he hobbled in and she banged him in the noodle so hard with the skillet it broke the handle off in her hand and damn near killed him."

Everyone in the booth was laughing when Ned collected his hat to head on back home and kill the rest of the day. "I'll see y'all later, and be careful Cody."

Cody absently rubbed the little badge on his shirt pocket. "I will."

Chapter Ten

Pepper and I looked forward to hunting Hootie with Grandpa Ned. But the day quail season opened, she was in one of her sad moods again. That gal was always the toughest girl I'd ever known, but she was hurt deep down inside and it wasn't healing like it ought to. Every now and then we'd lose her when she was staying with us. It turned out that almost every time, she'd be staring into the round mirror on Miss Becky's antique dresser at the arrowhead-shaped scar burned deep into the backside of her shoulder.

She and I had problems with what happened to us a few months earlier, but Grandpa said we spent too much time thinking on the past and to put it all behind us. He said we needed to think about other folks and their troubles to get our minds off of our own. He got that from Miss Becky, because as far as she was concerned, if you helped other folks, your troubles didn't seem so big.

After my time in jail, I was doing a little better in school, so on Saturday morning Grandpa told us to get our hunting clothes on. We joined Uncle James and Mr. Kip, and drove to Mr. Martin Davis' place like we've done since I was big enough to tag along. Mr. Martin had the best quail hunting in the country, Cody always said. Pepper loved Mr. Martin and called him a cute little old man, and he always made a big deal over her when we got there.

Every year we visited outside for a while with Mr. Martin. I was always excited and ready to go, but the old men piddled around and visited while the frost melted, like they weren't in any hurry at all. They about drove me crazy with all their talk, so Pepper and I usually played with the dogs until Mr. Martin came out with his beat up old Browning from behind the bedroom door, and we went hunting.

This time Uncle Cody was busy with law work and Mr. Martin wasn't waiting for us. Grandpa Ned had already told us he had lung cancer and was feeling bad, so when we got out of the trucks that morning, Grandpa, Mr. Kip, and Uncle James started up the porch steps. The screen door opened and a slim, homely woman met them at the door.

"Howdy." Grandpa stopped quick because he was surprised. "I didn't know anybody was here except for Martin."

She nodded and fidgeted with a rag in her hand. "He's inside. I'm his...we're kin, so I've been coming over to take care of him, clean house and such."

"How are y'all kin?"

"Mama is Anna Belle, used to be a Davis."

Grandpa nodded. "How's he doing today?"

"He's better. Seems to have rallied since he knew y'all were coming." She stepped aside. "Well, y'all go ahead in. I got some cleaning to do at Sammy's."

"All right, then. Good to see you."

She left, cutting across the yard to follow a trail through the pasture and disappeared from sight. They went on inside and left us in the yard to wait. Pepper didn't like waiting outside, she wanted to see Mr. Martin, but she did as she was told.

Mr. Kip and Uncle James came back out and milled around while Grandpa stayed and talked. After a while he came to the door and motioned for me and Pepper to come in. I'd never been inside before and didn't like it, because it smelled bad like a house does when someone is sick. The strong odor of cigarettes didn't help much, either. Pepper stuck her tongue out like she was yakking and we got kinda tickled.

"Shit, this stinks," she whispered in my ear.

I always get nervous when she starts cussing around grown-ups, but Grandpa didn't hear her. We went through the living room and though it smelled of smoke, everything was spotless and neat as a pin.

Mr. Martin was propped up in a big old four-poster bed and he raised up when we came into his room. "Howdy, boy." His voice was weak and phlegmy. He stuck out his big nicotine-stained hand for me to shake.

Cody taught me a long time ago to shake strong like a man, but when I did, I was afraid I'd break the old man's hand, it was so soft and bony.

"Hey, gal."

Pepper leaned over the bed and gave him a big hug. She moved funny in her oversize brush pants Grandpa gave her for Christmas, but he said she'd eventually grow into them.

Grandpa acted uncomfortable, shifting from one foot to the other at the end of the bed. Mr. Martin motioned for me to come over beside him. "I'm gonna do something this morning that'll make you mad at me."

I didn't know what to say, so I waited a minute.

"Your old grand-pappy here and the rest of them are gonna to hunt this morning like they always do, but I need you two to stay here in this room with me while they do it."

Our eyes met across the bed and Grandpa nodded.

Mr. Martin pointed out the window of his farmhouse toward the creek bottom pastures and fencerows where we hunt quail. "Sick old people like to have healthy young'uns around some-times, and I need a good dose of y'all today, so I've asked your grand-pappy to shoot a mess of birds this morning while the three of us sit here and listen through the window."

Well, that really made me mad and tears made my eyes hot, because Hootie was out there and I surely wanted to hunt over him. But I knew how Grandpa would feel if I made a fuss, and I didn't want Pepper to see me tear up, so I swallowed it back.

Not getting to hunt didn't seem to bother her much, but then again, I already knew that girls saw things different.

Grandpa gave us a little smile, patted Mr. Martin's bony foot under the sheet, and left.

"Sit right there in that rocker beside the winder so you can see." Mr. Martin pushed himself up and Pepper used a couple of feather pillows to prop him higher. She straightened the wedding ring quilt on his bed and sat on the edge to hold Mr. Martin's big old wrinkled hand in hers. "I like to lay here where I can see outside. The best time to watch is when the shadows start to stretch out in the evenin'.

"Up to a week ago, when I felt better, I watched deer come by, and an old hog ever now and then. There's a big covey of quail that works along that fencerow there. I see a lot."

He paused, racked with deep, wet coughs. He lay back and closed his eyes for a moment. "Shoot, about a week ago I even saw somebody slipping around the barn over yonder and heading down toward my cousin Donny Wayne's house that you can barely see through the trees there across the pasture. His old skull was nearly peeled like he was in the army. He walked like that Foster bunch, but I couldn't tell which one it was, if he was a Foster. He didn't have any business out there anyways, so I hollered and he ran off. Probably thought I had a shotgun in my hand."

I heard the men open the dog boxes outside and load their shotguns and the sound of those bolts, slamming closed like to have killed me. Grandpa and them walked through the gate, and into the pasture. The dogs ran across the grass to the first fencerow, histed their legs on fence posts and clumps of grass, and started working birds. That's when Mr. Martin lit another cigarette he didn't need.

"I bet you kids don't know it, but people were thick as fleas on a dog when we was all growing up here in the bottoms. Why, I bet there was probably a dozen different families living within hollerin' distance of one another. Each house had about ten kids each, plus their mamas and daddies, and usually a grandparent or uncle to boot. I don't cipher too good. How many folks would that be, Pepper?"

"Somewhere maybe around a hundred and thirty?"

"Don't surprise me none. Living close was good, because we helped one another when times got tough." He paused and thought for a moment. "Yessir, family is a powerful thing, but mine's about gone."

He finished the cigarette, crushed it out in a full ashtray beside the bed, and lit another one. "Son, I can't get up anymore and I can't hunt, neither, but what I need is for you to watch them out yonder and tell me and Pepper everything that's happening this morning. Don't leave nothing out, not even one little ol' sparrow flying past or one missed shot."

I walked over to the wooden window.

"Raise the winder there, Top, so's you can see and hear."

"It's chilly."

"I know, but I'm under all these quilts and y'all are dressed to be outside, so it'll be all right."

It was a struggle to raise the sticky old window, but I got it up. Mr. Martin didn't like screens, so I had a clear view of the pasture down below. I didn't have much spirit to talk, but I sat in the rocker and told him how the Brittanys worked the fencerow, running back and forth with their noses on the ground, and how they checked every berry tangle on either side of the fence. I described how Grandpa and them spread out and how they carried their shotguns. I told him how the sky and the land looked once I got the idea of what Mr. Martin wanted.

"That's right. Pretend you're one of the Colt Forty-five baseball announcers on the radio and tell me what you see. Is the frost melting yet?"

"Nossir. The ground is still white where the sun can't reach the shade."

"Are the leaves pretty down there in the bottoms?"

"They're turning, and a bunch're already falling. There's a big hawk setting on the top limb of a tree. He's watching the dogs work down below."

"He's waiting to see if anyone kicks up a bird. He'll sure enough take out after one if they don't get them all on the rise."

Cody's new Brittany, White Dog, would hunt with anybody. He didn't act like he missed Uncle Cody at all and pointed the first covey. Hootie did what he was supposed to do and that was to honor the older dog's point. The whole thing blew up when Uncle James walked up to flush the birds. We heard the little pops from the shotguns and I told Mr. Martin how each bird flew. A couple dropped into the deep briars and the dogs had to find them.

The men only hunted in the north pasture and around the edges within sight of the barn, but I finally figured out that they intentionally stayed right close to the house.

After a while, I got into the spirit of the whole thing and started reporting what was happening, like they do on television. Pepper climbed up on the bed beside Mr. Martin and curled up against him like a kitten.

"Taking the lead, I see Mr. Kip moving up behind White Dog and Hootie who are on point. I'm sure there's a covey ready to fly and he's walking slow and everyone else is ready and there… they…go! Birds are flying every-which-a-way. Grandpa drops one, Mr. Kip drops another one and looky there, Uncle James gets two with one shot!"

The sound of the shots reached us a moment later.

Mr. Martin got a kick out of it. I even stopped for a commercial break when the dogs worked the ground between coveys. I advertised a prescription medicine in a bottle sitting on the nightstand beside the bed. It tickled Mr. Martin and he laughed until he started coughing so hard tears came to his eyes. Pepper held his hand even tighter.

"Don't ever take up smoking, kids. Y'all ought not get sick and die on one another. Cousins need to take care of each other for as long as they can, because family is important."

He recovered and talked for a while about how bad cigarettes were for people, but it didn't stop him from lighting one after the other. Smoke hung heavy in the room, despite the open window. The men found one more covey and the pops came quick and soft. I went back to covering the action and pretty soon they finished and started back.

"They're done, Mr. Martin."

"I nearly am, too." He gave us each a long regard. "You know kids, I was your age once, but time passes and I got old. It's a misery now. I won't be around this time next year, and I want to give y'all a gift I never gave my own kids. They're gone now, and don't have anything to do with me for reasons of their own, but here's what I want you two to have. It's a couple of stories about my life for y'all to hold on to, because when I'm in the Forest Chapel cemetery, and all my memories are gone, that'll be the end of me, 'cept for a hunk of rock."

Those words sent a chill up my back, but I sat on the edge of the bed. While Pepper held his hand in one of hers and rubbed it with the other'n, Mr. Martin told about other hunts and birds he'd killed, and places he'd seen in the world. "Miss Pepper, you make sure you never quit hunting and fishing. It ain't just a man's world. Both men and women can love the outdoors, so you stay right in there with the men and show them how it's done."

He talked for a long time about hunting elk in Montana, and mule deer in Colorado, and even bear in Alaska. But mostly he talked about hunting quail, which he dearly loved.

"And another thing, you two. Y'all had a hard time last spring, and things that happened weren't right. That kind of thing weighs on the mind, but you two are young and healthy… not like me. If the memory gets too heavy on y'all's shoulders, remember I said that even though things seem rough, there's other things that'r rougher."

He coughed some more as Pepper's eyes welled, and I knew what she was thinking. I felt a lump in my throat.

"We all have our demons," Mr. Martin said. "But most other folks' troubles are worse than our own. We all have secrets we cain't tell no one and we'll all most likely take them to our graves. Why, I know one person…" He looked startled, as if he suddenly realized we were there. "Never mind, anyway, Miss Pepper, Mr.

Top, y'all stay away from these old cigarettes. They'll kill you. That's why they're called coffin nails."

He lit another by scraping a kitchen match alight with a rough thumbnail. "Listen, I can hear them quail calling to get the coveys back together. That reminds me of the time…"

After a while I realized that the men were back in the yard, listening through the open window while Mr. Martin talked. He finally got tired and started coughing again, and after that, he was finished. Everyone came inside, muddy boots and all and stood around the room.

Uncle James reached into his hunting vest and handed Mr. Martin a little rooster quail that he'd shot. The old man lay there in bed, stroking the bird's feathers while they laughed and talked about the hunt. Hootie stuck his nose in the door and came in and muddied up the floor. Grandpa's face got red, but Mr. Martin laughed his phlegmy laugh and called him over to the side of the bed to rub his ears for a while.

A few minutes later, Mr. Martin leaned back like he was really tired. Pepper hugged him again. I didn't know I'd learned anything, but I shook his hand and we left to take Hootie outside.

Grandpa and the men stayed a little while longer before they came outside. They were sniffley when they loaded up the dogs, like everyone was coming down with colds.

Grandpa put a hand on my shoulder and drew Pepper close for a moment. "Martin said he had a good time and to thank y'all, though he's sorry he ruined your hunt. He also said for y'all to try and remember what he told you, whatever that means."

We knew. Pepper and I didn't talk in the truck, but she held my hand the whole way back. "I know what Miss Becky means now," she finally said. "There's always more trouble out there than our own."

The problem was, I didn't know what *Pepper* meant with that comment. I wished I could figure out what grownups were talking about, even with us kids.

A week later and I heard Mr. Martin had died in the night. Pepper cried. I realized he'd taught me more than one lesson that day, but I hoped I wouldn't have to learn too many more things like that.

On the backside, though, Pepper started feeling a little bit better and she smiled more and more.

Chapter Eleven

Several stories above the ground, the rotting roof was patched with an old tire holding down a piece of rusty tin flapping and rattling in the breeze.

Cody was in the grip of another nightmare. This one was the worst. He thrashed, making soft animal sounds high in his throat, rousing Norma Faye from a sound sleep. He was drenched in sweat and tangled in the sheets.

An out-of-control wisteria vine wound its way up the support post and provided habitat for a variety of creatures.

He moaned, muscles twitching in terror. Norma rolled over and draped one arm across his chest to calm him. She felt his racing heart. "Hon, wake up."

Overgrown shrubbery hid the massive front porch, providing dark warrens through which rats and rabbits hid and reproduced. Feral cats moved through the clutter.

He stood before the monstrously large building of his dreams, but this time it wasn't a house and though familiar, it was unrecognizable. This wasn't his subconscious. It was real.

Leaves clogged the rain gutters so long ago the contents had turned to rich, dark compost.

Or as real as a dream could get.

Animals discovered the ready-made den and the entire yard smelled of cat urine.

He could smell? In a dream?

The garbage was a junk collector's dream. Deceased cars, boxes, crates, trunks, tires, motor parts, and raw wooden shelves full of jars prevented human entry into the structure. The warped double doors opened only wide enough to allow a small amount of light to reach the rear wall of a large room filled to overflowing.

An obscene force from below the ground pushed an oak sapling's roots into the air. As it fell, a dark burrow was revealed, leading to a warren of horrors.

He tried to shriek. At the high keening sound, Norma Faye propped up on one elbow and shook Cody until he quit struggling and opened his eyes.

"You were having a nightmare."

"Oh, lordy, you ain't a lying." He slipped an arm around her shoulders. She laid her red head on his bare chest and held him close until his heart no longer beat so rapidly in her ear.

"You want to talk about it?"

"No."

"You need to."

Cody turned his eyes into the dark shadows against the ceiling's corner. "Can't."

"Hon…"

"Shhhh."

Chapter Twelve

For the past week I'd been reading a book I'd checked out from the library about Indian burial mounds and wanted to find one. Indians lived and traded in Center Springs in the eighteen hundreds and arrowheads were everywhere, if you knew where to hunt.

We had a fair collection of arrowheads and spear points, but the idea of finding even more was fascinating to us. I'd never known anyone up on the river talk about burial mounds, but there was one interesting hump not far from the store that I was convinced might be what we were looking for.

Pepper didn't want to go and she dug her heels in at the idea. "I don't want to do no damn digging. That's work!"

"You'll dig worms for fishing."

"Fishing is fun."

"So is finding Indian stuff. What if we dig up a tomahawk, or a breastplate…or even a real Indian skull?"

I knew I had her with the skull idea, and she finally gave in on Saturday morning. We were riding our bikes past Neal's store when we saw Uncle Cody's El Camino in the parking lot. He was leaning over the side of a truck, talking to men Miss Becky called the Spit and Whittle Club. When he saw us passing the domino hall, Uncle Cody waved us over.

"What are you two outlaws up to this morning with them shovels?" I noticed he was a young version of Grandpa. He wore a blue shirt with his little badge pinned onto the pocket, right next to the inside seam. Instead of a revolver on his hip, Uncle Cody carried a big old 1911 Colt .45. It wasn't pretty like the Colts Grandpa carried. The .45 was oiled, worn, and looked pure-dee mean.

"We're fixin' to go out to a deep draw beside Mister Vern Taylor's pasture." I readjusted the shovel on my handlebars. "There's an old Indian mound at the bottom and we're gonna see what's in it. Maybe we can dig up a tomahawk, or a pipe, or maybe even a skull."

Uncle Cody studied us for a minute from under the brim of his hat. "You up for some digging, Pepper?"

"Sure, there's nothing else to do."

"Well, let's put them bikes in the back of the truck here and go on up to the graveyard instead. I'll get a shovel and we can all dig up a grave or two there. I bet there's been some folks buried in the Forest Chapel cemetery that are still wearing rings and necklaces and stuff."

The idea horrified me, and he saw it in my face. "We can't do that!"

"I don't know why not." Uncle Cody shrugged. "It's the same thing."

"No it isn't…we're going to an Indian mound, not a cemetery."

"That's what an Indian mound is, Top. You're talking about digging up our people. That might be a Choctaw mound with Miss Becky's great-great-grandmother in it."

Pepper rolled her eyes. "I *told* you this was a stupid idea, dumbass."

"Did not."

"Hey guys, how about we put your bikes in the back anyway, and y'all go to the bottoms with me. You don't have anything else to do now, do you?"

Her eyes lit up when Pepper thought about running around with Uncle Cody. "Let's go."

I wasn't really excited about it, but I went along with the idea. Uncle Cody pitched our shovels in the bed and laid the bikes on top. He waved goodbye at the men and we left. Pepper sat between us as he drove slowly past scattered farms. Uncle Cody rolled the windows down and let the breeze blow through.

We passed Isaac Reader's house and turned on a dirt road that led between pastures and woods. About a hundred mallards paddled around on the slash, a swampy low place that was always boggy.

Uncle Cody pointed toward another flock that turned to pitch in beside the greenheads. "We'll slip down here in two or three weeks and shoot us a mess of these ducks."

Nearly all the crops were in, and the fields plowed straight and true. Only a few bare stalks stuck up here and there. We drove over a plank bridge and turned right toward Sanders Creek. There was an old, unpainted tarpaper shack sitting in the middle of a corn field full of dead stalks, not far from Love Thicket. Uncle Cody parked in front of the house.

"What are we doing here?" Pepper frowned at the shack.

"I'm gonna visit for a second." A wrinkled little old lady stepped through the door with a dish rag in her hand. "Y'all stay right here." Uncle Cody got out. "Howdy."

He left the door open and walked toward the woman.

"Well, shit." Pepper flopped backward in the seat. "I didn't know we were going to sit in the car all day."

"Well, it ain't all day. He won't be a minute. What are you griping about? We'd be helping Miss Becky if we were still back at the house."

She crossed her arms and sulled up.

Instead of joining her, I turned the starter key. The radio warmed up and The Animals filled the cab with "House of the Rising Sun."

Pepper turned up the volume. "That's about whorehouses."

Shocked and embarrassed, I tried to turn the radio down. She slapped my hand away and sat there like she'd done something big. I'd never thought about what the song meant, and I knew we'd get in trouble when Uncle Cody heard it when he got back.

The song was almost over when he opened the door. He grinned and turned the radio down. "What's this world coming to when long-hairs are singing about cat houses?"

I started to ask what the song had to do about cats, but it dawned on me what he meant. My face went red and I felt the heat. Pepper saw it and reared back to laugh. Uncle Cody punched one of the buttons to change the station and turned back on the dirt road, this time listening to Roger Miller's song "Chug a Lug." We liked the part where he sang that "it makes you want to holler hi-de-ho" but when we all chimed in to sing along, Pepper changed it to "hiney hole" and I was shocked. Uncle Cody threw back his head and laughed, and after that, we sang it that way together.

He pulled into another yard, minutes later.

"What are we doing here?"

"I won't be a minute, Top. I got some information from that lady I talked to a little bit ago, so now we're stopping for me to ask *these* folks a few questions."

Pepper thought about working up a mad. "Are we going to do this all day?"

"Nope, one more stop or two oughta get it."

He got out of the truck again and waited by the fender. This time, a middle-aged man in greasy overalls left the tractor he was working on and shook his hand. They stood close enough for us to hear, so Pepper turned the radio down a little.

"Well howdy, Constable."

"Howdy Jess. I'm poking around today, visiting with folks to see if anybody's heard or seen anything around here that can help me. I'm needin' to visit with Kendal Bowden for a spell. You know him?"

"Yeah, I know of him."

"When was the last time you saw him."

"Like I said, I know *of* him. I've haven't laid eyes on him since we were knee high to a grasshopper. He used to play with Merle Clark and Randal Wicker and Josh…I'm sorry to hear about him. Do you reckon Kendal really did come back and kill him?"

"Can't say for sure. Do you know of anyone around here that might have seen him lately?"

"Naw, no one has said anything. I've been mostly working, so the only people I see are up at the store."

"I know the feeling." Uncle Cody caught my eye and knew we heard every word they said.

"He's kin to Donny Wayne Foster. You might go by and ask *him*."

The name jolted us. Back in the spring, Donny Wayne, his sorry brother Tully Joe and another guy joined in with Calvin Williams to jump on Uncle Cody up at the store, intending to whip him because he was seeing Norma Fay after she'd left. They needed more than the four of them, though, because Uncle Cody whipped them all. I heard Grandpa say that Donny Wayne put out the word that he intended to kill him if he ever caught Uncle Cody alone.

"Well, you know me and Donny Wayne don't gee-haw too good."

"I heard. He got his jaw unwired about a month ago and he says it ain't been the same since you broke it for him. He don't seem right no more with all them teeth missing that you knocked out. Says that shoulder you dislocated has been troubling him some, too."

"None of that was my idea."

"I heard that, too. He ain't home right now anyways. He took work out at Slate Shoals, hauling hay. You might go by his place and talk to his wife. She don't hardly go nowhere, but you be careful around him and don't let him get behind you."

Uncle Cody stared across the field, like he was studying the cut stalks. "You say Donny Wayne for sure ain't there?"

Jess shrugged. "I ain't sure of nothin'."

"All right. You call me if you see anything or hear about Bowden showing up here in the bottom."

"I ain't got no telephone here, Cody. You know that."

"Well, I'll let you get back to your rat-killin'. Holler at Neal up at the store, if you do. He'll let me know."

They shook again and in a minute he was settled back in the cab and slammed the door. Pepper turned the radio back up. "Where to now?"

"We're going to Donny Wayne Foster's house."

He must have seen how the name affected us. "Don't worry kids. He ain't there and I don't intend to fight anybody today. We're fixin' to stop by for a few minutes so I can ask his wife a question or two. When I'm done, we'll go down to a little persimmon patch I know. After that frost last week, they should be ripe and we can gather Miss Becky a quart or two."

Neither me nor Pepper liked persimmons. I always figured the texture and taste appealed only to older people, but going to the woods with Uncle Cody was always fun, so it sounded like a good idea.

A Chrysler was parked in front of the run-down farmhouse set at the edge of a field, with its back porch facing a thick stand of trees. The only pretty thing in sight, one lone red oak grew out front, the colorful leaves still hanging on. A tire swing hung steady in the still, cool air. A quarter mile to the west, neat rows of pecan trees extended into the distance, but they belonged to Old Man Tatum, and he'd call the laws if he knew anyone was even spitting at them.

"Y'all stay here and leave the motor running. I'll be right back." Uncle Cody got out of the truck, and this time he unsnapped his holster. I turned off the radio and leaned out of the open window.

Donny Wayne Foster's teenage son, Harold, opened the screen door. "What do you want?"

"Harold, don't act like your daddy. I dropped by to visit with your mama a minute to see if she's seen Kendal Bowden."

"Naw, she ain't."

"Let her tell me that."

"She ain't here."

"Well, who's that standing behind you, then?"

Harold cut his eyes to the side. "My cousin. She's visitin'."

The thin young woman stepped closer to the open door and by the rag tied on her head, I recognized her as the one who cleaned house for Mr. Martin Davis for the last few weeks before he died. "Oh, howdy. I'm Cody. Ned said he met you at Martin's house when they came out to hunt quail a while back."

"I remember."

"You doing all right?"

I could tell Uncle Cody was trying to make conversation at the same time he was checking the windows to see if Kendal or Donny Wayne was inside.

"I'm good. Donny Wayne ain't home, and neither is Shannon. She's over at Henrietta Dibner's this afternoon, helping with her sick baby. You can talk to her there."

"That's all right." Uncle Cody stepped back. "I'll come back later when Donny Wayne is here. It's him I need to talk to."

"He won't have nothin' to do with you," Harold said. "Not after what you did to him up at the store."

"Well, Harold," Uncle Cody was getting mad, so he stopped himself. "Tell Donny Wayne I'll be back again in a day or so. I intend to talk to him, because you know you aren't telling me the truth, so I'll keep dropping by from time to time…to visit."

The girl stepped back inside and I saw her hand come out into the light and rest on Harold's shoulder for a minute. He turned and snickered. "If there ain't nothin' else, I got business."

Uncle Cody turned toward the car. "So do I, and my business is with your daddy. You tell him what I said."

Harold stepped back inside and let the screen door slam shut. Uncle Cody had his jaw set when he got back in the El Camino. He reached over and turned the radio up loud, backed up, and we drove down to the creek, laughing at Frankie Valli singing "Rag Doll" in a high girl's voice.

Uncle Cody shook his head. "Folks oughta be boys or girls, and not both."

Chapter Thirteen

"How you doing, Mr. Jules?" Cody stepped into the courthouse elevator.

"Fair to middlin', Constable Cody. Goin' up to see Judge Rains?"

"Yep, he called for me this morning."

"Well, he's in a mood."

Cody nodded, remembering all the years that O.C. Rains had been part of his life. "Well, I don't believe I've ever seen him when he *wasn't* in a mood."

Jules nearly danced as he laughed. "Thass right, Mr. Cody. That man is always in a mood. Always in a mood, yessir."

The elevator stopped on the fourth floor and Cody gave the old man a pat on the shoulder as he stepped into the echoing corridor. O.C.'s secretary Thelma Lee Fletcher was away from her desk, so Cody quickly crossed the outer office to open the judge's wood and frosted glass door at the same time he rapped.

O.C. frowned in annoyance at the unannounced entry, but his eyes quickly crinkled at the sight of his newest constable. "Howdy young 'un."

"Thought I was Uncle Ned, didn't you?"

"It crossed my mind. I was hoping the old bastard would show up today. I've been a-missin' him lately. I haven't had anybody to argue with."

"Well, don't start in on me. I haven't had the practice, and you'd probably eat me for lunch."

"Naw, I'd go easy on you for a while, till you toughened up anyways. How's things going out in Center Springs?"

"Been doing good." Cody tilted his hat back and sat in the only wooden chair that wasn't full of papers. The joints creaked under his weight. "You needed to see me?"

O.C. picked up a wire fly swatter and leaned back in his own creaking chair. "Yessir. I didn't want to talk about this over the phone or the radio, but I heard tell where Kendal Bowden might be."

If O.C. was expecting Cody to interrupt, he was wrong. Ned would have barged in with questions, but Cody simply sat and waited. The quiet respect wasn't what O.C. was used to, and it annoyed him. He surely missed sparring with Ned.

He sighed. "Anyways, I got a call first thing this morning from somebody who wouldn't leave a name, but he said he saw Kendal fooling around the old Cotton Exchange building. He may be hiding there. I want you to run over and check it out for me."

Cody frowned and leaned forward to rest his elbows on his knees. "Sure will, Judge. But..." He chose his words carefully, unsure of how to pursue his thoughts. "Mr. O.C., my precinct is up on the river, not here in town." He watched the old judge's reaction. "Won't I be getting in someone else's business here?"

The fly swatter twirled in the judge's fingers. "You're wondering if you'll be stepping on Sheriff Griffin's toes, or Dub Moore's."

"Yessir. It's Dub's precinct and I don't want to get crossways with another constable over something like this. That big old building is right on the line...uh, right on the tracks, too. "

"Good point, son. But you forget who's sitting on *this* side of the desk. I can tell my constables what to do, and no one needs to make me mad. It'd be like poking a grizzly and I'm an old bear that's best left alone to do what he does. Dub won't say anything because he's in Dallas, and neither will Griffin."

"All right. I'd still like to take somebody with me. How about I ask Jeff Andrews to go? That way I'll have somebody from the sheriff's office if anything happens, and maybe Deputy Washington since the Cotton Exchange is on the tracks."

"Deputy Andrews. That's the boy Griffin hired out of Dallas here-while back?"

"Yessir. He's a good hand and I'd feel better if I had one of Griffin's men along for the ride, even though you're the one who sent me."

Having someone from Griffin's shop accompany him in town would go a long way in smoothing any potentially ruffled feathers. O.C. was impressed with the new constable's bureaucratic instincts.

"All right, then. Take him with you. Having Big John nearby is a good idy, too. Give him a holler. Have you heard about Randal Wicker? They found his body outside Tishomingo, Oklahoma, yesterday. His head was gone, just like those others."

"No, I hadn't. I wish I knew what Kendal is after, besides a bag full of people's heads."

"We'll find out, eventually. Randal had two little old kids that are sure going to miss him."

I'm sorry about him. He was a pretty good ol' boy."

"You got that right." O.C. twirled his flyswatter. "How's Ned?"

"Settling in to being a regular citizen, I reckon. He feels a little left out of things."

"I hate to hear that, but he earned his time off."

"Yessir, folks are still calling him when they have problems and that helps, but the weather's changing and he won't be plowing for a while. I hope he don't take to sitting around all day. That'll kill him."

"Ned's too mean to die. He'll find a way to keep busy. I imagine he'll buy a few more cows so he'll have something to complain about."

"I wouldn't put it past him." Cody stood. "I'll let you know what I find out at the Exchange."

"You do that. Y'all be careful."

"You bet. I'll get back to you later."

O.C. waved his hand and watched Cody leave. *He'll do fine, but dammit, talking with him ain't near as much fun as arguing with Ned.*

Chapter Fourteen

Chisum had changed since Cody Parker left for his senior trip to Vietnam.

His El Camino rolled slowly past the corner Stop & Grab convenience store. It drew out-of-work men as if the business offered free money. He felt the store's name invited shoplifters to load their pockets and wondered why they didn't change it to something more appropriate.

Jeff Andrews scarcely glanced out the window. "So I was in this little café late one night down on Harry Hines in Dallas when these three punks walked in and started giving a couple of middle-aged guys some grief."

He tilted the little Stetson back on his high forehead. "They ignored the little bastards and left. I paid my tab and left too, but them punks thought it was a good idea to follow me outside and one of them stuck a gun in my ribs."

Cody steered the El Camino with his right wrist resting on top of the wheel, wishing he'd chosen someone else instead of the blowhard in the seat beside him. Dictated by a long line of genetics, Cody's left elbow jutted out of the half-breed car's open window.

Andrews waved his hand. "I couldn't believe it. They tried to rob me…*me!* When I turned around, the second punk tried to job me with a little knife in his hand but it missed. The third one hit me in the mouth with a lead sap, like Mr. Ned carried.

It broke out these three front teeth." He pointed to the upper bridge for emphasis. "That pissed me off, so I reached under my shirt for this little .38 I carry and shot the one with the gun. He hit the ground and I shot the other'n before he could hit me again. The one with the knife run off. That's when I decided I was done with Dallas, and I came back here as a deputy."

Cody wondered how much of the story was true. He found it hard to believe that so much had happened to the man in the short time since he became an officer. Cody thought about his own hitch in the military and decided Andrews was full of hot air.

Finished with the story for the moment, Andrews finally watched the houses roll past.

Cody glanced down the street lined with giant elms shading old Victorian homes. He pointed through the bug-splattered windshield toward the largest structure in Lamar County, a full five stories, six hundred feet long and one hundred feet wide. "Good lord, this old place is falling down."

The crumbling brick Victorian Cotton Exchange Building sat on a railroad spur, south of the main tracks, the unofficial line between the white and colored sections of town. Despite its age, the neighborhood north of the tracks was owned by white folks and in mostly good condition. Past the tracks and the railroad depot, the streets crumbled, houses sagged, and tired people struggled to live from day to day.

They coasted to a stop next to the inset main entrance in the middle of the block and cut the motor. At their quiet arrival, someone ducked around the corner as the sun winked out behind the Catholic Church steeple several blocks away. The figure's quick disappearance failed to send a warning signal. It was the first error in a long night of terror.

The shadows cast by the ragged trees emphasized the desolation of the elderly neighborhood behind them. A tingle ran up Cody's neck as he stared at the dilapidated facade.

The snippet of a dream rose and burst like a bubble in his mind. *Scarce grass and lush weeds in the courtyard were knee high in the surprisingly warm fall weather.*

Repeating arches running the entire length of the first floor reminded Cody of buildings in Italy. They were covered in a nightmare of vines reaching outward to the curb, shading a wide sidewalk running along the entire street side of the building. The tangled vegetation gave the building a feeling of decay and depression.

Another bubble burst. *A house with many rooms.*

After examining the exterior, Cody was convinced the vegetation was all that held one corner together.

Still another bubble surfaced and popped. *A nest of yellow jackets, undisturbed for weeks, buzzed under the front eave.*

The wall nearest the car appeared to have been used as target practice by someone with a howitzer. The rubble of bricks littered the sidewalk and had been there long enough to crumble in place. Leaves and debris drifted against the rubble, holding water and allowing rot to find a foothold in the eroding bricks.

Outside of a junkyard, Cody had never seen so much trash in his life. The desolate building seemed to be a magnet for discarded garbage. It was piled against the exterior like sand blown by a hard wind.

Pop. *A Model A Ford at the curb rusted to dust on bent rims in a nest of weeds and dying grasses growing through the crumbling concrete...*

Dented metal trash cans and bedsprings, old bicycle and automobile parts, and stacks of decaying lumber lay in great tangled drifts up to the bottom windowsills. From outward appearances, the accumulated debris was the only thing holding the massive structure upright.

A rusty second-hand wire screen on the wooden door frame was full of holes. Obviously not original to the stately building, it defied gravity as the rails and styles warped in the weather.

"They said this was a showplace," Cody said, and then paused.

He remembered. He was staring at the physical reality of his nightmares!

His face flushed hot and drained of blood.

"What do you think?" Oblivious to Cody's growing feelings of dread, Andrews breathed deeply as cool air caressed his face. He enjoyed the season, tired of the recent dry north Texas summer. "Do you smell anything?"

Cody fought his rising unease. "Only the onions you had with supper. I bet a stray dog or cat crawled into all that junk and died." He glanced past the young man. "At least there's a little path to the door."

"This shouldn't take but a minute." Their visit was only a knock and talk, but Andrews had asked to do it alone. "I can't believe anyone actually lives in this spooky old place."

"Here if you need me." Cody called over the slamming car door.

The sour feeling in the pit of his stomach increased when Andrews leaned back through the open window. "You may have to help me after all, Cody. There's about a month's worth of junk sticking out of the mailbox slot. I'll bet you we've got a ripe one inside."

Cody stepped from the car and adjusted the hand-tooled holster that held his pistol. Settling the belt, he reached back through the open window without taking his eyes off the foreboding pile of bricks looming above them.

He lifted the microphone from its hanger. "Martha, this is Cody and we're at the Exchange building." He took stock of the immediate area before the light was completely gone. "You'd better send an ambulance. And we'll probably need uniforms here."

He heard the background discussion as the sheriff's office dispatch contacted an ambulance from Cobb and Oaks funeral home, and the Chisum police. "Gotcha, Cody."

"You coming?" Andrews started up the walk.

One more glance at the lengthening shadows and Cody rounded the front of the El Camino. Its cooling motor quietly ticked under the hood. He moved into step behind the deputy, dreading the disgusting job of dealing with another decomposing body.

They crunched in tandem up the crumbling concrete walkway. Chips of rock, gravel, and glass crackled under their brightly polished black cowboy boots. Andrews stopped before the entrance.

Despite his self-professed experience, he was grateful for Cody's company. Frankly, though he hadn't told anyone, he was terrified that one day he'd face the Nebraska killers. He was on edge from daylight to dark, worried that he'd come across the murderer of the entire Brooks family when he was by himself.

He hoped someone would capture the man so he could rest easy at night.

Cody scanned the area.

Broken tennis rackets, window frames, assorted lumber and bundles of newspapers accumulated against the outside wall.

He wondered how the material had gotten there in the first place. His stomach cramped. He was awake, staring at his own nightmares.

Ancient, matted wisteria vines hung from the support posts and exposed rafters like malignant green spaghetti. English ivy ran rampant, clinging tightly to every surface.

Cody shivered, suddenly enveloped by a sense of déjà vu. "My god. I've been dreaming about this place for weeks." This was the thing that all Parkers hated about the questionable gift they shared. They usually understood the dreams *after* they came to pass, or after an event was over and they recognized the connections.

Andrews snorted. "I swear, this spooky old place is right out of a monster movie. It never fails to surprise me that people can be so trashy."

"Have you ever seen anything so bad?"

"I've seen junk heaps, but this takes the cake." Andrews picked his way up the four granite steps to the warped board-walk. He looked left to right before stepping around a rusty car fender. "The front door is open a crack."

With one foot propped on the bottom step, Cody tilted his hat back with a thumb and glanced around the property. He scanned the block, seeing dozens of windows lined up along each floor and vertically to the roofline. Windows blocked by rotting plywood or yellowed shades once provided the only ventilation at the turn of the century, so each was separated from its neighbor by only three or four feet.

With growing unease, Andrews started talking to salve his nervousness. "This reminds me of a house over in Dallas when I first started this job. I was getting calls there two or three times a week from the neighbors who were concerned about this old nutcase lady's health. She lived alone and never threw anything away. Had little aisles everywhere, like narrow hallways through clothes piles of trash. You wouldn't believe what it was like inside. Newspapers, magazines, and cardboard boxes full of God-knows-what were stacked from the floor to the ceiling."

Cody half listened to Andrews' nervous rambling as he stepped to the side of the screen door's peeling doorjamb and knocked loudly. "Sheriff's office!"

"But the kitchen was the real trip," Andrews continued.

Oh lordy, I really do recognize this place.

"This woman cooked on a stove with only one burner not covered with junk. She barely had enough room to open the icebox." Andrews kicked the door with the toe of his boot. "Sheriff's office! Open up!"

Cody's hands shook.

"Imagine a house packed waist-high with trash and you'll get the idea. I handled that all right. It was the roaches in the kitchen that got me, though. They climbed up my pants legs like ants.

"I was standing beside this one table made from two-by-fours and realized what I thought was filler between the boards turned out to be live roaches packed so tight you couldn't see any light around their bodies."

Cody shivered, wishing Andrews would quit talking.

"It still gives me the heebie-jeebies to think about it."

Cody studied the mountain of trash around them.

Andrews slipped an index finger through the metal handle on the wooden screen door and gave it a tug. It opened with a screech of rusty springs. He pondered the sight before him. "Look here. Someone re-hung the front door so that it swings outward. I've never seen a front door that didn't open to the *inside*."

Foot still propped on the bottom steps, Cody leaned an elbow on his knee and rested his right hand on the handle of the .45. "Did you say it was unlocked?"

"Yup."

"Well, beat on it again. If no one answers we go to step two." He glanced to the right and thought he saw someone peek around the corner at the end of the long walkway, covered with broken glass.

His attention was on the corner when Andrews kicked harder, rattling the nearby remaining panes in the window frames. "Open up! This is the law. Open the door!"

Cody scanned the yellowed, water-stained paper shades hiding the interior from outside eyes. An unknown force pressed the shades against grimy glass, most cracked or broken.

Although the day had been over seventy degrees with no wind to speak of, not one window visible from the street was open. Cody listened, but not even the telltale hum of a water cooler broke the silence.

The sun slipped completely below the horizon, its glow reflected on the low clouds accumulating in the north.

"We need to get done with this, Jeff. That's a blue norther heading for us and I bet it'll be a booger when it gets here."

"Nobody home." Andrews turned the knob, opened the door, and visibly flinched at the interior. "What the hell?"

Cody tensed, his hand grasping the butt of his pistol. "What is it? What's the matter?"

Andrews held out his palm. "Relax, nothing's wrong, but I ain't never seen anything like *this* before."

Cody knew no situation was as it first seemed.

Their present situation required careful handling, in Cody's opinion. The unknown and unexpected got an officer in trouble, or killed. Andrews stayed where he was beside the peeling wooden door. Stepping to the right of the deputy, Parker placed his body in front of a solid wall between the entrance and the blocked window.

Buckets of machine parts and empty beer bottles sinking through a rotten linoleum floor popped into his mind. *This really is my nightmare.*

"What'cha got, partner?" Cody asked softly.

"Your guess is as good as mine." Andrews moved a step closer. "It's all blocked with bales of newspapers and old magazines."

Cody peered through rapidly collecting shadows. The entrance was completely packed with bound papers and tangled household items.

Andrews placed his open palm against the trash at shoulder height and pushed. The barrier wouldn't budge. He steadily increased the pressure and when he attacked with all his strength, nothing even *shifted.*

"We've got some tonnage in here."

"Seems pretty solid to me," Parker agreed.

With both hands Andrews shoved at the barrier, testing to see if he could find any give in the stacks. Kneeling on one knee, he shoved a ragged bundle of Life magazines dated 1944. A hollow-eyed American soldier stared at unseen horrors behind the camera. The magazines shifted.

"This one is loose. Gimme a hand here and let's see if we can work it out."

Parker knelt on one knee and they gripped the twine binding, finally working it out of the mass. When it fell free with a thump, an overpowering odor of death wafted from the hole.

The lawmen recoiled from the stench. Andrews turned and retched while Cody held his breath. He removed his light colored hat and used it to reflect the last of the sun's rays a few more inches into the hole they'd created.

"It's a tunnel!" Andrews exclaimed.

Cody replaced his hat, gritted his teeth, and choked.

Oh God, please let this not be true. I can't take any more tunnels in this lifetime.

Chapter Fifteen

Crumbling cardboard boxes spilled an assortment of rusty pistons into drifts of leaves.

While Andrews moved bundles of newspapers, Cody retrieved his flashlight from the El Camino. He returned to a two-by-two foot hole that gaped like an animal's burrow.

Cody's flashlight illuminated the waist-high tunnel. He paused, transfixed between the past and the present. The passage's design brought back horrifying memories he'd hoped to bury.

The dying light from the sky barely illuminated the entry as they peered inside. The stench dissipated slightly in the evening breeze which had almost completely stilled, an indication that the weather was about to change.

Satisfied with what he'd seen, Cody rose and stepped back to play the beam over the building. He mumbled to himself in an unconscious impersonation of his Uncle Ned. "We've got a crazy person living here."

Vietnam images of heat, humidity, water, mud, jungle, and terror rushed back like a freight train.

Andrews studied the dark hole in wonder. "This thing leads way inside. It goes for about five feet and then makes a right turn. It's a tunnel through garbage."

"I don't like this." Cody handed him the flashlight and hesitantly picked his way through the trash. "I'll call in and get the

Sheriff." He resisted the urge to turn and run back to the car. Cold dread settled into the pit of his stomach.

I'm sure as hell not going inside that thing. When I left the Nam I said I'd never crawl into anything like that again. Houses...I been dreaming of big old houses in neighborhoods like this one... but nothing like this evil thing here.

The mesmerizing hole beckoned. Andrews found himself drawn by the yawning maw. Like a child with a tantalizing mystery just out of reach, the temptation was too much to resist.

"I'm only going in far enough to peek around the corner."

Andrews' tone and the clatter of his belt as he dropped his holster sent a fresh feeling of dread through Parker.

He turned. "Uh, uh. Why don't you wait until Donald gets here?"

Donald Griffin had been sheriff for nearly twenty years. He also came to Chisum from Dallas, eager to get away from the big city's crime and politics. He found a home in the small town, but Cody's Uncle Ned Parker had little use for the man who was as territorial as a junk yard dog.

Ned felt Griffin had something crooked going on.

Andrews removed his hat and placed it on the gun belt to keep from soiling the light colored felt. He leaned inside, his voice muffled by the trash. "It ain't gonna hurt nothin' and I won't go all the way inside. This is like Alice in Wonderland. Down the rabbit hole."

Cody wasn't happy with the muscular, hard-headed deputy. *Was I ever this foolish? Yeah, I guess I was when they gave me a forty-five and sent me into the Vietnamese dirt. If you like this so much, Andrews, you should have been a tunnel rat with me because you'd have been broken pretty damn fast from crawling into small places.*

He jogged to the El Camino, opened the door, and sat inside with one foot on the ground. Twilight cloaked the neighborhood. Thick billows of dark clouds gathered to the north. The air stilled.

Keeping an eye on Andrews was getting harder in the fading light. Cody watched the lower half of his partner's body as he squirmed into the hole. He started the engine and angled into the street to position the car's recently installed spotlight directly onto Andrew's back. He clicked the button on the floor and the headlights illuminated the scene even more. He blocked the street, but Cody didn't care.

He keyed the Motorola's microphone. "Martha."

"Go ahead, Cody." Her voice crackled on the other end.

"Tell Donald that we have a possible dead body in the Exchange with the damnedest situation I've ever seen. He needs to get over here."

"Okey dokey."

He focused on a clot of greenery three feet deep. Ivy and grapevines grew from huge cracks in the foundation and side-walk, draping the exterior in a coat of vegetation starting to wither in the late season weather. The base of one grapevine was thick as a bat. Tired weeds grew past rusty bumpers piled lengthwise between the arches. A gritty maze of broken concrete surrounded the building. Paint peeled on the sagging shutters at ground level, and another service door further down hung on warped frames.

Hundreds of yellow National Geographic *magazines formed a multicolored floor leading into the burrow.*

The burrow wasn't high enough for Andrews to crawl on his hands and knees. He was forced to squirm in on his stomach. Feeling around with his left foot, he found a solid purchase and pushed farther inside. He instantly felt relieved when he saw the tunnel widened not far ahead. At the bend Andrews knew he'd be able to get room to move.

The flashlight illuminated bound stacks of yellowed and crumbling newspapers and magazines reaching up the right side. It reminded him of the hay bales he'd stacked by the thousands in barns all along the river bottoms. Only the smell wasn't as pleasant as sweet alfalfa.

The left side was old television picture tubes of various sizes, forming a solid wall of glass. Twenty-four inches overhead, doors and rolls of mildewed, carpet created a ceiling.

The gagging odor of rotting meat filled the burrow again, stronger than before, as if pushed from behind by a fan. Andrews' stomach contracted. Breathing through his mouth and supporting himself on one elbow, he fought down a wave of nausea, knowing that he'd be the butt of jokes for months to come if he puked in the shaft. In an effort to see around the corner, he shifted and twisted to gain more leverage.

He rolled to the side against the newspapers, raised his chest as high as possible, and called back over his shoulder. "Hey, partner!"

At the muffled shout, Cody quickly replaced the microphone and trotted back up the walk. He knelt beside the entrance. "What's up?"

"I've gone about as far as my nose will let me." His voice was muffled. "You'd better send for the meat wagon. Someone in here is pretty ripe."

"Already have. Can you see the body?"

Feeling a little more secure with Cody so close, Andrews grunted and scooted another inch or so. "No, but this tunnel bends up ahead. I can move around a little better once I get in there. I think the smell is coming from around the corner."

"Come on out." Cody's bad feeling intensified and over the years he'd come to respect his intuition. He was more spooked than he cared to admit.

I dream of tunnels that burrow deep into the earth.

He shivered and fought the need to run. "Get out of there."

Andrews shifted, already feeling the strain in his neck from the awkward position. "I'm about ready. One more push and I can see around this bend. Then I'll be out."

A low sound drifted through the fetid air, causing hair to prickle on the nape of Andrew's neck. "Cody, did you hear that? It sounds like somebody is hurt in here!"

Andrews moved his left elbow to rest on a large piece of crumbling cardboard. It gave slightly with a loud snap, like a bone breaking.

A nasty, grinding sound filled the tunnel. Andrews barely registered a pale face that appeared around the corner and widened into a leering grin. He knew that face. He'd seen it on a wanted poster just that morning under the white block letters that spelled the name of Kendal Bowden.

His own fears had been realized.

Driven by four bags of hardened cement mix, the front fork of a kid's bicycle plunged downward with savage force, ramming through his upper back and punching completely through the man's chest to bury nearly six inches deep into the garbage below.

Andrews was pinned as effectively as a butterfly on display. A scream forced itself through his blood-filled throat before shutting off as if someone threw a switch.

Chapter Sixteen

Hundreds of coffee cans full of nuts, bolts and nails.

Cody's heart pounded. He slammed backward into the exterior wall at Andrew's brief scream and quickly drew the big .45 from its holster, expecting an attack from any direction. Peripherally, he saw his partner's feet kicking spastically in the air. The liquid sounds coming from Andrews flushed ice into his blood.

"Jeff!" Cody swept the pistol toward the street, then knelt and grabbed his ankle. "Can you hear me?"

Andrews' convulsing elbow brushed a second hidden trigger, setting off a chain reaction in the mass of garbage above. A thin wire snapped, releasing a simple lever mechanism. Short but incredibly heavy pieces of railroad track slammed down with the force of a sledgehammer onto the television picture tubes.

Glass shattered from the force of the blow. The resulting detonation blew out the screens in a spray of razor sharp glass, slicing Andrew's face and neck to ribbons. Not one square inch of exposed skin on the left side of his upper face and neck remained intact. Blood pumped from his severed carotid artery and soaked the dust-dry newspapers and magazines below.

Parker jerked at the sound of the tremendous implosion. Andrews' legs ceased their spastic jerking as sparkling dust poured from the hole around his body, shimmering in the spotlight.

Cody launched himself back to the street, chased by illogical fear. Terror took the reins. He raced across the sidewalk and around the El Camino's hood to get a barrier between him and the building. Grabbing the open door with his left hand, centrifugal force slung him around and into the front seat. He snatched the microphone and pressed the key with numb fingers.

"Man down!" Cody's voice was full of panic. He kept his pistol pointed toward the Exchange, looking for nonexistent targets. "Martha, Jeff's hurt and there's been an explosion!"

With a gasp, he gripped the transmitter even harder. "I need help!"

"We heard you, Cody," said the calm voice Martha Wells. She'd been the dispatch operator for the past thirty years and was always cool in any crisis. They counted on her to handle an emergency without emotion. But afterwards, once the situation was resolved, she'd break down and weep great crocodile tears for at least an hour.

For the moment, she was all business. "All units. All units. Officer down at the Cotton Exchange Building on Howard. Repeat, officer down. Help is on the way, Cody. Hang on, hon."

Chapter Seventeen

Ned was so used to being constable that he couldn't shake the habit of hanging around town on a Friday night. He was standing outside of the brightly lit Grand Theater when Top and Pepper led the way out of the picture show. James didn't seem too surprised to see Ned and he winked at Aunt Ida Belle, like they knew a secret.

The retired constable stood a little taller when he saw them. "How was the picture?"

"Not bad for a Disney show," James said. "But I like Brian Keith in anything."

"Where y'all headed now?"

Ida Belle shrugged her round shoulders. "It's not too late, so I kinda wanted to go by and see Aunt Neva Lou."

The kids deflated at the thought. Miss Becky's only sister Neva Lou lived by herself in a house that smelled like cats. She didn't have any kids, there was no television, and it was too dark for them to do anything except sit still and listen to the adults visit.

James didn't seem that excited about it either, but he was going along with the idea to keep the peace.

Ned felt bad for his grandkids, because he didn't have much use for Neva Lou himself. High overhead, he absently registered the sound of geese complaining about the coming weather. "You kids want to go and get some ice cream with me instead?" Smiles brightened their faces. "Well, y'all c'mon. Pepper can spend the night with us."

"All right, but neither one of the kids have their coats and there's a norther on the way." Ida Belle always had a worry.

"That's all right. They'll be just as cold with you as me, besides, my car has a heater."

James hid a grin.

"Well, all right then." Ida Belle wasn't going to argue with Ned, but she wasn't going visiting alone. "Let's go, James. Pepper, you behave yourself." Without any further conversation, she turned and led the way to their car. James trailed sadly behind.

The kids followed Ned the short distance to Lane's corner drugstore just off the square. The soda fountain's white marble counter extended from the large front window and ran the length of the store's left side. Backed by gilded mirrors and thirty-year-old soda pulls, brightly colored pasteboard signs announced everything from Double Colas, Hires Root Beer and Grapettes, to Oak Brand ice cream sundaes.

Top and Pepper climbed onto the red vinyl stools and beamed. "Hidy Carlina," they said almost in unison.

Carlina had been the soda jerk there for years and knew everyone in town. Most of her customers thought she hung the moon. She crinkled her nose and popped her gum. "What you doing with these two outlaws, Ned?"

He always enjoyed visiting with her, because she popped her gum better than anyone he ever knew. "They're keeping me company. Y'all order what you want."

Top knew exactly what he wanted, because he'd had his mouth set for a chocolate soda all evening in the hopes that his Uncle James would stop by the drugstore on the way home. "Chocolate soda."

"Chocolate *malt*," Pepper ordered. "They're thicker."

"I could care less…" Top began, but Ned cut him off.

"Coffee."

Carlina watched them spin on the stools. "They're pretty busy company."

"Keeps me young."

"You're too damned old to be young," a voice said from behind.

Ned turned to see Judge Raines in his usual black suit. He didn't let on that he was glad to see the old judge. "You came in here for me to buy you a cup of coffee, didn't you? Why'n't you go on down to Frenchie's while me and these two have our ice cream in peace."

Judge Rains gave Top's hair a quick rub. He squeezed Pepper's shoulder, slapped his Stetson on the counter, and settled heavily onto the empty red vinyl-covered stool beside Ned. "I'm here because I wanted ice cream, too. It's Saturday night."

Carlina knew the pair well enough to ignore their bickering. The judge came in the drugstore every Saturday evening at the same time, so she had a fresh pot of coffee ready to go, in case he needed a quick pick-me-up.

With Ned's attention elsewhere, Top finally had the opportunity to show Pepper that he wasn't the titty baby she thought he was. He stuck a hand deep into his jean pocket and nudged his young cousin to get her attention. As she watched, he turned his back on the old men and held out a closed fist.

She sucked in a shocked breath at the sight of Ned's tiny gold constable badge in his open hand. Snitching cigarettes, taking a drink, and cussing were about the extent of her boundaries, despite the rough exterior she tried to show Top. But the thought of actually snitching, *stealing*, her Grandpa's most cherished possession was almost too much.

"What are you going to do with that?" she whispered.

Top leaned toward her. "Keep it. Grandpa don't need it no more. I'll always have it when he finally gives up trying to find it."

"You're a damned idiot. He won't never quit looking for that badge."

Ned turned slightly. "Did y'all say something?"

"Nossir." Top closed his fist.

"Well, it ain't polite to whisper in public."

"Yessir." He slipped the badge back in his pocket.

Carlina returned with the coffee. She thumped two thick white mugs on the counter. When Ned motioned with his finger, she set a tiny container of cream beside his mug.

Top loved the ounce of cream that came in the tiny clear containers and feeling brave, grabbed it just ahead of Pepper's quick reach. He downed it like a shot of whiskey in an old west saloon and slapped it back on the counter.

Judge Rains laughed. "Land O'Goshen, I'm glad I like my coffee black. It'd be hard work for a man to cream his coffee around this crew."

Ned shot his grandchildren a wry grin. "Who you got in jail tonight?"

"Kinfolk, mostly. Mine *and* yours. You'll be glad to know Cody caught Donny Wayne Foster's boy, Harold, racing outside of town again. He wouldn't have brought him in, but the little idiot gave him some lip, and Cody had warned him twice before already. I'm-a gonna let him spend the night in the hoosegow before I turn him a-loose."

"Don't surprise me. None of that Foster bunch has a lick of sense." Ned sipped his coffee as Carlina set the kids' ice cream on the counter with a flourish. Quick as a wink, he reached over and grabbed the cherry off of Top's soda. When the youngster opened his mouth to complain, Ned beat him. "Turnabout's fair play." He popped it in his mouth and chewed. "Others have been racing at night down by the creek bridge, knowing that I ain't constable no more. I told Cody about it, but they only race deep into the night, or when they know Cody's gone, and they're hard to catch."

Pepper about fell off her stool, laughing at the way Top bristled up over losing the cherry off his soda. She poked him with an elbow and turned to her own malt, pulling hard with her cheeks to get the thick goo through the straw.

O.C. nodded and watched Carlina construct a banana split for two of Chisum's oldest residents, Miss Dollar and her husband Arthur, who came by every Saturday night for the same treat. Miss Dollar wasn't eighty pounds fully dressed and soaking wet, and besides a cup of strong coffee and a piece of toast in the morning, the ice cream was her entire meal for the day.

"Cody'll get the rest of them, eventually."

"I hope so. It galls me to think I have to lay there in bed and listen to them engines."

"That's the best place to race in Center Springs," O.C. goaded him. The straight stretch from the creek bridge to where the highway curved around Ned's hill was almost exactly a mile, long enough to get a running start and shut down before the highway turned.

"Well, I don't give a ..." Ned's comment ended abruptly when a young courthouse secretary named Liz Jennings burst through the drugstore's glass doors, her Shelly Fabares hairstyle awry.

"Judge!" They turned at the stress in the woman's voice. "Martha over in dispatch is trying to find you. She's about frantic. She called me at home to come and find you. She even tried this phone, but nobody answered."

"That's because it's been on the fritz all week." Carlina dabbed whip cream on top of the banana split.

O.C. spun around on his stool. "That don't matter none. What is it, Liz?"

"She says one of your people has been killed tonight."

"Who was it?" O.C. reached for his hat.

"Jeff Andrews went to check on a bad smell coming from the old Cotton Exchange building. Somehow he got killed and they have them bad guys penned up." She cut her eyes at Ned.

"Who's with Jeff?" He stood up, stomach clenched, instinctively knowing the answer.

She had to tell him. "Cody Parker."

Chapter Eighteen

Wooden cases full of empty soda pop bottles, hand tools, handmade cedar chests and crude quilt boxes, fruit crates, chicken crates, clothes, clothes, clothes...

Sirens increased in volume with wails of urgency and fear. The brotherhood of lawmen takes immediate precedence when one of their own is in trouble. Every available officer in town rushed to aid their fellow brother in arms.

Cody stuffed his .45 back into the holster, jerked the shotgun from its awkward position between the seats...

...Oh God, please don't let him be dead...

...and sprinted up the glass-strewn sidewalk. He crouched momentarily behind a low pile of rotting lumber. After a quick scan without identifying any outward signs of danger, he sprang back up the steps and braced his back against the wall.

"Jeff!" He whispered and carefully squatted beside Andrews. He reached out, and gently shook a limp leg without taking his eyes off the surrounding debris.

Hurry up, guys. He's not moving!

"Jeff!" He gave Andrews' foot a shake. The heavy, unresponsive weight of his fellow lawman's leg was all he needed to know.

Ominous rumblings and deep wooden groans sounded as if huge objects shifted inside the building just as the first police cars screeched to a stop. Sirens howled, covering any further sounds. Flashing lights slashed through the peaceful dusk of early evening.

Momentary terror gave way to absolute panic as Cody rushed toward the friends who would understand his horror. At the sight of the fleeing constable, armed and anxious officers scrambled around to the safe side of the vehicles and leaned over their shotguns.

"Someone inside killed Jeff!"

He virtually flew around the bumper of a newly arrived patrol car. His feet slipped on loose gravel. The terrified young man fell hard, smelling leaking antifreeze and burned brake pads.

"How many?" came a grim voice.

"I don't know," Cody gasped, urgently shoving with his feet and coming to rest with his back against the blackwall's hubcap. "I don't even know *how* he was killed, but he's dead."

There's not a whole hell of a lot I do know about this situation, except that there's this tunnel made of trash and something killed Andrews and for all I know it's gnawing on his head like a peach pit right now.

More help arrived in answer to the call, along with the first ambulance, a glorified station wagon operated by the Cobb and Oaks funeral home. In minutes, Howard Avenue was impassable, jammed with white cars. The strobe effect lit the entire the street with revolving lights.

Homeowners emerged, drawn toward the action and noise. Police officers frantically waved the idiot gawkers back. "Get down! Get back inside!"

…or at least stand in the clear so the creeps in there can have a clear shot at you and I can see where they are…

Slow moving residents backed away from the frustrated officers. Car radios crackled with orders. Men scrambled for cover and waited for something to happen for several long minutes before tension began to bleed off. Finally, the lack of activity sparked the first arrivals to check on the injured deputy.

Under the cover of more than a dozen cocked weapons, two ambulance drivers and two armed sheriff's deputies broke cover, ran through the main arch in the gathering darkness, and jarred to a stop on either side of Andrews' legs. A dim yellow glow from his still burning flashlight washed an eerie incandescence around the still body. Carlton Evans, the oldest and most experienced of the ambulance drivers shook the officer's leg.

Getting no response, they tried to drag Andrews free. He didn't budge. Still not sure if they were going to come under fire, Carlton quickly cut Andrew's pant leg, reached in and felt the inside of his thigh for the big femoral artery. He pressed firmly with his fingertips, praying for a pulse.

Carlton removed Andrew's left shoe and sock while Harvey Glasscock opened a folding knife and passed it to his partner. Carlton pricked the sole of Andrews' foot with a sharp knife in an effort to elicit a response of pain.

He shook his head at his partner when he detected no signs of life.

When that failed they soon realized they were poking a cadaver.

The scared and frustrated men retrieved their gear, and still covered by the two officers, backed slowly to the safe zone behind the patrol cars.

Not sure what to do in the bizarre situation, everyone waited for a supervisor outside of the silent, surrounded warehouse.

Chapter Nineteen

I'd never seen those two old men move so fast. They shoved off from the counter in a flash and headed for the doors without a word.

"Shit!" Pepper said as we spilled off our own stools. Grandpa stopped and turned around as he reached the door. "You kids cain't go. Carlina, you're about to close. Take them home with you and…"

She gave him a horrified look. "They can't go home with me tonight, Ned. Darren ain't working and he's been mean as a snake this week. I can't have him drinking around these little ones."

I'd heard of Darren's meanness. He drank a lot and folks said he was known to hit Carlina, but I couldn't see how anyone could hurt somebody like her.

Grandpa searched for someone else to help, but the only customers left were the old couple, and he didn't know them well enough to ask.

"Fine, then. Y'all come with us, but you ain't-a stayin' long. I'll find somebody to take you to Neva Lou's after a while. Now, c'mon, we gotta git!"

Him and Mr. O.C. led the way into the darkness and around the corner, heading toward Grandpa's car parked in front of the picture show. Pepper and I ran easily behind them as they cut across the street, holding out their hands as cars squalled to a stop.

We dove into the backseat as Grandpa and Mr. O.C. slammed the front doors. I knew how Grandpa drove, and if we hadn't already been in the car, he would have left us standing on the curb. As it was, he hit the starter, then reverse, and shot out of the diagonal parking space, nearly hitting a pickup that barely swerved out of the way.

The truck's driver set down on the horn.

"Don't kill us driving over there." Mr. O.C. spoke as calm as you please.

Grandpa ignored him and snapped the radio on. It worked for once and we heard the excited voices of lawmen driving hard to help one of their own.

Chapter Twenty

Bald tires, shredded tires, and rotten tires, stacked and tossed...

Police officers worked their way down the potholed streets, beating on doors to wake neighbors and escort them to a safe area behind the hastily erected barricades far away from the ominous scene.

They cleared the nearest homes on the south side of the trail station. White officers shouting orders at the black occupants immediately scared half of the residents and made the other half fighting mad.

"Mister Officer, y'all gonna have to let me take my time," one heavyset gray haired old woman begged as she struggled to keep her thin house dress closed.

A white deputy did his best to hustle her down the street. "I don't *have* time. We need to move!"

"But I cain't walk fast."

Deputy John Washington appeared from nowhere. "Dale, take your hands off Miss Sweet."

Only the second black deputy in Chisum's history, Big John was an almost mythical presence on both sides of the tracks. He handled the law work that Sheriff Griffin's biased officers usually ignored, and involved himself in any case where his people found themselves in the crosshairs.

The deputy turned toward Big John. "She's got to listen to what we're saying. One of our people is dead over yonder and we need to clear this entire area!"

"I know it." John's deep voice rumbled low and calm. "But Miss Sweet didn't have nothin' to do with that, and she's old. She cain't walk fast." He gently removed Dale's hand from his old aunt's arm and replaced it with his own, putting himself between her and the Exchange. "Now, everybody just needs to calm down. Miss Sweet, hold onto me and c'mon."

"I cain't walk far John."

"Yessum, we're going right over yonder to Leroy Douglas' house and he's gonna put you in his car and drive you to Miss Peaches."

"Well, I cain't leave without m'sack. It has all my jars and medicine herbs."

Miss Sweet acted as a healer in the colored community. She doctored anyone who asked, black or white, and often acted as a midwife for both black and white folks as far away as Center Springs or Tigertown.

John stopped and waved at a skinny cousin he recognized. He knew nearly every colored person in Chisum, and was kin to a good number of those who lived there. They all listened when he spoke. "Nehemiah, run back in Miss Sweet's house and get her medicine bag. Where is it Auntie?"

"I set it by the table when I was eatin' my supper."

He turned back to Nehemiah. "It's on the floor, and hurry."

Miss Sweet held onto his big arm. "This ain't right, what they're doing, draggin' folks out their houses without a by-your-leave. What's going on?"

Big John smiled down at the wrinkled face of Miss Peaches' twin. "What they're doing is fine. It's the right thing, Auntie. They just going about it the wrong way."

"What are these white Laws hollering about, John?" A young man with thick glasses asked, mad at the rude treatment. More frustrated people gathered around John. He felt the rising anger on the street.

"They scared of something. Other'n that, I don't have any idee, but we'll find out. Go on down out the way and find somewhere's else to wait." John raised his voice so the others could hear. "Y'all listen to these men here and I'll be back directly when I know something."

Nehemiah came back out with the heavy muslin sack. "Is this what you wanted Miss Sweet?"

"That's it. Bless you child." She took the sack, hooked the long strap over her thick shoulder, and fussed at the contents for a moment while John and Nehemiah patiently waited. "Lawdy mercy, I can't go nowhere 'thout my medicines. Somebody might need them 'fore we get back. What if somebody has a spell, or somebody gets hurt? In fact, baby, I 'spect y'all should let me stay close by in case you need me. What if you get hurt, John? These folks ain't-a-gonna take care of you like I can. Now you *know* that's right."

"Yes, ma'am, but I don't need to worry about *you* gettin' hurt. You go with Leroy and he'll bring you right back if something happens, or they'll bring me to Miss Peaches' house and y'all can doctor away. Is that all right?"

She thought about his suggestion as she finished her brief inventory. Satisfied that everything was in place, she handed it back. "That'll be all right, hon. Now, Nehemiah, you tote this for me honey."

"Yessum."

Wearing only his pants and undershirt, Leroy Douglas was already outside. He took over for John and helped Miss Sweet into the front seat of his car. Four others climbed into the back seat as Leroy slipped behind the steering wheel and carefully drove his frightened passengers through the gathering crowd.

As Big John turned, the sheriff's cruiser passed slowly through the barricade and stopped beside the makeshift command post. Deputy Washington officially answered to Sheriff Donald Griffin on paper, but in reality, he worked for Judge O.C. Rains. "Now, y'all simmer down till I find out what's what and don't nobody go acting the fool tonight. We don't need that kind of trouble. Looks like we got enough up there by the tracks as it is."

Sheriff Griffin turned off the engine and stepped out, radiating authority. "All right, what have we got here?" He settled his belt and joined a cluster of uniformed patrolmen behind one of the first cars to arrive on the scene.

The beefy Griffin was the image of a Texas lawman from his Stetson hat, crows-feet in the corners of his eyes, and a heavy gray mustache. The entire affectation, along with the pearl handled Colt .45 revolver on his hip, gave rise to smirks behind his back.

"I want all these vehicles out of here right now. Clear this out all the way back to the intersection."

His men jumped at the order, glad to do something productive. They untangled the haphazardly parked emergency vehicles. The growing crowd of residents waited to see what would happen next.

"Why are all these…Negroes…standing around here in the way?"

A couple of the men hid grins behind their hands. Others shifted uncomfortably.

It was nothing new to John. He scratched at the short hair underneath his hat brim, in an unconscious imitation of Ned Parker. "They live here, Sheriff."

Surprised that John heard him, Griffin simply nodded. "Tow them cars if you can't find someone with the keys." He turned toward the massive building, talking almost to himself. "I've always hated this place." He saw a very unnerved Cody squatting against the wheel of a nearby police car and walked over as men rushed between the cars. "What have we got here, son?"

Cody raised his eyes and ran shaky fingers through his hair. He'd lost his hat when he slipped and fell. "We came by to check on a report that Kendal Bowden might be hiding out here."

Griffin listened with a troubled expression until Cody haltingly told his story. When he finished, the sheriff frowned. "I'm sure I heard you wrong. The Exchange is full of what?"

Cody shifted uncomfortably. "Junk from all over town, I guess."

Sergeant Thomas Blair shifted a chew of Redman into his right cheek. The rock-solid police officer took stock of the situation as soon as he arrived and began to sort out the details. A fireplug of a man with abnormally short arms, Blair quickly saw that no one had taken charge of directing the scene. Though he officially answered only to Police Chief Mayhew, the lack of organization was more than he could stand. He immediately issued orders and planned to continue until the police chief told him to stand down, or Sheriff Griffin assigned one of his own men to act as the incident commander.

"Sheriff, he's right." Blair waved a hand toward the Exchange. "My guys poked around as much as they could, and from what we've been able to see, this entire floor is filled with trash all the way to the ceiling. Someone has been stacking garbage inside for months and maybe years. From what Andrews said before he got…well, they might have left a way to enter and move around through tunnels in there just like the one he's trapped in."

"Garbage," Griffin repeated flatly trying to understand the situation. "Like tin cans, bones, coffee grounds…"

"No, sir. Well, yeah, I reckon, there might be some of that." Blair tried to find the right words to adequately explain the situation they faced. "It's like someone packed this place with stuff they wanted to save. So far we've identified bundles of newspapers…lots of newspapers, televisions, rolls of carpet, magazines, furniture of all kinds, household items, cardboard, papers, and that's what we can see around Jeff's body. You can see it in the windows, pushing through the paper shades like them they tore off over there."

Blair spat a stream of brown juice onto the ground. "I guess the best way to describe it is if somebody hauled everything from the town dump and filled the place up."

Griffin nodded. "That's the damnedest thing I've ever heard of. Williams!" he called to a deputy across the street. The lawman had already lost his temper and was ordering a family to leave their barking dog and get down the street, out of whatever danger was nearby. He turned his back on the angry and confused family to join the men standing beside the car.

"Sir?"

"Get your people to start questioning these folks and find somebody who has an idea about whether anyone lives here or not. I need to know a lot more. At least find someone who's been inside." He turned to the men behind him, immediately dismissing Williams and knowing the patrolman would get the job done. The Exchange had been there for decades. Surely a neighbor remembered the layout, or knew what was going on.

"Thomas," Griffin continued, "You see if you can get me current information on the owner of this place, too."

Sergeant Blair nodded, leaned into his car, and picked up the Motorola's microphone. Before he could key the mike, Griffin stopped him with another question.

"Have we heard anything from inside?"

"No, sir. Not since we arrived. We haven't gotten much out of Cody either except Andrews is dead."

Griffin didn't like surprises. A familiar knot gripped his stomach. Dealing with domestic disputes, drunks, traffic violations, and even bank robbers was fairly easy for the experienced lawman, because he'd trained for it. He knew what to do in each case and if the situation changed, he knew how to change with it. The ominous structure in front of them was a mystery, completely baffling, and frightening.

"They should have torn this place down years ago."

Big John nodded and stared past the patrol car at the body in the front door. "They probably would have, but it's on *our* side of the tracks, and that don't make it too important."

Griffin ignored him and turned to his men. A generator growled to life and harsh trailer-mounted floodlights bathed the scene in stark, white luminescence. Spotlights snapped alive and crisscrossed the exterior to the roofline, five stories overhead. Andrews' bare leg glowed in the harsh light. The door in which he was pinned appeared tiny in comparison to the building.

Griffin studied the brick edifice. The 360-degree view from the high roof would be perfect for keeping watch on the community and was an ideal shooting platform. From the high perch, anyone with a good rifle, and everyone in Chisum had a deer rifle, could control an incredibly large area around the Exchange.

"Get a scope on that roof line. I want to know if even a chi-chi bird lands on a window ledge. And I want to know for sure what's inside. If those tunnels are like you said, I want to take this slow and careful. Call Carlton White and have him bring that German Shepherd of his out here. We're going to need him."

He turned from his dead man pinned in the door. "We may have to send a dog in once we get Andrews out. Dogs are expendable. My deputies aren't."

Chapter Twenty-one

Equipment identifiable only to morticians, wooden barrels of all sizes, wagon wheels, singletrees, doubletrees, blacksmith billows, filthy clothing, buckets...

Deputy John Washington stayed close to Sheriff Griffin at the now bustling command post. "This is your part of town, John. Tell me what you know."

"I don't know nothin'. I heard Cody's call while I was checking on things in Sugar Bear's parking lot, then I run right over here and when I saw he was all right, I came to you." He made no mention of the sudden flaring tempers when the deputies hurried people from their homes. It wouldn't have made any difference, because Griffin would have listened politely, then ignored the entire incident.

"All right. You have any ideas about what's been going on here?"

The big deputy scratched his temple. "Nawsir, but this old Cotton Exchange has been rotting down for years. Me and about everybody else has been wondering why so much trash is collecting around here."

He gave Griffin a brief history of the historic building. He didn't mention that on numerous occasions he'd brought his concerns about the decaying Exchange to individual members of the city council, who usually wouldn't listen to a colored man, but nodded solemnly out of respect for the legendary law officer. Unfortunately, the Council wasn't interested in the old building, or for that matter anything else across the tracks. It had always been that way.

Surrounded by deputies and patrolmen, police chief Tommy Mayhew joined them. He scowled at Sheriff Griffin when he ordered police sergeant Blair to update the crude map taking shape on a fold-out card table. The incident originated within the city limits, but originally involved men who worked for the county. Instead of challenging Griffin's authority, Chief Mayhew reluctantly allowed the county sheriff to direct the activity, though it galled him. He tolerated the complexity of the circumstances and stood by to support the sheriff's department...for the time being.

Big John saw Cody standing nearby. He stepped close and placed a huge hand on his shoulder. "How you doing?"

"I'm fine, except for being scared to death. I knew this was going to happen for months, John." He glanced around to be sure no one overheard. "I been dreaming about it."

Big John knew about the Parker family's strange gift. He recalled the connection between Top's dreams that lasted for months and ended in the river bottoms back in the spring. He nodded sympathetically. "Nightmares, or dreams?"

"Is there a word for what's in between?"

"That'd be life, son."

"If y'all are through, or unless you want to throw some voodoo bones, I'd like to get busy here," Griffin interrupted. John turned an impassive face toward his boss and waited.

Griffin pointed at a rough plan drawn by a sleepy old man who had last been in the Exchange twenty years before. "Cody, get yourself together and tell us what you know."

Taking a deep breath, Cody gave them a quick rundown of what happened after he and Andrews arrived at sunset. He stabbed a finger at the drawing. "The entrance here in the front was probably a dummy to sucker anybody poking around into a trap. It worked pretty damn well. We didn't get any farther than there."

Sergeant Blair, who'd been talking with other officers that checked out the Exchange, had a little more information. Earlier, firemen under the protection of rifles tore down a brittle paper shade to discover a layer of boards nailed to the window from the inside. When they hacked through the boards they found a wall of furniture barring their way. It was packed so solidly, the amazed investigators could see only inches into the interior.

He packed a big chew into his cheek. "There's an entrance around back here that's been used quite a bit." Blair pointed with a strong forefinger. "This one at a back door seems to be the main way in and out. There's a pretty clear path where someone's walked it down."

Griffin nodded. "Good work. Can we get in?"

"You can if you don't mind another tunnel. A couple of our boys poked around and opened the door to find the same thing. From what I can tell, it's filled as solid as everything else. We didn't try to move anything out of the way, after what happened with Andrews."

"Damn. What is this all about?" Griffin asked.

Doors slammed behind them. They saw a large German Shepherd jump to the ground from the back of a pick-up. Sheriff Griffin turned to his men. "We'll send the dog in and figure this thing out."

The other car contained Ned, O.C., and the kids. Every officer in the county knew the old men and showed their respect by stepping aside as they passed through the crowded street.

Relief washed over John Washington, realizing that he felt responsible for Cody. Now that Ned was present, the old man would make any decisions that involved his nephew.

At the same time, Ned's knees grew weak when he saw that Cody wasn't injured.

Griffin frowned. "What are you doing here? You're retired, ain't you Ned?"

"Not so's you'd notice." He breathed a sigh of relief and spoke to Cody. "You all right?"

"Yessir, shook up some."

Satisfied, Ned turned his attention back to the sheriff. "I came to see if I can help. I heard you had a booger-bear hemmed up in this old place, so I thought I'd drop by and watch a good job well done."

"Well, you can't." Griffin drew himself up. "We have way too many chiefs around here as it is. And what are them kids doing here?"

Ned appeared surprised to see Top and Pepper behind him. Before he could answer, O.C. stepped forward. "They were all with me when we heard what was going on. I brought them."

Griffin caught the set of O.C.'s jaw and knew better than to argue with the old warrior in front of his men. He'd wait and hash it out with him later.

"We'll all stay out of the way and watch from over here until I can find somebody to take them off my hands." Ned took one step back. He'd be damned if he gave that pompous ass Griffin two steps.

Griffin wanted to tell him to leave, that any decisions he made would be second guessed by the men under his charge if Ned and O.C. Rains were present. He didn't want either of the old men to have anything to do with the crisis at hand. But at the same time, he knew better than to order the old constable and his grandkids away. It would only make O.C. Rains mad, and he didn't need that in his life right now.

Rains was a tough old bastard and Griffin knew he'd lose in a pissing contest with the judge. Besides, he wasn't sure Ned would listen to him, either. He'd dig in his heels about going. If Griffin backed down, he'd lose the respect of his men and no matter how the night turned out, he'd lose the election next year.

"Sheriff Griffin." Sergeant Blair interrupted the standoff, hung up his microphone, and stepped out of the car. "I have a little more information. The city has issued official clean-up orders at least six times in the last year. In fact, someone brought in two dump trucks and parked them in the driveway, but they were removed for nonpayment."

"So someone authorized the trucks at one point. Was it the occupant?"

Blair recognized Ned and O.C. standing nearby and nodded hello while Griffin talked. "Apparently not. It was the city. Last fall, the Health Department initiated a complaint that stated the inside was filled with garbage throughout the first floor and declared the place was uninhabitable. But the signing individual took another job in Ft. Worth before action was taken. The city also began condemnation procedures through the assistant city attorney, but the paperwork got lost and everyone forgot all about it."

"I love bureaucracy." Griffin's voice dripped with sarcasm.

"That's how it is on this side of the tracks."

Griffin snapped toward the sound of humor in John's voice, but with O.C. Rains standing behind the big deputy, he didn't say a word. "Cody, now that I think of it. What'n hell are *you* doing here in the first place?"

"I sent him." O.C. scowled.

Griffin felt a tightness in his chest. Heat rose in his face. "What for?"

"I heard somebody might have seen Kendal Bowden snooping around here and told Cody to come check it out."

"Well, dammit, O.C., you should have told me, or at least let Chief Mayhew know what was going on." He turned his attention back to Cody. "So Judge Rains told you to come into town, get one of my deputies, and come across the tracks here to ni…to the colored side and check out an abandoned building?"

"Nossir," Cody spoke up. "That was my idea to ask Andrews, since we're in town, but the rest is right."

"You should have brought John. This is his part of town."

"I don't believe John can fit in that little half-breed car of Cody's," O.C. said. "Besides, he told me he was bringing Jeff, I forgot to tell you. He thought about asking John, but it looks like he changed his mind."

"I intended to call John when we got here, but things happened too fast," Cody explained.

Griffin wanted to chew both Cody and the old judge out, but there was no point in it. What was done, was done. He turned back to his men. "Can someone please tell me who owns this spooky old place?"

Blair referenced his notebook. "George Hart."

"That sounds familiar."

O.C. rubbed the back of his neck. "Yep, he and his brother Alvin ran a funeral home way back when, long before you moved to town. One day Cobb and Oakes moved in with lower prices and a newer building in the north side of town. Hart and Hart went out of business."

The men surrounding him shook their heads.

"Alvin's been an invalid for years." O.C. wagged a forefinger back and forth. "For a long time you'd see George pushing him around town in his wheelchair, but I doubt I've seen George in a coon's age."

"I saw him last about a year ago, slipping down the street late one night here on our side of town." John jerked his thumb toward the south. "He was carryin' a car battery on his shoulder. I thought that was a little strange, because I don't believe he owns a runnin' car, but he was always peculiar anyway. Haven't seen him since, though."

Sheriff Griffin chewed his bottom lip. "All right. I want to hear from the people in the neighborhood. Talk to everyone and find out when was the last time they saw George. Find out from the city about who pays the property taxes and go to the power company and see what name is written on the checks each month. Let's get a handle on this place we've ignored for so long."

"You know who George's boy is?" O.C. asked.

Griffin sighed. "Who?"

"That feller that helped break Kevin Jennings out of the nut house in Tulsa and then killed him up on the river. His name is Kendal Bowden."

"Oh, hell, I think I knew that." Griffin turned his eyes toward the sky, as if seeking help from above.

They turned toward the Cotton Exchange, giving Ned a moment with John. The old constable flicked a hand toward the kids. "Think Miss Sweet is feeling good enough to watch these two while we're here?" He knew her house was only half a block from the Exchange.

"She was feelin' just fine when they emptied all these houses and put her in the car to stay with Miss Peaches."

Trapped, Ned took off his Stetson and ran a hand over his bald head. "Now I know what an old sow feels like when she has trouble weaning her pigs off the tit." He turned to survey the tangled mass of parked cars blocking everything nearly as far as he could see. "I need to get these kids out of here."

"I'll find somebody to carry them home for you, Mister Ned."

"Naw, that ain't your job. I'll find somebody here in a minute who can run 'em over to Neva Lou's." Ned stared down at them, wishing for a moment he was young enough to run off with them.

Chapter Twenty-two

When we first got to the Cotton Exchange, Pepper and I saw Mr. Andrew's legs sticking half out of the door. It was strange, one leg was covered by his britches and the other one fish-belly white, like he never got out in the sun at all.

There was a lot of excitement around us, and we stuck close to Grandpa and Mr. O.C. A couple of the deputies I didn't know frowned at us. One of the men who knew us mouthed Grandpa's name and jerked his head in our direction, so that made it ok for us to stay there for a while.

For once Pepper didn't have much to say, from fear I reckon, because at first the whole thing scared her to death. As the men talked, we kept ourselves between Grandpa and Mr. John, who rested his big hand on Pepper's shoulder and gave us a grin.

We were safe, though, because nearly every law in town was standing within spittin' distance. More searchlights arrived and soon the Exchange was lit up like the castle in Disneyland. It was spooky. The gray exterior made me think of vampires. While I was staring at the second floor, something caught my attention. I poked Pepper and pointed it out. Grandpa noticed when I waved my hand toward the building and instead of frowning at us to be quiet, he raised an eyebrow toward the Exchange.

Chapter Twenty-three

The discarded possessions of a city were packed tightly in the enormous building.

Less than a half hour into the situation, they ground to an impasse. The men around Sheriff Griffin usually dealt with issues in a straightforward manner. Most felt that an assault or entry into a barricaded building was authorized only when the officers came under fire.

Police Chief Tommy Mayhew wanted to wait until morning, but after making his views known, he simply backed off to let Griffin hang himself. Mayhew was experienced enough to pick his fights, and this wasn't one of them.

His frustration rising, Griffin drummed his fingers. "We need to get that boy out, and I want to find out what's going on." He turned to study the faces of the officers around him. "Any suggestions or observations?"

Sergeant Blair worked at his chew for a moment. "From what I can tell, every door and window in the place is either boarded up or packed solid with junk. I'm afraid George blocked all the windows and doors and booby-trapped the entire thing."

"Why would he do that?" Griffin watched the building, not expecting an answer.

"To keep something out?" John mused.

After a long period of silence, Griffin finally made a decision. "Since we aren't getting any response from inside, I guess we need to send the dog in there." He glanced at the faces of the men around him, hoping to find a supporting expression. "If that don't work, we'll need someone who is an expert in barricaded buildings."

Chief Mayhew laughed harsh and dry. "Expert? Where are you going to find a booby trap expert in Chisum?"

Griffin raised an eyebrow and waited for an answer.

A very much calmer Cody Parker had an answer. "I know a guy on the Mesquite police department who was a tunnel rat in Vietnam. We can probably call and have him here in two hours."

Mesquite was a growing town on the outskirts of Dallas, a hundred and twenty miles away.

"He did what?" Griffin snapped, not understanding. The tension and bizarre answers frazzled his nerves.

"He was one of those guys who went down into VC tunnels with a flashlight and a forty-five."

"I never heard of such a thing. You really think there are tunnels through all that mess?"

"That's what we saw before the booby trap went off. Andrews is stuck in a tunnel made of trash."

Sheriff Griffin stared at the row of arches and shuddered. Now that he thought about it, he remembered hearing about guys on Japanese-held islands who cleaned out their stronghold tunnels during the second war. Anyone willing to go in there all alone had to be nearly as nuts as the lunatic inside. He was frankly unsure what to do next. "All right, call Mesquite and see if they'll work with us on this. While we're waiting on them, Blair, send the dog in to nose around. It's a lead pipe cinch that *I'm* not crawling into any tunnels inside a *building*, and neither is anyone else right now."

"You want me to use the back entrance to get the dog inside?"

"That's the only one I see here on this paper."

Ned cleared his throat. "Why don't you use the one up there on the second floor corner? The one on the right, I mean?"

Griffin was annoyed at the seemingly ridiculous suggestion. "I guess you know another way in?"

"Donald, when was the last time you went squirrel huntin'?"

"Dammit Ned. We're talking about a *situation* here, and you want to discuss the last time I hunted *squirrels*? Have you lost your mind?"

"Well, I probably don't have much mind left to lose, but if I was huntin' squirrels, I'd find a slick spot on the trunk of a tree to see where he's getting in and out of his hole."

Griffin could barely contain himself. "What…are…you…talking…about?"

"Hell Donald. Even Top standing here knew what he was looking at, once he really paid attention."

Cody suddenly realized where Ned was going with the conversation. "When you're squirrel huntin' you either set still and let them come to you, or find a nest, or where they crawl in and out of a hollow tree. When they do that, they wear the bark away from the hole. Ned calls it the slick spot."

"You find a slick spot, Mister Ned?" John Washington knew good and well Ned didn't ask such questions unless he already had the answer.

"Yep, saw it right off, once Top pointed it out. You can get in by climbing that skinny little trellis made of two-by-fours and covered up with that ivy. I don't reckon I've ever seen a vine trellis made out of wood that thick. What paint there on the sill has been worn off, too."

"A slick spot." Griffin glared at the only trellis on the building. He wondered why he hadn't noticed it before, because now that he was paying attention, it was more like a ladder than a trellis and it was the only one of its kind on the south wall.

Ned grinned. "Right."

The sheriff sighed. *Whatever happened to the old days when all we had to worry about were family disputes and bootleggers?*

Chapter Twenty-four

Moldering shoes filled crevices and holes in the tunnel and canyon walls. A figure wriggled confidently through the darkness, and waited.

Deputy Carlton White and his dog Shep crouched behind a car near the covered sidewalk. The pair had been partners for over two years after White transferred to the newly created K-9 unit from street patrol. It was the first pairing of its kind in northeast Texas, and all based on his experience in the Korean War.

White's dog handling training in Dallas covered six weeks when he was paired with the huge German Shepherd. They immediately bonded and White learned to communicate with the dog using German commands, a holdover from the second world war. Once he was comfortable with the foreign words designed to prevent a criminal from giving the animal counter orders, White and Shep practiced together every day.

As the weeks passed, they became inseparable. They understood each other and, in time, successfully worked the streets with confidence and authority. More often than not, the department loaned White and Shep to other towns and communities along the Red River where they tracked felons through towns and woods and cleared buildings at night

In the short time they'd been together, White learned to respect the animal's intuition. It made White nervous when

Shep whined as they came up to the Exchange, a sound that he'd never heard before.

Neither liked what they saw…or felt.

O.C. picked up on their unease. "What is that dog gonna do in there? Grab somebody by the collar and drag 'em out?"

Feeling that for once he was on safe ground with the old judge, Griffin hooked both thumbs in his tooled western gun belt and rocked back on his heels. "White will call through the window that he has a dog and will send it in. If whoever in there don't come out, he'll release the dog, who will find, hold, or incapacitate the individual, until White can join up."

Ned frowned toward the Exchange, forgetting the men around him. He fell into the familiar habit of talking quietly to himself. "Apprehend. Individual. In-com-pass-it-tate."

Pepper snickered and Top glared at her. He didn't want to attract any attention that would cause them to be sent away.

"What was that, Mr. Ned?" Washington also heard him and gently brought Ned back to his surroundings. Ned glanced at the lawmen around him and sheepishly raised an eyebrow.

"What *are* you doing here?" Griffin asked Ned. "You ain't…"

With growing irritation, Ned knew he had no business there, but he held himself in check. "I know. I ain't a constable anymore, but Cody is, and he's my kin and…"

"We've already chewed this fat." Judge O.C. scowled at Griffin. "Don't forget he's with me."

The three-way confrontation ended as the gathering crowd watched White cautiously approach the Exchange and ascend one of two wide-stepped ladders officers previously leaned together against the bottom of the window frame.

Carefully, expecting to be shot off the ladder, White quickly reached the second floor window and opened it. He ripped down the paper shade and exposed a tunnel of trash similar to the one holding Andrews' body. He stared into a shoulder-width aisle through sagging stacks of wooden crates, doors, refrigerators, boards, and a warped wooden file cabinet, all cemented together with cloth and other debris jammed into every crack and crevice.

Once he was settled, White called the dog. Shep whined and ascended the rungs. He'd been trained to climb ladders, but it never came naturally to him. White calmed the dog and murmured soft words of encouragement in his ear. He shifted to the side and the dog stepped through the window, hesitating nervously and waiting for instructions.

Two bolt action 30.06 caliber rifles covered them from the roof of the train depot across the street. From there, the officers could see directly into the window. Despite their guardian angels, White glanced uneasily around the starkly lit building and the shadows surrounding the streets that led to darkness.

He'd been briefed about what they might find inside the window, but he was unnerved by the bizarre tunnel leading into the building. He stroked the German Shepherd to calm his quivering muscles.

Finally, White shouted into the opening. "This is the law! You are under arrest! Come out now!" Without waiting for a response, he continued. "If you do not immediately respond I will send in a dog!"

Overcoming his fear, Shep barked into the opening, suddenly ready to do the job he loved.

White waited for another moment, listening. When there was still no response. He leaned into the window and shouted again. "I am sending in a dog! Do not *run*! Do not *fight*!"

He urged the dog in. "*Du gehst!*" Shep hesitated at the dark entrance, quivered in anticipation, and sniffed the stale air. He stepped delicately over the debris and following the beam of White's flashlight, quickly disappeared around a sharp left bend.

White watched until Shep was completely out of sight and gave a thumbs-up. Positioned where he could see clearly, Blair relayed the message to Griffin. "Sheriff, the dog is in. Carlton is going to stay up there until contact is made."

Sheriff Griffin nodded and hoped the dog would find someone so they could wrap up the macabre scene. The neighborhood was becoming a circus. The area bustled with activity. High intensity lights illuminated the besieged building and huge generators filled the air with noise and exhaust.

"TV is here," someone said in a flat voice.

"It took them longer than I expected." Griffin swung around to watch two well-dressed men in narrow lapel suits weave their way through the crowd. One struggled to carry a huge television camera attached to a wooden tripod. The other carried a note pad and was busy adjusting his thin tie.

"Sheriff! Can you tell us what's going on here?" the reporter called over the roar of the generators. He extended a microphone attached to a long cord toward Griffin, expecting an immediate answer. The photographer opened his tripod, steadied the camera, and started filming, panning across the area and coming to rest on the annoyed lawman.

Completely ignoring the obtrusive reporter, Griffin turned his back on the camera and jerked a thumb over his shoulder. "Keep those ambulance chasers back behind the cars." He ground his teeth. "And don't let them get close enough to film that boy in the door."

At the top of the ladder, Deputy White was joined by Deputy Billy Roy Davis. "Anything yet?"

"Naw, and I haven't heard a sound. What are you doing up here?"

"Thought I'd keep you company, and besides, if Shep tangles with anyone in there, you'll want some help."

Despite the expert riflemen watching from behind, they continued to glance uneasily over their shoulders.

White reached into the window and ripped down the rest of the stained shade. "My lord. Have you ever seen anything like it?"

The tunnel floor was covered by debris that extended into the darkness. Billy Roy worried that the entire thing might come tumbling down with the slightest invitation. "This whole nightmare could fall in any minute."

The gaping entrance remained silent and dark. Nerves jangling, White checked his watch. "It's dangerous as hell. What is that? Boxes stacked up so high those on the bottom are crushed and giving away."

"That side is made from furniture thrown every which-a-way. If those drawers weren't jammed in there like that, the whole thing would come down."

"Hope it don't come down on my dog."

In the passageway, disturbing odors assaulted Shep's sensitive nose and he was nervous, because everything was enormously *wrong*. Though uneasy, his training held true and the dog advanced, even if he didn't know what he was supposed to be looking for.

The darkness ahead was almost complete. Shep turned again, relying heavily on his sense of smell. The touch of a real wall against his right shoulder made him feel somewhat secure.

The passageway rose sharply.

His toenails scrabbled for purchase on smooth cardboard, which soon gave way to stairs covered with mildew-slick carpet. The police dog climbed higher along the incline. Darkness was complete. The wall against his shoulder suddenly stopped and he paused, uncertain of which direction to take.

Indecisive and apprehensive, he whined uneasily. At that moment, Deputy White called into the tunnel. The dog's sensitive ears perked at his master's faint voice. "It's all right boy. Seek. Go on."

With the encouraging words, the Shepherd made an unconscious decision to take the right fork. The roof of the tunnel lowered even more and Shep ducked under a rusty car fender bulging downward, only inches above his head.

The tunnel again turned right and the grade continued upward. He sensed a slight movement ahead and he squeezed into an even smaller opening, now moving quickly.

A rustle, barely discernible in the trash ahead made a soft shuffling noise. This was what Shep did for a living. He barked and charged, front paws scrabbling for leverage on slick cardboard. His rear legs dug in and sensing an open area, Shep gave one last lunge to escape the claustrophobic passageway. His sudden weight caused a flimsy piece of cardboard beneath his paws to collapse.

In absolute darkness Shep plunged over twenty feet into the bottom of what was once a closet, now thick with sharpened surveyor's stakes. The dying animal only managed one sharp yelp of terror and pain before the deadfall did its work.

◇◇◇

Deputy White heard the dog bark at the fork, then the bellow of his challenge. "Got him!" The enthusiastic words died on the man's lips when they recoiled in horror at the dog's shriek of terror, and the immediate, ominous silence that followed.

A frightening high, thin giggle drifted out of the darkness.

"Shep!" White shouted after his partner. He unconsciously leaned into the window to rush in and help his partner. Billy Roy grabbed his belt and held him firm.

◇◇◇

Sheriff Griffin jumped at Billy Roy's sudden shout back over his shoulder. "The dog is down! We're pulling back! Keep us covered!"

The terror in his voice brought other deputies behind the barricade of cars to lean expectantly over their weapons. Something else had happened. Guns in a dozen hands rose toward the façade, seeking targets but finding none. They watched the building, radiating fear like heat from fire.

Whatever was *inside* might come *outside*.

Superstition and darkness preyed on frayed nerves and the combination does not mix well with people who live so close to the land.

The two riflemen at the rear watched the gaping window, covering the officers' frantic retreat down the ladders and back to safety behind the police car barricade.

Sheriff Griffin was almost beside himself when the stunned K-9 officer joined them in the shelter of a fire truck. "What the hell happened?"

"I think he's dead, sir." White stifled a sob. His partner was gone and the loss was intense. Losing the dog was like losing a human friend. "I heard him yelp, and then nothing."

"Could you make out what was going on?" Ned asked.

"No, he was out of sight." Deputy White barely controlled his anguish.

Billy Roy made a vague motion with one hand. "He yelped, but that sound was cut off pretty quick. I believe he's dead."

Deputy White turned his leaking eyes away from the activity around him. Seasoned officers and deputies gathered to touch his shoulder or his back, extending their sorrow, but maintaining a sense of decorum in the midst of an ever-mounting horror. They understood his grief, and didn't want to intrude.

"And then we heard somebody in there laugh."

John Washington stood amid the scattered deputies. "This ain't right."

Griffin leaned wearily on the fire truck and stared down at the crude floor plan. The Motorola in his car again squawked to life. He walked around the open door, slumped in the car seat with one foot outside, and spoke into the microphone. "Go ahead."

"Sheriff Griffin, Mesquite PD said to inform you the officer you requested can't respond. He broke his leg last week playing baseball."

"All right," Griffin answered and rubbed the back of his neck. "Now what?"

Sergeant Blair turned from the bizarre warehouse. "I know one more man who used to do tunnels, but I bet he won't go."

"Who?"

Blair jerked his thumb toward the back seat of Griffin's car, where Cody Parker sat half in and out, elbows resting on his knees.

Cody heard him and lowered his eyes to the ground. They lost focus as he tried to block out the world before him.

no, no, no,...

Chapter Twenty-five

Mountains of flattened cardboard tied with cotton string. The dark figure wriggled, crawled, and scooted through the tunnels. Animal heads on walls, heads in jars. Kendal learned at Daddy's knee. The art of collecting was deeply ingrained, but the need for organization was just as strong while Kendal was so personally disorganized...

Griffin considered John Washington for a moment. "All right, deputy, this is your side of town. Do you have any suggestions for a warehouse full of death traps?"

"Well sir," John drawled. "I don't never remember anyone talking about junk piles in particular. But I reckon if y'all turn off the power and water right about now it might get that feller inside to talking."

Sergeant Blair turned his attention from his radio. "Won't work. Company says there ain't no power to this place and hasn't been for years. Don't even ask me about phones. The last time they had phone service was during the war."

"Unbelievable," Griffin sighed.

"I was afraid of that." Washington watched the Cotton Exchange. "I disremember the last time I saw lights on in there. How 'bout tear gas. That way we'd know if anyone was holed up inside. They won't stay there very long, unless they have gas masks."

Sheriff Griffin weighed the consequences of gas. "No. Tear gas is liable to catch the place on fire. We don't need to take any chances until we know what's going on for sure. I don't want to lose what's left of that boy there in the door, neither." He cut his eyes toward the bulky news camera on top of a nearby station wagon. The dark lens was fixed on the Exchange at the moment. He turned back to his men. "So far all we have are booby traps. So I guess we either wait him out or go in."

"We could try to make entry." Blair didn't like the suggestion, but it was all he knew to do.

"You forget the tunnels?" Griffin asked. "You boys haven't exactly practiced anything like this."

"No sir, but they're good, experienced men. I can pick a team and have 'em check it out."

"Call in the National Guard." O.C. had already gotten his fill of the whole situation. "This is too much. We don't know nothing about anything such as this. Let the Guard take care of it."

Griffin's face turned red. "I ain't calling the governor. Who ever heard of calling in the army over a killer?"

"Whoever heard of a killer holed up in a trash pile?" O.C. quickly flared at the man whose only concern was reelection.

The sharp report of a gunshot from the Exchange immediately resulted in a barrage of return fire from nearly every officer on the scene. Bullets ripped through windows, shredding everything piled there. Brick powdered under high-velocity rounds. The area flashed with hundreds of shots.

The noise was tremendous.

Ned grabbed the kids and with his back against the fire truck, hoped it and his body would be enough to protect his grandchildren. Big John yanked O.C. against him and they covered Ned's family from the other side, fearing a missed round from the frantic return fire.

The reporter rolled off the station wagon, landing hard, nearly knocked unconscious. Firemen and other onlookers scrambled for cover.

"That's enough! Cease fire! Cease fire!" Sheriff Griffin realized the lawmen had emptied their weapons and were reloading.

Blair took up the shout, along with other cooler heads.

Hands shaking and ears ringing, Ned ran his hands over the kids to make sure they were all right, and then released them.

"Who fired that first shot!?" Griffin shouted.

"It came from the Exchange!" Blair pointed.

"Anybody hit?"

After a moment Blair answered. "Nossir, don't think so."

Ned drew a long, deep breath and pointed toward O.C. "Well, that tears it." His blood was up and he wanted something done. "Call in the National Guard and let them handle this."

O.C. was mad and agreed with him. "Griffin, if you don't call the governor, I will. We need the military here and we need them now."

Cody Parker stood beside the car and rested his hand on top of the open rear door, slumped over as if he'd been beaten. He chewed the inside of his lip, giving himself a moment to think. "No. I'll go in and see if I can find a way to get Andrews loose. Blair is right. I've had experience in this sort of thing."

I can't believe I'm doing this.

Fear was a heavy stone in Ned's chest and he wished he hadn't said anything. "Now that ain't what I meant."

Amid a swirling sea of flickering emergency lights, camera flashbulbs, and tense men, Griffin pondered the frightened constable. With no other alternative available, he finally agreed. "All right, if that's what you want to do."

He felt it would serve the young upstart right for getting them into this mess in the first place.

Chapter Twenty-six

Two splintered 4x4 posts braced one of many sagging ceilings. They rested upon a foundation…of four bricks.

◇◇◇

In a white sleeveless undershirt tucked into his jeans, Cody stood beside Ned and John. The young constable's gun belt and khaki shirt lay on the table. In his left hand he held a flashlight and gripped the .45 automatic in the other. A lit cigarette dangled from the corner of his mouth.

Ned thought for a moment, then reached into the pocket of his slacks and withdrew his Colt 32.20. Griffin raised an eyebrow when he saw the revolver, but Ned ignored the man and slipped the small handgun under the waistband in the small of Cody's back. "Just in case."

Arms crossed over his massive chest, Washington frowned at the idea of Cody going in alone.

O.C. couldn't remain silent. "You sure this is what you want to do? Personally I think you're nuts if you do. There's a better way coming."

Sheriff Griffin watched the press of spectators and reporters milling around behind the barricade. He was sure the phone lines were hot. "Of course I don't want him to go. But I don't know what else to do. The longer we wait, the worse it's going to be."

"No one here knows what to do with this," Cody offered. "Even if the National Guard shows up, they won't have anyone with my experience."

Ned absently stared at his grandchildren who were dwarfed by the tall deputies. More excited than frightened, Top and Pepper knew the wrong word or action would get them banished from the scene, so they remained silent, and listened. "Crawling in that hole over there won't make any difference to that dead man, son."

Cody looked into Ned's blue eyes. "This has been coming a long time, Ned. For months I've been dreaming about tunnels and houses and buildings and attics. Whatever sight our family has, it's been working on me. It's like when Top was dreaming about the Rock Hole, and I have to go along with it."

Top jumped. The mention of the Rock Hole was a wallop of electricity. He took a step backward, as if to run, and then steadied like a wild colt once again under John's big, calming hand.

Pepper quickly crossed her arms and turned away, unconsciously rubbing the back of her shoulder with her fingertips. For a moment she almost bolted from the crowd of men. The intensity of the situation was simply too much, reminding her of that terrifying night in the bottoms. Her chest tightened and she stifled the tears burning her eyes.

Ned saw the reaction in his grandchildren and wanted to gather them up in his arms, but he didn't have time. Instead, he put his hand on Cody's shoulder and hugged Pepper against his side with the other. "Let Griffin send in a couple of his boys. You don't have to do this. You're a constable, not a policeman or deputy sheriff. Wait for O.C. to call the National Guard."

Cody shifted back and forth on his feet, bleeding off energy. "I doubt it'll be much anyway."

Griffin knew the longer he hesitated, the more intense the questioning was going to be from the reporters. "Those people back there are having a grand old time. The mayor is already pressing me to settle this thing before dawn, O.C.'s wearing my ass out, and we can't use teargas for fear of burning the place down, not with a deputy lying there in plain sight, so what else can we do? And besides," he waved a finger toward Cody, "*he* volunteered."

"Like hell he did, Griffin!" Ned snapped at the sheriff, who took a half step back. John and O.C. moved with Ned, intending to step in if he started to swing. Instead, satisfied that Griffin had backed off, Ned sighed and turned to Cody. "All right, but don't you forget, somebody's in there and it's probably Kendal. He's tied up in this mess. For all we know he's watching us right now and I wouldn't put anything past him at this point."

He turned toward Griffin. "How long will it take for the Guard to get here?"

"Hours?" Sergeant Blair shrugged and spat. "Even if they get called out tonight, they won't be here 'til tomorrow."

"Not on your life…" Griffin knew the implications of military action in a civilian situation. "There's a whole crew of folks in Oklahoma that's been chasing Kendal, if that's who you think is involved here. They'll be back here from Oklahoma at first light."

"I know what to do, sheriff." Cody dropped his cigarette butt on the ground and ground the cherry out on the cracked concrete.

"All right. I'm open to suggestions."

"I had quite a bit of experience with VC booby traps. Close to the same kind that killed Andrews." Cody felt the familiar dread in those humid jungles so far away. He also remembered what to expect. "What we need to do first is see if there's another way in, or spider holes."

"What? *More* entrances?" O.C. asked, shocked.

"Yeah, I'll bet if this guy is crazy enough to fill this junk pile full trash and a maze of tunnels, he's liable to have holes all around the building."

"Jeeze." Sheriff Griffin mentally kicked himself for not considering that possibility, distracted by everything else going on around him. Alarmed, he turned away from the Exchange toward the growing crowd beyond the barricades.

The news of a crazy person near downtown Chisum had spread like wildfire. Spectators congregated in the street, straining to catch a glimpse of the activity near the Cotton Exchange.

At the edge of their normally quiet neighborhood, the excited and frightened neighbors crowded behind the officials, talking loudly and asking questions no one could answer.

Each of them was a potential target for a sniper.

"Shooting ports! Blair, get these people back and watch the crap around the outside!" Griffin looked over a patrol car toward the drifts of refuse under the sheltered walkway. "I guess this means you don't think we've found the only entrances?"

"Not likely." Cody waved his arm toward the building beyond the fire truck. "I bet there's two or three spider holes or entrances hidden in all that stuff piled around the outside. If we were back in-country, there could be lines running from the entrance to homemade bombs all around. The idea was that if anyone opened the entrance, the lines would pull the pins and boom."

Blair shrugged. "We didn't find anything outside at first."

"Your men probably didn't try that hard," Ned said. "Nobody told them what to watch for."

"Well, we need to look harder before I try to go in." Cody managed a weak grin for Top and Pepper. "It ain't so bad, kids." He shifted his attention to Ned and O.C. "We used to send two-man teams underground to check it out. The first guy in front watched for triggers as the second man supported and stayed in touch with the commanding officer on the surface by radio.

"While all that was going on, the section commander kept track of their reports to either map the tunnels, or to know where to dig the guys out in the event of an emergency."

"But first, step one is to clear the entrance," Griffin said.

"Yessir,"

"Check it out."

Blair sighed. "Yes sir. C'mon boys, we're going creepy crawling."

Chapter Twenty-seven

Stacks of rotting lumber, a Model A hood, tons of damp, moldy clothing, rotting saddles, water coolers, wooden soda pop cases, salvaged sheet iron…and one insane trophy collector named Kendal Bowden.

They watched the men erect a blind under heavy guard to block the view of Jeff Andrews' corpse from the ever-increasing crowd. Two heavily armed men had taken up positions beside the fallen deputy who was covered with a sheet supplied by the funeral home.

Deputy Washington moved up beside Cody. "I heard when you said y'all used two people over there. I'm going in with you."

Shocked, Cody's head snapped around. "No you're not. I'm not going to be responsible for you. I'll have enough trouble without worrying about you, John. Besides," Cody grinned wanly, "you're too damned big."

Before John could respond, Ned interrupted the argument by waving toward a constable he'd known for years. "Milton, would you do me a favor?"

Unsure of himself around Griffin and his deputies, Milton Williams stood uneasily beside the sheriff's car. "Sure Ned."

"Good. Would you take these kids of mine over to Neva Lou's house?"

"Shit," Pepper said under her breath.

"Grandpa, I want to stay here," Top argued.

"I know you do, but things could get even rougher, and you kids don't need to see any more. I don't have time to fool with you. Besides, it's getting too dangerous. Y'all can stay at Neva Lou's, or James and them might still be there. Be sure to call Miss Becky. She's probably getting worried already, because I bet the phone lines are hot. Milton, is that all right?"

"Sure, as long as I can get back through."

"You can come back," O.C. said.

"Grandpa, we want to stay."

Ned answered Top without expression. "Well, you cain't."

Pepper saw under the surface of Ned's expression. Instead of arguing, she pulled Top away and they followed Milton. Top took one look at her and knew his cousin was up to something.

"Cody, you and John quit your arguing and come here." Sheriff Griffin motioned for everyone to rejoin the officers.

Temporarily abandoning their continuing disagreement over how best to handle the situation, they joined the others bent over a fresh, hand-drawn map.

"All right. The guys are finished. You were right, Cody. They found at least two openings at ground level. One is here."

With a hollow thump in the table, Griffin pointed at a position near the southeast corner of the building, across from the train depot. "But it's blocked with junk that fell in. They found the second on the southwest side after my people cut down a thicket of brush and vines. My guess, someone busted through the section of the brick foundation and that's where the nutcase goes in and out. There are fresh scuff marks everywhere."

"Another slick spot," Ned said. The men stared at the map as if committing it to memory.

"Y'all, it's right over yonder where that spotlight's pointed toward the foundation." Griffin handed a pair of binoculars to Cody.

He stared long and hard at the hole hammered through the long seam where the foundation and the sidewalk met. Cody passed them to Ned. "Well, there it is. I've been seeing that hole in the ground in my sleep."

Ned felt a chill go down his spine as he squinted at the reality of Cody's nightmare. The men within earshot stared at the young constable, wondering if he'd lost his mind. Ned knew better. "Tell me."

"The opening leads in and down for a ways. It'll take me in the building all right, into rooms I'll probably recognize. I can see them right now, little pieces of the dream that haven't faded away, but," Cody shrugged, "anyway, it'll all lead to what's been bothering me for months."

Ned spoke softly. "How'd them dreams come out?"

"I don't know. I always woke up before I got finished." He managed a half smile.

Blair offered the only help he knew. "The chipped out bricks are padded with an old quilt to make it easy for Kendal get in and out."

"This is nuts," Chief Mayhew snapped. "Now we're back to basing this operation on squirrel hunting and nightmares."

Cody grimaced. "You ain't a kiddin'."

Mayhew glanced at the men surrounding him. Though he was police chief of Chisum, it was the sheriff's department running the show. He knew if he wanted to make a fight of it, Griffin might turn the operation over to him, and he for sure didn't want that. "I hope you're right about all this, because I'm with Judge O.C. on this one."

Cody shut off the disagreement. "Chief, I know these old places. There's probably a trap door in the floor somewhere, to get underneath and fix pipes or whatever. My guess is that whoever we're after enters the building through the trap door. It probably comes up in a closet. That's how it was in the house I grew up in. It should be the same here in the Exchange.

"This opening is close enough to the door, though, that I might be able to crawl to where Andrews is pinned and figure out a way to get him loose. Once that's done, I can get out and we can wait on daylight and the whole U.S. Marine Corps if that's what it takes."

"I agree this is damned dangerous, Mayhew." Griffin turned back to Cody. "But I don't have much to go on. So here's what you do. Take a quick look-see inside, but don't go in very far. I want you to be able to back out real quick. See if you can find that trap door you're talking about, or a way that leads to Andrews, then get out. We'll talk about what to do next to free his body. Let's take this one step at a time. Be careful."

"You don't have to tell *me.*"

Sergeant Blair joined them, accompanied by a young officer who appeared to be no more than a year out of high school. Despite the hour, the man's tie was properly knotted and he looked fresh as a daisy.

"Sheriff Griffin, this is Officer Malcom Baker." Blair made the introductions. "He's new to our department, and he's older than he looks. You might want to hear what he has to say."

"All right, you have five minutes. Cody, wait a minute."

The crowd shifted aside to make room for the slim, bespeckled policeman who looked frail beside the beefy men surrounding him. He cleared his throat and calmly addressed the group as if they were a room full of college freshmen. "Well, I heard what was happening from my grandmother who called. Even though I'm not on duty today, I may have information that will help in this situation."

Everyone beside the fire truck was keyed up and ready to get started, but the confident young man with the slicked-back hair captured their attention.

"What do you have for us?" Sheriff Griffin asked.

"I recognize the personality, or personalities, of those inside." Baker fidgeted with the knot in his tie. "When I heard you found a warehouse packed with junk it was immediately clear that you were dealing with a situation for which you probably aren't prepared. See, I'm working on my doctorate in psychology and I've done extensive research in this area. I'm familiar with this type of pathology. I'm confident that the individual or individuals here suffer from a disorder called disposophobia."

Ned snorted and shifted his feet. "Son, you're gonna have to speak a little lower to the ground for us country boys. I can't even pronounce that last word you just spit out. Can you break it down a little into a language I can understand, say, English?"

"Sure, Mr. Ned. Disposophobia is a clinical term for hoarding, which means to never throw anything away, or even to collect castoffs from other people to add to their own possessions." Gaining confidence with his subject matter, Officer Baker began to enjoy the attention. "Most victims of a similar obsessive compulsive disorder are compelled to repeatedly wash their hands, or perform ritual tasks again and again before they can move on to the next aspect of the day. In this situation, though, it means the people acquire and keep objects to such an extent that it impacts and impairs the use of normal living space."

O.C. grunted. "We're pretty impacted here."

The men snickered, more from tension than the feeble joke.

"You're right…oh, hello Judge Rains." Baker adjusted his tie again. "The person living here has an anxiety toward disposing of any physical items. That anxiety, combined with intrusive thoughts that occur regarding their possessions, can and does become dangerous."

"I feel like I should be taking notes," Sheriff Griffin said dryly. "What does this *mean?*"

"It *means* the spaces inside are probably filled with materials such as paper products, which are a hoarder's commonly saved items, even paper with notes written on them, or shopping lists. And you must remember I'm not talking about a shoebox full of papers. I mean entire *rooms* filled to the ceiling with material. They can include everything from junk mail to newspapers, magazines to books, even trash. They simply can't throw anything away."

"This place covers thousands of square feet." Cody thought aloud about what he might encounter inside.

Baker beamed at the thought. It was easy to tell he was the kid back in school who always raised his hand to remind the teacher she'd forgotten to give her students their daily homework assignment. "That's right, and it'll be filled if the exterior is any indication. Hoarders keep food, furniture, calendars, dishes, or even lumber scraps. Patients have saved tires, car parts, even entire vehicles inside their homes.

"One woman I researched for my dissertation kept pictures of kittens which she felt her children would some day want. One man collected newspapers that his invalid brother could read once he regained the use of his eyesight, which of course would never happen, because his brother was permanently blind. But that's how these people think."

O.C. briefly worried about the numerous piles of files and paper in his cluttered office. "Is this common?"

"No, these are radical cases. Most people simply junk up their houses. Their collections aren't limited to personal possessions. They save broken household items, thinking they might be useful. They store clothes, toys, machinery, books, dolls, tons of unused material…truthfully anything that reminds them of happier or better days. It isn't rational to us, but to them it makes perfect sense. I've read of extreme cases where hoarders even save such things as prepared but uneaten food, fingernail clippings, urine, or even their own feces.

"These people have been known to bring junk back to their homes by either picking through the trash, or actually stealing from their neighbors. Collecting refuse in this manner can quickly fill entire houses or buildings, which probably happened here."

Frustrated and nervous, Cody was ready to go, but the soon-to-be professor was on a roll.

"Back in nineteen forty-seven two Manhattan brothers, Homer and Langley Collyer, disappeared. The police investigated and found a three-story brownstone similar to this building here, but much smaller. It took them three *weeks* to sift through nearly a hundred and forty *tons* of junk that filled the brownstone from floor to ceiling. They actually had to remove the roof and dig downward.

"That's what I expect here. I've been watching this place since I first came to Chisum. I'm confident the building is filled to capacity with his personal items and whatever he's collected and brought in through the years."

Cody digested the information for a while. "Where you from, college boy?"

"Dallas."

"Figured. Are these people violent?"

"Not usually, but as we know from experience, every case is different."

"This one is," Sheriff Griffin said.

For the first time Officer Baker noticed the obscured front door where men worked to free Andrew's body. "What happened?"

"They found a tunnel into all that trash you're talking about. The deputy crawled partway inside and apparently triggered a booby trap."

Baker nodded, shaken. He absently tugged his ear. "That's part of the delusion. They often feel they need to protect their possessions from intruders. If the building is as full as it seems from here, there may well be trails through the 'collection' and those trails may be protected by deadfalls."

"Great," Cody said in disgust. "I think we're way past the '*may be*' stage when it comes to booby traps and deadfalls."

"Can you stay with us for a while?" Griffin put his hand on Baker's shoulder to let him know they needed to get moving. "We may need you later."

"Of course. Do you plan to enter the building?"

"Thinkin' about it. How did they do it in New York again?"

"Simple, they used a crane to remove the roof and ceiling, and excavated from above. But then again, they didn't have…" he gestured with his hand, "a victim to deal with."

"We can't do that tonight." Cody thought back to his military days, trying to come up with an alternative plan. "When someone discovered a tunnel in Nam we tried to force smoke into them to find entrances and exits. Once we identified an entry point and it was secured, we used tear gas to flush out any enemy troops. Then we destroyed the entrances with explosives."

"We don't have any smoke grenades on hand, and I'm afraid we might set fire to the place," Griffin reminded him. "This isn't war, Cody."

"Not yet."

Blair spat. "I know a guy who keeps bees."

"There ain't enough beekeeper smoke in the county to find out what's going on in there." O.C. waved at an annoying fly in front of his face.

"None of that matters right now." Cody's thumb absently rubbed the safety on his pistol. "I'll go in and see if I can get to Andrews. If it doesn't work, I'll come out and you can push the place over with a bulldozer if you want, or pull it apart with a crane."

"You'll need to hurry. We don't have much more good weather." Ned pointed upward. There wasn't a breath of wind. "That norther will be here in a few minutes and it's gonna get ass-chillin' cold. And me without a coat."

Chapter Twenty-eight

Piles of tin cans, broken desks, stacks of surveyor's stakes, thousands of moldering books…

Police Chief Mayhew picked up a brand new three-channel Realistic radio from the card table and held it out to Cody. "Here. Take this in with you."

"A walkie talkie? I've never see one like this before. You sure it ain't a kid's toy?"

"Nope, it's a radio. It's the newest thing out there and we only have two of them on the force. When you talk in it, I'll hear on this one, along with everyone from dispatch to our car radios. We can keep in touch while you're inside."

Cody held the heavy radio in his hand, thinking it probably wouldn't work. "I can give it a shot. I really wish I had one of them wrist telephones they draw in the Dick Tracy cartoons."

"They aren't likely to come up with a telephone you can put in your pocket before tomorrow morning, so forget about the funny papers," Ned said.

Griffin met Cody's eyes. "You ready?"

A shiver ran down Cody's spine and he stared at the old building with a heavy sense of dread, knowing if he didn't start right at that moment, he wasn't going.

Memories washed over him like ocean waves as he finally trotted across the brightly lit street, dodging around a dented washing machine. He jumped lightly onto the sidewalk, moving past a rusting refrigerator and a rotting kitchen cabinet like the one in Miss Becky's kitchen. The entire time he expected to feel the impact of a bullet or the blast from an explosion.

He stepped past a watering trough full of bald tires and arrived at the hole in the foundation. The entrance was so narrow he found it hard to imagine it was intended for people at all.

In Vietnam, entering a tunnel system was a very risky, and potentially deadly, business. Usually armed only with a pistol or a knife and a flashlight, Cody Parker spent uncounted hours in the pitch black, suffocating hell, playing a deadly game of hide and seek with a usually unseen enemy.

In one fluid movement Parker crouched and wriggled inside. His body blocked most of the illumination from the spotlights. He flicked on the flashlight and aimed it into the darkness ahead.

Brows knit, Cody searched for potential dangers. In Nam, the Viet Cong sometimes mined tunnel entrances or concealed firing positions within the first few yards.

Back then, carefully probing the subterranean passageways was second nature to Cody and his fellow tunnel rats as they gently inched their way along. Any number of indicators would cause him to hesitate or even back out; wires, unusual tree roots, or a glimpse of something that simply wasn't right. Anything that could detonate a booby trap had to be rendered harmless.

The same triggers might be hidden in the drain-size burrow around Cody. Like the rest of the building, the thirty inch crawlspace was packed to the joists only inches above his head. Bundles of magazines and cardboard boxes pressed in from all sides. One of the rotting boxes had split, spilling bushels of musty-smelling walnuts still in the hulls. The cramped, littered aisle led directly toward the center of the building.

Growing up in an old pier-and-beam house, Cody was confident the passageway ended under a trap door, probably located somewhere deep inside the Exchange. Unlike most of the houses in the northern part of the country, very few homes in Lamar County had basements. Poor soil conditions and shifting clay required support structures designed to move and breathe with the ground's expansion and contraction during wet or dry seasons. The open foundations allowed air to circulate beneath the southern structures while at the same time making electrical and plumbing repairs much easier.

Cody was confident that large buildings were constructed in a similar fashion and he'd find the same underpinnings, only made of larger and more substantial materials.

Grunting, Cody slowly dragged himself along on his elbows while used and stained paper plates gathered around his body. Each time he pushed with a knee, garbage rustled underneath. It smelled like an animal burrow, musky and humid. He constantly moved the flashlight and peered into darkened crevices, searching for anything suspicious.

His combat instincts returned without thought. Every movement came with natural ease, as if crawling through trash was an everyday act.

The tunnel made a left turn…a secure move for the builder. If there had been any doubt about why the tunnel was created, it was eliminated by predictable engineering. The passage angled, weaving around a variety of obstacles such as support pillars, stacks of building materials, and an unimaginable collection of refuse. The layout made shooting in a straight line impossible and helped deflect explosive blasts from grenades.

Common sense said he should heed Griffin's warning and back out when he encountered the curve, but like Andrews, Cody simply wanted to see around the corner.

Progress was slow. Crawling through what he came to think of as a narrow burrow, and knowing an armed enemy wanted to kill him, was a stressful, nerve-racking job, pushing his mental state to its limits.

Pressure plates would be the obvious triggers to booby traps and it dismayed Cody as he turned the corner to see that someone had covered the tunnel floor with slick cardboard to make crawling easier. Unfortunately, it also hid any number of tripping devices. His sweaty right hand full of pistol, Cody searched for hidden tripwires. He knew pressure-sensitive panels would be undetectable until it was too late. Cold sweat gathered on his forehead at the thought of explosives. Had someone been able to get their hands on dynamite or grenades?

Besides explosives, he also worried about other, equally nasty surprises. In the Viet Cong tunnels, living booby traps ranging from scorpions to snakes were a constant threat.

The frightened deputy stopped to rest. Already his neck ached from the awkward angle, another reminder of the past he longed to forget.

I can't believe I've gotten myself into this. All because Andrews opened a door that should have stayed shut.

Chapter Twenty-nine

Antiquated farming equipment, dozens of plowshares and hames; nuts, bolts, and screws in every conceivable container; tube radios, boxes of 78 rpm records beside a windup gramophone were only a few items filling one entire story all the way to the ceiling....

"John." O.C. Rains waved his deputy over.

"Yessir?"

"I don't like him in there by himself and he's already gone past where he should have stopped."

"I's thinking the same thing myself Judge."

Ned joined the two. "What are y'all whispering about?"

John picked at his shirt buttons. "I don't like Mr. Cody in there alone, Mr. Ned."

"Well, you're too damn big to go in after him."

"Y'all keep telling me that. But I believe I'll strip down and join him anyways."

"You sure that's a good idea?"

"Wouldn't-a said it if it wasn't." John finally reached a decision and unbuttoned his shirt.

Griffin finally overheard their conversation. "It'd be bad to put two men in danger."

"One can help the other'n," Ned said.

Griffin picked up the walkie talkie and weighed it in his hand. His indecision was obvious. "Y'all think that's what we ought to do?"

Chief Mayhew shrugged. He was through making suggestions that no one listened to.

John peeled off his shirt and draped it over a hood.

Griffin keyed the button. "Cody, can you hear me?"

Inside the tunnel, the disembodied voice caused the agitated young man to nearly fire off a shot in the darkness. He'd carefully worked his way around the corner and was faced with a slightly wider but very similar tunnel. He fumbled with his walkie talkie and pushed the transmit button.

"*Goddamn* it!" he hissed into the speaker. "Who is this? You do that again and I'll crawl out of here and shoot your ass off, understand?"

Down to his sleeveless undershirt shirt, Big John grinned at Sheriff Griffin's shocked expression. The angry outburst was heard by everyone within earshot of a radio. Griffin quickly realized the open channels would be a potential problem when he heard Cody's voice from every direction. The crowd around him chuckled at the young man's raw comments.

Shamed by his thoughtlessness, Griffin keyed the mike. "All right. Sorry. We weren't thinking."

"I contact *you*!" Cody snapped. "It doesn't work the other way around. What do you want?"

"I wanted to tell you John Washington is coming in with you. If you get into trouble he can help."

Cody closed his eyes and rested his forehead on his forearm. He didn't need someone outside to think for him. "No way. This tunnel is too small and he doesn't have any experience. If I get into trouble, he won't know what to do. He'll be in the way."

John overhead the conversation and quickly stepped around the patrol car. He unbuckled his belt and removed his holster. Glancing back over his shoulder, John thumbed the safety strap and drew his .38.

"Let me borrow that for a second, Leon." Before the surprised deputy could respond, John grabbed the flashlight from his hand and hurried toward the burrow's entrance.

Blair frowned. "I'd listen to him sir…"

His sentence was cut short when Sheriff Griffin saw John running toward the Cotton Exchange. "Hey! John! Stop! Wait a minute, Cody don't want you in there!"

Without a backward glance, John knelt at the foundation, flicked his hat off with a finger, and entered the burrow behind Cody.

"Somebody stop him!"

O.C. Rains held up a hand. "They ain't none of y'all man enough to stop that deputy."

"Cody!"

Deep inside the tunnel, still another unexpected voice only yards away nearly gave Cody's a heart attack. He'd carefully worked his way around the corner into a slightly wider, but very similar tunnel. He jerked at a sudden sound behind him. Because the burrow was so narrow, he was unable to turn around.

"*Goddamn* it!"

"It's only me!" John crawled quickly through the burrow to catch up with Cody.

"Shhhh. Talk lower. What are you doing in here?"

"They was fixing to send somebody in." John's deep voice, though soft, still filled the stale air of the tunnel. "I figured you'd rather have kinfolk helping."

Cody almost grinned at the reference. "No way. This tunnel is too small and you don't know what to do."

"Too late. I'm already inside."

Cody thought for a long moment. "Kinfolk?"

"Yeah, you know how it is. Woodpiles and all."

Thinking, Cody lightly tapped his flashlight against a bundle of yellowed newspapers beneath his hand before he realized what he'd done. "Great. Now I can blow *two* of us away." Once he was forced to stop and think about his situation, the horrific mass filling the structure raised goose bumps on his arms. "Get out of here."

"They'll send somebody else."

"Tell them I don't want anyone in here with me."

"Listen Mr. Hard-head, let's you and me get through this mess and get it over with, or go back out right now."

The hairs on the back of Cody's neck tickled. It wasn't John's uncharacteristically forceful comment. It was that sixth sense people often have in strange or stressful situations. "John, don't move."

"What is it?" John whispered.

"I don't know." Cody's voice was so low John could barely hear him. "But I got a bad feeling. We need to get out of here and not after a while, either. We've got to get shut of this place right now."

"Just 'cause I'm in here…"

"No!" Cody said sharply, louder. "We have to get out now. Back out *right now*!"

They heard a slithering noise. Cody couldn't figure out where it was coming from, but it sounded like someone else was crawling through the mess with them, mere feet away, through the other side of the stacked and piled junk wall.

Hearing the terror in his voice, John knew something bad was about to happen. He began to worm backward, knowing instinctively that it would be a slow, painful process.

A soft, muffled giggle came through the boxes above and to the right, followed by a quick rustle and sudden silence. Cody mimicked John's actions and scooted backwards until John's left foot hung on a piece of junk that momentarily refused to yield. When it did, a small *thunk* made Cody's stomach drop.

A frantic scrabbling not far away was drowned as a hidden release triggered a deadfall behind them, dropping nearly a ton of debris into place over the burrow's entrance, effectively blocking their escape.

The very real horror of being buried alive almost overwhelmed them. Choking dust rolled through the burrow like a tidal wave, dimming their flashlight beams and showering the two men with debris. John yelled into his folded arms and ducked, expecting to be crushed under tons of common, everyday junk.

The resulting cave-in sounded as if the Exchange was falling in. Timbers creaked deep inside the structure like those of a wooden sailing ship as they accepted and adjusted to changing stresses far overhead.

They were sealed inside.

Chapter Thirty

Empty cans that once contained a variety of foods, worn out hand tools, bedsteads, china cabinets; rolls of use chicken, hog, and barbed wire...

Chisum's local Channel 12 claimed the prime location when they first arrived, and the Sherman station was setting up across the street. The radio station's reporter crept as close as possible with his recorder to the knot of lawmen surrounding the folding table. Reporters from *The Chisum News*, *The Sherman Democrat*, and the *Greenville Herald-Banner* interviewed the neighborhood's residents, crowding the perimeter held by Chisum police.

The calm weather ended. A hard wall of jarringly cold wind suddenly blasted through town. A Texas blue norther can drop the temperature fifty degrees in an hour. One minute the night was still and comfortable, then with a rustle of leaves the wind howled out of the north, chilling everyone.

It snatched up everything not held down and carried it off in seconds. Voices shouted in shock. Cursing, men quickly rolled down their sleeves. Those prepared for the weather hurried to their cars for coats and jackets.

Despite the chaos around them, the sheriff's department and Chisum's police force worked calmly toward a solution. Sheriff Griffin and Judge Rains huddled against the arctic air behind a fire truck and were deep in conversation when a muffled explosion came from inside the Exchange.

Dust and debris poured through the heavily guarded entrance to the crawlspace as if shot from a cannon. The silence outside was deafening for a full five seconds. The stunningly cold wind forgotten for a moment, everyone stood stock still and stared at the Exchange colored by flashing lights from police cars, fire trucks, and ambulances.

Someone screamed. A searchlight found the blocked opening and the dust cloud that was quickly snatched away. A cacophony arose from the spectators and news people when wind swept the huge cloud of dust over the crowd as they squinted to protect their eyes.

Already chilled to the bone, Griffin examined the foundation through his binoculars. "It's completely blocked." He motioned at one of his deputies. "Get me a couple of engineers on site. I want to find out how long it'll take to clear that entrance. And somebody get me a damned coat."

Hands in his pants pockets, Ned stared in shock at the Exchange. "I hope those boys have air, if they lived through that."

O.C. shivered, but he couldn't tell if it was from the cold or unease. "My lord."

Chapter Thirty-one

Lard tins carefully saved in pasteboard boxes, wormy candy decades out of date, a free-standing kitchen cabinet, a wooden icebox, broken dishes, crockery, panes of dusty and streaked glass. The plan had been to draw Cody inside all along, and Kendal was ecstatic to find him there after all.

Thinking the roof was coming down, Cody and John remained still, faces buried in the trash, until they were sure nothing else was going to fall. Cody's lungs tightened from the dust. Like Top, he was asthmatic from birth, though his symptoms were usually much less severe.

Coughing and eyes watering profusely, Cody kept his face buried in his arm and waited until the tension in his neck eased. Several minutes passed before he blinked at the motes floating in their flashlight beams.

"I swear." John coughed, dislodging the filth in his short hair.

"I've been in here less than twenty minutes and we're already trapped." Cody spat grit, gagging on thick dust. "I don't believe I'm good at this anymore." He regained control of his fear and panned his light around the claustrophobic burrow. "We have only one option. It's pretty clear we aren't leaving the same way we came in. I suppose we can wait right here until someone digs us out, or we can see about crawling out somewhere else."

Heart thumping, he picked up the dropped radio and keyed the thumb switch. "Griffin, can you hear me?"

The radio crackled, weak, full of static and tinny. "It sounded like a mine caved in behind y'all and a butt-load of dust rolled out. You boys all right?"

"That depends. What do you see out there?"

"It's completely blocked. I have a couple of guys beside me who say it'll take hours to clear the entrance, and then there might be another collapse. You boys have air?"

Creaks, pops, and groans told them the Exchange was still settling overhead.

"Yep, and right now it smells like a garbage can full of dust and stink. The deadfall was around the corner behind us. The whole floor collapsed. We can't stay right here for long, but I don't want to chance it if y'all start digging us out." He released the transmission key.

"Any suggestions?" Sheriff Griffin and his men huddled over the expanding layout, stabbing fingers at various points. "We have someone here thinks George Hart has more than one way out of that place."

Cody and John exchanged glances. "Yeah, we're about to act like moles and find one of them. I bet we can get out the same way George does. We heard someone moving close by before the cave in. For sure somebody's in here with us and I bet he has some other way out."

"There might be more booby traps, too."

"No kidding."

"Y'all hold it for a minute. Let me study on it."

Cody played his light ahead, pondering their next move in the narrow passageway, and wondering if the Exchange was structurally sound. The entire building was built to support the enormous weight of cotton bales, but even so, if the joists or timbers had rotted, or were open to the elements, the whole thing could be spongy throughout. If that was the case, unimaginable weight loomed precariously overhead.

Logic dictated the main access tunnel wouldn't be trapped again until farther ahead. Whoever had created this horror wouldn't want to trip their own ambushes if they needed to get inside quickly. That would come later, once a pursuer was deep in the burrow and out of his element.

But then again, there was that one tunnel with one punji pit right after another, he thought. *I'm too rusty for this crap, and we just tripped a deadfall at the entrance, so my logic ain't worth a hill of beans.*

Behind him, Cody heard John puffing as he slithering along on his elbows to get closer. He turned and pressed against the wall to peer back past his feet. The glow of his flashlight illuminated John's sweating face.

Cody realized that he was also getting hot. "All right, now listen carefully. As long as you're with me, you have to do what I tell you. This is not *your* mission and *I* am in charge. I don't intend to die in here." It felt uncomfortable to speak to his old friend in such a forceful tone. He'd grown up respecting John and the badge he wore. Young men didn't order their seniors around, even though in their sharply divided world of black and white people, it was completely acceptable.

John paused. "Yeah." He wormed closer until Cody's feet were only inches from his face. "I'm with you on that."

"You also don't question a thing I say, John. Please. And when I tell you to do move, you act instantly, got it? I mean it."

"Got it. My people are used to doin' what we're told." John's weak joke broke the tension.

"All right." Now Cody was responsible for the two of them. The knowledge was nearly too much to bear. He had to train John as quickly as possible. "This burrow winds around through here, so try to follow and do exactly what I do. Move exactly the way I do, and don't touch anything I don't touch."

John played his own beam around Cody's legs, already feeling claustrophobic. Sweat rolled through his eyebrows and he wiped it away with a bare forearm. "Right."

The passageway they followed reminded Cody of a Colorado mountain road. It switched back tightly and wound around ancient piers made of crumbling red bricks. The refuse underneath rose slightly until overhead, the rough, hand hewn bodark joists threatened to bump his skull each time he raised too high.

After twenty minutes of huffing and crawling, they were completely disoriented. Once, they came to a Y and the right-hand path angled sharply downward into the ground. The black hole reminded Cody of an animal's burrow leading to a den and woke up the sense of dread that had been revealed by his nightmares. He shivered at the sight and considered his options for a long time before choosing the left fork.

Cody's flashlight finally illuminated a wooden trap door set into the floor directly above, recessed in a square of shadow. The burrow itself continued past the overhead access panel and widened into an open thoroughfare, compared to what they'd been in. It ended in a horizontally positioned door.

Despite his gut-wrenching terror, Cody grinned. "You sneaky son-of-a-bitch. That's your second trap. It's too comfortable, and someone chasing you would head right for the wider tunnel. You really know how to set up a sucker play."

"What do you mean?" John was unable to see past him.

"This is the trap door I was looking for. We go up. Don't go any further, understand?"

"Why not?" John mentally kicked himself for the question.

Hating what he had to do, Cody twisted to the side and directed the flashlight between his feet and into the other man's dilated pupils. "Because I *said* so."

John closed his eyes. Bright spots swam before his eyes. "Got it."

Cody once again sucked in a deep breath, trying to control his emotions. He sounded like Ned, and it made him sick to speak to John like that. He valued his friendship far more than the big deputy knew.

"There's something not right about this tunnel. An external door laid sideways under here ain't exactly natural, and besides, there's too much space around it. He *wants* us to turn that knob up there on top and drop the door toward us. Whatever's back there, we don't want to know about." He twisted onto his back. "I'm going to open this trap door, and my bet is it'll take us into a closet so we can get inside and maybe out of this mess. Now, you be ready to get out of my way if anything starts to happen."

John wiped the sweat from his brow. "There may be more booby traps once you get the door open."

"Prob'ly are. You want to sit right here without knowing what's going on? I wouldn't doubt more traps, but I don't think we have a choice."

Thankfully, the ground beneath the entry panel was scooped out, providing easier access. The trap door was designed to drop open upon the release of a small wooden slide. Maybe George had left himself a fast, easy, safe way into the building, and this was it.

Cody grasped the handle, feeling wood polished from much use. "We're going to have to open this up."

"Do what you gotta do." John forcefully exhaled a lungful of air and watched thick dust motes dance in the beam of his flashlight.

"All right. Wiggle back down a ways so I ain't directly under this when it falls."

He waited as John wormed his way backward until he was safely away from the door.

Cody yanked the release, praying that he was right.

Blocked by John who was effectively a cork in a bottle, Cody couldn't respond when the door dropped with a screech of rusty hinges and Shep's bloody body fell through the hole. Constable Cody Parker screamed and tried to backpedal. The dead dog hung suspended on the sharpened stakes affixed to the trap door. His limp head swung slowly back and forth, blood and mucus dripping onto the damp cardboard.

"Son of a bitch!"

"What! What!"

I'm getting too old for this.

Regaining his shattered composure, Cody keyed the mike. "We found your dog."

Chapter Thirty-two

Mr. Milton Williams wasn't real happy that he had to leave with us kids. We felt the same way. He watched us in his rearview mirror as he drove through the streets of Chisum. "You know where I'm taking y'all?"

Pepper and I exchanged glances in the back seat of his car. "Sure do." She pointed. "Turn up there at the corner."

"Where are we going?" I whispered. She pointed west. Aunt Neva Lou lived north of the Exchange, not far from the town square.

"Shut up, ignern't," she hissed, then her tone changed to sugar. "Take the next left, please?"

We didn't know that neighborhood from a hole in the ground, but I real quick figured out what she was doing.

She was setting us up for a butt whoopin'.

Mr. Williams turned left and drove for a while until he slowed down, knowing something was wrong. "Missy, you sure you know what you're doing?"

With wide eyes, she looked for a minute like Betty Boop. "Oh, no. I must be turned around." She gave him a big smile and pointed. "It's that way."

"Are you sure this time?" Mr. Williams sounded frustrated. "I don't intend to drive all over town tonight."

"I am now."

He sighed and we passed the Harper House, which was a mansion once owned by one of the richest men in north Texas, and then she had Mr. Williams stop at a much smaller house.

"Right here on the corner with the lights on the porch. She's waitin' on us. She always leaves the light on because she was attacked one time when she went to the door and her husband had to run a feller off with his shotgun."

I shot her another glare, because she was laying it on way too thick, even for her. We had no idea who lived there.

Constable Williams parked at the curb, turned the car off, and gave his door handle a yank. Pepper stopped him. "Oh, you don't have to get out, Mr. Williams."

He hesitated, glancing back toward the searchlights slashing in the sky. I opened the back door and stepped out. The cold wind cut through me like a knife.

I could tell Mr. Williams was thinking about walking us up to the house.

"Me and Pepper are fine right here." I felt a little better that I hadn't actually lied, but it didn't help much.

I went partway up the walk and waited for Pepper. She slammed her door and waved. "Bye now."

We waited for a second on the walk, but Mr. Williams sat there without moving. "Well shit fire." She grabbed my arm and we went on up the porch. I figured we'd get to the door and he'd drive off so we could skedaddle and go back toward the Exchange, but he didn't.

Pepper's next move was completely unexpected, even for her. She reached out and opened the front door like nobody's business. My mouth fell open when she walked inside like we lived there.

Still stunned, I turned around, waved, and followed her in. Apparently satisfied, Constable Williams finally started his car and drove off. The warm air felt great, but I expected to be shot at any second. There was no one in the neat living room, but almost every light they owned was burning.

I heard water running in the bathroom around the corner. A woman's voice came from the kitchen, along with the rattle of pans. "I'm about finished with the dishes, Larry! I'll bring you a towel in a minute."

I peeked back out and saw the street was dark and empty. I yanked the door open and jerked Pepper back outside to safety. The door slammed way harder than I intended.

"Wow!" Pepper's eyes went wide. "That was close…"

She was interrupted when the door swung back open and a gray-haired woman in a faded house dress stood there with a dish towel in her hand and a surprised expression on her face. "I *thought* I heard someone out here. Can I help y'all?"

My brain quit working. "Uh."

Pepper put on that stupid big sweet smile of hers. "Is Tammy home?"

The woman frowned. "I'm sorry hon, but you have the wrong house."

"Oh, sorry."

"Who you trying to find?"

"Tammy Stafford. I've been to her house before, but we must be turned around. Sorry to bother you."

Pepper led the way back to the sidewalk as she watched. "You two better hurry on back home and get your coats."

"Yes, ma'am."

"Lands. Them kids out after dark on a night like this, what are folks thinking?" She shut the door behind us and in a flash we ran down the street.

Pepper shrieked into the wind. "That was neato!"

I swung at her, missed, and we raced around the corner and ducked behind a pickup parked on the street. It broke the north wind, but didn't do much to warm us up.

"Now what are we gonna do, you idiot?" I was scared and cold.

"We're going back to watch."

"Grandpa will see us and give us a whoopin' you won't believe. It won't be like getting your mouth washed out with soap."

"Quit your whining. We're having an adventure."

"A *cold* adventure. I'm freezing to death and I didn't want one in the first place. I just wanted a chocolate soda."

"Come on. We'll be warmer if we walk. We ain't that far from the Exchange."

"What are we going to do when we get there?"

"I haven't figured that out yet, either."

I followed her down the dark sidewalk, wishing we had our coats. Lights from the Cotton Exchange glowed off the low clouds. Pepper led the way and I followed, shivering, hands deep in my pockets.

Twenty minutes later, we came up to the backside of the Exchange. Two police officers stood beside their cars, bundled up with their hands in their coat pockets.

It didn't take but a second before they saw us. They stepped onto the sidewalk to cut us off. "Where do you two think *you're* going?"

Luckily, we didn't know either one of them. "Home," Pepper said.

"Well, y'all can't go any farther," the tallest officer said. "We're sorry missy, but everything around here has been evacuated."

"But we're freezing. We didn't bring our coats."

"I can see that. Where do you live?"

"What's going on?"

"Don't make any difference to you girl." The tall officer's patience was short in the icy wind. "Everybody left, so you're going to have to go back where you came from until all this gets sorted out."

"Is my mama all right?" Pepper asked with wide eyes.

"I'll ask you two again. Where do you kids live?"

She waved vaguely toward the Exchange. "Right over there."

"What do you think, Ed?"

The short one shrugged. "We can't make them stay out here and freeze to death."

With their backs to the Exchange, they didn't see what caught my eye. Behind them, a dark, huddled figure stepped out from behind a car and quickly walked toward us. I hadn't seen anyone else with the officers, but I figured it was another cop.

The two policemen stepped closer. Ed ducked so his hat could break the wind from his eyes. "Which house is yours?"

Pepper pointed over his shoulder. "It's over there."

Ed turned to look. He saw the man walking toward us. "Hey, come here!" He gestured with his hand and jogged across the street to intercept him.

"Y'all get on back now where you came from before you turn to a chunk of ice." The tall officer was finished with us. "You can call for somebody to come pick you up there later."

Before she could answer, I heard Ed shout. "Hey! Don't shoot! Herb!" A quick exchange of gunshots echoed through the neighborhood.

"Run!" Herb shouted at us and fumbled under his coat to free his revolver. "Get him, Ed! He's a-runnin' between them houses!"

"Come on!" Pepper wanted to run toward the action, but for once I wasn't having any of it.

I grabbed the back of her shirt and yanked, nearly pulling her backward off her feet. "No! That's enough. We're going to Neva Lou's right now!"

She hesitated for a moment, and then deflated. "All right, but we're missing everything."

There was another scattering of shots.

"I hope we miss a whipping." I ran, leading the way, and dreading the cold, miserable time it would take us to get there.

The cold was the least of our problems, because we soon learned that Kendal Bowden got away that night, probably because of us.

Chapter Thirty-three

Broken and cracked dishes in cardboard boxes, broken furniture, Christmas lights, empty wooden file cabinets, drawers full of car parts, ball jars, crates of tractor parts, cigar boxes full of medals and ribbons…

"Now what?" John already knew the answer, but dreaded the response that would make it real. The building creaked and popped around them like a live thing.

Cody swallowed hard and stared at the dog's impaled corpse. "We got to get out of here." He moved his flashlight around the claustrophobic burrow.

John simply nodded.

Heart thumping, Cody twisted and wormed his way into a position to lever the dog out of the way. Using the spotty glow of John's flashlight around his own body, Cody thumbed his own light off and fumbled with the animal's limp carcass, lifting it off the stakes and wincing at the wet noise. He pushed the dog's corpse deeper into the tunnel to be recovered later.

One by one, Cody snapped the pointed stakes off the trap door and tossed them aside. Once the way was clear, he cautiously stood upright in the closet, and flicked on the light. For the moment at least, the immediate area appeared to be clear of more traps. "Come on partner, it's time to go up."

John inched toward Cody's feet. It was a tight fit, and Big John would have to contort himself for a moment, but Cody figured there was room enough for them to get out of the confining tunnel.

"All right. Stand up here beside me and let's see about getting started." He moved aside to make room. Grunting and straining, John worked his way into the small opening. He continued to wriggle upright until they stood side by side, waist high in the narrow confines of the enclosed closet.

Cody put his hand on John's broad shoulder and wedged the edge of his boot on a six-inch wide section of the sub floor. "Brace yourself."

John spread his feet and tensed. Taking a small jump, Cody simultaneously used his big shoulder for leverage until he stood on the thin ledge. Setting his feet carefully, he extended his hand and helped John climb beside him. Together, they leaned back against the tiny closet's crumbling plaster and lath walls.

"George may be insane, but he knows all the tricks." Cody glanced upward. "Each time he passed through, he raised this trap door with the punji sticks into place behind him."

"You said George."

"Right."

"I been meaning to ask you. I thought you's after that Kendal Bowden."

"We are, but Kendal didn't make all of this. It took years, and he was in the nuthouse most of that time, so George and Alvin probably brought all this crap in here." Cody thought back. "Kendal may be in here, though. When me and Jeff pulled up in front of the Exchange, I saw somebody ducking around the corner. I knew he was about my age because of the way he moved. An old man like Hart wouldn't move that smooth."

"Did you get a good look at him?"

"Naw, he disappeared pretty quick."

"So we might have two or three different folks in here, all workin' together to kill us."

Cody nodded. "That's about the size of it." He pointed his flashlight at a ragged hole in the ceiling. The beam illuminated a clot of papers and trash jammed into a shaft stretching five stories overhead. Bits of paper drifted downward, falling like giant dirty snowflakes. "We could climb straight up, if we could get good handholds."

John added his light. "You start messin' with that clog, the whole thing'll fall on us. We don't have any idy what fell in there after the dog dropped through."

Around them, dust particles swarmed in the beams, sparkling and dancing in the still air. Cody forced himself to breathe slowly and deeply.

"It must have been like the trap door on a gallows." John tested the moldy wall behind them with the palm of his hand. It didn't give. "I'll bet less than half the dog's weight would have been enough to blast him right through."

"Prob'ly. Be careful. We're in for a time."

Cody examined the closet's old fashioned four panel door. He pressed the wood and saw it give slightly. He carefully pushed it open, thinking of the possibility that someone could be lying on the opposite side with a shotgun.

He peered through the opening. "It's clear."

The inverted V-shaped passageway made of rubbish appeared open and empty, providing a long view of brightly colored clothes filling gaps in the "walls" like mortar between bricks. Beyond, the thin aisle vanished into total darkness.

"You first." John eyed the rickety stacks leading into the interior.

"Uh huh. Don't shoot me in the back."

Cody led the way, stepping cautiously into the opening, tense and alert. Holding the flashlight in his left hand, he aimed the pistol along the flashlight beam. Though narrow, the aisle was noticeably wider than the previous drain-size burrow they'd struggled through.

They moved in a crouch through a dramatically different passage. Loose papers and trash rustled underfoot as the men slowly advanced. John pointed his flashlight overhead. Papers and bulging boxes stretched twelve feet to the moldy, peeling ceiling. The walkway made a sharp right turn ahead.

Startled by the light, a rat shot from a hole in a disintegrating trunk to disappear across the aisle into a gap stuffed with rags. Cody's stomach clenched in fear. He had a deep-seated horror of rats after seeing some in the Viet Cong tunnels as big as cocker spaniels.

He instinctively aimed at the motion and nearly squeezed the trigger before he realized it wasn't human.

Someone with an engineer's mind had worked to arrange packing boxes and cartons in interlocking walls of the ominous tunnel. Splitting and decaying boxes of garbage, small appliances, department store catalogs, and strewn clothing filled every crack and crevice. The air smelled of urine, mildew, and rot.

Rodent droppings covered the debris beneath their feet and Cody shivered at the thought of what lay ahead. He recognized the distinctly identifiable scent of dead rats. Covered in sweat, their hands and arms were already scratched in dozens of places, picking up God knew what in the open wounds.

At the aisle's bend, they paused beside a new passageway. After an eternity, Cody knelt. "I wish I could see around this corner."

"Go low," John suggested. "I'll go high."

Cody quickly peeked around the corner and jerked back. Startled vermin rustled through the garbage, but nothing else moved in the darkness. Adrenaline pumping, Cody turned and followed his line of sight over the cocked pistol.

John stepped quickly behind him and swept the area with the muzzle of his revolver. He relaxed and exhaled deeply, finding the way clear. The much shorter passage dead-ended in a solid, compacted wall of trash. Another burrow barely two feet in diameter appeared like a waist-high cave entrance in the side of a wall.

Cody wondered if the worm-like tunnel had been intentionally created in the trash, or if piles of boxes and discards had collapsed to form the soda-straw narrow passage. He finally decided that digging a labyrinth of tunnels through the preexisting mass of trash was virtually impossible, so he figured it had been intentionally constructed as a crawlspace.

Bundles of newspaper, magazines, and lumber shaped the entrance, along with cartons, grates, wire, leather trunks, suitcases and furniture. The opening reminded Cody of Carlsbad Caverns' entrance.

Steel fifty-five-gallon barrels acted as columns holding up walls made of boxes and wooden crates, all containing even more discards. Through it all, filthy clothes in the cracks acted like chinking in the log walls of a pioneer cabin.

"I really never was much into crawling into caves." Uncle Ned said smart remarks were Cody's way of dealing with fear. Every muscle in his body twitched with unconcealed anxiety.

The complexity of the labyrinth was as amazing as the ant farm he ordered from a comic book as a kid. He wished for a Lucky Strike, to calm his nerves and to watch the smoke indicate air movement throughout burrow. Only feet behind, the sudden reverberation of collapsing junk caused them to crouch. Their movement through the precariously stacked aisles moved the rotting boards enough to cause a shift in the mass of material that resulted in an accelerating domino effect.

Heavy thumps, and then an even deeper wooden crack shifted the floor. "This place is giving way." John's voice was full of dread.

"No telling what's rotted through here through the years."

The stacks around them suddenly tilted dangerously under tons of moving weight. Cody's face went white and he shouted in fright. Dirty air full of dust and powdered rat droppings quickly clouded the flashlight beams. He pressed both hands against a rusted barrel in a futile effort to stop its movement.

John suddenly lunged and spread his huge arms to brace the debris on either side of Cody. His muscles bulged with the effort of preventing the falling mass from crushing them.

The song "Big Bad John" popped into Cody's mind when he saw the huge deputy straining in the aisle, holding the walls still with pure effort.

Big Bad John, or Samson.

Finally, their tiny world once again settled into fragile stability. John felt the change and slowly reduced the pressure from his shaking arms. When he felt it was safe, he finally dropped his hands, bent forward, and succumbed to violent, racking coughs.

The dust impacted Cody as well. He used his undershirt tail as a filter, taking deep breaths to open his lungs. Luckily, adrenaline acted as a natural antihistamine and the attack faded.

John was the first to recover. "I cain't take much more of that." With quivering fingers, he picked up his dropped flashlight and examined their surroundings. The filtered light showed the wreckage had settled by at least three feet, pressed from above by the weight of the garbage that had fallen the same distance through the rotting floor.

Around them, the Exchange was a living entity. The continuous muffled creaks and snaps of timbers told how the massive building was shifting and adjusting to the redistributed weight.

They were trapped into moving forward.

In the burrow's cave-like entrance, Cody's flashlight illuminated the right hand wall of identical cardboard shipping boxes. *Sanderson Farms* logos stretched into the darkness. The raw odor of rot and mildew from cartons that once contained raw chickens rendered the air thick and nauseating.

John added his light. Roaches scurried throughout the tunnel, crawling through trash and cardboard walls. Rats and mice flickered through the filth, appearing and disappearing through tiny openings. A cloud of choking death enveloped them.

"You going in there?" John knew the answer.

"Have to." Cody spit, hawked, and spit again.

"I really, really hate this."

Breathing through his mouth, Cody squirmed fearfully into the tiny burrow. "I don't like all these boxes beside me. They're too perfect for this place. You wait right there until I get to the end of this run."

"You don't have to tell me twic't." John pointed his light over Cody's shoulder and watched the younger man wriggle on his stomach. Like the first tunnel they'd been through, the diameter was only large enough for Cody to scoot ahead, using his elbows to pull his body along. His shoulders had only scant inches to spare on either side and he was forced to duck his head to avoid the precarious garbage pressing down.

This reminds me of the one that killed Andrews only a few hours ago…was it years…like maybe back in the Nam…or did I get that mixed up…was it Nam…did Corporal Richards die in a tunnel like this???

Disturbed by the men's presence and the sudden light, giant waterbugs skittered over Cody's legs, crawling in and out of the dark cracks in the trash. Loose paper collected under his body, and pieces occasionally separated from the roof like skin peeling from a harsh sunburn.

Darkness, isolation, stench, and sweat that reeked of fear weighed heavily on the two men. Instead of giving in to doom, John concentrated on his surroundings, focusing his mind. In stark contrast to the assorted garbage, the disturbing wall of identical interlocking boxes on the right side of the burrow stood out like a well-constructed brick wall.

"You're right, Cody. This wall don't make no sense. Them boxes was laid out smooth until a few minutes ago when everything moved."

The ordered arrangement of the packing boxes worried John and he knelt before the opening, painting the wall with his flashlight and frowning in concentration as Cody finally pulled his entire length into the horizontal shaft.

He examined the crushed containers.

"Why are all these alike?" John's gaze traveled from Cody's boot soles to the boxes on his right. He slowly directed the light from one box to the next and froze at a glint of light near Cody's right leg. "Freeze! Don't move!"

Mentally stretched to the limit, Cody jumped at the sudden shout and then became a statue. His left arm holding the flashlight lay folded underneath his body, his right hand full of pistol extended inches above the litter under him.

John bent awkwardly at the waist and eased his huge shoulders into the narrow burrow. "You've got a treble fishhook caught in your right britches leg. When you bent your knee it set the hook and there's about six inches of tight line that runs into the boxes beside us."

Cody forced himself to breathe normally. "Dammit…damn *damn*. Careful. If there's one, I can guarantee there'll be another. I didn't see any fishing line."

"I ain't surprised. It's that new stuff they came out with a few years ago that's clear, like plastic."

They found themselves whispering, as if a normal tone of voice would set off the device.

"No wonder I didn't see it. Monofilament line is supposed to be invisible to fish. It sure was to me."

"Hold on a minute." John carefully reached in with two fingers and delicately moved pieces of paper and plastic Ideal bread wrappers to get a clear view of Cody's leg. "He hid about three hooks that I can see. They're set with the points aiming backwards toward me so that whoever crawls along here will get caught."

"All right." Cody's heart felt like it was beating out of his chest. "The only reason it hasn't gone off is because the line hasn't broken or been stretched far enough to yank some kind of trigger. Find a way to tie it off so the tension will stay the same before you can cut me free."

"I was afraid you's gonna to say that." John wiped his sweating brow. He closed his eyes and thought for a moment. Mentally forcing his hands to quit shaking, he delicately ran the monofilament between two fingers and gently followed it from Cody's leg, tracing the clear line to where it disappeared into boxes stained with chicken blood. The harsh light made it difficult for John to see the nearly invisible connection.

He moved his flashlight until the line suddenly jumped into sharp contrast.

"I see it now. I need to put this down so I can use both hands. Be still."

Cody had no intention of moving.

John carefully wedged his light between a headless doll and a pair of dirty khakis, angling it toward Cody's hooked leg. He planted his feet and leaned even farther into the burrow. Pressing his right hand against the cardboard box, he cautiously grasped the fishing line with his thumb and forefinger to maintain the tension.

"Shift your leg to the right a little to give me some slack to work with. I think I can work the hook out."

"You *think?*"

"How 'bout I do my best?"

I hope he knows what he's doing.

What am I doing? John fretted. *I'm shaking like a leaf.* His forehead beaded with sweat. It quickly collected in his short hair and ran into his eyes. His nose and chin dripped with perspiration.

With infinite care, Cody adjusted his leg, wincing when paper rustled and crunched under his knee. John set his jaw and wrapped the slack around his thumb. With that slight anchor, he was able to work at the hook to get it free. The tiny cotton fibers of Cody's pants kept snagging on the hook's barb. Once, when John thought he'd finished, another of the three hooks caught in the material, causing him to repeat the process once again.

"Stay with me, son. This damned barb keeps catching."

"Take your time." Cody tried to keep the situation light. He rested his forehead on his arm. "I'm not going anywhere. You sound scared, big guy."

"That's probably 'cause I'm as afraid of this thing as I am of a snake." John stuck his tongue out like a kindergartner with a coloring book. He frowned at the predicament as he worked to free the hook. When it was done, he finally drew a long, deep breath.

"All right. I got thissun out, but don't you move until I tell you."

Still maintaining the tension on the trigger with the line around his thumb, he picked up a small piece of broken packing crate and buried the hook's point into the wood. Twirling the piece between his fingers as if rolling a cigarette, he wrapped the remaining free line around and around the chunk until it was tight. As the line shortened, he followed it toward the cardboard wall and worked his thumb free. When the wood no longer turned, he thought he'd finished, but there was an inch of slack left over and the line would come unwound.

"I'm pretty close to being done," John said. "But I've got too much slack here."

"What do you need to do now?"

"Hard to say." He paused to think of a way to finish securing the line. Then he remembered how he and his grandfather used to tighten sagging fences by twisting the slack out of the barbed wire. "Got a pen?"

"You gonna write me a note?"

"Gonna write a will. I need something like a pen or a pencil.

"I don't have anything like that in my pockets."

They thought for a moment. "All right," John said. "I'll have to use my knife, but I might need yours in a few minutes." Digging in his pocket, he located the small Case folding knife.

The next step required three hands, but he'd have to do it with two. Keeping the line in a fixed position, he released one loop from the roll around the wood. John created a loop around the closed pocket knife and twisted it until the growing knot drew the line tight.

The whole thing fell apart when he released it.

"Dammit!"

"What?"

"It didn't work."

"Try it again." Cody voice rose slightly.

"I'll have to start over and do it another way." John realized it wasn't like the movies where the hero knew how to do everything. "I believe I know how to fix it this time."

Still maintaining the pressure against the boxes with one hand, John halfway opened the blade until the knife made an L shape. He abandoned the piece of wood and carefully wrapped the curling line around the handle until it drew tight. Fingers shaking, he pressed the point of the sharp blade into the cardboard wall, burying it to the hilt. He wiped the sweat off his forehead and slowly released the knife.

It held.

The only thing left to do was release the line itself. "You want to scoot on down the tunnel in case this thing don't hold?"

"No, I can't risk moving any more until we check everything around us. If I do, I'll hang another one and we'll be right back where we started. Go ahead on and we'll see what happens next."

Tension became a physical presence. John blinked sweat from his eyes onto a rat-chewed page from *The Chisum News*. He leaned to the side as far as possible, hoping that if the booby trap exploded, the trash beside him would deflect the charge. He slowly relaxed his fingers.

They waited for the detonation that didn't come.

John released a long breath he hadn't realized he was holding. "Made it."

Cody relaxed his shaking muscles that had been taut since John discovered the fish hook.

They rested their aching necks for a moment.

There was still work to do.

Chapter Thirty-four

Soiled mattresses, broken furniture, dishes, boxes and boxes of unopened mail, drifts of empty tin cans and bottles…

Outside, Sheriff Griffin ground his teeth in frustration. The men surrounding the walkie talkie watched it as if it were a television.

"I couldn't do it," one ambulance driver whispered.

Another officer shuddered, feeling his fear of tight places rise like gorge. "What are they doing?"

"Trying to get out," a fireman answered. "They shouldn't have been in there in the first place."

Sheriff Griffin didn't answer. He was mentally kicking himself for the insane idea of allowing the officers to enter the spooky building. They hadn't made radio contact for the last thirty minutes, and he desperately wanted to speak with them. Griffin knew from his earlier experiences with the new untested radio that reception was temperamental at best. Cody might have turned it off so they wouldn't be startled by an unanticipated voice. A silent radio wouldn't give their position away if someone happened to be nearby.

And he wasn't sure those new-fangled radios would work from inside a building full of trash.

But they could at least try and call every once in a while! He hadn't heard a word since Cody reported the missing police dog. For all Griffin knew, if it hadn't already happened, both men might soon be dead, the life crushed out of them inside the garbage-filled building.

The tired sheriff rested amid the chaos surrounding the Exchange and his men. More television crews arrived from the towns nearest Chisum. It would only be a matter of time before the Dallas stations showed up. Radio reporters moved from one interview to the next in the hopes of finding someone with a different slant on the activities. Newspaper photographers popped bulb after bulb at the heavily armed deputies and whatever else caught their eye.

It was a long time until dawn.

The wind continued to batter the town, cold settled deeper, and the dark clouds spit icy rain.

Griffin's car radio squawked. He pushed the button. "What?"

He was interrupted by the sound of muffled gunshots. Prepared this time, he dropped the microphone and held up his hand. "Don't shoot! Hold your fire! Where did that come from?"

"Sounded like from behind the Exchange," Ned said. "Them was pistols."

"Get somebody around there! Go!"

Lawmen from every branch broke from the cover behind cars and raced around the building. Cars that weren't blocked in started up and wailed away. Another scattering of shots echoed off the surrounding buildings before fading into silence.

"Sheriff, the tee-vee people have already broken in to the programs and announced some crazy person is barricaded up here in the Exchange. They're going on and on about it like they did when Kennedy was shot."

Blair waved his arm from the front seat of his car. "Two of our officers think someone left the Exchange from the back way."

"I reckon we have enough men around back there. Did they get him? Is anyone hurt?"

Blair spoke into his microphone. "Whoever it was got away. Two of our men were involved, but no one was hurt."

Sheriff Griffin felt his blood pressure rise and thought his head was about to explode. All the flashing lights from the emergency vehicles around him didn't help his headache any. "Well, how the hell did that happen when we have men watching this place like a hawk?"

"They don't know, sir, but I think it was because they were talking to a couple of kids at the time."

Ned sighed with relief when he remembered Constable Williams had taken Top and Pepper to the safety of Neva Lou's house. He was glad to get them out of danger and didn't want to have to face Miss Becky over bringing them to a dangerous crime scene.

He didn't want to cross that little Choctaw woman over anything.

Chapter Thirty-five

Used tires, boxes of light bulbs, books, and paper…paper…paper…

◇◇◇

Cody and John had been in the building full of twisted passages for hours. Once again they stood upright in the semi-darkness of the small pocket of space beside the booby-trapped chicken boxes. Hearts pounding, the men trembled from fear and exhaustion. Three more large treble fishing hooks, a tangle of monofilament line, and three large-bore, home-made shotguns lay before them on the tunnel floor.

The crude but effective weapons were nothing more than pieces of iron pipe with shotgun shells forced into one end. The triggering mechanism made from a strong spring and a nail was primitive, but certainly deadly in the small confines of the burrow.

"Zip guns. I wouldn't-a thought of that in a million years." John wanted to sit until his legs quit shaking.

His mouth cotton-dry, Cody shivered and hoped George hadn't been able to locate the necessary parts in their town to make explosives. Even a small bomb would be deadly in the tiny confines, isolated from medical help.

"Was this son of a bitch in Vietnam?"

"Not sure."

"Really wasn't talking to you." Cody dug grit from the corners of his eyes. "I was thinking out loud."

He recalled the sweating dynamite he'd found in the bottoms when he was a teenager. It was in a crumbling cardboard box tucked into a littered corner of an abandoned shack in the river bottoms. He'd been killing a boring Sunday afternoon, poking around one of the many collapsing sharecropper shacks that littered the fields.

Cody found Ned at the store and told him what he'd discovered. With the leftover World War II army camp only a few miles away, everyone in the county grew up with warnings about unexploded shells that littered the countryside from years of artillery practice.

Hours later, military experts from Camp Maxey detonated the unstable dynamite, blowing the house to splinters.

Oh god I hope he didn't pick up shells at the army camp...

Cody had no other alternative than to climb back into the same burrow. "We move slower. I've got a good idea George or maybe Kendal is denned up nearby. All these traps are designed to stop an intruder before they can get to his hidey hole."

John noted Cody's reference to a lair. He'd already begun to think of George as an exceedingly cunning animal.

He'd come to think of the Exchange's tunnel systems as an aboveground ant hill.

It was obvious George was an experienced builder, probably from trial and error. The air was breathable, which would have been impossible without some kind of ventilation system. Without fresh air, the decomposing matter inside the burrows would have been downright deadly, if not explosive. Cody expected the vents were probably constructed with an angle to prevent rains from flooding the system. Or maybe not. He glanced up, wondering again if decades of rain had seeped into the aging building to rot the studs and joists holding the structure together.

"Oh, man, I don't want to do this any longer than we have to," John sighed.

Cody stopped and thought. "Me neither."

He keyed the walkie talkie, not expecting anyone to answer.

Chapter Thirty-six

Paper shotgun shells, black powder kegs, cylinder grease, half a shebang, canvas, canvas tents, dishes of all kinds, dozens of cracked wooden covered wagon hoops, cast iron stoves, rusty cast iron pots and skillets...

The sheriff's handset finally crackled to life.

"Anybody still out there?"

Griffin snatched his radio from the table, hearing the tinny voice from half a dozen cars within earshot. "It's about time you peckerheads called in. We're ready to send in gas or another team."

"Well, don't do either one. We've been kinda busy and I haven't had time for much visitin'."

Griffin grinned, relieved to hear Cody joke despite the situation. "We've been pretty busy out here, too. What the hell happened? What have you found?"

"This place is a rabbit nest of shafts and aisles. Baker was right. It's packed solid. You get the idea someone crammed this place with garbage like a trash can, and then packed it tighter and dug tunnels through the whole thing. George never threw anything away. In fact, I'd be willing to bet he brought most of it in from the outside. No one person could save this much junk in a lifetime."

Overhearing the conversation, Officer Baker rubbed his hands together. "Amazing!"

"Hold on, guys," Griffin said into the radio. He turned to the academic. "What is so amazing about junk?"

"This individual switches back and forth between predictable symptoms and mental afflictions. He's both a hoarder and a pathological collector of rubbish. The clinical name for the disease is Diogenes Syndrome." He waited, as if expecting Griffin to try and pronounce the difficult word. When he didn't respond, Baker continued. "With this individual's past life experiences and his acute anxieties from various types of psychosis, he may be nearing maximum overload."

"I don't know what the hell he said," Ned told O.C. "But you need to get him an office in the courthouse tomorrow morning. Thissun might replace you one day."

Hands in his pockets, O.C. frowned. "I swear."

Griffin didn't understand, either, but he didn't let on to Ned. He did understand one word. He chewed the inside of his cheek, wishing he hadn't stopped smoking last year. "What type of overload?"

"Any number of possibilities may exist. We might find he's even more violent than merely placing a booby trap at the entrance. He's going to control his life, protect himself and his possessions at all costs. The line has blurred between garbage and what's essential to sustain life. To them, it's *all* essential. These people can't throw anything away, and if even a family member tries to throw out one bag of what is literally garbage, the hoarder will accuse them of throwing away his or her 'stuff' and will retrieve it and actually redistribute it across other piles of trash. Have they encountered any more traps in the burrows?"

Griffin keyed the mike and repeated Baker's brief lecture. "Have you boys found any more traps?"

Cody snorted, his voice tinny over the radio's tiny speaker. "The damn place is full of them. I don't have time to give you a list right now, but you can bet we're being extra careful after the last hour or so."

"That's right." Baker spoke directly to Sheriff Griffin. "George is living in another world. Now he's trying to find meaning in the mire. The chaos he's created is his and his alone. This isn't clutter in the traditional sense. This is a massive building turned into a fortress and what they find in there is probably incomprehensible to a rational mind. I can't believe we have this here, right in our own backyard. I can see it in a big city like Dallas, or Chicago, but here in Chisum? This is classic, and it'll be studied for years."

Griffin stared at the young patrolman for a long moment before turning back to the radio. "Can you give me any idea whereabouts y'all are in there?"

He heard Cody breathing heavily in the musty air. "It's hard to tell exactly, because these tunnels backtrack on themselves and wind around. They go up and down without any particular reason, except to get around big pieces of crap he's got stored in here. I swear, I think we crawled around a steam engine a while ago. This is like a red ant hill and for all I know we're close to where we started. We followed one tunnel and it led us back in a big circle." He paused to think. "We might be near an outside wall."

"What makes you think that?"

"Because we have a pretty fair radio signal. Deeper inside, I doubt we'll get any signal at all, but I can't tell you I'm right about that, either."

"Any sign of George?"

"Not yet, unless you mean the traps. He hasn't dropped by to introduce himself."

"Well, he might have got out. Somebody left the back of the Exchange and traded shots with a couple of my officers. We're sealing the city right now while we root him out."

"So while we're crawling around in here, the person we're after is out in the fresh air?"

"Yep, and fresh ain't no name for it. We've had a norther blow through and it's trying to sleet. So, all right. What's your plan? I know you aren't going to listen to any of my suggestions."

His immediate anxiety subsided and John grinned, knowing the younger man better than Cody would have believed.

"Suggest all you want. It won't make any difference to us. He wants to keep us confused and disoriented. We're not exploring, we're trying to find a way out and if I don't make it soon, I'm gonna lay here and die."

"Got it. Can you think of anything we can do out here?" Griffin felt he had to offer some kind of support, however futile it might be.

Cody's voice crackled out into the darkness. "Yeah, get us some roach spray."

The anxious men beside the radios chuckled nervously and continued to watch the building. They were frightened by the entire horrific night, the Ghost Man, a demented murderer who had already taken one man's life, and a frightening building that was possibly digesting two friends at that very moment.

Chapter Thirty-seven

Furniture piled to the ceiling, lamps, dozens of new caskets and the crates they'd been shipped in…many more used caskets…and some still crusted with crumbling dirt…

Cody rolled his head to relieve the tension. "You ready to go partner?"

John directed his flashlight through the gloom and into the hole. "Not really." They waited for a long minute. "I sure could use a drink of water."

"Me too. In fact, I'd even settle for a sip of Doak Looney's moonshine."

John's smile flashed. "We're liable to find a quart or two in all this mess before long."

"Ain't that a fact? Well, now's as good a time as any if we're gonna go."

"No choice. Let's do it."

Cody once again leaned into the gaping hole and entered another burrow. John followed after a few moments, giving Cody time to gain some distance.

The burrow angled to the left. They grunted and wormed their way forward, making slow time in a building as full of holes as Swiss cheese. Unknown to them, at several points during their exploration, even more burrows crossed their path mere feet above and below, depending on their location. No sane person could imagine the extent of the tunnel system.

They progressed without conversation, each with his thoughts and fears. John's world encompassed only the sight of Cody's feet and the peripheral view of the surrounding garbage. Progress was slow in the musty shafts, nothing more than inches at a time. It was move the elbows, pull and shuffle a few inches, and do it all over again.

Cody stopped when he reached a relatively clear rise of damp wooden stairs. The entire area was suddenly wet, indicating years of water percolating through the building.

"I'm telling you. This feels more and more like a cave. This wall is wet."

John waited. "What do you want to do?"

"This ain't right. Give me a few minutes."

"Go ahead on. I'll read this cereal box right here."

The burrow in front of Cody rose at a sharp angle, following the steps as if someone had installed a drain pipe on the staircase. The plain wooden banister supports on his right seemed to hold up a tenuous ceiling only inches above. The tunnel split halfway up and after breaking through the supports, angled downward. Cody knew for certain that it led deeper into the bowels of the Exchange.

No way was he going down there.

The wall beside the stairs appeared to be solid enough, but the plaster and lath had bulged outward. Cody couldn't tell if it was due to the burden from above, or intense compression on the other side. Peeling remnants of wallpaper hung slimy with mold.

Two of the nearest splintered steps seemed to be more warped than the others. He gently tapped the wood with a knuckle to test the step.

"This don't sound right. I'm pretty tight here. Hang on while I see if I can reach my pocketknife."

He worked his knife free, snicked the blade into place, and slid the sharp edge into a crack between two boards. "Let's see what we have here."

Minutes later Cody stared at a gaping hole revealed by the newly removed tread. At first, the step's wood appeared normal, but had been roughly chipped away on the bottom side so the piece was as thin as a fingernail.

The trap was simple. Anyone wriggling through the burrow would break a knee or elbow through the thin veneer, dropping onto ragged pieces of glass and sharp slivers of broken mirror standing on edge.

Cody wiped his face. "That could hurt."

"What's that?"

He broke the shards with the butt of his flashlight and described what he'd found. Still worried about the glass, he carefully collected great handfuls of paper and clothing from the walls, and stuffed the mass into the gaping step. "Now be careful when you crawl across here, in case I didn't get this packed good."

John shivered. "This place is the Devil's House." He followed, worming over the vicious ambush that had been laid for them. Despite the packing inside the step, he held himself above the dismantled trap.

They struggled like moles through the darkness. Surprisingly, the odor of decay had dissipated until it was barely noticeable. Cody was again convinced George had designed an ingenious ventilation system, which kept the air from getting dangerously stale.

A door at the top of the stairs was halfway open. It was the only indication they had reached a real room, instead of packed warehouse floors. At first glance it looked like the exit to a broad hallway only three feet high.

Then Cody realized the illusion was created by empty wooden cable spools creating near perfect crawlways. He stopped in amazement. As far as he could see, the gigantic spools extended far into the distance. Like stubby buttresses only six feet apart, the open area was in direct contrast to what they'd just been through.

He moved out of the way so John could join him.

"Sweet Jesus. This thing goes on forever!"

"It sure looks like it goes for the entire length of this madhouse. How long is this building, five hundred feet?"

"More like six or seven, and maybe a quarter as wide. These big spools are all around us."

"What's up there?"

John rolled onto his back and directed his light into the open intersections and found the bottom of another spool stacked on top. For all they knew, they may have reached as high as the ceiling. John wiggled around to shine his light through the open forest of wooden mini-columns.

Speechless, they had no choice but to continue. Unlike the previous burrows covered with paper, clothing and cardboard, the rough wood caught their pants with dozens of splinters, tearing holes and puncturing flesh.

They scooted among the buttresses, trying to maintain as straight a line as possible. After what seemed like hours, they once again came to a familiar burrow that quickly led to a large room where they could finally stand upright. They rested for a moment to stretch out the kinks and knots of fear.

Their flashlights picked out ragged furniture in the large, chaotic room. Unafraid, rats scurried through shredded newspaper in yellowing drifts.

Once again the smell of decay hung heavy in the air. John breathed through his mouth. "Something died."

"Yeah, but it was a while ago, I'd think."

"How do you know that?"

"Because that dog carcass chained to the sofa there isn't fresh."

John's light found the couch. The sight of the long dead animal had a profound effect on the men. Neither wanted to think about what it would have been like to die from starvation while alone in total darkness. The bowl George once used to feed the pitiful animal had been gnawed to plastic shreds by the starving dog. Cody lit a skull full of broken teeth. Large patches of dried skin and hair peeled from the bone.

When they moved the beams around the area, a nightmare version of normality leaped into focus. Toy trains, a tricycle, lamps, Christmas trees, an upright piano, musical instruments, mountains of rotting drapery material, pots and pans, thousands of foam egg cartons, milk crates, tin cans, paintings, a standup radio, an engine from a 1948 De Soto, doors, board games, a complete medical library, National Geographic magazines dating back to 1918, a wagon wheel, letters, shovels, baby carriages, plaster statues, dressmakers dummies, a primitive X-Ray machine, and much more filled the space around a large, musty chair.

Though seemingly random, the items were carefully selected and in many instances, displayed in a bizarre sense of order. "This is his *living room!*" Cody said in wonder, eyeing stacks of photo albums and old pictures.

"He might come back, then." John checked over his shoulder in case George suddenly appeared.

"I don't think he's been here for a long while."

They examined the room, crushing scurrying roaches underfoot. Mice skittered through stacks of old cigar boxes wrapped with hard rubber bands.

"Which way now?"

"Through there?" Cody pointed at a tall, dark arrowhead-shaped opening. Two enormous stacks of bundled newspapers arched high overhead, creating a peaked entrance.

"That *slick* look again?"

Cody shrugged. "I don't have anything better to go on." He bent and entered the short passageway. It didn't take long for the men to traverse the short length of the narrow canyon leading to a filthy mattress between stacks of decaying books.

"Must have been a reader." John directed his light over the eccentric hoarder's collection. The stained mattress was almost buried under a tangled mass of soiled clothing and food containers. The oily pillow was a dark smudge. He picked up a copy of Hemingway's *Old Man and the Sea*. "I've already read this one."

Surprised at the announcement, Cody wondered why he'd never pictured John reading books. He'd have to think about that idea later, when he had the time to wonder about the big deputy's hobbies.

The room smelled faintly of perfume and old cigar smoke.

"You're talking about him in the past tense." Cody's beam skipped over the rotting walls, finding a full kerosene lantern leaning haphazardly against the mattress. A table lamp without a shade sat on a wooden crate piled with soiled women's underwear. Empty bottles caught and reflected the light in patterns of color and shapes.

"Well, I'll be." Cody pointed to a magazine. "World War Two is over. Hitler is dead."

"So is Oswald," John held up a more recent Dallas Times Herald newspaper. The front page was filled with a photo of Jack Ruby gunning down Lee Harvey Oswald.

With no other way out of what they thought of as the bedroom, they returned through the same burrow and back into the living area.

"That way." John pointed toward a dark entrance and Cody ducked into what reminded him of a mine shaft.

The pathway wasn't as tall. On their knees, the reluctant explorers continued until it branched in two directions. One was obviously dusty and long unused. He decided on the more heavily used right-hand tunnel that angled sharply higher.

"Wait here."

There was enough room at the fork for John to get reasonably comfortable. He squatted to rest his forehead on his hands while Cody probed ahead. Only inches away, the peeling plaster and lath ceiling stretched into the distance. The hair prickled on the back of John's neck when he once again remembered that five stories of solidly packed garbage surrounded them.

The suffocating burrow made a gradual turn ending in a dead end. Cursing, Cody backed out, grunting and wiggling. Scooting forward was much easier than backward.

He rejoined John in the wider turnaround. It was large enough to sit upright and rest. The space was supported by stacked volumes of hardback books, many of them medical encyclopedias dating back to the turn of the century. The rotting spines separated and hung like dried strips of dead flesh.

Soaked in sweat, they panted in the dim glow of their flash-lights. "Let's turn these off while we rest for a minute," Cody suggested. "These batteries won't last forever."

Giving the idea a moment's consideration, John saw the wisdom of the suggestion, despite the need to see. They clicked the switches and absolute darkness immediately descended, again reminding Cody of Carlsbad Caverns.

In the bowels of the spooky old Cotton Exchange, he shivered as the impenetrable darkness wrapped around them. The ticking of John's wristwatch sounded like full size grandfather clock, the luminous dial a bright beacon in the blackness.

"This guy is full of tricks." Sweat dripped off Cody's nose. Their undershirts were soaked and black from crawling over unimaginable filth.

"I hope we've seen them all."

"Not hardly. If this was Nam there could be a hundred other things waiting for us, anything from snakes to deadfalls."

"Anything but snakes." John heard his own heart beating. Silent and still for the first time since they entered the maze of tunnels, they heard a variety of soft sounds generated by the tons of waste around them. Small creaks and groans evidenced a subtle shifting of the building's contents. Small mammals scurried through the rubble in which they'd lived for generations.

"Let's turn on the walkie talkie and check with the World," Cody said, falling back into the slang they used when referring to anything outside of Vietnam. He flipped the switch and keyed the talk button. "Can y'all hear me?"

He immediately received a dim and crackling response from Sheriff Griffin. "You boys all right?"

"For now. We're taking a breather."

"Any idea where you are?"

"None at all. We've twisted and turned so many times that I doubt we'll ever know where we went."

The radios went silent as they pondered the situation.

"What's your plan?"

"Our *plan* is find a way out of this nuthouse."

Griffin was hamstrung on the outside. Cody didn't know it, but the sheriff had his hands full. Hundreds of spectators crowded into the once quiet neighborhood, pushing against the barricades. Questions continued to be raised about his handling of the event. The mayor was demanding action and no one knew what to do.

Every broadcast referenced the fallen deputy now covered by a sheet and blocked from view by makeshift curtains hung from thin wire stretched between the supporting arches. Men covered by rifles still worked to free the deputy's body.

Sheriff Griffin scanned the brightly lit area, wondering how the night would finally end. He focused his attention on the boys inside. "See if you can make enough noise so we can hear you if y'all find an outside wall. We may be able to break through and get you out."

"That was our idea, too. I'll be damned if I know where we are. We're moving now. I'll contact you later." He flicked on the flashlight, covering the lens with his hand at first to lessen the shock to their eyes. "Ain't this a mess?"

John agreed. "Sho' nuff. At least you knew what you were doing in Vietnam. I guess your time there is keeping us alive, 'cause I doubt I'd still be breathin' if I was alone. Was it like this?"

Cody scanned the stacks of garbage around them.

"It worked the same way there, but in reverse. The entrance tunnels were simple, but the farther down and away from the trap doors, there were drops, twists and turns, and parts like the u-drain under a sink. For all we knew, we'd go through one of those drains and come up through water to find the whole North Vietnamese Army.

"I heard they had such a wide tunnel system that a USO show was going on topside, and directly underneath, the Viet Cong were having a meeting."

He shivered.

"Think about it. If this crazy feller tapped into the drain system under the street, it could go forever. A friend of mine found tunnels under a shack that had one main room nearly twenty feet square, one of the few places we had the room to stand upright and walk around. It was an ammo bunker full of weapons, ammunition, mortar shells, grenades, clothing, and documents. Half a dozen other tunnels branched out of that main room, which was the center hub of a giant wheel, and popped up in huts, under logs, and even in a chicken coop. One had a trap door so small it was hidden under the feed trough in a hog pen."

"I don't know how you made it." John wondered at their near normal conversation in such bizarre surroundings.

Cody thought for a long moment. "I'm not sure we did." He stared at an empty detergent box and momentarily drifted away before shaking off whatever had gripped him. "You rested enough?"

"As much as I can be."

"All right. Let's get out of here."

"That'd tickle me to death, but this time I want to lead."

Cody shrugged. "You have to learn some time."

On his hands and knees, Big John crawled into the burrow that tightened until they found themselves on their stomachs. Constructed this time through wooden pallets, the sagging roof of rotting, split plywood bulged downward, at one point scraping their backs. It snagged John's undershirt with a quiet rip. They continued crawling slowly through splintered wood.

The pallets gave way to bound stacks of National Geographic magazines which formed the walls. A haphazard spray of angle iron bed rails planted deeply into the substructure below served as an unplanned support system that kept the great weight from falling in on them. Grunting and panting, Cody pulled himself along with his elbows, following John's huge shoes. The burrow widened ahead, and he was anxious to get out of the narrow tube and into the inviting open area.

They suddenly found themselves in a soft, almost comfortable burrow made of rotting bales of cotton. "Cotton." John shook his head in wonder. "Of all things."

The burrow through the five-hundred-pound bales was almost glorious. The softness was a blessing under their much abused knees and elbows, as long as they avoided the thick wires holding each compressed bale together. It reminded Cody of playing in Ned's hay barn when he was a kid.

"It only makes sense," he muttered to himself. "Lord knows how much of this stuff was left. This whole level could be cotton all the way to the ceiling and George just dug through it like a mole."

Hundreds of small rat and mouse tunnels branched off through the soft burrow. Rodent droppings collected on his bare forearms as he crawled, and Cody again wondered what diseases they would leave with, if they survived.

Despite the relief to his knees and elbows, John was nearly frantic from the narrower confines. He almost tumbled into still another open area and immediately realized there was enough room to sit upright inside what he quickly realized was a huge chamber excavated in the cotton.

This animal has lived with these rats long enough that he's even making nests like them.

Even there, as usual, stacks and stacks of newspapers and collected litter lay half buried in the loose fluff.

With enough room to turn for once, John reversed his direction and extended his hand to Cody, who was struggling to pull himself through. John's eyes widened in the dim glow. The mountainous stack of bales atop Cody's emerging body *moved*, making the big man's head spin for a moment. Sensing disaster, half a dozen squeaking rats frantically squirted out of the rapidly compressing burrow. They scampered across the open pocket to escape into holes on the far side.

A cold finger slipped up John's spine. He grabbed for the younger constable's waving hand and gave a tremendous pull. With a quiet, *solid* whisper, the mass dropped in a frightening, muffled sigh as tons of cotton caved in, burying Cody from his chest down.

"Oh god!"

Choking dust roiled into the area. John's dropped flashlight lit the scene, casting musty shadows from below.

"Hang on!" He hauled at Cody's arms, trying to free him from the collapsed bales. The immense weight slowly crushed the air, and life, out of the young constable. Frantically, John clawed at the cotton, grabbing great handfuls of the stuff, but it was like trying to claw hard sand. His fingers found one of the heavy gauge baling wires and he gave a mighty tug, but nothing moved.

"Hang on, Cody! Oh lord, can you hear me!"

"Can't breathe," Cody gasped, voicing the exact phrase Top used only months before in the bottoms.

Had he been alone, the situation would have ended only one way. Still, without help, John wasn't sure he'd be able to pull Cody free before he suffocated. There was the further danger of even more of the heavy cotton coming down, and the very real concern that the entire cavity would soon be a deathtrap.

"Can you move your legs!?" John desperately dug great handfuls of cotton, throwing it behind him. But the large heavy bales slowly compressed Cody's lungs. "How far back was the cave in?"

"I can't bend my legs," Cody fought to breathe. "I can't… get…any…air."

More cotton piled up around John's feet as he desperately tried to dig Cody free. The yellow light gave the whole scene an otherworldly effect. Drifts of loose fluff came up to John's knees, while in direct contrast, the heavy, packed bales continued to press downward.

Despite his efforts, Cody's torso refused to budge. John retrieved the flashlight and quickly cast the beam around the open space behind him. The walls of the dirty white canyon ended nearly two feet below the twelve-foot ceiling. The frame from an antique iron bedstead angled apart from the others.

His fear and sense of urgency intensified when the wooden ceiling shifted with a crunching sound from the rotting joists suddenly relieved of their cotton supports.

John threw himself against the freed bed rail and worked it loose, praying silently that nothing more would fall. When he was sure it was safe, he turned and inserted the end of the angle iron in the narrow space between Cody's left side and the collapsing bales. Jabbing it firmly inside, and making sure the end wasn't resting on any part of his trapped friend, John put his huge shoulder under the sharp rail.

Like a power lifter, he used his legs to push, applying pressure to the fulcrum. For a horrifying moment he thought his feet weren't going to quit sinking in the cotton below, but he finally felt the soft material solidify under his shoes. The hard edge bit sharply into his shoulder. Ignoring the pain, he squeezed his eyes shut and pushed harder.

Nothing happened. At first he thought it was useless. It was like trying to lever the Great Pyramid from its foundation. The pain was incredible as the edge cut into his trapezius. Needing relief, John pulled at great wads the very substance that was killing Cody. He quickly shoved a thick cushion between his shoulder and the iron, then braced himself, and heaved again.

This time the heavy bailing wire worked in his favor, giving the angle iron a firm foundation for leverage, and his massive strength moved just one of crushing bales. It was enough. Barely conscious, Cody drew a shuddering breath.

"Get out!" John quivered with the effort. "Crawl out now! Use my legs and pull!"

With an instinctive will to live, Cody grasped his thick calves and used the anchored deputy to drag himself free of the death trap. He kept the momentum by pushing with his almost numb legs as the pressure released, until he fell between John's feet.

John slowly lowered the impromptu lever, allowing the dead weight to settle a little at time into the opening. Wood snapped overhead with a muffled sound. The ceiling dropped slowly with a terrifying groan until it rested on the huge cotton bales, which compressed even further into the gap Cody vacated only moments before.

Thoroughly exhausted, John could do no more than retrieve his flashlight and aim the shaft of light directly overhead. "Oh lord, I don't think it's gonna hold."

The young man knew the giant hero beside him was for the moment at the end of his rope. This time there would be no Big Bad John to hold the ceiling up if enough joists snapped.

He could do nothing but reach out and take the big man's hand. Two adult males holding hands would have been ludicrous outside. But in the house of horrors, the human touch was all they had left in their last moments before their world collapsed.

Emotionally and physically spent, they could do nothing but pray that the ceiling held. Deep grumbles, muffled rustles and sharp pops both above and below filled the room until finally dwindling into silence.

John settled onto his haunches and caught his breath.

In the harsh illumination, a grimy brown plastic Mr. Potato head with one yellow arm and a black mustache stared back at Cody with a single eye.

He finally released John's hand and picked it up. "I had one of those once."

He closed his own eyes in exhaustion.

Chapter Thirty-eight

"These yours?" an irritated young police officer asked. "They say they belong to you, Mr. Ned."

He and O.C. turned toward the voice behind them. The officer had Top's shoulder under one hand, and Pepper's under the other.

Ned took off his Stetson and rubbed his forehead where the leather band made it itch. The kids stared at their feet, knowing their grandfather's blue eyes would be flashing. "They are for the time bein'. Where'd you find them?"

"They were on the side of the Exchange, about a block away. A couple of our men found them walking in this weather without coats when everyone was looking for the one who shot at our officers a little while ago. They said they were coming here."

Griffin glared at the children. O.C. stifled a chuckle and shifted his body slightly, putting himself between the sheriff and the family dispute.

Almost spent, Ned knelt, grabbed the kids, and roughly pulled them toward him. "I'll take them."

"Yessir." The officer gratefully released the two young outlaws and wove his way back through the cars and emergency vehicles.

For the next five minutes, Ned spoke with quiet fury. No one knew whether the kids shivered from fear or cold, but most of the officers within earshot were glad it wasn't *them* getting dressed down.

After he finished what he had to say and cooled off, a thought occurred to Ned. "Was it you two that was on the other side of the Exchange? Did y'all have a part in letting that feller get away?"

Pepper shrugged. "We were over there."

Sorrow filled Ned's eyes. "I don't need this right now. I'god, when I tell you two to do something, you do it. You know what's coming when I get y'all home."

Pepper's eyes leaked. "I know, but can you get us some coats, first? We're freezing."

O.C. turned completely away so the kids couldn't see him laugh.

The kids looked up at their grandfather who didn't know what to say other than, "Girl..."

Chapter Thirty-nine

Rusting washing machines lined the wall in a parody of the Western Auto's appliance showroom floor.

Resting, Cody painted his flashlight along the fluffy bales towering over them. The only way out of the soft cavity was an irregular hole behind them. He stuck his light into the opening to find another room only feet away. "I hope this doesn't dead end. If it is, we may be here a long while."

"Sorry if it was me that done it." John sucked in a deep breath, feeling the pain in his lower back from the tremendous effort only moments before.

Cody coughed. "I don't think you tripped anything. Maybe it was me. The stuff probably shifts from time to time. You got me out so I didn't end up like Andrews out there. Thanks."

They rested in awkward silence for a moment, each man with his own thoughts.

"How does a place get like this?" John thought aloud, asking the air instead of Cody. "This ain't right. It's like one of them picture shows."

"Who knows. Sometimes people's brains go haywire and they throw up their hands."

"This has been going on a long time and nobody said a thing. My people talked about the Ghost Man, but nobody paid a lick of attention to what he was doin' here."

"I don't know John. It sure ain't natural." Cody winced, feeling his muscles complain. "You ready to go?"

"As ready as I can be."

On rubber legs, Cody crouched and stepped through the opening. John's own legs trembled as he followed into still another room piled with trash and filled with a familiar scent.

John recognized it at once. "This smells like my old Auntie's house. It smells like old people."

"Old furniture is where that comes from, for one thing, but the air is surely getting rank. What's that?"

"Where?"

Cody shined his light on a dark patch of polished wood behind stacks of boxes and a chiffonier. "Is that a desk, or paneling?"

John pushed himself to his knees and rapped the small section. It sounded hollow. "This isn't furniture. It's a door."

"That's the first closed door we've found since the closet when we came in." Cody joined him against the far wall. "Maybe it's a way out. Let's try and see. Careful. Watch for tripwires."

Using only John's light to save their dying batteries, they moved trash from one side of the small nest to the other, packing it in the cotton chamber. They finally cleared enough room to fully open the door.

"Finally," John sighed. "Think it's booby-trapped?"

"Doubt it. There was too much trash against it." Cody slowly gave the antique oval knob a slight turn. It worked easily. He flicked on his flashlight and cracked the door to peek inside. It stuck for a moment and he gave it a jerk.

The stench that rolled through the small opening was thick and putrid. Gagging, Cody slammed the door, but not before he caught a glimpse of the filthiest bathroom he'd even seen. In that brief second he saw the pedestal sink, toilet, and claw foot bathtub filled with waste. Insects carpeted the horrendous floor in a seething mass while rodents scurried for escape through unseen holes. Mold grew in thick, luxurious clumps from the walls and ceiling. Bats shuffled overhead and squeaked in a writhing mass as guano dripped like rain.

"Sheew, that stinks. What was it?" John gasped, swallowing to regain control of his stomach.

Cody retched again, bringing up nothing but a thin drool. "A bathroom. I don't even want to *describe* it. Bats found a way in. Things I don't even want to think about are growing against the door and filled in the cracks, sealing the room off. My god, how can anyone live this way?"

"I don't have any idy." John turned toward the only remaining opening behind him, breathing through his mouth. "I guess we go this way. Let me lead."

"Hurry up so we can get away from here." As long as they moved carefully through the extremely narrow aisle, it shouldn't be a problem. He put his hand on John's shoulder. "Watch for trip wires. I don't want to sit in here for a week next to *that,*" he indicated with a thumb over his shoulder, "while they dig us out."

John shuddered, but he advanced slowly. His dimming light continually flickered over the trash, searching for any clue to another deadfall or booby trap.

They crept through even more bundles of paper and boxes, making hard right angles and often turning back on themselves. Underfoot, piles of tin cans, pasteboard, and clothing shifted with a dry rustle, making progress difficult.

The narrow aisle followed the wide perimeter of a concrete water fountain nearly reaching the tall ceiling. They stopped to examine the strange object that should have been in a fancy yard, or in a town square.

"How'd he get that in here?"

Cody rapped it with a knuckle. "In pieces, I guess. Or maybe this room is so big it had its own fountain. Who knows? Right about now it seems normal."

A column of mismatched boxes leaned tiredly against the top of the fountain's cherub. They had to shuffle sideways and bend between the large dry bottom reservoir and the smaller one above to scoot past the obstruction.

"This may be a doorway." John painted his light across still another pathway taking them through an opening. The packed garbage led steeply upward. Cody aimed his light toward the crest of the rise and realized it stopped at an open transom less than eighteen inches below the top of the doorframe. His own weakening beam illuminated a once highly polished mahogany frame, a tiny indication of the building's former opulence.

"We've probably gone through a dozen doors since we came in here," Cody said. "And didn't see a one of them."

"I'm about tired of this funhouse."

"More like a madhouse."

They struggled to gain purchase with their feet, climbing what would have in the open appeared to be a simple, though enormous, pile of trash. Papers, magazines, clothes hangers, clothing, and even dishes shifted underfoot and sloughed off in a small landslide.

Cody dropped to his knees and finished the climb, directing light through the transom and beyond. "There's a room in here."

He studied a large area completely devoid of trash, marred only by the garbage spilling from their access point. It was as if George wanted at least one room relatively free of clutter.

John struggled uphill beside Cody to share the odd sight. Other than a dozen battered metal garbage cans, the room was an oasis. Each can was fitted with a lid, bringing a strange order to the chaos around them.

Cody slid over the top and dropped heavily onto the floor, where he unconsciously reached to the wall and flipped the light switch. For the first time since they entered the Exchange, a single fixture in the ceiling came on. Cody cringed at his own stupidity. The switch could have triggered any number of booby traps. Instead, the miracle of electric light illuminated the area.

A doorway on the opposite side was blocked with clean, carefully arranged boxes. Two familiar burrow entrances, one directly over the other, led into another mass of rubbish. A four-foot length of bed slat leaned against the wall.

"Another trap?" John asked from the transom opening.

"Who knows? This feller is so crazy that every guess I can come up with sounds wrong."

"We have to go through."

"Yeah."

"I like the light."

"Yeah."

"What do you think is in the garbage cans?"

"I don't want to know."

"Do you think we should find out?"

"No."

They paused.

"You first," John said.

The overhead lights dimmed.

He looked at the fixture. "Electricity doesn't act like that."

"Battery lights do. Come on down. We need to get moving."

John eyed the passageways. "Umm humm." He wriggled around, worked his feet through the opening and dropped heavily to the floor with a loud grunt.

"All right. We move slowly and carefully through here, one at a time."

"Which hole are we going to take?"

"I'll decide when I can see into them. Stay right here until I call you."

"Like I have anywhere else to go."

Cody stepped gingerly onto the tongue and groove oak. It felt solid and safe underfoot. He glanced upward at the ceiling, anticipating a collapse. When nothing happened, he relaxed slightly and concentrated on the two yawning black holes directly across, one at knee and the other at chest height.

For a moment the decision was almost overwhelming. Self confidence waned and Cody didn't know how long he could keep it up. The maize of burrows was much larger than he'd first anticipated and he wasn't sure he had the mental presence to keep his composure much longer.

To stall until he made up his mind, and to touch the sane outside world, he removed the walkie talkie from his back pocket and pressed the button.

"Can you hear me?" He didn't expect it to work, and was surprised when he heard Sheriff Griffin's voice almost lost in the static.

"Did you want me, or was that an accident?"

"No, I'm resting for a minute."

"Y'all all right?"

"Hell no, we ain't all right. Do I have to remind you of what's going on?"

Griffin sighed. "No, I don't know what to say."

"Well, neither do I. We've come to a fork in the road here, and I can't decide which way to go."

"What do you mean?"

"We're in a big, empty room, and the only way out is two tunnels in front of us. One goes up, and the other angles back down." Cody was quiet for a moment, pondering the insanity of their situation. "We really need to get out of here." His voice rose perceptibly. "I'm too tired to decide and right now I don't think I can take much more of this madness."

Griffin's eyes found Ned. They exchanged a glance. "Settle down son."

Even though he begrudged the old man's presence, he knew it would help if Ned talked to his nephew. He'd just finished reading the riot act to his grandchildren and probably would have given them a whipping right then if there hadn't been so much going on around them.

"I have someone here that may be able to help. Wait a second."

Cody closed his eyes and squatted before the two tunnels. The next voice through the tinny speaker was old and familiar.

"You're in a mess, huh?" the old voice asked.

"Ned?"

"Yep?" The concern in Ned's voice was evident. "How you doing, son?"

"I've been better."

"Well, you've been in a tight before. You never got into anything you couldn't handle overseas, and you won't now."

"That's because the tunnels over there made sense. They dug 'em in the ground and we knew how those people thought. They had living quarters, connecting tunnels, and storerooms. Most of them were level, or at least they changed levels for a reason. These tunnels go up and down just for the fun of it."

"No, son, think about it. If George filled that place up and set traps, he had a plan and a damned good reason for doing it."

Feeling oddly calmed by the old man's voice, Cody's mind shifted gears. "You're right. I know a few of these tunnels are diversions, and others were made for booby traps, but I'm tired and second-guessing myself. I might get us both killed."

"Quit thinking so hard, son. Close your eyes, listen to your gut, and don't worry about John. He's in there 'cause he wants to be. John crawled in while Griffin was-a-hollerin' for him to stop. He's full growed and knows what he's doing."

On the other side of the room, John dropped to one knee to rest and closed his eyes. "Maybe."

They chuckled, despite their situation.

"Now, think about it. You likely learned something over there in those tunnels to find your way around. What was it?"

Cody loosely held the radio in his hand and thought back. What had he forgotten? Traps. Tunnels. Ammo dumps. Access and escape hatches. Then he recalled a peculiar symbol the VC used to indicate the direction of an exit.

"Son of a bitch!"

John opened his eyes. "What?"

Cody keyed the radio. "That's it Uncle Ned. I've been missing signs because this madhouse isn't as clean as a tunnel. I bet there have been signs all through here that George used to get around. I just didn't see them."

"I knew you'd figure something out." Ned met O.C.'s eyes and gave him a grin. "Think it'd be all right if you went over and hammered on one of them walls?"

"I guess."

"Well, get to beating on it and let's see if we can hear you out here."

John crossed the room and picked up the bed slat. Taking a good grip on the one by four, he slapped it sharply against the wall. Plaster dust exploded and revealed the lath underneath. He hit it again, and again, until he was out of breath.

"Did you hear any of that?" Cody asked. The dim over-head lights made the scene surreal, reminding him of the dark alleyway in Saigon where he shot a woman who was supposed to be his friend. He quickly repacked the painful thought for another time.

There was a long pause before Ned came back on the radio. "Nope. Is there another'n to hit?"

"Yessir, here we go again."

This time John went to the opposite wall and banged away, gaining momentum with each strike as his frustration and fear took over. After five minutes, Cody waved for him to stop. "Anything that time?"

"Nope. You boys are in a real pickle. We didn't hear a thing."

"Looks like we're back where we started."

"Remember, put yourself in George's place," Ned told him. "Where would he go? Where would a squirrel or an old coon den up?"

"I doubt it would be too low. I'd imagine he'd run for high ground."

Ned grinned at the men around him. He pushed the talk button again with a leathery forefinger. "That's right. He might have a den dug a little lower in there, but my guess is that he'll run to high ground if things get hot. That's what I'd do. That way he'll be able to get out easier. He's not going to get himself in a bind where he'll have his back to a wall with no way out."

"Glad you're here. We'll keep going up when we can."

"You do that. Hurry up. Top and Pepper here are about to freeze to death and it's sleeting. One good thing, though, is Kendal ain't in there no more. He got out, but that don't mean there ain't somebody else in there with y'all." Ned watched the tense faces of the deputies and wondered if he'd ever see Cody or John again. "Now, you boys be careful."

He handed the walkie talkie to Griffin and turned away from the Exchange, a hard lump in his throat.

Baker, the young academic officer, stuck out his hand. "Constable. I'm Malcom Baker. I heard a lot about you when I was growing up. I always wanted to be the kind of officer I heard you are."

"Well, thanks, but I ain't a constable no more."

O.C. turned from his conversation with a police officer and patted Ned's arm. "Yes, you are. I been meaning to tell you, ever since we got here tonight you're back on my payroll."

Ned was surprised. "Why, I retired and Cody was elected."

"You think I don't know that? But I'm a judge. I say you're a constable again. Raise your right hand."

"Now wait a goddamn minute," Sheriff Griffin snapped. "You can't do that."

Chief Mayhew bit his tongue. He realized the old judge meant business.

"I can, Griffin, and I'm-a doing it now because I'm the county judge. Ned, raise your right hand. Do you swear to uphold the laws of the state of Texas and this county and this country as a sworn constable of Lamar County."

"It ain't *legal*," Griffin argued.

Despite the cold, fear, and anger, Ned held his hand up and felt better than he had for months. "I shore do."

"Now you're a constable again and you're assigned to me, permanent."

Wearing adult-size coats, Top clapped and Pepper jumped up and down with joy. The lawmen gathered within hearing distance knew better than to respond in front of the furious sheriff, but they exchanged happy glances at the sudden outcome.

O.C. smiled at the kids, then frowned toward the Exchange. "I wish I had a badge to pin on you."

Top dug in his pocket. "Mr. O.C.?"

"What son?"

Top held out the little constable badge. "Here it is. You can pin it back on him right now."

Ned's blue eyes twinkled. "I wondered where that went."

"I been carrying it."

"I see that."

O.C. pinned the badge onto Ned's shirt pocket, near the seam. "Now you're official."

Ned raised an eyebrow at the kids. "Y'all are still gonna get a whoopin' when we get home, if we don't freeze to death first."

"If that don't beat all," Griffin said in disgust.

Chapter Forty

Rotting drifts of leaves filled the rain gutters. Vines rooted in the moist material and covered the potholed roof like a steadily creeping jungle fungus.

◇◇◇

Buoyed by the conversation, Cody carefully examined the two entrances. Ned was right. Signs had been there all along, plain as day when you knew what to look for. Now that Ned had reminded him, it all made sense. The descending passageway beckoned at a forty-five degree angle. He had no urge to go back down, so he chose the second tunnel, because it was marked with a clear indicator pointing upward.

The battery-fed overhead lights finally dimmed to darkness.

He clicked on the flashlight and illuminated the burrow barely big enough for their shoulders. "Uncle Ned says we're heading up. See that mark scratched there on that piece of cardboard? It points to where we need to go, just like he said. I can't believe I've been missing them."

"Well, there's a lot of trash in here, and it all seems to fill your eyes up."

"I'm sorry, John."

"You ain't got nothin' to be sorry for. Now, we oughta listen to Mr. Ned, and get ourselves out of here." The big man swallowed the lump that suddenly rose in his throat.

With Cody leading, they wriggled deep into the oppressive burrow once again. It eventually led into a man-size nest containing still another stained and filthy mattress littered with yellowed, rodent-shredded bills, letters, and receipts. Rats scurried to hide in the dark crevices.

"Nice bedroom."

"You want to rest?" John played his light across the mildewed mattress.

"Yeah, a long ways from here."

"Foller me."

John snapped the dying flashlight off and followed his partner into still another passage. Wiggling on their stomachs, it narrowed down so far they could barely move.

John inched forward. Each movement elicited a grunt, sounding as if they struggled with a great task. Cody's shoulder brushed what he felt was a doorframe, but it was hard to tell.

Minutes later, a highly polished but stubby wooden leg supported a solid roof only inches overhead. He heard John grunting along behind him. Momentarily forgetting himself, Cody rapped on what he took for plywood. The knock was answered by a slightly harmonic sound.

Cody gave a harsh laugh. "I don't believe it."

"Now what?"

"I'm under a piano. This fool has covered a piano and we're crawling underneath."

"Hope it don't fall on us." John remembered as a kid when he sat with other colored youngsters in the Grand Theater's balcony and watched cartoons where the characters dropped pianos on top of each other. "You don't see an anvil up there anywhere, do you?"

"I'll be damned." Cody picked up his pace. "I wouldn't have believed it."

"You found an anvil?"

John followed behind, scurrying as quickly as possible. He spilled into still another open space illuminated by Cody's flashlight. They found themselves standing in a dark room filled with bookcases.

"We're in a library!" John flicked his flashlight on and aimed it past the unusually sparse clutter.

Books extended to the ceiling without benefit of shelving, one row sitting squarely upon the others below. Roaches and silverfish moved freely among the volumes. Every square inch of wall space was packed tightly with moldy and mildewed books. The floor was covered with rotting papers and magazines. George had shaped a library in the litter.

"He was a reader all right." John moved the beam around the room.

"Incredible. Why did he keep this room open?"

"There ain't no tellin'."

Hundreds of volumes dealt with engineering and mathematics, evidence of a scientific mind. In the gloom, Cody was convinced that the secret to George's madness lay in the rotting pages.

The makeshift library felt as big as a rodeo arena after their travels through the crawlspaces. Cody gaped at the room's width and breadth, a rotting shrine to knowledge. He advanced cautiously, watching his footing, since many of the covers sloughed off under his feet.

John turned back the way they came. It was true. A grand piano was covered in books and bags of papers and magazines, leaving only the small burrow underneath as an entrance, or an exit. Awed by their surroundings, he stepped toward the nearest wall, reached out one hand, and gently tugged one of the thousands of shelved volumes toward him.

The movement caused the rows of rotting books to fall inward. The shift in pressure dissolved them into soggy mush, and they in sequence crushed their lower neighbors. With a wet sigh, the entire section melted into damp mush at their feet.

Casting his eyes upward, Cody gaped at the ceiling that bowed downward, like a canvas tarp full of water. He quietly placed a hand on John's arm and pointed up.

John glanced back toward the destroyed mound of pulp, following the structure with his eyes to its junction at the ceiling. It sagged even more, now that the delicate support was gone.

"We have to leave," Cody whispered, his eyes hard on the ceiling. "Now."

They moved as rapidly and carefully as possible across the room toward a dark doorway. Still too stunned to speak, they quickly entered another passageway which immediately narrowed and lowered overhead.

Crouching, their progress stopped when the burrow abruptly ended at a wall. Beneath Cody's nose, a black pit yawned, reflecting the light. He carefully reached down into the opening, fully expecting something to come roaring out of the darkness.

"What is it this time?" John feared the answer.

Cody's fingers felt water. Ripples distorted the light. When nothing bit him, Cody stuck his hand even deeper. "It's a damn bathtub full of water."

"What fer?"

"He's cut the floor out here under this wall and wedged an old claw foot bathtub underneath it." Cody examined the wall where it appeared to rest on the tub's edge. "This is a u-drain, like under a sink. Dammit! Wait a minute."

He suddenly realized the purpose of the tub. Still nervous about what might be in the murky water, Cody pushed his arm even deeper and bent his elbow to feel under the wall. The primordial fear of the opaque water was almost too much for him. He shivered, the hairs once again rising on the back of his neck. On the other side, his fingers emerged into the air. He splashed and quickly jerked his arm back.

"You aren't going to believe this, but to get past, we're gonna have to go underwater and come out the other side."

"Not gonna happen. Is there enough room for me to get by? I want to see this."

Cody pressed himself against the garbage, allowing John to ease past. He didn't care if John thought he was seeing things. One look at the bathtub was enough evidence.

"Uh uh. Ain't a-goin' in there."

To Cody's surprise, John doubled his fist and punched the plaster and lath above the tub. Determined, angry, and scared to death, John attacked the wall. Shards of lath exploded under his hammering fists. He recited a litany of curses, born of fear and frustration fueled by the last few hours in the honeycombed garbage heap.

Dust billowed in the yellow light. Tougher pieces refused to yield and John tore at them with his hands, grunting and cursing, finally kicking them out until he created an opening big enough to pass through.

Minutes later, exhausted and strangely satisfied, he turned back to Cody and jerked a thumb toward the ragged opening. "*Here's* the door."

Once the other side, Cody interpreted the symbols beside two burrow entrances. "This one."

Again on his hands and knees, he led the way, moving as quickly as the terrain would allow. The tunnel was pocked with cubbies and alcoves, each filled with items collected from the streets. Shoes, detergent boxes, empty prescription bottles, and folded city maps jammed the openings like offerings to strange gods of commerce. To their left, waxed bags full of an unknown putty-like substance bulged outward. John decided he'd rather not know what was inside.

"Goddlemighty!" Cody exclaimed and backed up quickly. His shuffling was accompanied by muffled curses.

"What? What?"

"Rats. These huge rats ran right over my hands. I can handle seeing them, but can't *stand* it when they touch me."

"Didja get bit?"

"No. But they scared the *shit* out of me. They ran from between all these bundles of newspaper up here and disappeared into the other side."

John rubbed his sweaty palms together. "What do you think scared them to come so close to us?"

Sweat dripped off Cody's nose. "I wish I knew."

They waited a few more minutes to settle their nerves. When nothing else appeared, they soon found themselves in a pocket with just enough room for the two officers to sit upright with their backs against the refuse, facing each other. Cody crossed his feet beside John's elbow and keyed his walkie-talkie.

Chapter Forty-one

Car fenders, an engine block in a puddle of grease, stacks of egg crates, bundles of material and cardboard boxes…

"I want you guys out of there," Griffin said into the radio. "This is a damned circus out here and y'all aren't making any headway."

"We'd love to come out," Cody told him, exchanging disgusted glances with John. "But we've already *told* you, *we don't know where we are*. This place is like a rotten apple full of worm holes. The only thing I know is that we're headed for the attic, if there is one. When we get there, we'll either find George or we can beat on the roof until someone hears and cuts us out."

"We're ready when you are."

They paused as a rustling sound jolted the tired, strained men.

"Rats again?" John wondered aloud.

"It's something alive."

"I believe we better get going." Without waiting, John turned and crawled into still another tunnel. Surprisingly wide and clear, it angled sharply upward through still another hole in the ceiling, putting him at the base of a set of dark wooden treads. John realized they were probably just below the attic.

He heard Cody huffing behind him and waited in the relatively open area. Cody soon emerged and John stood. He pointed at the stairs leading to a dark, open access. "Looky here."

"We finally found what we were looking for."

Cody keyed his walkie talkie. "Boss, we're near the roof. We're pretty sure now that our little friend has holed up in the attic."

Sheriff Griffin stared at the sleet bouncing off every hard surface within sight. The wind thrashed the trees, sending leaves raining down to mix with the ice. "What are you going to do? You have a plan?"

"Not much of one. We're just going up." Cody's voice quivered with tension.

Griffin scratched his neck and wished the night were over. "If the attic is empty I want y'all out immediately. Understood? Find the underside of the roof and beat on it until we locate you. I'll have my men ready to cut you out."

"You sound louder than you have since we came inside. There ain't as much static, so I bet we're about out. We'll let you know what we find."

They rested quietly for a moment. "Damn," Cody grunted.

"What?"

"I'm getting a fever blister."

John grinned. "I'll go. It's my turn."

"You sure?"

"No, but get out of my way before I lose my nerve." He cautiously climbed the creaking steps. Not knowing what was waiting for them, he held his revolver with the muzzle pointed upward. Cody knew full well that if anything happened, he would be virtually unable to help from his vantage point.

Pausing below the opening, John directed his dim yellow light onto open rafters.

"Careful." Cody kept his eyes on access, watching for movement that would indicate trouble.

When his light failed to initiate any response, John took another step higher and stopped.

"See anything?"

"Nope."

John gained another step and placed his left hand, the one with the flashlight, on the edge of the opening. He stepped again and slowly peeked into the attic, trying to see all directions at once. Finally, he sighed. "All right. I reckon I'm going in." He didn't notice the faint crack that released a counterweight and tipped a 55-gallon barrel onto its side. It crashed only feet away from the entrance and the metal lid popped off.

Half a dozen nearly dead snakes spilled near John's hand. They'd been without food or water for so long the reptiles were slow to respond. Some lay still. The largest, a rattlesnake, coiled weakly and shook its tail with a dry, dusty rattle.

A small copperhead regained its wits first and quickly struck at the first movement it saw. Lucky for John, the half-dead snake only managed to hang one fang in the meaty part of his thumb, but it was enough. Already wired to the limit, he jerked backward, slinging the snake toward Cody below.

"Snake! I've been bit. Aw! Damn, I've been snakebit." Stumbling backwards down the steps, John would have landed hard if Cody hadn't broken his fall. They went down in a tangle and Cody momentarily saw stars when his head cracked against the floor.

Tasting blood, he struggled to his feet and painted the light quickly around John's prone body until he found the disoriented snake. It moved lethargically, and had barely managed to turn over when Cody stomped again and again until it was unrecognizable.

He turned to John. "It's all right. Take it easy."

John's heart rate was already accelerated from fright, and it wouldn't take long for the venom to travel throughout his body. Cody had heard stories about people who ran themselves to death after being bitten by poisonous snake. Knowing the trip to St. Joseph's Hospital, only a few short blocks away was impossible, Cody reverted to his earlier training.

Kneeling, he again fished the razor sharp knife from his pocket and flicked the blade open with his thumb. It was hard to see in the failing light. "Hold still, this is gonna hurt." He grasped John's wrist, and made a small incision directly over the single puncture before John even registered the action. He jerked back at the stinging pain in his thumb, but Cody held tightly and made the second cut across the first.

Blood and clear venom leaked from the wound.

He picked up his flashlight and shined it on John's hand. "Keep that bleeding for a minute."

John's initial panic subsided and he consciously calmed himself, knowing what would happen if his heart didn't slow. He watched as blood dripped onto the paper below them.

Cody removed the lace from John's shoe and tied it in a slipknot around his thick forearm, firmly enough to indent the skin. "Don't pull the knot too tight. You need to loosen it every couple of minutes or so, or you'll get gangrene. This is supposed to help slow the spread of the poison."

Still frightened, John nodded.

"He only got you with one fang, and it didn't go too deep, so you may not have gotten a complete load. We'll be out of here pretty quick."

"I sho' do hope you're right."

"I am." He felt less confident than he sounded. John sank heavily to his haunches.

Knowing there was no other way, Cody climbed the steps, ready for anything. He repeated John's actions and carefully examined the entrance. At eye level, he could clearly see the barrel turned on its side, but because of his low angle, the snakes were virtually invisible. Not knowing what else to do, he probed the entrance with his light. When nothing happened, he risked a peek over the edge.

Two snakes lay belly up, obviously dead. Another weakly tried to crawl away. The rattler remained coiled, staring into the light with obsidian eyes.

"This is going to be loud."

He shot the rattler first. The .45's report was deafening. The snake separated two inches behind its triangular head. He shot at another, missed, then another. The reports hammered in the confined space as loud as grenades.

The last snake almost slipped away, but Cody vaulted over the edge and stomped it to death. Keeping one eye on a closed door at the far end of the attic, he returned to the trap door and called down to his partner. "Can you make it up the steps now?"

"All them snakes dead?"

"Yep."

"Then I can make it."

John climbed up and stepped delicately on the dusty raw planks, watching for live snakes and keeping an eye on the dead ones. He methodically kicked the limp bodies through the opening. "How much time do you think I have?" His hand was already swelling.

"That's up to you. How you feelin'?"

"I'm fine right now, except my thumb hurts where you chopped it open."

"It could have been worse."

"Prob'ly. Maybe it'll take a while for me to start feeling the poison."

Cody shrugged and glanced back at the door. "We have to get out and the only way is through there."

John glanced at a makeshift door at the far end of the attic and back to Cody. "You do it. I'll cover you."

A normal aisle led between furniture, trunks and bedsprings. "You're going to shoot past me in this?"

"No, but after this crazy feller shoots you and you drop, I'll shoot *him*."

"Thanks."

"Don't mention it."

"Here I go." Cody wiped his mouth. "Try to let *him* kill me, it'll read better in the paper." They knew that if George were in the attic, he would be ready. Cody cautiously approached the door.

The whisper of quiet rustling came again from the other side. "There's something back there," Cody said more to himself than anything else, realizing he'd been hearing a soft background noise, like the hiss or static from a television. He glanced at the wooden shiplap overhead. "That's sleet. We made it to the top."

"Well, we can't reach the roof from here."

"No, but it's angling down and I bet we can reach it once we get past this door." The rustling grew louder.

Bracing himself on one leg, he gave it a hard kick and drew back immediately. Deceptively easy, the door swung on well-oiled hinges. A crude guillotine of quarter inch steel plunged downward, then toppled inward.

Beyond the opening was still another nightmare created by a demented mind. Cody shivered at the vision of Hell. Recoiling, he stumbled backward in revulsion, barely keeping his feet. "Son. Of. A. Bitch!"

A large metal table sat in the middle of the room. Cody recognized it as an autopsy table by the drains around the edge. His head reeled at the sight of half-dried fluids, caked substances he dared not consider, and crusted galvanized buckets full of drying organs.

An ancient medical cabinet filled one entire corner, along with sinister equipment unfamiliar to the men. Dusty medical glassware lined the perimeter of the attic. For once, aisles between stacked boxes provided clear avenues to walk.

Looking down from the only vertical wall in a room full of angles, dozens of stuffed animal heads hung on mismatched boards, giving the impression of a mixed herd observing the scene with dry, dusty brown eyes.

The rustling noise they'd been hearing became louder as hundreds of rats scrabbled from burrows and holes to skitter across the dusty wooden floor. The earlier gunshots and the crash of the sheet metal panicked a swarm of terrified rats that had been feeding on the remains.

The rodent squeaks and scrabbling added to a much louder noise coming from the attic roof, now only a few feet overhead. With no insulation of any kind, the rattle of sleet was much, much louder.

They poured through the attic in a fluid mass and rushed toward the only opening large enough for them all to escape at one time, the area around John who knelt beside the trap door in the floor.

"Goddlemighty!" Cody jumped back and tripped. He landed hard and buried his face in his arms as the rats swarmed over him like a warm, hairy river.

Not knowing what was going on, John saw a wave of vermin covering his partner before they swirled around his body like filthy water, tumbling through the opening by the hundreds.

His finger involuntarily twitched on the trigger. The materials around them did little to deaden the sound, and the concussion pounded John's ears with more than enough force to momentarily deafen the deputy.

The bullet plowed through several escaping rats before it hit a sealed tin full of long-stored body parts in formaldehyde. It exploded, spewing vile, reeking contents into the small hovel.

Chapter Forty-two

Cotton mattresses, boxes of cotton sacks, thousands of 'toe sacks, unimaginable mountains of torn, dirty, stained, unusable clothing...

Cars, fire engines, and ambulances idled in the bitter cold, white exhaust boiling in clouds from hot exhaust pipes. With the heater going at full blast and waiting for James to make his way back to Chisum, Top and Pepper listened to the radio in the luxurious warmth of Ned's car.

Huddled in his yellow slicker against the sleet, Sergeant Blair broke away from a group of equally cold men. "Sheriff, we've got some more information on George and his son."

"OK what is it?" Griffin didn't take his eyes off the building. Ned and O.C. stepped closer to listen.

"George and his brother lost the funeral home nearly twenty years ago and moved here into the Exchange. Alvin hasn't been seen for most of that time, but he did visit Dr. Townsend once or twice, who said his mind was about gone."

"We know that. Is there more?"

"Well, George Hart was always a strange cat, and once they got out of the funeral business, and dodged going to jail, they stayed pretty much to themselves. Baker here has some more that he knows. Tell him."

Officer Baker had finally abandoned his own self-imposed dress code, loosened his tie and was wearing an oversize cloth coat. He pointed to a house beyond the railroad station. "I went over there and used those folks' phone to talk with my old professor, who made a few calls to a doctor he knows that works at the sanitarium in Tulsa. He told me Kendal Bowden Hart was sent there when he was a kid because he almost killed George Hart one night while he was asleep, to pay him back for sexual mistreatment."

"I'll be damned." O.C. slapped the back of one hand into the other. "That explains a helluva lot. That's what I couldn't dig up, and here he makes one little phone call up to the Territories and finds out."

Unsure of what O.C. was talking about, Baker continued, keeping an eye on the old judge. "Well sir, the doctor wasn't supposed to talk about this, but since Kendal got out and started killing folks, he figured we needed to know so we can catch him. Kendal's mental disease is worse than we imagined, and it's because, according to the doctor, for years George, and others, sexually mistreated Kendal. When Kendal tried to cut him up one night, screaming about human reanimation, George had him committed to the institution in Oklahoma."

Griffin turned his eyes to the deputy. "A crazy undertaker committing his crazy son? I guess Kendal came by it natural, but this gets nuttier by the minute."

Baffled by the professor's conversation, Ned cleared his throat. "What's human reanimation?"

"You've read the book or seen the movie *Frankenstein*?"

"Um hum. Saw that silly movie on television."

"The doctor said Kendal came at his daddy with a knife, saying he was going to cut him up and bring him back as a nice person. When he got to the hospital, Kendal told the doctors that others had mistreated him as well, and he intended to kill them all for what they done. He kept saying they all wanted to look, whatever that means."

"How'd all this happen without us knowing about it?"

"It's easy when they have someone committed like that," O.C. said. "George probably put him in the car and drove his crazy ass to Tulsa. Once the paperwork was done, and because Kendal was a minor, they sealed all the records and none of us could find anything about it, especially after Val Jackson got involved and knotted everything up with paperwork."

"What'n hell does he mean '*look*'?" Ned began, but was cut off by muffled gunfire coming from the Exchange.

Dampened by the storm, the shots sounded as if they originated near the roof. They had no way of knowing it was Cody shooting at snakes. From the outside, in the midst of a sleet storm, the idea was ludicrous.

The tired deputies jumped at the sudden noise. From Sheriff Griffin's right, a puff of smoke appeared from the ground near a police car. A tear gas grenade streaked toward a second floor window and crashed through the pane, lodging against the ancient paper window shade which immediately burst into flame. Fed by even more dry paper and wood, the blaze virtually exploded.

"Who fired that round?" Ned snarled and waved his hands. "Hold your fire, goddamn it! We've still got people inside. Griffin, get aholt of your men and get some water on that winder now!"

"Oh, lordy," O.C. whispered and turned to the now flaming window.

Griffin turned to his deputy. "Blair. Get those boys on the walkie talkie. Tell them the whole place is afire!"

"Already tried. No answer sir."

Helpless, O.C. wished he knew what to do. "They've tangled with something awful bad in there."

"I know those boys." Ned watched the firemen scramble in front of the brightly burning building. "Whatever it is, I'd hate to be on the business end of them pistols."

Chapter Forty-three

Stacks of telephone directories, an upright piano, a nine foot grandfather clock, a child's toy box, paper, wood, cedar chests, cloth material...all incredibly combustible...

"God, oh god!" John screamed. "What is all that?"

Cody lay on his back, gasping in horror. "I don't know, I don't know." Suddenly he remembered their reason for being in the attic. With an effort he rolled over and surveyed the room, aiming the pale glow of his flashlight and pistol at every corner, but knowing full well if George were present they would already be dead.

In the farthest corner of the attic, stacks of decaying medical books, files, and newspapers almost hid a stained mattress covered by bundles of rags.

Evidence of George's unstable mind rested on rough shelves lining the attic opposite the trophy heads; sealed glass jars full of human organs preserved in murky fluid.

In stark contrast, five clean bell jars were lined neatly on the obscene embalming table. Each sparkling jar contained a recently collected head floating in crystal clear liquid.

"What the hell?" Cody smelled the unmistakable odor of fresh moonshine whiskey that had been used as the preservative. Moving closer, the small bones of uncounted rats, picked clean of flesh, crunched under his boots.

The covered jar on the left contained the wide-eyed face Cody recognized from wanted posters as Kevin Jennings, the owner of the body he and Ned had pulled out of the Red River only days before. The second trophy trailing a very fine tendril of blood in the clear liquid was Josh Brooks. Next was that of the missing person reported by his wife, Merle Clark, then Randal Wicker. The last, bearded and wrinkled beyond imagination from a lifetime of abuse and neglect, was George Hart.

Cody stared at Hart's dead, dull eyes. "What the hell have you started here?"

In the center of the stained mattress Cody finally recognized the bundle of rags as George's emaciated trunk. Lying at a contorted angle, he was dressed in ragged shorts, work brogans, and layers of shirts. A burlap sack resembling a shawl was pinned at the stump of his throat with a garish broach. The rats had been busy with George's corpse, but Cody realized it wasn't all there. Understanding dawned, and he knew the drying organs beside the filthy embalming table belonged to George.

"Kendal did for you, didn't he, Hart? But for what? What did you do to *him*?"

"You talking to me?"

Cody turned toward John and swallowed. "Naw, just talking to a dead man is all."

John panned his weak flashlight over the mounts ranging from whitetail deer, to elk and wild boar, to sable antelope and kudus. "I don't know why you people always want to put trophies on the walls."

The observation made Cody grasp the clear explanation to the human heads floating in jars mere feet away. "Kendal's daddy collected those kinds of trophies, and it looks to me like the son of a mortician was collecting his own. Now we partly know why he took those heads."

"You reckon that's George?"

Cody studied the grisly head for a long moment. "Yep, that's him right there." He paused with a stunned look on his face. "My god, John. I know what this is all about now. George did all this to keep *Kendal* out, not us. He's crazy all right, but in his own way, because he spent all these years building his version of a fort. He did something to that boy and knew Kendal would eventually come after him, and this is how he intended to stay safe!"

John ran a shaky hand across his sweaty face. "Well it backfired and Kendal still got in and killed him for sure."

"There's no telling what he did to Kendal to make him so afraid his own kid would come back to kill him. My god, undertakers are scary enough when they're normal, but what'n hell did he do?"

"My people heard stories, but they didn't intend to spread nothin' that wasn't theirs to tell. White folks wouldn't have listened no-how, but it don't make no difference now, we need to get out of here so we don't end up the same way."

"He's done now that George is dead. Kendal sucked us into this nightmare after he finished his collection because we got too close to him on the outside. He's gone."

Curious and light-headed, John breathed the fetid air through his open mouth. He knelt on the floor as the poison made him dizzy. "Lord have mercy."

Chapter Forty-four

All or most of it combustible...

The entire front of the structure virtually burst into flame as decades of loose paper ignited with ferocity no one outside would have predicted. Smoke and crackling flames sucked through the network of burrows, racing through the Exchange. The highly combustible refuse was flawlessly ventilated, creating the perfect bonfire.

The result was nothing less than catastrophic.

"Keep trying to get those boys on the radio!" Sheriff Griffin shouted. "Tell them to get out the back way!"

The scene on the street was chaotic. More fire trucks screeched into position as firemen frantically unrolled hoses and turned streams of water into the billowing smoke. Smoke boiled from the windows and seeped in roiling clouds from under the eaves.

Ned could already tell there was no way to contain the conflagration.

A white curtain of sleet descended in a hissing rattle, bouncing off the firemen's protective gear and gathering in drifts. Water that didn't turn to steam ran down the façade and gathered in pools before draining into the gutters sluggish with ice. Vapor from the tailpipe of every vehicle in the area added to the misty scene.

Anxious and frustrated that he could do nothing for the men inside the Exchange, Ned paced and talked to himself. O.C.

desperately wanted to go to his old friend, but knew there was nothing he could do or say. For the moment, they felt powerless, forced to allow others to work while they simply stood by, and fidgeted, and watched.

From inside, squeals and detonations disclosed the existence of containers exploding in the heat. Fire raced through the burrows, quickly reaching every floor.

The crackling roar increased and glass shattered.

O.C. blamed himself for sending the young, untested constable to the Exchange.

Sheriff Griffin blamed himself for not handling the situation better and wondered how badly the outcome would affect the next election.

Chief Mayhew blamed himself for not taking a stronger role in the events leading up to the fire. "Back those cars up! Get them away from the fire."

Ned blamed himself for allowing John and Cody to enter the building. He watched the firemen direct another hose onto the flames. "Get that water up higher! That's where they'll come out if they can! They'll head for the roof!"

The fireman turned sad eyes toward the old constable. His look crushed all Ned's hope. "We're doing the best we know how, sir."

O.C. stepped up beside Ned. "Let 'em work, Ned."

"Them boys are still in there. They'll burn." Ned wiped tears with the heels of his hands.

"The good Lord'll get them out, that's what Miss Becky would say, wouldn't she?"

"You're right about that, but she's always been stronger than me in that way." His eyes dropped down to Andrews' smoking legs. "My god, what's next?"

Slowly, reluctantly, they backed away from the increasing heat as the fire became a living thing, consuming all it touched.

Chapter Forty-five

Smoke from the fire filtered into the tunnels. Fresh air from George's ingenious ventilation system fed the flames, turning the bizarre design into a giant, self-fed blowtorch.

The shrieking mass of rats fleeing the smoke-filled tunnels below once again engulfed them, pouring back through dark unseen openings like water. The two horrified lawmen jumped to their feet, but John immediately fell back to his knees, struck with weakness from the poison circulating through his system.

His head swam. "What the hell is happening?"

Smoke billowed into the attic. The crude ventilation system Cody had suspected was very real and efficient, pulling in fresh air to feed the ferocious fire below. Cody knocked a large rat off his leg using his flashlight as a club. "This place is on fire!" He grabbed John's arm and struggled to pull him upright.

"The roof! We have to break through now!" Rats, mice, rotting human body parts, and bitter, toxic smoke nearly pushed Cody's tired mind to the edge. With an effort from deep within he choked down the panic that rose like bile. His eyes focused on the lowest section of the roof sloping to within reach.

"I need to call them so they won't shoot us when we break through the roof!" Cody pushed the button the walkie talkie. "Boss, you there? Hey, somebody answer this thing!" He shook the walkie talkie, not realizing he'd accidentally turned it off.

Another rat clawed up his leg, and he danced sideways to kick it off.

John tried to clear his mind. He staggered weakly to his feet and kicked his way to the closest underside slope of the roof. Cody picked up a plastic palm tree with one hand and slapped at the rats trying to climb John's legs.

"No more!" Cody shouted and dropped the tree. He aimed his pistol upward, emptying the magazine into the shiplap only inches above their heads. When the slide locked open on the big .45, he ejected the clip, slammed another one home and repeated the process, finishing the ragged circle. When the slide locked back again, he snatched Ned's six-shooter from behind his belt and emptied it as well to further weaken the wood.

Despite his weakness, John understood his role. He pushed Cody aside and punched at the dark, splintered boards with his huge fist. He quickly broke out a large section only to find a layer of sheet iron still holding them prisoner.

"Son of a *bitch*!" Cody shouted.

As smoke filled the attic, the rats retreated from the two men and scrabbled for escape through a hole in the corner behind George's rotting corpse. As more and more squirming bodies piled on the remains, George sank deeper into the vile, soaked mattress.

Chapter Forty-six

Fire, everywhere, fire…

◇◇◇

Sheriff Griffin stood huddled miserably in the cold. Sleet had finally beaten the leaves off the surrounding trees and turned the world white around them. The fire moved at an unimaginable rate and quickly overwhelmed the puny efforts of the small town fire department.

"Can't you get anything on the radio?" he shouted over the wind. Flames shot out of the windows as the inferno ran wild.

Ned could barely contain himself. "Get that water higher!"

"You let me do my job!" a fireman shouted.

Behind the firemen, dozens of men surged forward, offering to help. O.C. held his hands toward the crowd of civilians, both black and white. "There ain't nothin' y'all can do. We don't have any more hoses, and a bucket brigade would be like pissin' on the fires in Hell. Let these men do what they know to do, and y'all get ready to start emptying them houses here on this side before the fire jumps the street."

The conflagration was a physical presence the men felt, and heard, and smelled. It roared with an angry life of its own. The north wind blew a toxic cloud over the emergency responders and the crowd of onlookers.

Fire Chief Nate Jackson crunched through the sleet and stopped beside O.C. "The fire won't jump, not in this sleet storm. But what we're breathing might kill us all. *We* can't leave, but these people need to get out of here."

"I know it, but John's in there and they're anxious. They don't know what to do."

"They can pray."

"You can bet they're already a-doin' it."

"Chief Jackson! There's smoke coming from that house over there."

O.C. turned from the shout to see a small frame house across the street from the train station. Smoke boiled from vents in the pier and beam foundation, and around loose, ill-fitting wooden windows. "Jackson, I thought you said the fire wouldn't jump in this storm."

"It won't. It couldn't have!"

"Well it by-god did!"

"I bet somebody left the stove on and it caught fire. I'll get somebody in there."

Chapter Forty-seven

The well-fed flames turned The Cotton Exchange into a five-story hell smack in the middle of Chisum, Texas.

Cody finally realized he'd turned the walkie talkie off. He flicked the switch. "Boss, you there?"

The radio crackled to life in his hand. "Yeah, son, we're here. Y'all have to get out! The building is on fire!"

"No sh…," Cody began. He was cut off as an explosion in the attic not far away partially took out a section of the roof.

A potato chip can, tightly packed with gunpowder, nails and pieces of metal, worked perfectly. George's deranged mind planned for it to take out at least one person and hopefully more. But his plans hadn't covered the unlikely event the device would be covered by a body and hundreds of rats. As the corpse collapsed inward, the metal trigger released with an audible click. The explosion that should have showered the interior of the attic with deadly shrapnel was absorbed by the mass of rats, and George's own rotting body. Deflected like a giant shotgun shell, most of the blast went straight up.

Cody staggered and caught himself. He was covered with a fine red spray. Most of the blood was from the rats, but a few small pieces of steel struck his right side.

John was luckier. From the corner of his eye he'd seen the mass collapse and remembering what Cody had said about booby traps, crouched just as the corner exploded.

The radio in Cody's hand cracked through a coating of red. "What's going on in there? John! Cody!"

Coughing from the smoke, Cody tried to answer but something was wrong with the radio. He glanced down and saw the send button was completely gone, along with a chunk of his right thumb.

The wound was numb for the moment, but he knew it would only be a few minutes until feeling came screaming back into the damaged hand.

"You all right?" John's words were muffled through eardrums hammered by the explosion.

Mentally disconnected and also half-deaf, Cody turned toward the center of the attic, barely registering his partner through the swirling smoke. Holding up his damaged hand, his eyes filled with tears. "Define all right."

The new hole in the roof acted as a flue, drawing more thick smoke into the dark attic. Another dampened sound was added to the melee. They instinctively realized if the sound had penetrated their damaged eardrums, it was monstrous and terrible.

It was the roar of an oxygen-fed blow torch.

"Get out that hole!" Cody shouted and pointed to the opening. "The fire will be here any second!"

The flames roared up the tunnel like an open furnace.

Chapter Forty-eight

An open volume by Robert Frost burst into flame and the words, "Some say the world will end in fire, some say in ice," were consumed...

From their position overlooking the backside of the Exchange, the two riflemen were temporarily blinded by the detonation. Blinking to clear their sight, the youngest of the two keyed his military walkie talkie as flame and smoke billowed into the storm. "Boss, this is Red. I thought for a minute the whole roof back here blew out."

Griffin strained to see through the smoke and flames. "Any idea what's going on?"

"Nope. Somebody was shooting holes in the roof, but there was an explosion about forty feet away. I can't hardly see a thing from the flash and the smoke...wait a minute." He stopped and closed his eyes for a moment, then opened them and peered through the scope again. "Jeeze!"

Another explosion blew out the right front corner of the Exchange, taking out most of the major support on that side. The front of the warehouse sagged and fell outward. The firefighters dropped their hoses and ran. The crowd outside finally saw for the first time what the interior was like, as if someone had ripped the outside corner off a wax paper milk carton, revealing an ant burrow made from trash.

Every eye strained to see, hoping they wouldn't find their fellow deputies in the rubble. Flames roared outward, burning hot and bright.

On the opposite side, aiming over the roof's ridge line, the rifleman tightened the sling wrapped around his wrist, positioned the stock snugly against his shoulder and lined the crosshairs on the ragged hole.

Though the volume of sleet was already steady, the skies opened, and ice pellets rattled so hard the brick building was nearly obscured across the street.

The horrific sight emerging onto the roof shocked Red. He was back on the radio in a second. "Sir, I've got two people crawling through the smoke onto the roof through about a million rats that are coming from everywhere and sliding right over the edge."

Griffin clutched the radio in a white-fisted grip. "Do not fire, deputy. Do not fire! What do you see? Are they our men?"

The second rifleman squinted through his scope and two completely unidentifiable, smoke-blackened apparitions crawled out of the hole.

"I can't tell yet."

Griffin cursed. Would nothing go right this night? "Hold your fire unless they shoot first, understood deputy?"

"Yessir."

Ned snorted in disgust. "Oh hell, Griffin. Ask that boy if one of them is a skinny white kid and the other one a big *black* bastard."

Chapter Forty-nine

The fire was out of control, intensified by accelerants such as kerosene, paint thinner, alcohol, gas, and oil. Support beams, studs and joists weakened and collapsed…

John crawled out first, pushed from behind by Cody. As soon as his partner rolled out, Cody hauled himself onto the frozen roof, cutting himself on the jagged edges of the metal blown outward by the explosion. They immediately slipped toward the edge, and the drop five stories below. Luckily, the ice hadn't yet formed a strong crust. Cody jammed his boot heels into the rusting sheet iron to gain a foothold. John slipped for a terrifying second before his shoe sole caught against a nail that had worked its way free over the years.

With those precarious anchors, they lay gasping in the sleet. Their breath made thick clouds in the cold air.

Flame shot outward and then sucked back inside to be replaced by thick, acrid smoke. The ice beneath their bodies quickly melted from the intense heat only inches below. With a groan Cody closed his eyes and lay still for a moment, oblivious to the sleet stinging his face, and the increasing temperature underneath.

The wind sucked the black smoke from the hole, blowing it away behind them toward the front of the Exchange. Cody twisted to look back over his shoulder. Flames leaped into the night air.

"We need to get off this roof before the fire catches us."

"How we gonna get down?"

Cody peered through the curtain of sleet and saw two men waving from the roof of a house just across the street. It felt odd to wave back, but he raised a hand, and then saw the rifles. "They had a couple of snipers over there, watching."

"Think they'll shoot?" John closed his eyes under the clean, icy downpour.

"They better not. Not after all that."

Chapter Fifty

The fire fed indiscriminately…

◇◇◇

Griffin's radio crackled to life. "Sheriff, it's them. Our guys crawled through the roof and they're working their way to the edge. Send us a ladder truck around here real quick."

"Well, *glory!*" Ned shouted.

O.C. clapped in applause. The men surrounding the car radios heard the good news and a cheer went up around the Exchange.

Griffin nearly leaped for joy. "Great! Keep an eye on 'em."

"Yessir."

Sheriff Griffin turned to the only reporter he trusted. "Our boys are out. We'll have a statement for you in a few minutes."

The *Chisum News* reporter nodded. "I appreciate that. Do you have a statement about the house?"

Griffin went cold. "What house?"

"The one across the street here. Someone noticed smoke coming out of it a few minutes ago and I heard a fireman say it's blocked like the Exchange." He pointed to the house now totally engulfed in flame.

Griffin turned around and watched the firemen direct their hoses onto the little structure behind them. Flames licked along the eaves and smoke boiled from the windows.

"No. I don't have a thing to say, except it looks like it's on fire."

Minutes later, Griffin heard a shout and saw Cody and John get out of a police car and limp toward Ned. O.C. put his hand out to hold Griffin in place. Ned rushed forward on shaky knees and met them halfway.

His stomach unclenched with relief when he finally hugged them. "You boys look like you've been through the wringer."

"Yeah, and now I know just what that means." Cody let the old lawman hang on for as long as he wanted.

Ignoring O.C.'s orders not to watch, the kids saw the two filthy men step behind the safety of the cars and fire trucks. They shot out of the car and raced through the crowd, nearly knocking Cody down.

"Uncle Cody!" Pepper grabbed his waist. "You're safe! And *damn*, you stink!"

Top hugged him tightly. When he saw John alone, leaning against a police car, the boy let go of Cody and tapped Big John's leg. "You all right?"

Exhausted, he grinned down at the youngster and roughed his hair. "I am now."

"Y'all don't go in that other house." Top pointed at the smoke across the street. He'd been watching the firemen as they fought the flames.

"Not likely," Cody agreed.

Smoke billowed from the storm drains as slush poured in. The rich odor of burning pitch from hundred year old pine almost smelled good, compared to the filthy air they'd been breathing all night.

"Griffin!"

The sheriff turned toward Cody's voice.

"Kendal didn't get in and out through the Exchange. That house is the entrance. There's a tunnel under there which connects everything and he walked in and out of there as open as you please, probably passing right by y'all and laughing the whole time. Let it burn Griffin, just like the Exchange. Both fires will burn everything clean and we'll be shut of all this."

John didn't comment. Two ambulance drivers rolled a stretcher toward the worn out lawmen and he sat down to let the cold, clean air wash over his tired, filthy body.

"He's been snakebit," Cold told one of the drivers.

"What?"

"John was bit by a copperhead in there. Y'all need to get him to the hospital."

"We're waiting on someone to take him."

Cody stood. "You take him now. The ambulance is sitting right there."

"He's colored."

Cody saw red. He grabbed the man's coat and threw him to the side. "Get him to a doctor!"

Two colored men in overalls stepped forward and took John by his arms. "We'll take him, Mister Cody."

"I ain't-a goin' to no hospital." Feeling fuzzy, John shook his head. "Ain't a goin'."

The tallest man in khakis and a red cloth coat didn't like that idea at all. "You'll die, or at least you'll lose that thumb."

John wiggled his swollen fingers. "Take me to Miss Sweet. She's been curing snake bites all her life. She knows what to do."

"You gonna make it, Cody?" John had no intention of leaving until he was sure Cody was all right.

"I'll be fine."

"Then I reckon I'll go." Without another word, they hurried the big deputy into an old car that shot off south of the tracks, detouring way around the burning house the firemen had all but abandoned.

The ambulance driver regained his feet and disappeared into the crowd. A policeman handed Cody a cardboard cup of lukewarm coffee.

Griffin finally joined him, shifting his weight from one foot to the other. "What did you find in there?"

The tired young constable sipped the weak brew and contemplated the burning house while a different ambulance driver wrapped his thumb and examined the shallow wounds in his chest and side. "Dead people, or parts of them."

He told Griffin about what they'd encountered in the house of horrors. When he finished, a crowd of silent men had gathered to listen. "We didn't find Alvin, but I have a good idea it was him we smelled when me and Andrews moved that first bale of papers. If they can get that fire put out, I imagine you'll find his body not too far from the front door. He probably just died and George left him, or he might have been able to move enough to drop one of the deadfalls on himself. If that happened, George wouldn't have been able to get him out, so he probably just left him."

"Did you ever get a look at Kendal?"

"Never laid eyes on the man, but I think we heard him a few times. You said he got out."

"We believe he did, but we haven't found him yet."

"Them reporters keep asking to talk to somebody," Sergeant Blair interrupted. He nodded toward the jostling crowd gathered behind the barricades.

Griffin shrugged. "I'm not talking to the bastards."

Ned's eyes flicked toward the Sheriff.

"Here comes Wayne Brewer." Blair recognized the Channel 12 News reporter, followed by a cameraman.

"Dammit."

Ned frowned at his grandchildren. "Y'all need to get back in the car where it's warm."

Pepper pulled the oversize coat up tight around her neck. "I know."

"Grandpa?" Top tapped his grandfather on the side.

"You too, boy."

"I know, but I have something to tell you."

The old man looked down at the worried boy. "Hum?"

"I know where that Kendal feller might be."

Chapter Fifty-one

Before I could explain my idea, flames and small explosions shot from holes cut in the foundation of the Exchange as even more booby traps cooked off. The deputies waited where it was safe behind their cars and watched the firemen work. Great clouds of white steam rose up against the low, heavy clouds.

The heat drove everyone back, and they moved the whole shebang back past the tracks. The two ambulance drivers tried to talk Uncle Cody into going to the hospital, but he wouldn't leave.

"Not until I know John's all right."

"*You're* going to the hospital right now," Grandpa told Uncle Cody, looking at the huge white bandage on his hand that was blooming red. "You need to get your own thumb worked on. John's gone to Miss Sweet and she'll doctor him up just fine."

Uncle Cody flashed us a grin that told me everything was going to be all right. "Blair called and Norma Faye is on the way. I ain't riding in no ambulance that won't take John. She'll carry me to get it stitched up, and then I'm gonna sleep for a week."

"All right, then. There she is now."

The terrified redhead I still had trouble thinking of as Aunt Norma Fay rushed through the crowd and nearly knocked Cody over in her relief. He gave her that grin that I still practiced in the mirror and held her with his good arm while the ambulance drivers stood around looking like they didn't know what to do.

She was crying and carrying on, and I knew that someday I'd have me a wife that wore tight shirts and made a fuss over me if I got hurt.

"Sheriff Griffin!" A television reporter finally squeezed through the crowd and got close enough to the sheriff for questions. "Why aren't you trying to save that house?"

"It's beyond help."

"I see that, but do you have any comments about that house on the other side of the tracks?"

Griffin turned on his heel, and only I heard the comment the reporter could have built a career on. "I hope it burns to the ground and takes the rest of this sorry end of town with it."

Grandpa didn't hear it either. He was ready to go. "They don't need us anymore."

Mr. O.C. took one last look at the Exchange. Fire shot from every window. Tall, graceful flames leaped from the collapsed roof and almost touched the low clouds. Smoke and steam caught against those same clouds and spread overhead. In the spotlights, thick streams of water from the firemen's hoses crisscrossed, but did little to slow the fire.

A rumble in the distance made everyone stop. I saw panicked looks on the faces of the men around us, and then the railroad lights began to flash as the crossing arms started to come down.

"God almighty!" Mr. O.C. yelled. Cars were parked both on and very close to the tracks. One ambulance sat almost on the rails.

I've never seen anything happen so fast in my life. Men shouted, women screamed and half a dozen people ran toward the cars and trucks on the tracks. In the distance, I saw the engine's headlight through the falling sleet, bright and round, coming fast.

The train whistle shrieked, adding to all the noise, yells, the flashing lights on the cop cars and fire trucks, and people running every which-a-way. A truck plowed through a wooden crossing arm, knocking it spinning. A couple of men opened a car door, shifted it out of gear, and slipping and sliding on the ice, pushed it off the tracks where it rolled across the street and into the side of the house that was still burning.

The whistle shrieked again, this time sounding to me like it was scared. Grandpa grabbed me and Pepper and held us still. In seconds it was upon us, and we felt the wind from its passing.

It was a fast moving passenger train and I saw shocked faces at the windows when the cars flashed past the burning Cotton Exchange. Colored lights and the fire flickered on the shiny cars' steel skin. Cold wind blasted against us and seconds later, they shot down the tracks and were gone.

Just then one whole corner of the building slumped, collapsing in a blaze of sparks as decades worth of trash burned uncontrollably. We felt the intense heat as Grandpa and Mr. O.C. hurried us kids into the car and finally away from the nightmare.

We slid into the back seat of Grandpa's car and some men moved the barricades. Grandpa didn't stop until we reached the town square. The norther had already moved on through, and the sleet tapered off, but it was still painfully cold. Melting ice from the tall buildings around us splashed onto the concrete. Paper trash washed along the gutters. I wondered if the drains were helping put out the fires back behind us, down deep underground.

I'd never seen the square so late at night. It was empty and with all the sleet on the ground, it made me think of Christmas, which was still over a month away. The car hadn't had time to warm up good, and the side and back windows were still fogged.

Grandpa angled into a stop beside the big icicle-covered fountain in the middle of the square and shifted the car out of gear. Grandpa and Mr. O.C. needed to get cleaned up and rested, but they wanted to hear what I had to say, too. He turned around so he could see me sitting behind Mr. O.C. "All right, tell us what you know."

I have to admit, it made me feel pretty big to have those two old men pay so much attention to me. "Well, you remember when we went fishing last summer, while it was still cool?"

"Does fishing have anything to do with all this and Kendal Bowden?"

"I reckon it might."

"You're so full of bull your ears stink." Pepper rolled her eyes as I tried to explain my thoughts so's they'd understand. She shrank back when Grandpa turned his expressionless blue eyes on her. When they were dead like that, it always scared us to death. "I meant… he's just talking out his a…he wants attention."

"He's got it, Missy, now you hush a minute," Mr. O.C. said. "Go on Top."

"We were following that deer trail, remember, when that little old mama quail took to flying crooked like she was hurt?"

Grandpa nodded. "I remember."

Early one summer afternoon, right after our troubles at the Rock Hole, me and Grandpa slipped off to go fishing on the river. We threw a couple of Zebco 33s into the truck bed and drove through the bottoms, past the fields until Grandpa pulled under a wide pecan tree not far from the timber leading down to the river bank.

He parked beside a cultivator and shut off the engine. It ticked quietly as the motor cooled and we got our fishing rods from the truck bed. It was pretty warm in the sun, but a lot cooler in the woods. Grandpa led the way and I followed down a game trail leading down to the river.

When we came to a small clearing in the trees, I nearly jumped out of my skin when a quail flushed from cover almost at our feet. But instead of whirring away like they do on a covey rise, the little bird fluttered and tumbled across the clearing, dragging one wing.

"That bird's hurt." I dropped my fishing rod and darted around Grandpa. "I bet I can catch her."

"Bet you can't." He stopped and waited in the shade. He was right. Every time I got within inches of the quail, she regained her strength and flapped away on the ground, barely out of reach. I chased her across a little meadow and into the trees, always a foot or two away, but never close enough to get ahold of her. I finally gave up and walked back to Grandpa's shade.

"Where's the bird?"

"It got away."

"I knew it would."

"How'd you know? I wanted to catch it and see what's wrong."

"There wasn't nothing wrong, son. That bird isn't hurt, she's trying to lead us away from her nest. All that commotion is to get your attention, so that you'll see her and nothing else."

"How do you know that?"

"'Cause I'm old. Come here and mind where you put your feet." He led me a few yards off the game trail. "Now, stand right here for a minute." It didn't take more than a few seconds until he found what he was after. "Here it is."

I joined him beside a thick clump of tall bluestem grass hiding a neat little nest containing nearly a dozen tiny eggs.

"That's what she was trying to lead you away from. Birds and animals know how to protect their young'uns. She acted like she was hurt to draw us away from her eggs in this here nest."

"Will she come back?"

"Sure will. As soon as we're gone, she'll be right back to set. Before long there'll be a bunch of little bitty quail running around here."

"Let's wait for her."

"Nope. I'm of a mind to catch us a mess of catfish for our supper tonight. I don't intend to waste any time waiting for no mama quail to come back to her nest."

I filed that experience away and followed Grandpa Ned down to the river, where we caught half a dozen blue cats before a thunderstorm drove us back to the truck.

That's how I knew what Kendal was doing, because I saw a little ol' mama bird do the same thing.

Mr. O.C. scrunched his face up, like he was about to bust as I told him the story, but he kept listening.

"You said she wasn't really hurt, she was leading us away from her eggs, Grandpa. You said all birds and animals did that sort of thing. Well, when Kendal got away, it felt the same way to me, but different."

I struggled with the words. I knew what I wanted to say, but it didn't seem to make any sense out in the open, like a nightmare that scares you to death in the dark and still seems real when you're first waking up. Then, when you're sitting up in bed the next morning and want to tell someone about it, the whole thing feels silly.

"It seems to me like that Kendal feller ain't been seen one time, but when y'all got too close to his nest somewheres, he led you away…up here to the Cotton Exchange."

Pepper couldn't contain herself. "That's stupid. He wouldn't have led everybody to where he's hiding if he wanted to lead them right back away from it."

"Hush for a second, Pepper," Grandpa said softly. He turned to Mr. O.C. "He's half right. I think Kendal has been hiding in the bottoms, because that's where his people are and that's where Cody has been looking. But when he got too close, Kendal lit out and led us away from his nest straight to the place where his old man went crazy twenty years ago. He knew them tunnels, because he learned them after he killed his old man when he got back to town, then he led Cody into an ambush. Now Kendal thinks he's dead and he went back to Center Springs while everyone is here in town."

I heard Pepper take a quick breath. "Grandpa, when we were sitting with Mr. Martin while he was dying, he said he saw somebody slipping around his place one day that he didn't recognize and the way they walked reminded him of family. He said how funny it was that our people all lived within a mile or two of one another."

"What does *that* mean?" I was frustrated that Pepper was going in an entirely different direction.

"*That* means, stupid, that Kendal Bowden …."

"…is in the bottoms for sure." Grandpa said.

"Sounds right to me, Ned." Mr. O.C. shivered and reached over to turn up the heat. "There's folks down there that will hide kin, no matter who they are or what they do. I'll call up to Tulsa and see what else I can find out from the hospital while you poke around and see what you can kick up."

"Well, it ain't gonna happen quick. They'll lie for sure, and hide him out with somebody else until the coast is clear."

Mr. O.C. turned back toward the clearing windshield. "Then Cody'll have to keep an eye peeled, along with a constable fresh out of retirement."

Chapter Fifty-two

Grandpa and I went to the store a couple of days later. The norther had done its job, bringing in fall. He called it jacket weather, because even though it warmed up during the day, the nights were cold and everybody needed more than shirt sleeves.

It was my idea to go, because I overheard Grandpa and Bill Morris talking at the post office the day before about how Center Springs was slowly dying. I was always interested in history, and the conversation had wandered from the long gone Rawhide Theater to the blacksmith shop that my great-granddad once owned. When Mr. Morris said Uncle Neal's store was once the original courthouse for Center Springs, it brought the building into a new light.

Grandpa sat on the two-by-six that served as a combination seat and porch rail, talking to a collection of the local farmers. I went inside and slowly turned round and round, trying to get a feel for the old building when it was a courthouse.

On my last spin, I saw a little wooden tray full of loose cigarettes on the counter.

We called them onesies, and I remembered that Pepper had snitched a couple of them a few days back. Uncle Neal was running the slicer with his back to me, cutting rat cheese. On impulse, I dug a quarter out of my pocket and laid it on the cigarettes. Twenty-five cents was way too much in repayment, but it made me feel better.

I'd barely gotten my hand back down when he turned around with the cheese wrapped in white paper. "Well howdy Top. I bet you could use a cold drink." He glanced down and picked up the quarter with a slight frown. He used a blunt forefinger to punch at a key on the cash register. He hit a larger key with the heel of his hand. The cash drawer popped open with a loud chunk and he dropped the quarter into the tray and removed a dime. "Here, get you a drink."

That's how he was. Everybody said Uncle Neal was tighter'n Dick's hatband, but he always had something for us kids. I wasn't going to turn down a free RC, even though it was my quarter. The drink box was beside the front door and I'd already dropped the dime into the slot and was sliding the RC bottle along the metal track to pull it out when I heard Pepper's voice.

I popped the cap on the opener, and went outside. She'd apparently walked to the store and was sitting on the opposite end from Grandpa, talking to Cale Westlake, a kid I'd gotten into a fight with a few months before. I stopped outside the door and he saw me. I could tell he wanted to punch me again, but he turned his back and kept talking with Pepper.

I didn't want any trouble, so I sat down on the wooden steps to listen, off to the side so I wouldn't be in anyone's way coming in and out of the store. Grandpa was standing at the far end of the porch, near the domino hall, so he could see up and down the highway and the oil road behind the store at the same time.

"I'd never seen nothing like what was in that old Exchange building."

Mr. Ty Cobb Wilson was whittling on the pine two-by-six seat with his pocketknife as he listened to the conversation. The legs on his overalls were full of sheep burrs, because him and his twin brother Jimmy Foxx spent most of their time hunting.

"Say it was full of trash?"

Grandpa was wearing his bib overalls like the other men. The only thing different was the constable badge pinned on his blue shirt once again. "That's what Cody said, and from what I saw when the front fell off in the fire, that place was packed as tight as if you'd jammed a 'toe sack into a coffee can. Then them crazy fellers either dug tunnels through that mess, or they made them while they was filling the place up. Damnedest thing I'd ever seen."

"But the one y'all are chasin' got away."

"Sure did. Old George and his brother Alvin didn't make it out, but George was already dead when Cody and John got to him. Kendal had cut his head off, too. They found what was left of his brother's burned body this morning, but it wasn't the fire that killed him. Cody was right. He was crushed to death under a pile of junk that fell on him a while back. They know, because…well, because there wasn't any flesh left on the body. He'd already rotted away. Anyhow, Kendal got out and we're still trying to find him."

"Is that George's kid?"

"Yeah. He was in the nervous house up in Oklahoma and got away. There's a lot of folks after that nut."

Jimmy Foxx shifted to lean his back against a support post. He stretched his legs along the rail and crossed his feet. I could see that he wasn't wearing socks. He stuck his finger in a hole in the leg of his overalls and scratched. It was unusual to see the brothers during the day. They usually ran the bottoms, hunting whatever would run from them.

"That feller was always odd, even when he was kid. I was never able to put my finger on it, but he just didn't seem right."

Ty Cobb kept on carving without taking his eyes off the knife. "Him and them running buddies of his came over a time or two to play with our cousin Carl. They seemed all right to me."

"I reckon he wasn't, and he ain't," Jimmy Foxx said. "He's done killed all three of them same friends, plus another feller or two. That ain't all right in my book."

"You think Kendal might have been the Skinner and now he's come back?" Ty Cobb was worried.

Grandpa stood. "Naw, he was locked up when all that was happenin'. I done checked, and the sad truth of the matter is, we aren't for sure he did it. But it seems that way to me. That's why we're trying to find him. You boys see Kendal anywhere around, or hear tell that he's down there in the bottoms, you let me or Cody know."

Jimmy Foxx laughed. "I knew you wouldn't stay retired. Now we have twice as much law around here as we once had."

Grandpa took off his Stetson and momentarily examined the band. "Well, I don't rightly know what I am now. Cody was the one y'all elected. I've been…told…that I'm an *appointed* constable, for what it's worth."

Cars passed on the highway, but Grandpa barely paid any attention to them. We heard an old truck rattling down the oil road that came up back of Uncle Neal's store and Grandpa perked up.

Ty Cobb kept talking, but Grandpa wasn't listening. The truck turned off and into the bottle cap parking lot between the store and the domino hall. I didn't know who the driver was, but as he slowed, he saw something he didn't like. He shifted into first gear, turned left on the highway, and drove off.

"Wasn't that Donny Wayne Foster?" Mr. Ty Cobb asked.

"Sure was." Grandpa put his hands in his pocket and watched the truck disappear to the east.

"Must have changed his mind about stopping. C'mon son, let's go." He glanced in our direction. "You too, Pepper. Come go with us."

"I don't want to."

He studied Cale for a second and made up his mind. "I know, but I didn't ask if you wanted to go. C'mon."

I followed Grandpa to the truck and after a few seconds, Pepper did too, with a sullen slump to her shoulders. She gave out a peeved sigh and slid onto the seat and scooted over beside Grandpa. When I got into the cab, I saw Cale still standing where she'd left him. He pointed his forefinger at me like a gun, and fired with his thumb.

I fired back, but didn't feel as confident.

There was a wooden case of cokes in the floorboard and I rested my feet on them as we rode in silence. Before we got up the driveway to our house, a weaving car passed us on the two-lane highway.

"I'god, that's Lonnie Wells and he's drunk again." He jerked the wheel into our drive and slid to a stop. "Y'all get out and take them cokes out with you. Hurry!"

I jumped out of the passenger door and Pepper piled out after. I grabbed the handle on the case and tried to drag it out, but being full of cokes, it was too heavy for me.

"Hurry boy!"

"I'm trying," I said through gritted teeth, but the edge of the case caught the door frame and stuck.

Grandpa got more and more aggravated. "I got to git! He's gonna kill somebody."

"Dammit!" Pepper whispered as she leaned in with me and we both gave it a yank. It shot out of the door and crashed onto the gravel at our feet. Two bottles broke with a hiss and we drug it another foot to finally get out of the way. Grandpa threw out my half-empty RC, barely missing Pepper's nose. It hit the ground, spewing itself empty.

With the passenger door still open, Grandpa shoved the gear shift into reverse, backed out on the highway and shot away in a cloud of rocks and dust. The door slammed shut as the old engine coughed and caught with a growl.

"Son of a bitch!" Pepper shouted, angry that she'd been hit with rocks when all she really wanted to do was sit up at the store and make eyes at Cale Westlake.

"Pepper!" Miss Becky called from the porch. "You and me need to have a talk with a cake of soap while Top carries them bottles up here."

I grinned at her as Miss Becky slammed the screen door closed. "She's gonna wash your mouth out again."

"How'd she hear that?"

"I've already told you that little woman can hear better than she lets on."

"Well, shit.

Chapter Fifty-three

It didn't take more than a minute to catch up with Lonnie Wells. Ned was right, the six-foot-six, full-blood Comanche was drunk as Cooter Brown. The chase might have been longer, but Lonnie was hungry after spending all day at one of the beer joints across the river in Oklahoma, so he coasted into the parking lot at Neal's store to get a bite to eat.

Ned slid to a stop right behind him and was out of the truck before Lonnie could fumble his own door completely open. Ned grabbed a handful of Lonnie's shirt collar and roughly yanked the drunk out of the seat.

"What the hell are you doing, Ned?" He staggered on the rusting bottle caps and held onto his car for support.

"Arresting you because you're drunk." Ned reached into the deep pockets of his overalls for his cuffs. In seconds, he had Lonnie's hands secured behind his back.

"Well, I'd like to oblige you, but you ain't constable no more. What is this, a citizen's arrest?"

Ned leaned the drunk over his own trunk. "Nope. This is official…" He drifted off as Donny Wayne Foster drove by again, this time turning his face away from Ned and his prisoner.

Still loafing at the store, Ty Cobb and Jimmy Foxx joined Grandpa beside Lonnie's car. "Bet you're surprised, aincha' Lonnie?" Ty Cobb laughed.

"Did you see that?" Ned asked the two men.

Jimmy Foxx watched the highway. "What, Donny Wayne going past again?"

Ned stood beside Lonnie, his hand against his back so that he stayed bent over the car's trunk. "Yeah. He's acting like Charlie Rollins."

They all knew who he was referring to. Charlie Rollins was one of the most peculiar men in Center Springs, and he'd rather turn away from anyone he passed so he wouldn't have to wave.

"Wonder what that's all about?" Ty Cobb asked.

"I have an idea. Get in the truck, Lonnie. You're going to jail."

"For what?"

Ned sighed. "For being stupid, Lonnie."

Chapter Fifty-four

Ned was frustrated that he had to drive Lonnie back to the house and change cars to take him to jail. He shot up the long gravel drive and parked beside his sedan. Lonnie was lucky that it was a crisp, fall day, because Ned moved the complaining drunk out of the truck and tucked him into the back seat of his sedan while he went inside.

He almost wished he hadn't come back, because the table was full of sticky coke bottles. Top was in the kitchen, dabbing at a cut on his hand from one of the bottles that had exploded when the wooden case fell to the ground. Blood dripped into the sink and the youngster was mad enough to spit nails. Hootie whined and anxiously rushed from one child to the other.

Pepper was in the bathroom, gagging and squalling as Miss Becky calmly lectured her on the evils of cussing while washing her granddaughter's mouth out with soap.

He stopped for a moment, confused at the commotion. "Mama, I'm taking Lonnie Wells to jail and I'll be back directly."

"That's fine. You can bring him in here and I'll give him the same as Pepper. A good mouth washing will do him good in the eyes of the Lord."

"I don't doubt it, but I have other things to do. Oh, Top's bleeding in the kitchen."

"Oh my lord. Is it bad?"

"Naw. I've cut myself worse shaving."

Popping gravel told Ned someone was coming up the drive. He stepped outside to see Cody coasting to a stop in his El Camino. "Well, looky who's here. Howdy boy, I was about to give you a call on the radio."

"Heard you had a little excitement." He got out and slammed the half-breed truck's door.

"Yep, I got Lonnie cuffed up in the back seat there. How's that blowed-up thumb of yours?"

Cody held up his bandaged hand. "Sore as a risin', but it'll heal." He leaned over to peer into the car. "Howdy Lonnie. You look kinda green. Don't you puke in Ned's car."

"He better not. Listen, I'm gonna carry Lonnie to jail, but I want to run by Donny Wayne Foster's, too. You got time to go with me?"

"Again? I was over there a few days ago and didn't see nothing."

"Well, we need to go again. I'll explain it later, when Lonnie's out of earshot. We'll go when I get back."

"Whenever you're ready."

"All right then, go inside and save Pepper. Top might need doctorin' and I'll be back directly."

Cody frowned. "Top's hurt? What's the matter with Pepper?"

"You'll see."

The twenty minute drive to Chisum gave Lonnie time to pass out in the back seat before they got there. Ned drug him out of the car and had him checked into a cell faster than it took to accept the congratulations of those who found out that he was back in business.

He didn't even hang around long enough to visit with O.C. Ned never did like to go in the courthouse in his overalls. It didn't feel right, so he left as quickly as possible to get back home.

He felt a little better as he drove back toward Center Springs. The recent norther had loosened most of the leaves, and the highway was covered in red and orange. As he topped the hill leading down to the creek bridge, he saw four cars preparing to drag race down the arrow-straight county road, toward the curve at Ned's house. He stopped on the shoulder and watched the drivers rev their engines.

A slender teenager walked between the cars on the yellow dividing line and turned back toward the first two racers, raising his arms. Seeing Ned across the creek bridge, he pointed and made a comment that caused heads to pop out of the windows.

Ned knew they were laughing.

So was he.

He picked up the handset from the hanger on the dash and keyed the microphone. "Cody. Can you hear me?" He waited, hoping Cody was close enough to hear his Motorola. Below, the racers were deep into conversation. He heard the engines rev once again.

The speaker crackled. "Go ahead Ned. Glad you finally got that radio fixed."

"Suppose so. You still at the house?"

"Yessir."

"Pull your car down the drive and block the road right quick."

There was a pause. "All right. I'm doing it. You wanna tell me why?"

"Because we're about to bust up a drag race. You got a '55 Chrysler and a new Ford heading your way."

He replaced the microphone. The signal man raised and quickly lowered his arms. White smoke billowed out from under the racer's rear tires and they shot down the straight highway, accompanied by the scream of straining engines.

The signal man raised his arm and waved at Ned, who waved back.

He shifted into gear and coasted down to the other two waiting for their turn at the starting line.

The first pair of racers reached the sharp curve and slowed. They disappeared around the corner. Seconds later, the Chrysler shot back toward the creek with a shriek of tires. When the escaping car saw the bottleneck of his friends and Ned's sedan, he made a hard left turn and raced down the only escape available, a dirt road between two fields, leading north into the bottoms.

Ned caught a glimpse through the open side window of two people in the front seat. He recognized Harold Foster driving the Chrysler. The passenger was a girl with her hair tied up in a blue bandana, the young woman Ned met at Martin Davis' house who kept house for him before his death.

"Got the Ford," came a crackle through Ned's speaker. He keyed the microphone to answer, but to his frustration, the radio wouldn't work.

The kids in the other cars didn't know what to do. One of their friends had disappeared, and the other sped off toward the bottoms. They waited as Ned stopped his car behind the Studebaker and got out.

He stepped up between the cars. "How you boys doin'?"

"Fine, Mister Ned," the signal man with a flattop answered.

"Y'all want to get out?" He peered into the Plymouth, then the Studebaker. "Well hidy Thomas, Pete, Seth. Y'all wanna kill that motor for a little bit?"

The three nodded sullenly. Flattop, whose name was Eric, stayed put on the dividing line.

"Y'all want to get out of them cars?" Ned asked again.

"What for?" Thomas asked.

"Well, 'cause I said so, mostly."

"You ain't the law no more, Mr. Ned."

"You'd better think again, Seth." He tapped the badge on his shirt with a forefinger. "I done hauled Lonnie Wells to jail for being drunk half an hour ago, so I guess I'm back in business."

"Aw, naw." Eric suddenly deflated.

The redheaded driver in the re-bored Studebaker started to let off the clutch when Ned put his hand on the door. "Won't do you no good, Pete. Cody has the road blocked up there, and running off down in the bottoms will only make me mad. I know where you live, son. Shut that motor off and let's get done here so I can go on down there and get Harold."

When they killed their engines, Ned knew things had returned to normal.

278 Reavis Z. Wortham

Fifteen minutes later, Cody drove down to the creek bridge, made a U-turn, and parked on the shoulder behind Ned's car. They finished with the racers, and turned them loose with a stiff warning.

Cody watched them drive off. "I'm surprised you didn't want to haul them in, Ned."

"No need. They're kids who like to race, and racing ain't much of a crime."

"They'll line up again when you're gone."

The old constable shrugged. "And people will keep drinking, husbands and wives will keep fighting, and folks will keep making whiskey. It gives us something to do. Catching them was most of the battle. Now they'll find another place to race, or we'll catch them again and sting 'em a little harder."

"Did you see for sure who was in that car that got away?" Cody stared down the dirt road.

"Yeah, it was Harold driving, one of that Foster bunch."

"That's what I thought, but he wasn't in there alone. He had a gal in there with him that I saw at Donny Wayne's when I went there a few days ago." Before Ned could answer, Cody's radio crackled. He picked up the handset through the El Camino's open window. "Go ahead, Martha."

"Cody, where are you?"

"I'm standing here at the Sanders Creek bridge."

"Good. Get ahold of Ned and y'all go over to the Oklahoma side and meet Sheriff Matthews. He's found a body."

"Does he know who it is?"

"Well, I should have said the *rest* of a body. They believe its Merle Clark. Now they can join him up at the funeral home with his head."

Overhearing the conversation, Ned glanced northward as if he could see the river a mile away. "Or what was left of it after the fire."

Cody told Martha that he'd be along directly and replaced the microphone.

"We ain't going across the river right now," Ned told him.

"But the sheriff is waiting for us there."

"I know it, but I don't believe Kendal's in Oklahoma, and we don't need to see what they have over there. My radio must be about blowed up. Get John on yours and have him come meet us at Donny Wayne's."

"Well, if that's where we're fixin' to go, we don't need John just for a visit."

"We might. I know where that little quail has her nest, now."

Chapter Fifty-five

After I told Grandpa what I suspected on the square that night, he agreed, but told me to hold my horses. "I'll need more than a suspicion before we go over to that man's house and start accusing folks."

It made me mad that he wouldn't do nothing. On those television shows, they always figured out who the bad guy was and everybody hurries over to arrest him. After the commercial, he'd confess on the stand like on Perry Mason, and they'd send him to prison.

"Mighty fine thinkin', hoss, but give me time to study on this for a while. Then we'll see."

Then we'll see. From adults, that usually meant they didn't want to do what you asked, or they'd let whatever you asked them lay for a while before they forgot it.

Pepper's mouth was still soapy and I'd quit bleeding when we heard the engines revving up down by the bridge. We went out on the north porch with Hootie, watching the race, because you can see the straight run from the creek bridge to our hill. Uncle Cody was in the yard, hoorawing us about bleeding and soap bubbles and such, when he heard Grandpa's voice on the radio. He trotted over and answered. About two seconds later he whipped the El Camino around and shot off the drive.

We heard the squall of tires as the race started up, and saw Uncle Cody round the hill below us and cut off the cars. The

Chrysler whipped around in the middle of the highway leaving streaks of hot rubber on the concrete and shot back the way it came. I saw a woman in the passenger seat hanging on for dear life, but she didn't seem scared and it looked like she was yelling at the driver to hurry.

He must have been listening, 'cause he tromped that accelerator and the Chrysler's carburetor sucked air as the motor roared. I knew neither Uncle Cody nor Grandpa was going to catch a suped-up car like that, and sure enough, he turned left between two fields, pitched off in a cloud of dust, and was gone.

Uncle Cody spent a few minutes talking to the kids in the Ford before they started their engine and drove toward the store. He went on down to the creek bridge where Grandpa was still talking with the people in the other cars. We watched the tiny figures for a long time. They all milled around for a while, and then the racers slowly scattered and drove off. It was a surprise that no one went to jail.

"Grandpa must have got soft while he was off," Pepper said.

"Naw, they don't want to arrest anybody today."

I might have been right, because he and Uncle Cody stood there visiting on the shoulder. They finally got into their cars and took off toward the bottom, throwing up dust like the Chrysler had done a few minutes before.

"*Now* what are they doing?" Pepper turned to me like I knew the answer.

Surprisingly, I did. "They're going to Donny Wayne's."

"Bullshit. How the hell do you know that?" Pepper flinched when she said it, and watched the screen door to see if Miss Becky was going to come boiling out. She was still spitting soap and didn't want any more.

I couldn't explain it, but I knew after seeing how Donny Wayne acted at the store. She hadn't been paying attention to anything but Cale Westlake. "That was Harold driving. They're gonna go down there and arrest him, and it serves him right. But I think Donny Wayne is up to something, and Grandpa will find out when he gets there."

For a long moment she didn't say anything, but suddenly her eyes lit up. "Are you sure?"

"Of course I'm not sure."

She turned her face toward the north. "Donny Wayne's old shack ain't far."

My stomach fluttered. "Oh, no."

"What?"

"We ain't going over there. Grandpa will wear us out again, and my butt is still sore from the whipping we got over the Exchange."

She spat out some more soap. "Don't you want to watch him arrest Harold?"

"Not really."

"We can go down and stay on the road. He won't get mad at us farting around down there. We do it all the time."

"Not when he's on the way to put somebody in jail."

"Well, I'm going." She hurried toward the gate. Hootie followed and almost tripped her in his excitement. "I'll let you know how exciting it was when I get back, 'fraidy cat."

I'm not sure how it happened, but I inhaled a big dose of medicine off my puffer and suddenly found myself walking alongside and arguing with her. The next thing I knew, we'd gone through the little wooden gate into the pasture and slipped through the barbed wire on the other side.

Long before they built the highway from the creek bridge, the original dirt road from Arthur City to Center Springs cut through a slight hill on the north edge of Grandpa's property. Though it was grown up and fenced, the road was still clear, if you knew where it was.

I stopped in the middle of the open cut and watched Pepper climb the steep bank to the top where she crossed still another fence into Joe Daniel's pasture. "Don't."

"We can be there in ten minutes if we run."

I surprised myself when I sounded like Grandpa. "Oh, hell."

Chapter Fifty-six

With Cody leading the way for once down the dirt road, Ned followed far enough behind that the rooster-tail of dust didn't completely obscure his vision. They crossed a plank bridge, and when his front tire dropped off into a deep pothole with a hard jolt a minute later, his radio squawked and came back on.

"...read me, Ned?"

Cody turned left between two plowed fields and for a moment Ned had a clear view of the fringe of bare trees lining the river. "That you, John?" He turned to follow and Cody again turned right.

"Yessir. Did you want me?"

"Sure do. Where are you?"

"Turning off two-seventy-one toward Center Springs. I'm heading your way."

"Well, put your foot in it and meet me at Donny Wayne Foster's house. You know where it is?"

"Cain't say as I do."

Ned thought for a minute. Donny Wayne didn't live more than half a mile from a little scratch farm occupied by a colored family who worked the fields for anyone who had enough money to pay them. Ned struggled to recall their name as he spun the wheel to follow Cody. "They's some of your folks lives down here, not far from the pecan orchard."

The radio was silent for a moment. "You talking about where Lawrence Walker lives?"

"That's it. Wasn't that where Miss Sweet delivered a baby back in the spring?"

"Yep. I know where you're talking about now. I'll be there in a little bit."

"Come a runnin'. I might need you."

"Mr. Ned!" The mention of the bottoms and John's people suddenly reminded him of a snatch of conversation, a brief exchange between himself and a prisoner the day Ned put Top in jail. The memory tied in with a conversation an hour earlier, when Miss Sweet told him about delivering the misshapen Hart baby, Kendal.

That's why John was so close. He had important news for Ned.

Norbert said "…it's in the bottoms" when he was layin' in the cell. Something ain't right.

Miss Sweet weeping over the secret she'd kept for years about a disfigured child who had eventually gone insane.

A secret so horrifying that she promised God she'd never tell a soul…

…until she realized the ugly truth about Kendal.

"Mr. Ned! Dammit!" The old man's radio was on the fritz again.

What's in the bottoms?

Trying in vain to remember the rest of the song Norbert was singing that day, John stomped the accelerator and knew Ned would need him, soon.

Chapter Fifty-seven

Ned followed, confident Cody knew exactly where he was going, but with the angle of the river cutting through the fields, a direct route was out of the question. He was sure anyone staying with Donny Wayne would see them coming long before they arrived.

They weren't exactly in a rush to go charging up in the yard, so when they got close, Cody slowed and waved for Ned to come around in front. The Chrysler was parked under the tree, beside the tire swing. Ned pulled his sedan up behind it and killed the engine. Cody stopped his El Camino on the dirt road and stepped out so he could see if anyone came outside and tried to run for the leafless trees not far away.

Dang, that's familiar. He squinted at the distant pasture and field leading to the river sparkling in the distance.

Ned opened the car door, put one foot on the ground and tapped the horn with the heel of his hand. It was always good manners and a safe way to approach any house in the country. At almost every farm, there was at least one yard dog whose job was to keep wild animals and intruders out.

A mangy mix of skinny bird dog and hound crawled from under the steps and set up a racket until Donny Wayne stepped through the screen door. He picked up a chunk of firewood and threw it at the dog, hitting it in the ribs. It yelped and slunk back under the porch. "Shut up, dog!"

Ned stepped out and spoke over the roof. "Hidy, Donny Wayne."

The middle-aged man ran his fingers through dirty, tangled hair in need of cutting. "Ned."

"Isn't that Harold's car?"

Cody grinned to himself. Ned already knew the answer. Cody stepped to the rear of his El Camino so he could see around the corner. He wished he'd parked a little farther back to keep an eye on the rear, but he also needed to hang close to Ned.

Donny Wayne pointed a finger at Cody. "What's that son-of-a-bitch doing here?"

"He's the law. Same as me."

"I done said what I'd do if I had the chance."

Cody spread his hands. "I ain't alone, like you wanted, but here I am. Get to doing."

"Uh uh!" Ned said, interrupting their crowing. "I asked you about this car. You take up your business with Cody some other time."

The irritatingly familiar memory kept itching Cody's brain. *Have I been in that pasture?* He might have hunted it in the past, because most folks in Center Springs let you on their property if they knew you, or if you asked.

"You know it belongs to Harold," Donny Wayne said. "And that's my truck parked right there. Now, what do you and that wife-stealer want?"

Ned ignored the barb directed toward Cody. "Well, Harold's been racing again on my side of the creek bridge."

"He's full growed. Why are *you* here?" Donny Wayne pointed. "Ain't that Cody's job now?"

Aggravated that people kept asking him that question, Ned rubbed his forehead. "I'god, people kept saying they thought I was working when I was retired, and now that I'm working again, they think I'm not. We're both constables today."

"I don't remember no election."

"Oh, hell, Donny Wayne. It don't make no difference no-how, y'ain't voted since Roosevelt died and you probably ain't even registered in this state since you moved down from Oklahoma. O.C. Rains made me constable again, but this is Cody's precinct now. I'm helping him out."

"Then I don't need to talk to you. Ain't that right, Cody?"

He shrugged. "Well, I reckon you need to talk to any of us that ask you to."

Ned leaned his forearms against the sedan's roof. "What difference does it make? We're here to see Harold anyway. Whyn't you go on and call him out here?"

"You already knew we were on the way," Cody said. "Didn't you? You could have already had him out here instead of arguing with us."

Donny Wayne was having trouble focusing on who he needed to address. First one, then the other constable kept talking to him, and Donny Wayne didn't think that fast. Mean as a snake, he was only slightly smarter than his brother Tully Joe. Anyone could give him a hoe, tell him to chop an entire cornfield, and he'd do it without a problem, but any type of complicated thinking caused his head to hurt.

"Harold! Come out here!"

"Donny Wayne, what was on your mind earlier today?"

"When, Ned?"

"When you passed me twice and didn't wave nor nothin'."

If there was one thing Donny Wayne did know, it was to tell Ned the truth, because he wasn't good at keeping track of lies. "Well, I had something on my mind."

"I bet you did," Cody said. "I also believe I heard you have somebody here visiting for a while?"

The different line of questioning completely threw the man off. The only thing that came out of his moving mouth was an exasperated breath. He glanced over his shoulder. "Uh, Harold, Ned wants you."

From the corner of his eye, Ned saw John's car speeding down the dirt road.

Donny Wayne stepped to the edge of the porch when he heard the engine. "Who's that?"

"Don't matter." Ned saw a figure through the dirty living room window. Inside, a young woman wearing a blue bandana watched the men in the yard. "I see your company standing in there. What's her name?"

"That's Barbara, she's my wife's cousin."

Ned knew most of Shannon and Donny Wayne's kinfolk, but he couldn't remember ever hearing Barbara's name. "Well, I recognize that blue bandana. I met her a while back before Martin passed."

"That's right. She took care of him because he always favored her when she was little."

"All right, then. She was in the car with Harold a few minutes ago, too. Is he gonna come out?"

"I done called him."

"Well, call him again." Cody's thumb ached and his patience was wearing thin.

Donny Wayne's face flushed. "Harold, get your ass out here!"

Barbara retreated from the window when he shouted through the rusty screen. Finally, Harold stepped through the door and leaned against the frame. He cupped a match around a cigarette, shook it out, and thumped it toward Ned.

"What?"

Ned felt his temper begin to rise. He had no tolerance for rude people, especially rude *young* people who didn't have enough sense to comb their hair. "You was racing on the highway."

"So?"

"So here's the deal. I'm here to warn you that I'm carrying a badge again and I don't want to catch you racing no more, not anywhere, or I'll take you to jail. Y'hear me?"

The young man drew a deep lungful of smoke, blew it out and glanced toward the deputy sheriff's car. He saw Big John get out of his sedan.

Uncertain whether to stay where he was, John shifted from one foot to the other. "Mr. Ned! I got something to tell you *right now*."

"In a minute, John."

Harold jerked his head toward John. "What's that nigger doing here?"

"That *deputy* is here because I called him."

"Well, he ain't got no jurisdiction in Center Springs."

No one hated to have someone tell them their business more than Ned Parker. He stepped around to the back of his car and paused there, his left hand on the deck lid. "That'll be enough out of you about law work. Now you listen, boy. Racin' is over, and John and Cody will help me keep it that way."

"Don't let them talk to you like that, Harold." The voice came from inside.

Ned had enough experience to know what happened when a woman kept provoking her men when the law arrived, and it worried him.

"Have her come out here for a minute."

"She won't do it."

"Tell her anyway."

Harold snickered and turned toward the rusty screen door. "He wants you out here."

It was a standoff. Donny Wayne stayed where he was, close to John and Cody. Harold leaned against a weathered porch post.

Barbara finally stepped thought the screen, drying her hands on a dish towel.

Now I know that pasture. Cody kept feeling a tickle of memory that barely escaped capture.

Only yards away, the scene was all wrong, but Ned couldn't figure it out. A chill ran up the back of his neck. He stared hard at the woman dressed in a man's shirt and jeans one size too large. A leather belt puckered her waistband and she had the cuffs rolled high.

Ned's radio sputtered to life though the sedan's open windows. He was surprised to hear O.C. Rains on the other end, and he sounded anxious. "…ammit..Ned…hear me…"

"I'll call him on mine." Cody half sat in the El Camino's seat with his left foot still on the ground. As he picked up the microphone, Ned's radio finally settled down and O.C.'s voice was crystal clear to everyone in the yard.

"...and that young officer here in town that knows so much and I've been talking to the folks up in Tulsa sanitarium. We finally got a judge to release all the information on Kendal Bowden. You've been after the wrong person...Ned, Kendal may be dressed like a woman. He's one of them...*morphodites* and that's why y'all couldn't catch him. Can you hear me?"

John heard. "That's what Miss Sweet jus' told me, Mr. Ned. She helped deliver a mixed-up baby with both sets of parts. That's what Norbert was a-sayin' when he told me *it* was in the bottoms."

The idea ground everyone to a halt. It became so quiet they heard a squirrel scrabbling in the oak tree beside them. Ned studied the ground for a moment to process the information. "A woman?"

Cody rose from the sedan, his stomach clutched in fear. *Oh God, now I recognize this pasture. That's the one I dream about, where a tunnel comes up from the back of a house and leads out toward the pasture...but what does it mean?*

He groaned in frustration because the premonition wouldn't come clear.

Two kids and a dog appeared on the ridge behind the lawmen, and the sight of the children jolted those on the porch into action.

Ned's head snapped up.

The people on the porch reacted and as if choreographed, everyone moved at once.

All hell broke loose.

Chapter Fifty-eight

I knew we'd made a bad mistake when Pepper and I came over the ridge. The little gray house was clear in the bright sunlight. A woman and two men stood rock still on the porch. Grandpa, Uncle Cody, and John stayed by their cars and they all seemed to be squared off.

It seemed pretty calm at first, but when the people saw us suddenly appear, we could feel the change all the way up on the ridge.

"Shit!" was all Pepper had time to say before they all went crazy down there.

Chapter Fifty-nine

When Barbara saw the kids in the distance, she stopped fidgeting with her hands, and that's when Ned realized what was wrong with her cup towel. Like falling dominos, the pieces rattled into place.

She'd been at the window long before she stepped outside, so her hands couldn't have still been wet.

The thin flour sack material was too stiff, because there was a pistol under there.

Kendal was a name for either a boy or a girl.

Bowdens, Harts, Davises, and Fosters were all kin.

The final domino fell.

The murderer wanted by the law in four states was right in front of him, and he wasn't a man, well, not completely anyway. He'd been hiding in a woman's clothes. Ned's head snapped up and he met Barbara's eyes.

Not Barbara, Kendal!

A blue jay shrieked twice from the nearby oak tree, harsh and clear.

"Don't you move!" Ned shouted and pulled the revolver from the front pocket of his overalls. "Put that gun down!"

Cody saw Ned's reaction and awkwardly tugged at his own pistol. The bulky bandage on his thumb made him fumble the automatic from the holster.

The click when Kendal thumbed the hammer back on her gun was crisp in the autumn sunlight.

With a grunt, John ducked toward the rear of his car for cover, almost losing his pump shotgun because of the bandage on *his* swollen hand.

Still wrapped in the dish towel, Kendal raised the pistol toward Ned. The explosion was sharp. The towel blackened and burst into flame. Donny Wayne dove headfirst into the house through the open window.

Unnerved, Ned's first shot missed and splintered one of the weathered wall boards, leaving a wound of raw yellow pine. At the same time, Harold threw himself back through the screen door.

Before Ned could react, Kendal shot again. Slinging the towel aside, she swung toward Cody and fired three more times.

Ned flinched as the second bullet cracked past his ear.

Cody fired quickly, but his aim was off because of the bandage. Kendal vanished into the house behind a cloud of gun smoke.

There was a brief moment of silence. Then a shotgun blast erupted from the open window, smacking holes all across the right rear fender of Ned's sedan and blowing out glass in the back passenger door. He ducked and scurried behind the car for cover.

The shotgun turned toward Cody and he heard the load of shot whistle overhead. He returned fire, walking his rounds across the wall beside the window.

As the sounds of gunfire rolled across the yard, Harold leaped out of a window on John's side of the house. He rolled to his feet with his hands high. "Don't shoot! I ain't armed! Don't shoot!" He ran toward John.

"Get down, boy!" John shouted. "I'm fiddin' to shoot you!"

Harold flung himself over the hood of the car and jumped to his feet, charging John. "Don't shoot me!"

Unable to figure out what the teenager was doing, John reversed the shotgun, stepped into the charge, and flattened him with a vicious butt-stroke to the chest. When Harold hit the ground with the wind knocked out of him, John flipped him over and dropped a knee onto the back of his dirty neck, then peered through his car windows.

More gunfire rattled in the front, and John was dismayed to see that he'd been distracted long enough for Kendal to crawl out from under the pier and beam house and bolt toward the bottoms.

He stood, put his foot on Harold's back, and threw a wild shot in her direction. He shucked another shell into the chamber, but Kendal ducked behind the outhouse that absorbed the second load and kept it between them as she ran. "Ned! She's gone out back!"

More gunshots erupted from the front of the house, this time all directed toward Cody. He rapidly emptied his .45 in a roll of thunder. Chips of unpainted wood exploded as the big slugs punched through the warped planks. He squatted behind the car and awkwardly used his left thumb to push the button that dropped the empty clip. He slapped another into place.

Ned saw movement as someone ran past the shot-up window. He fired twice, flipped the cylinder open and slapped the eject rod. He quickly reloaded from a handful of loose shells in his pocket.

The house was silent.

For the moment, the gunfight was over.

Chapter Sixty

A solid wall of sound reached us when the shooting increased, sounding like hunters around a dove field.

I grabbed Hootie's collar so he wouldn't run down there, and watched Harold jump out of the window. I thought Mr. John was going to shoot him, but when Harold ran at him, he jammed the butt of that pump into Harold's chest so hard it looked like he'd run into a tree. He hit the ground just as a woman in jeans ran from the back and sprinted toward the woods. Mr. John cranked off two quick shots that missed.

"Shit-a-monkey! What the hell was that all about?" Pepper asked when everything quieted down. "Were they trying to shoot that *girl*?"

My heart was beating so hard I could barely breathe. I sucked in a good dose from my puffer and waited for my lungs to ease. "Maybe she shot at them first."

"Girls don't shoot at the laws."

"I think that one did."

"We'd better get back home."

I thought for a minute. "We can't."

"Well, why not?"

I pointed toward the bare trees below. "Because we can still see her running and they can't. We'll have to tell 'em where she's gone."

"We'll lose her in a minute when she gets into them woods."

I pointed to a tall pecan tree on the ridge with us. "Not if I climb up there. I can see all the way to the river from the top."

"You'll fall out and kill yourself."

"It'll be better than another whippin' if I do. It's the only thing we can do to help."

Pepper made up her mind. "I'll give you a boost to that lowest limb."

We ran over to the tree. Hootie had already forgotten all the excitement down at the house. He must have thought we'd treed something, because he started running circles around the big pecan.

Pepper hooked her fingers together and I stepped in, like we'd done a thousand times before. I pushed off with the other leg, she lifted, and for a second I was floating. I grabbed the lowest limb and pulled myself up.

From there it was easy to shinny up higher, using those big limbs like rungs on a ladder. Because the leaves had all been beaten off by the sleet days before, I could see clear to the river.

"See her!?" Pepper called up.

"Nope. I've lost her."

My heart was pounding out of my chest from the fear of being up so high, and for all the excitement down below. I wrapped my arms around the trunk and held on. Grandpa taught me that to be a good hunter, you didn't watch for something shaped like a deer, a bird, or a squirrel. You watch for movement. That's what gives game away every time and it was what kept my attention on that little mama quail trying to lead me from her nest back in the summer.

With that in mind, I stared past the house at nothing. It wasn't no time until I saw a squirrel moving out of the corner of my eye. It was in the big tree in Donny Wayne's front yard. Birds flickered through the woods farther on.

After a minute, I shifted my focus to another tree way on the other side of the pasture, and fixed on it again. More birds, an old mama cow walking along the fence line, and then I saw a familiar sight. A covey of quail exploded past the little strip of woods between Donny Wayne's pasture and the field on the other side.

"See anything?"

Instead of answering, I kept my eyes hard on where the quail flushed. Like magic, there she was, slipping through the trees along the fence row leading to the river. I recognized the river bend where she was headed, because that's where Grandpa used to take me and Pepper out on a long, wide sandstone ledge just above the waterline to splash in potholes when we were little.

"I know where she's going!"

"Where?" Far below, Pepper's white face was tiny.

"I'll tell you when I get down." I worked my way from one limb to the other, and believe me, it's harder than going up. I was making good time until the last one, when my foot slipped. I grabbed for a nearby branch, and missed.

The last thing I remembered was seeing the trunk flash past.

Chapter Sixty-one

Harold was in cuffs and Donny Wayne was cussing and bleeding from a bullet wound that broke his collarbone. "One of y'all shot me, Ned. You didn't have no call for that. I's just puttin' up kinfolk, that's all."

"You was shootin' at us," Ned snapped.

"I was shootin', but I wasn't tryin' to hit y'all, just shootin' to give Kendal some runnin' room."

"You knew what Kendal done." Ned rolled up the blackened and partially burned dish towel Kendal had dropped and pressed it against Donny Wayne's shoulder. "And you knew *what* she was."

"Kendal's kin, that's all. We kept our shame quiet, them that knowed, and that weren't many. It ain't something you talk about, because she's cursed."

"Is it a he or a she?"

"She's both, you know, that's what morphodite means."

"No, we don't know, and the word is hermaphrodite." Cody yanked Donny Wayne's belt from his loops and used it to hold the compress in place.

Donny Wayne hissed at the pain. "I don't give a damn how to say it. It was one of them family secrets only a few of us knew. Her business ain't natural down there. It looks different with both parts all mixed up. That's enough to drive somebody crazy, and I reckon it did."

They paused for a moment, stunned by the shocking idea.

"Are y'all gonna take me to the hospital?"

"We'll get around to it," Ned told him. "What else can you tell us about Kendal?"

"I could talk all day about that crazy bastard. For years George raised him as a boy, up to when he sent Kendal to the crazy house, but Kendal figured the best way to hide when he got back was as a female. It was easy, since she's slight."

"You keep switching back and for between he and she."

Donny Wayne snickered with hateful confusion. "See what we've had to deal with all these years?"

"So you knew her when she got back? She's been gone a long time."

"Of course we did, when she showed up here at the house. I ain't sure I'd-a recognized her on the street, but it's her sure enough. I *looked*."

Hands shaking from adrenaline, Ned ran a palm over his forehead. "She's been killing people and cutting off their heads. Don't tell me you didn't know that?"

"I know what they say she did, and I wanted to tell you. That's why I passed you a couple of times today, but I couldn't find the words."

"Barbara is Kendal and she's been doing the killin' would have worked for a start."

"Well, hell. I done told you she's crazy. She'd-a killed all of us if she knew we'd let it slip out."

Working quickly so he could go after Kendal, Cody stuffed a second compress under the belt crossing Donny Wayne's shoulder blade. "Tell me, you knew what was going on at the Exchange when me and John almost got killed in there."

"I knew Kendal was gone to settle up with George and Alvin for what they done to her when she was a kid. She wanted to pay them back."

"This is making my head hurt," Cody said. "Why kill all the others?"

"Because they'd wronged her, too...shamed her I guess you could say. Kendal is damaged in more ways than one, and she wants to pay everyone back who's hurt her or talked her into letting them look at her business over the years.

"It don't matter how, whether they teased her for being kind of sissified when she was a boy-kid, or played mean tricks, or called the boy-kid a squat-to-pee, because he'd do that out in the woods or in the outhouse, so no one could see how he was made. Or like Josh, who married the girl Kendal wanted.

"She has thoughts all mixed up in her head about what people have done to her, and the kind of life she's missed, and the way George mistreated her when she was little."

John stuffed Harold in the backseat of his car and joined them. "Why take folks' heads?"

"I'm-a tellin' you, she…is…*crazy!*" Cold sweat broke out on Donny Wayne's forehead as shock began to set in. "You know George had all them trophy animal heads on his walls? Kendal wanted to do the same. She kept telling me she was going to learn how to mount deer heads and she figured to do the same with people. She wanted her own trophies to pay folks back.

"It's pitiful, ain't it? She hated George Hart enough to kill him, but in that way, she wanted to be like him. Now, can y'all get me to the *goddamn doctor?*"

Ned was about to answer when he suddenly heard Pepper's voice calling. He stepped away from the house. "What'n hell?"

The kids came down the ridge a couple of hundred yards away, followed by the dog, but they staggered slowly downhill with Top leaning on Pepper's shoulder, his left arm dangling.

Ned's heart nearly stopped. "Oh, lordy! Cody, get up there. Top must have been hit by a stray bullet!"

"What are *they* doing here!?" Cody shouted and raced toward the ridge.

They stopped seconds later when he met them and Cody snatched Top up. He frantically searched for blood. "What happened?"

Pepper was breathing hard. "He fell out of a tree and broke his arm."

"And you brought him all the way out here?" Cody asked, incredulous.

She pointed behind her. "No, he fell out of *that* tree."

Cody scooped the boy up and hurried toward the cars. "What was he doing up there?"

Pepper ran easily beside him. "We came to watch y'all arrest Harold, and when we got there, we saw all the shooting and saw somebody run from the back of the house."

"What's the matter?" Ned called. "Is he hurt bad?"

"Pepper says he broke his arm falling out of that tree over yonder." Cody reached the house and sat Top on the hood of Ned's sedan to examine his arm. "These crazy kids followed us out here and saw it all from the top of the ridge."

Ned turned to Pepper. She shrank back. "What'n hell was he doing in a tree way out here?"

She explained everything while Cody stripped his own belt from his waist. He strapped the boy's broken arm to his chest. "Top, is that all that's hurt?"

Though his eyes watered at the pain, Top didn't cry. "Yessir. It's broke pretty good, though."

"I'm gonna beat the whey out of you two when we get home," Ned said.

"I know it, Grandpa. But you need to catch that woman that shot at you first. I saw her get away. That's why I was in the tree, to see where she's going for you. She's heading for the river, where the bathtubs are."

Ned and Cody exchanged looks. They knew exactly where Top was talking about. Ned grabbed Harold's shoulder and pulled him out of the car. "John! Cuff Harold to my bumper and we'll leave him here. We'll take Donny Wayne with us and hope he don't bleed to death. Call it in and tell O.C. to send a car here to pick him up. Then you drive us like hell to the river."

Cody saw the bandage on his thumb was leaking blood. "What about the kids?"

Ned paused in indecision. "Put them in the car with you. Now let's go. Kendal's-a tryin' to get across into Oklahoma, and I don't intend to let her do it."

"We saw a woman run off. Who's trying to get away, Grandpa?" Pepper asked as she followed Cody. He carried Top in his arms.

"Kendal Bowden, whatever *that* is."

Chapter Sixty-two

Cody had the gas pedal to the floor and they followed John's car through the bottoms, ignoring the cloud of dust he threw up.

For once, Pepper didn't have anything to say. Though Top's broken arm hurt, he didn't complain. He sat quietly with Hootie between them while tears rolled down his cheeks.

It didn't take any time to get to the river. Near the sandstone ledge and the steep river bank, John slammed on his brakes in the middle of the dirt road. He and Ned jumped out of the car before the El Camino stopped only a foot from their bumper.

Cody killed the engine and pointed his finger. "You kids stay in here! I mean it, and hold that dog!"

They had no intention of getting out. Pump shotgun in hand, John warily trotted along the dirt road ahead of the cars, scanning from side to side and searching for footprints leading to the steep riverbank. On the other side of the road, a plowed field shimmered under a cool sun.

Pistol in hand, Ned went the opposite direction, watching the tree line for movement. "She's probably already down to the river!"

The .45 in his undamaged hand, Cody dodged between the cars and slipped down the bank to search the tangled drifts fifteen feet below the edge. An overhanging limb slapped his hat off, but he ignored it, working carefully through the trees and overgrown vegetation.

The river gurgled fifty yards away, running high. An occasional branch or bobbing log swept past. Cody trotted across the sandstone ledge, until he was close to the muddy water. He knelt behind a jutting outcrop and turned back toward the bank to carefully scan the trees lining the Texas shore.

He suddenly realized their mistake when he saw the cars. They'd left the kids unprotected up on the road.

Then he saw Kendal's blue bandana when she appeared beside John's car.

Chapter Sixty-three

My arm was throbbing deep and it hurt like thunder. Pepper sat beside me, scared to death of what was going to happen. Hootie kept whining between us, wanting to get out, but Pepper had a good hold on his collar and wouldn't let go. We knew she wouldn't be blowing bubbles this time and my butt still remembered the whipping I got after we got back from the Cotton Exchange.

I glanced over my shoulder and saw Grandpa through the glass, watching the trees across the field.

Mr. John was about a hundred yards in front, walking back in our direction with his shotgun across one shoulder.

Feeling queasy, I closed my eyes for a second.

"Shit," Pepper said.

When I opened them, Kendal was standing on the driver's side of Mr. John's car.

"Time to pay up," we heard her say. Then she shot Donny Wayne with her pistol.

I saw him fall over in the seat.

"That's for your part too, you son-of-a-bitch!"

She shot him again, turned and walked toward us as slow as you please, like Mr. John wasn't hollering and running toward us with the shotgun at his shoulder. I knew he couldn't shoot, because I was staring right down that big open barrel and it would get on us if he pulled the trigger. With the shotgun still aimed in our direction, he darted into the field and stumbled through the rows to get a better angle.

Grandpa shouted behind us, but I knew it was the same for him. We were too close.

As calm as if she were on an afternoon stroll, Kendal walked over to the El Camino's open window. She gave us a sad little smile that would have been pretty on any other woman, but her coarse features made it more scary than nice. I swallowed at the light in her disturbed eyes. I wanted to be brave, but I barely held back a whimper. Hootie growled low in his chest and I felt the rumble.

"Girl, don't you never let anyone touch you the wrong way, like they did me. You understand? I'm only different on the out-side and them others that knew treated me…they kept wanting to look and some did more and…well…it's their fault. I've done for them all, but it don't change nothing, nor what they did."

I might have felt sorry for her, but deep down I knew from that evil light in her eyes she was plumb crazy and had been long before they took her off. We could hear Grandpa and Mr. John yelling for Kendal to get away from us.

Pepper was scared and her voice trembled. "Donny Wayne was just settin' there. He helped you get away."

Kendal casually raised her pistol and shot once in Mr. John's direction without aiming and then again toward Grandpa the same way. The sound hammered our ears in the tiny space. I turned to see over my shoulder and saw Grandpa fall heavily toward the tall, dry weeds beside the road.

"Family secrets be damned. He just *had* to see and feel like the rest of them." Kendal might have said more, but Hootie had all he could take. He snarled and lunged at the open window, causing Kendal to jerk upright.

A loud gunshot from the river made her head snap back. The concussion felt like we were slammed by a fist, because Uncle Cody wasn't that far away.

The bullet cut across her scalp like a sharp butcher knife and her bandana fluttered away like a dying bluebird. She wasn't bald, but her hair was barely half an inch long and stuck up all over. Blood sprayed, but she kept her feet.

Laying half on the bank, Uncle Cody stuck his arm over the edge and shot again, but the second one completely missed. That one didn't hurt so much, because our ears were already ringing so loud.

She fired again in Uncle Cody's direction and sand exploded into his face. He fell back out of sight.

Pepper and I were sitting smack dab in the middle of a gunfight.

When she turned to throw another shot toward Grandpa, I heard him cuss. That's when I saw the blood pumping from her scalp in a thin, high-pressure spray. The big .45 nicked an artery in her head. The left side of her face and shoulder was already bright red. I don't know how she was still on her feet,

I heard Pepper gasp at the sight while she held tight to Hootie, who was roaring and trying to fight his way free to attack Kendal. She forgot us then, darted between the cars, and flew feet first over the river bank like someone jumping into a swimming pool.

Mr. John finally got the angle he wanted and fired like he was shooting at a covey rise. I heard the shot hiss through the air and then she disappeared just as Pepper lost her grip and Hootie launched himself through the window.

Chapter Sixty-four

Cody wasn't hit, but he lost his balance and fell with a crash backwards through a tangle of driftwood, losing his .45. A limb slapped his forehead, and blood immediately covered his left eye.

The gunshots from the road told Cody that Ned and John were still in the fight. He thrashed in the dried wood, trapped like a fly in a spider web. Kendal leaped over the steep bank and landed on her feet halfway down the bank. Like someone running down a sand dune, she made two more long jumps until her shoes slapped hard on the sandstone.

She dropped to her knees from the momentum. Her pistol skittered away. Blood poured from her head wound. More welled from three pellet wounds in her back, but she was far from dead. With bullets and #4 shotgun pellets exploding in the sandstone all around her, Kendal regained her feet and staggered the open forty yards to the river with Hootie right behind.

He sank his teeth into her calf just as she reached the water's edge. She fell onto all fours and the dog released his hold to get a better grip.

Kendal kicked free and regained her feet just as Top shouted from the bank. "Don't you hurt my dog you bitch!"

Hootie was distracted by the boy's voice and quit fighting long enough for Kendal to take two steps before she half-fell, half-plunged into the thick, fast current.

Cussing, Ned carefully slid down the bank and met Cody as he thrashed in the tangled limbs. John followed. He grabbed hold of Cody's arm and gave a heave, yanking him free of the drift.

The blood covering Cody's eye scared him. "Oh lordy, you shot!?"

"Naw, limb-slapped." He saw a bullet hole in Ned's shirt. "*You* hit!?"

Surprised, Ned glanced down. "Naw, just went through my shirt. Glad my belly only sticks out to the front."

They rushed to the water's edge where the furious dog barked and raced back and forth on the sandstone peninsula that prevented him from following Kendal.

She was in the strongest part of the current when a partially submerged tree swept past. Realizing a quick means of escape, she reached for the trunk and grabbed onto a broken limb. Her weight shifted the balance of the tree and it rolled in her direction. Like an iceberg, most of its mass was underwater. With a lazy spin, the limbs caught and dragged her below the surface.

The three men watched until the current swept the tree out of sight.

She never re-surfaced.

Chapter Sixty-five

Instead of the crop report on the radio a week later, the Beatles were singing that they wanted to hold someone's hand. The phone rang seconds after everyone sat down for Thanksgiving dinner. As usual, Miss Becky suffered Ned's glare and answered. She listened as she watched her family through the open door into the kitchen.

Ned sat in his usual place at the head of the table, facing the living room. To his right, Cody filled his plate. Beside her uncle, Pepper buttered a biscuit. Miss Becky's plate was still empty at Ned's left elbow. Across from his girl cousin, Top, his left arm in a cast, was eating a chicken leg. James and Ida Belle had their backs to the living room door. Cody's laughing red-haired wife, Norma Fay, circled the table, filling jelly glasses with sweet tea from a forty-year-old crock pitcher.

Hootie lay under the table, patiently waiting for one of the kids to sneak him a bite.

Finally, Miss Becky put down the receiver. "Ned, it's for you. It's that Oklahoma game warden, Homer Williams."

Mumbling to himself, Ned left his dinner and sat at the telephone table. "Hello!"

"You mad about something, Ned?"

"Only that my dinner is getting cold, Homer. What's the matter?"

"Well, I thought you might want to come over here and meet me where you did the last time, beside Cody's Sportsman's Lounge. You won't believe it, but we have Bill Caldwell dead to rights. He's been caught netting in the river."

"You don't need me. That's Oklahoma jurisdiction, not Texas."

"I know that, but I figured you'd be interested to know that we have him because he caught a body in his *net* this time, and not stuck on empty trotline hooks."

Ned sat down on the telephone table's seat. "You know Jennings' body was put there later, after Bill caught it in his net, don't you?"

"Yeah, I know you suspicioned it, just like I did. This time, though, I was watching him through my binoculars when he hauled up the net and saw the body. Get this Ned. He untangled it, drifted downriver to one of his trotlines, and hooked it on just like before. Then he went downstream to the Sportsman and called the sheriff's office."

Ned smiled. Now everything made sense. "Who's body is it? Anyone we know?"

A chuckle came through the receiver. "As a matter of fact, Sheriff Matthews says it's Kendal Bowden. I'll see you at the river."

Ned heard the click as Homer hung up the phone. He waited for a long moment. "Now Miss Whitney, I don't want you telling that before me now, y'hear?"

He grinned when the old eavesdropper gasped and slammed down the phone.

Cody glanced up from his plate. "What was that, Ned?"

"Something I need to study on while we finish our dinner." He rejoined the family at the table and half an hour later, nothing remained but dirty dishes. Cody, Ned, and the kids escaped the kitchen in a flurry of cup towels and flying aprons, and settled in front of the snowy television to watch the Oilers play a little football. Sprawled on the couch, Cody could tell Ned had something on his mind.

They sat through an entire quarter to let his dinner settle, until Ned couldn't stand it any longer. He grunted to his feet and put on his felt hat. Shrugging on a coat, Ned pinned the little badge onto his shirt and picked up his holstered revolver from where it rested on top of the television.

He stopped in the kitchen door. "C'mon Constable Cody. You and I are going across the river to Juarez."

"What for?"

"To watch the Oklahoma laws arrest Bill Caldwell for netting in the river."

"Well, if that don't beat all." Cody stood with a sigh.

"That ain't the half of it."

As they opened the doors of Ned's bullet-ridden Chevy sedan, a strong gust nearly snatched their Stetsons. A single snowflake struck his cheek and Cody shivered, but not from the chilly wind. It came from last night's suddenly remembered dream of snow, woods, rivers, and Mexico.

Damn this family curse.

Author Note

Thank you for the reading this second book in the Red River series. These novels are largely fiction, but they all contain a few grains of truth gleaned from old stories and my own experiences. Chisum, as many of you know, is my version of the real Paris, Texas. Those who know the area recognize many landmarks, and might question a few changes, but they were necessary to advance the story line. No, there is no Cotton Exchange, and never was, but at one time the Speas Vinegar plant sat on that spot I described, directly across from a train depot on the south side of Paris. The block is in reality too small for the gigantic Exchange in this book, but that's where fiction takes over from fact.

In addition, because this isn't a history book, I have taken the liberty of compressing certain events and timelines within this mystery, specifically Cody Parker's experiences in Vietnam. Though American troops were already involved there at the timing of this book, I believe "tunnel rats" were in their infancy.

Again, the characters in this story are the result of the author's somewhat twisted imagination.

January 10, 2012
Reavis Z. Wortham
Frisco, Texas

To receive a free catalog of Poisoned Pen Press titles, please contact us in one of the following ways:

Phone: 1-800-421-3976
Facsimile: 1-480-949-1707
Email: info@poisonedpenpress.com
Website: www.poisonedpenpress.com

Poisoned Pen Press
6962 E. First Ave. Ste 103
Scottsdale, AZ 85251

DISCARDED BY
FREEPORT
MEMORIAL LIBRARY